I0736204

# FROM HERE TO THERE

**7 stories across time, space, and reality**

# FOREWORD

Oof. The last time I wrote one of these we were in the middle of lockdown, and a lot has clearly changed.

But what hasn't changed is that I'm sure we could all use a little escape now and then. And that's where Mirror World comes in.

Last year, we ran another contest. This time we were looking for stories that put journey above destination, that told of people in transit between one place and the next. And boy, did the writers who submitted deliver!

The seven stories you are about to read are the best of the bunch. They run the gauntlet from pockets in time and space, portals, time travel, and space travel, to just plain walking to get where you're going. As in Far, Far Away, the first volume of this anthology series, we've included introductions and bios from each of the winning authors so you can get to know the talent behind these fantastic adventures.

So key up your time machine or spacefaring vessel, and get ready for a wild and bumpy ride through the multiverse.

## *Justine Alley Dowsett*

*Publisher, Mirror World Publishing*

# ITINERARY

### "Embedding" by Elana Gomel

Told in alternating points of view by an unlikely couple whose only connection is their young son, "Embedding" is a story of math and monsters. Anika, a creative writing student, meets Roy, an older mathematician. When their son Michael is five, Anika wakes up one morning to find that they have been transported into a strange enclosure surrounded by the impenetrable Wall. The rules of the enclosure are simple: stay indoors after the dark. If you go out, you die.

### "The Impossible Man" by Kelly D. Holmes

When temporal archeologist, Xiomara Lopez, encounters the same man 1200 years apart, she is baffled by the impossibility. And it doesn't help that this Impossible Man keeps interfering with her assignments, much to her annoyance. But in amongst the streets of Pompeii, medieval Hungary, Victorian London, and a Chicago speakeasy, they'll both learn that some things are worth the wait.

### "The Repositioning March" by Buddy Young

The final survivors of an army from a nation of mask wearers confront issues of surviving in both the body and the soul as the Soulless enemy who disdain masks pursue them relentlessly through a remote jungle.

## "Industrial Honey" by Rhiannon Lotze

When the bees begin dying, a bumblebee named Glykiá travels to the Underworld to beg Queen Persephone to fix the mortal realm with her magic. However, unable to use magic because of a treaty between gods and humans, Persephone devises another way to help. Side by side, goddess and bee leap into time, in a quest for the ages.

## "Night Music" by Jane Lupino

A young woman is heading back to her car when she hears music. She follows the sound and finds herself outside a large mansion she's never seen before. There is a party going on and she is invited to join them. Once there, things become a little strange and she discovers that she has somehow gone back to 1942...and that's not the only thing that isn't as it seems.

## "From Above" by Roy Sarkar

Caught between a crash site on a Jupiter moon and a ship rocketing through space, Amla Ghosh finds herself stuck between two worlds. With the distance between the two closing fast, both woman and machine remember the better parts of each other.

## "The Harajuku Crevasse" by Taylor Calder

After being taunted by an online rival, Noa resolves to get to Harajuku by 'hopping' – illegally travelling through the network of portals that conduct almost all travel on post-invasion Earth. Easy, right? Unfortunately for Noa, a mistaken hop leaves her deep below the ocean in a crashed alien vessel belonging to Aoi, the only alien to survive the Earth's brutal counterattack.

My father was a mathematician, and from an early age I loved math. Unfortunately, my love was unrequited. Math is like poetry or music: you need to be born with the capacity to visualize multiple dimensions, juggle algebraic abstractions, or be at home among infinite sets. I did not have this gift. Instead, I had another ability that bewildered my entire family. I created monsters.

Not conventional monsters, like zombies or vampires. I was endlessly fascinated by prehistoric creatures, the more grotesque the better. I devoured fairy tales with dragons, shapeshifters, and shadowy things that peeked through the window at night. I read classic ghost stories and watched whatever horror movies were available. As a child, I had a little notebook where I would write down descriptions of my monsters, either borrowed from books and movies, or made up from shreds of my nightmares. And my love affair with monsters bloomed as I grew up. Not just as a writer but also as an academic, I dedicated myself to studying and cataloguing the fauna of the imagination.

But I did not forget my father's topology lessons. And so "Embedding" was born: a tale of math and monsters. I tried to visualize an impossible multidimensional space swarming with grotesque lifeforms. I delved into my own fears as a child, lying in bed and hearing the soft footsteps of some padding creature, neither human nor animal, as it circled our summer house.

A child's imagination is the most powerful thing in the world: untrammelled by adult prohibitions, it can conjure new realities out of thin air. In my novella, a handful of strangers are locked up in a pocket universe populated by nightmarish creatures. How this topological cage came to be, who is responsible for its creation, and what happened to the rest of the world are the question that are gradually answered as the story unfolds through alternative narratives of Anika, a would-be writer and a single mother, and Roy, a mathematician and the father of her son.

But besides math and monsters, the novella is also about choice. Some mathematicians believe that the future is predetermined, and time is an illusion. I find this philosophy abhorrent. We always have choices, no matter how hard they may be. Roy, Anika, and Michael, the unconventional family at the heart of the novella are not playthings of impersonal forces. It is precisely

Roy's attempt to pin down the future that has broken reality itself. And what is broken can also be mended.

## *Elana Gomel*

Born in Ukraine and currently residing in California, Elana Gomel is an academic with a long list of books and articles, specializing in science fiction, Victorian literature, and serial killers. She is also an award-winning fiction writer and the author of more than a hundred short stories, several novellas, and four novels. Her latest fiction publications are Little Sister, a historical horror novella, and Black House, a dark fantasy novel. She is a member of HWA and can be found at https://www.citiesoflightanddarkness.com/ and social media.

# EMBEDDING

by Elana Gomel

## Anika - Now

I open my eyes when the edges of the curtain light up and I know I am safe.

Michael is downstairs and I hear him clatter pots and pans in the kitchen.

"I'm coming!" I yell, impatient to see my son, his face dappled with the gold of dawn. He would have pulled the curtains open already, no matter how often I tell him not to. What if he wakes up too early before the sunrise? The thought gives me chills, but I push it aside. He knows better. He has been conditioned for the last three years to live by the sun, pulling his blanket over his head when shadows begin to pool in the garden and jumping up the moment the top of the Wall glows pink. I don't think he remembers the urine-yellow of electric lights and the night stippled with scowling windows.

I push away my own blanket, noticing that it has a rip in the corner where I must have twisted it too hard as I tried to block my ears. Maybe I should ask Melissa for that herbal potion she brews from the weeds in her garden. She says it keeps her entire family sound asleep through the night, including five-year-old Carol. The potion smells of rotten hay, but if it works it would be worth trading for a pound of my Granny Smith apples.

Smoothing up my blanket and hoping for a new one from the Box, I paddle downstairs and indeed, Michael is already in the kitchen. He is pottering around at the woodstove, which I have forbidden him to do lest he sets the cottage on fire, but his proud smile kills my rebuke.

"Mummy!" he says. "I made porridge for you!"

I hug him and we sit together in our nook where the sun is strongest in the morning, warm and bright and safe. The burnt porridge tastes of ashes, but I would not exchange it for the fanciest meal from Before.

Of course, there are days when the sun does not shine, when the sky above the Wall is iron-grey, and the air is murky with the residue of darkness. On such days, Michael and I cuddle in front of the fire and talk. I have exhausted the supply of Grimm fairy tales, Greek myths, and Marvel superhero comics I remember from Before, and now I have to make up new stories to feed my son's inexhaustible hunger for questions as to what happened next. Well, I wanted to be a writer once, didn't I? Even if Michael's birth put an end to that dream, I can still spin a good tale in which the hero triumphs, the evildoers are punished, and the monsters are defeated. I have to be careful about the last point. I don't want to give him ideas. I have to keep him safe.

Still, it pains me to think he is growing up with no knowledge of numbers. Considering who his father is, it is a real deprivation, but I cannot teach him what I don't understand. It was always clear between us: Roy's math versus my stories; the division not only of parental responsibility but of character.

I tried to organize homeschooling for Michael, Carol, and Holly, but the age gaps between them are too wide. And while our tiny settlement contains adults whose educational accomplishments range from PhD's (the Carters) to a high-school dropout (Melissa's husband Buddy), nobody volunteers to teach the kids. Emily Carter is drifting into chronic depression, and her husband is preoccupied with his increasingly mad theories about our whereabouts. Melissa seems curiously unconcerned that her eldest daughter Holly (five years older than Michael) and youngest Carol are growing up functionally illiterate and innumerate. And Buddy spends most of his days in an alcoholic haze.

There were no books in the garden cottages when we woke up on the first morning. No electricity. No fridges or dishwashers. Pantries, yes; and a full complement of gardening tools, which I have learned how to use by trial and error. And the Box attached to the porch of each house: a large wooden chest with a hinged lid. It was empty, then. Three days later I found mine rattling with new potatoes in a cloth bag, a blue T-shirt, and a couple of knives. At unpredictable intervals, a new Boxing Day fills our Boxes with a seemingly arbitrary selection of useful objects. Buddy tried to organize a barter system, but it is floundering because the Carters refuse to leave their house and seldom open the door when Ruth Miller, the charitable soul that she is, visits with her daily portion of fire-and-brimstone. And anyway, how do you establish comparative value? What is worth more: a pound of fresh peas or a fork? We are too small for a society, too fragmented for a family.

I dread the moment when we can no longer work in our gardens. Last winter, Michael was still small enough that I could keep him occupied with my stories, toys made of kitchen towels and broken crockery, and snow-fights on crisp mornings. But he is growing up quickly. What will happen when the days grow short? When the interval of light dwindles to a sliver of safety bracketed by interminable stretches of howl-infested darkness?

Last winter was very long, dragging on as if unwilling to let the sun out of its seasonal jail. What if the coming one is longer?

No, I must not think about it. I must concentrate on what is now: the fresh light of the morning streaming into the kitchen, the green of my kitchen garden, the sour but plentiful plums on the contorted tree that I have watered so assiduously, working the hand-pump until my shoulders ached and sleep was easy to drift into.

And my son's face.

I eat the oatmeal, trying not to wince at the bitter taste. We have become vegetarians by default. The Box sometimes contains a couple of fresh eggs or a wheel of hard cheese. No meat. And like everything else, the cheese is not commercially wrapped or stamped.

Nothing in our homes bears any mark of industrial civilization. No labels on the clothing, no manufacturer's logos on the cutlery.

"Can we go for a walk, Mummy?" Michael asks.

"Sure. Let's just wash the dishes and then we can walk in the garden".

"Can we go to other gardens?"

Oh boy! My son is getting cabin fever. But as long as the sun shines, this should be perfectly safe.

"We can visit Holly and Carol," I say after a pause. Melissa will be glad to see me, even though Buddy, unshaven, morose, and surrounded by the fug of his fermented-fruit moonshine, is a poor role model for Michael.

Michael makes a face.

"Granny Kathy's garden?" he suggests. I pale. I did not know he even remembered her – the little elderly lady who seemed so perfectly fit for our circumscribed life and who was the first one to open her door after nightfall. Now her garden is overgrown, a riot of rank weeds and dying trees, and her cottage is quiet and shadowy, twilit rooms filled with the stench of mold and abandonment. And what lies in her Box does not bear thinking about.

"We are going to visit Holly and Carol," I say firmly.

## Roy – Before

He woke up screaming.

The nightmare was already fading when he turned on the bedside lamp and sat wrapped up in the blanket, shivering, even though the night was soft and balmy, the chirping of crickets coming through the open window as soothing as white noise. Only broken slivers of images remained imprinted on his retinas: a shaggy black dog with a human smile, yellow teeth behind his puckered smoker's lips; an arm lying on the pavement, blood seeping from the ragged end where it was torn off, the manicured fingers scrabbling restlessly; a baby in the crib, a stone hand, as large as the world, rocking it with an increasing amplitude, the tiny fragile body about to be catapulted into the vague space...

The baby was not Michael, he was sure of it. His son was almost five, not a helpless infant but a curious, mischievous, smart boy. Roy glanced at the antique bureau inherited from his own father where a large framed picture of Michael stood among the photos of the grandparents and uncles he did not remember. He wanted Anika to be in the picture too, but she demurred. She had made it clear from the beginning that they were not a couple. Just…what? Co-parents? He was not sure what the right term was nowadays and did not want to ask her, afraid to let the age gap between them yawn even wider. He was almost twenty years older than Anika. With some stretch, he was old enough to be her father.

Roy got up, his knees creaking, and went to the kitchen to get a drink of water. He paused to look at the gibbous moon shining through the lattice of black boughs, silver confetti sprinkling the new grass beneath the trees. His house stood on a large plot of land, which Roy let fall into its natural state, even though the splintered remnants of his father's barns and toolsheds reminded him that once upon a time it had been a working farm.

His father died both proud and ashamed of his only son. He was proud because Roy had made good, retired at the age of forty, and never had to work his fingers to the bone by the hard and thankless labor of growing corn and raising livestock. He was ashamed for the same reason.

Jim Hunter had hoped for grandchildren to take over the farm, but Roy had never married. The existence of Michael hung in the balance when lung cancer caused by the dust in the wheat silos claimed Jim's life. He never knew that parts of his DNA were busy molding a new life in a strange woman's womb.

Roy knew he would not sleep, so he went to his home office and powered up his newest Mac. Several others sat on the tables around the room, hooked up to large monitors or purring like sleeping cats. That was home: the space beyond the physical, the pure and timeless world of shapes and numbers. The farm was just a gatehouse, as comfortable and unnoticeable as a favourite pair of worn jeans.

The manifold, the topological multidimensional space, was where Roy had made his money and where he could find what he craved without the distraction of people and things. He smiled as he saw his latest visualization: a projection into the three-dimensional space of a complex multidimensional model. It looked like an orchid with many petals nesting around the embedded domain in the middle. False colouring sprinkled the petals with green, purple, and red, but the more one looked into it, the more the gaze was lost in the labyrinth of fractal recursions, as fragile and unrepeatable as rime patterns. Roy knew it was an inadequate and simplistic representation, but he admired the beauty of his creation. His mathematical lace.

Roy was a topologist. Initially, he used multidimensional geometries to model the stochastic processes of the stock market. His parents had been appalled by their only son's obsessions with math, his inability to form social attachments, and his total indifference to sports. He owed it to his father's stubborn distrust of "lib'ral nonsense" that he had never been diagnosed with some form of detachment disorder and medicated out of his mind. His mother may have been more insistent, but she had died young and Roy barely remembered her. Once his father bought him his first computer, Roy knew where he belonged. And the old man was both shocked and vindicated when his strange son's strange hobby brought in more money than Jim Hunter had ever seen in his entire life.

Roy still did a bit of day trading but only as an entertainment. His entire life now revolved around his new project. A project so useless in practical terms and yet so consequential that it consumed every moment of his waking existence.

He was happy: the solitary and self-content king of his own domain. Never burdened with a strong sex drive or desire for companionship, Roy felt best on his own. It was only the existence of Michael that complicated the purity of his existence like a butterfly flapping its wings among ice crystals.

Roy loved his son. His birth had been the spark that started his project. Somehow, that helpless red-faced bundle of infinite possibilities had made him want to know the future. To tame the uncertainty that threatened Michael on every side. A freak home accident, a careening car out of control, or a stray virus could rob him of his son. Every time Ron added a new curve to the manifold, reducing the terrifying blankness of the future to topology's reassuring simultaneity, he was doing it for Michael.

And then there was Anika. Roy was not in love with Anika and believed he had never been, but she also niggled at his awareness as a vague regret for what might have been. And because she was Michael's mother and his primary caregiver, Ron felt responsible for her as well.

Was his concern for them the reason for his nightmares? But how were his night terrors connected to Anika and Michael, who lived more than a hundred miles away in West Des Moines? Roy did not believe in premonitions. He believed in knowledge. His frequent debates with Anika about the future always ended with the same standoff. She thought that the future was open-ended. He did not. Time followed a necessary and predetermined trajectory. It did not meander into dark byways and accidental dead-ends.

Roy forced Anika and Michael out of his mind as he focused on the spinning undulating spirals and blooming Mandelbrot sets on his monitor. Somewhere in this bright forest of fractal shapes lay a key to erasing time.

## Anika - Now

The kids are playing outside, while Melissa and I are sitting in her kitchen, drinking herbal tea. Thankfully, Buddy is nowhere in sight. Probably snoring away in the master bedroom. Serves him right if he won't be able to sleep tonight!

Melissa does not look well. She has lost weight and her hair is unwashed. There is no justification for letting yourself go. We get soap (though not shampoo) in our Boxes.

I put one of her luscious raspberries into my mouth. Our gardens are all roughly the same – rows of leafy vegetables, apples and plums, apricots and peaches – but there is some variation. I have scraggly blackberry bushes; Melissa and Buddy – flourishing raspberries. We could all pool our resources – if there were enough of us, if we were not hemmed in by the Wall, if the nights didn't drain us of energy through the spigot of fear. If, if, if…I squelch my train of thoughts.

"Do you think we are dead?" Melissa asks out of the blue.

I choke as I take a sip of tea. Hot liquid shoots up my nose.

"Don't tell me it did not occur to you!" she says truculently.

I don't say anything. She turns away and rearranges the plates on the table. They are white-glazed, plain, with no ornament or trademark. And chipped. They look old. It suddenly occurs to me that so does everything else in our cottages: old, worn, second-hand.

"My mom was Catholic," she continues. "Believed in the Purgatory."

"We are not in any bloody Purgatory!" I scoff. "Really? A suburban family, a couple of academics, a churchgoing lady, and a single mom! That's your idea of unrepentant sinners?"

She shrugs.

"Where is Buddy?" I ask to break the uncomfortable silence.

She glances at me, and I finally wake up to the fact that her eyes are red and swollen. How did I not notice it before?

In bright sunlight, you don't want to see bad things. You cling to whatever tiny moments of joy you can find. But now the light is getting dimmer as if fine dust were being stirred into the air. The sun has vaulted the zenith and is now sliding down toward the Wall. The shadows are beginning to rise in the garden, unfurling from their lairs like hairy snakes.

"He woke up last night," she whispers.

I know what is coming but I still need to ask – as if pretending to doubt the inevitable can hold it back. But if it could, night would never come.

"The curtains were closed, right?"

It's impossible to lie still through the night, pretending to be asleep and listening to the stealthy cacophony outside, matching every discordant noise to the worst shape your imagination can come up with. Even with the nerves of steel, which none of us can boast anymore, mundane needs intervene: using the bathroom, hearing a child whimper in their sleep, getting a drink of water. I navigate the cottage by touch when I need to get up, careful not to yank off a curtain accidentally. We don't know if this will let the monsters in, but nobody is eager to find out.

Melissa nods, miserable.

"I heard him go down into the kitchen. I thought…you know."

His moonshine. I tried it once: a vile concoction that I could not drink even with the promise of temporary oblivion. And of course, I could not let Michael see me drunk.

"But then a door slammed. The front door."

The horror of it stops my breath.

"What did you do?"

"I was…I just couldn't. The girls were sleeping in the other bedroom."

Her daughters: thirteen-year-old Holly and five-year-old Carol. I imagine Michael in their place and bite my lips to stop myself from screaming. I realize what blessing it is that I am alone with him.

"I lay in bed," Melissa whispers. "I couldn't move. And then I heard the turn of the key. He locked the door from the outside."

"How did you unlock it in the morning?"

The doors of the cottages have no latches. You have to use a key in order to lock the door from the inside or outside.

"We have two keys. I found his lying on the porch."

We also have two keys, but I have hidden the second one and Michael does not know where. Every night, I put the remaining key under my pillow.

"Did you…find anything else?"

She shakes her head, and then tears come, streaming down her face in an unstoppable flood. I don't think she is crying for Buddy. She is crying for herself, and for her girls, and for the price of their survival.

"He is gone."

Of all of us, I did not expect him to be next. Just shows how little you know your neighbors! He locked the door behind him as he went into the darkness filled with howling, and tittering, and words screamed in no human language. In those last moments, he thought of his family. Poor Buddy: foul-mouthed and dim-witted but a husband and a father.

I open my mouth to ask another question and close it again. I have never told Melissa, or anybody else, what I have found in Kathy's Box.

Melissa breaks out in sobs. Holly walks in, dragging Carol by the hand. Michael follows, looking peeved.

"She doesn't want to play anymore," he says accusingly, pointing at Holly. One look at her face tells me that she knows.

I grab Michael.

"We are going home!" I say.

"But Mummy…"

I point at the sky where the clotted yellow light is beginning to fade, and this is all it takes. I squeeze Holly's hand on my way out.

"Take care of your mom," I whisper – an injunction as useless as it is hypocritical.

## Roy - Before

He stood in the dewy grass, squinting into the murk of the woods that spilled into the backyard. They needed some upkeep, he decided. While silence and solitude were the most precious things he bought with his money, Roy felt he needed to take care of the property in memory of his father. The farmhouse boasted a newly shingled roof, which the recently hired contractor finished putting in just a couple of days ago. Roy had been dubious about the man who seemed rather too fond of the bottle, but he had done a good job. The barns and the toolshed were next.

Roy drew in fresh air, trying to center himself. The bad dreams refused to go away, lodged in his memory like a bullet. Normally, he never remembered his dreams; why wouldn't he forget these disturbing ones? He would understand if they were connected to his manifold; after all, stories of mathematicians solving tough problems in their sleep were not altogether groundless. The mind was a powerful thing, the most powerful thing in the universe. But those dreams were about monsters, and Roy had very little interest in the organic deformities of evolution, and even less interest in horror-movies' predictable creature features. Michael was beginning to exhibit some signs of night terrors, and Anika asked Roy not to tell him spooky stories. Roy retorted that stories were her specialty. He never conveyed anything to his son but the pure truth of math.

He felt off-kilter somehow. The silence that always gifted him with clarity and calm now seemed pregnant with unexpected eruptions. Roy concentrated and seemed to hear…something. The silence of the woods was stippled with whispers just on the edge of audibility. Roy listened intently but could not decide whether the whispers were real or just a carryover from his disturbed sleep. Or was he developing tinnitus?

His dog Ada bounded out of the woods, her tongue hanging out as she ran toward her master. Roy liked dogs only marginally more than he liked people, which was not at all. Immersed in the purity of topology, he distrusted the messiness of organic existence, but having grown up on the farm and forced to help his father during the calving season, he knew how to handle animals. Even savage dogs accepted him, as if his matter-of-fact attitude made him one of them.

He absent-mindedly patted Ada's shaggy head as she circled around him. Named for Ada Lovelace, a famous mathematician, Ada was a large placid collie who followed Roy in his daily walk in the woods with the self-assurance of her namesake. But now she was agitated, whining, and growling deep in her throat.

Something bit into Roy's hand that rested on Ada's fur. It was as if the dog suddenly developed another set of teeth on top of her skull. Roy snatched his hand away and stared, uncomprehendingly, at the scarlet stain on his palm. His hand looked abraded, skinned, and scoured with deep scratches that dripped blood.

"What the hell?"

Ada whined. Roy dropped to his knees, grasping the dog's head. Nothing seemed to be amiss. Ada was agitated, but she had not grown a coat of steel wool instead of her long silky hair. Suddenly she jerked away with such force that Roy lost his balance and fell into the wet grass. Ada took off, flying toward the woods.

Roy scrambled to his feet, yelling her name. Ada was usually an obedient dog, instantly responding when called. But not today. She tore through the fringe of the undergrowth and disappeared among the trees.

Roy stared after her. It must have been a visual illusion, a hallucination, though he had never had one before. But there is the first time for everything, they say. Better to believe that the delicate machinery of his brain gave way under the unrelenting strain of his research than accept that what he had glimpsed was real.

As Ada was running, it seemed to Roy that her body lengthened and stretched, shedding her tawny fur, and flashing raw red like a skinned piglet, her jaws forming into a toothy beak, her flattened skull sprouting protrusions like porcupine spines. Just before the murk swallowed her up, she had become a monstrous sausage on skittering legs, a pink wormy thing, and the distortion seemed to spread away from her in concentric circles, pulling the swaying poplars into the vortex of deformity. Their trunks lengthened and curved, inscribing some impossible, outrageous geometry. The branches were pulled into the maelstrom of bubbling space that hurt his eyes to look at and his brain to process.

Roy mashed his fists into his eyes, and when he dared looking again it all appeared normal. The poplars were straight lines on the dappled background of sun and shadow. The perspective was ordinary. The space was not distorted. And his dog was missing.

Roy studied his bleeding palm. Something had injured his hand when he had patted his dog's familiar head. And if reality could betray him in such an everyday moment, what other treason was it capable of?

Roy went back into the house to disinfect and bandage his wound, while mentally going through a litany of plausible explanations – thorns in Ada's fur, a sudden quick snap of her teeth, some injury he had not noticed before – and rejected them all. The habit of clear thinking was too deeply ingrained. He could no more deceive himself than he could deceive others. There were only two options: either he was going insane – or the world was.

It was not him. Despite the opinion of school counselors and disappointed girlfriends, Roy had no doubt about his mental balance. But what he had seen, in a bubble of blinding, roiling light, was impossible. So, was his brain, that finely tuned and precious mechanism, giving way under pressure?

The sting of his oozing palm dispelled his doubts. No, that was real. And unless Ada had somehow acquired porcupine spines, there was no way a dog's fur could inflict such injuries. The laws of physics were immutable: hard and soft, solid and liquid, up and down. And underlying them all was the precise structure of the manifold, immutable and eternal.

He went back out, realizing he had to find Ada. The dappled sunlight swirled around him in thick patches like snowflakes. The juicy grass crawled with hidden movements. And the whispers that he had heard were getting louder, weaving into a tapestry of nonsense: impossible to either understand or ignore.

He squeezed his eyes shut and took several deep breaths. It worked. The patches of sunlight settled down into the grass, losing their three-dimensionality and becoming again just variations in luminosity. The grass stopped swaying. And the whispers receded, so he was able to convince himself they were only the susurrus of wind-whipped branches.

Something was lying at his feet, a light wooly mass. He lifted it.

It was a hunk of Ada's fur, so thick that it must have been ripped out by force. Indeed, the roots glistened with droplets of blood. And in the middle of the tangle, a blue human eye stared fixedly at him.

## Anika - Now

Twilight.

As the sun dips below the Wall, the air in the garden grows colder and fills with furtive smells: freshly turned earth, rotting green things, mold and earthworms. Smells of darkness.

Large hairy moths fly around the porch, one of them beating against the window, its shaggy wings leaving dirty smears on the glass. Why is it doing this? Night moths are attracted to light but there is no light inside the cottage. We have no lamps or candles. I always bank up the fire in the stove, leaving the smoldering embers under the coat of ash.

Michael is subdued. It breaks my heart to see how he is trying to be brave for my sake. Children are afraid of darkness. Perhaps they have always known something that adults prefer to forget.

I push a cup with herbal tea toward him, but he shakes his head. Even an additional dollop of plum jam won't tempt him.

"You'll sleep better," I say.

"I'm not sleepy, Mummy."

My heart skips a beat.

"I'll sit with you," I say.

Until a year ago Michael slept in my bedroom, but then he decided to be independent and relocated to the second bedroom despite my objections. Rationally I know it makes no difference. If the Rat-Wolves and the Walkers want to break in, flimsy partitions won't stop them, and I won't be able to defend my son against a horde of monsters.

But if we hide in the dark, safe in the cocoon of our own warm breath, with the door locked and the windows curtained, they will leave us alone.

How do I know it? I just do. This place has its laws, and they are just as ineluctable as the laws of physics. So what if I am no closer to understanding the rationale for them than I was three years ago when we woke up in the cottages? What did ancients know of the rotation of the Earth? But they had no doubt that the sun would rise every morning.

I stroke Michael's silky hair. The day is almost done; stagnant darkness is lapping at the ceiling as if the bedroom was an aquarium filling with unclean water. Darkness robs me of the sight of my son. It would be enough reason to hate it, even without the stealthy movements and the braying noises outside.

"Mummy," he asks, "is my dad alive?"

My heart skips a beat, and as if in response a thin howl dribbles in through the chink in the curtain. I call the howlers Rat-Wolves, the name that came from some forgotten sci-fi novel of my youth. I have no idea, of course, whether they look anything like wolves – or rats. Nobody has seen them besides Kathy and Buddy, and the dead don't tell tales.

Anyway, the Rat-Wolves are not the worst, not by a long shot. The trilling, nauseatingly sweet notes emitted by the creatures I call Canaries conjure up images of featherless birds the size of an elephant. Not to mention the Yakkers who are the only ones to speak – if this can be called speech – jagged syllables shattering against the walls of our house like handfuls of broken glass. But the Canaries and the Yakkers don't normally show up until much later.

"Do you remember your dad?" I ask, stalling for time.

Roy and I were never married; we were not even a couple, just friends with benefits. Or were we even friends?

I met him at a public lecture on topology at the University of Iowa. I was doing a degree in creative writing – as useless as a diploma as you can imagine. But of course, at the time I fancied myself the next Margaret Atwood. That was the reason why I wandered into that lecture on multidimensional topologies. I was thinking of writing a science-fiction novel. Nothing came out of it except…well, except the rest of my life. My son. And now I am living in what could be a science-fiction novel but is not. The laws of science are cool and comforting in their predictability. The laws of the Wall-bounded enclave where I am huddling in the stuffy bedroom, pulling the blanket over our heads, are those of a fever-induced nightmare.

I did not understand half of what was said by the lecturer despite the fact that the lecture was advertised as "popular and accessible". The slides he projected were beautiful – the Mandelbrot set, the Klein bottle, the Moebius surface – but also vaguely disturbing because I could not connect them to any shapes in real life. Triangles and squares are everywhere if you look. These things were as alien as deep-sea fish.

My concentration lost, I was considering how to make my exit without disturbing the man who had taken the last seat in the row despite the fact that there were plenty of empty seats closer to me. He was so much older than the rest of us that I decided he must be a professor. Slight and balding, he listened with a kind of absolute immersion I could never achieve even in the most absorbing classes. And then, right in the middle of a sentence, he got up walked to the exit, unconcerned about making a commotion. The lecturer glared at him while I slipped out, grateful for the cover. We almost collided outside the lecture hall.

"Nonsense!" he declared to the universe at large. "This guy has no idea what he is talking about!"

"Has he?" I asked.

He started as if just noticing I was around and then smiled. He had a nice smile and what I mentally classified as a "white-bread" face, common in Iowa where my own Indian features were considered exotic. His balding forehead and crow's feet betrayed his age, but he was slender and moved with a kind of fluid ease that made him look younger.

"No," he said. "He claims topological spaces are imaginary."

"Are they not?"

"No. Topology is the study of the underlying mathematical structure of space and time. How can it be imaginary?"

"I never thought of math as real."

"Math is more real than real. It is the language of God."

"I am an atheist," I said bluntly. I was tired of people inquiring if I was a Muslim with the kind of inflection you would use to ask: "Are you a serial killer?" I was born in Des Moines and though my parents were Hindu, my mother abandoned any attempt to teach me the basics of their religion after my father's death. We did not even follow a vegetarian diet at home. Ironically, I do here, in this demon-infested jail. I suddenly remember the Sanskrit word for demons: Rakshasas.

"So am I," he said then, unflustered, "but the universe still speaks the language of God, even if He does not exist."

After this enigmatic remark, I knew the conversation had to continue. And it did.

Now, cuddling my son, I am searching his face for his father's. It is easy. Michael looks much more like his dad than he does like me. He has inherited his pale complexion and no-nonsense features from Roy. The colour of his eyes is somewhere in-between Roy's hazel and my dark brown. My butterscotch skin and black hair got lost in the genetic lottery that has randomly reshuffled our chromosomes to create this unique and unrepeatable miracle. My baby.

My mother could not warm up to her grandson whose birth derailed her daughter's academic career. Could it have been different had Michael looked more like me? The thought of my mother comes with a jolt of pain and guilt that is not dulled by its frequency. Is she still alive? Is anybody still alive outside the Wall? Marvin Carter believes so. His wife does not.

"I remember my dad," Michael says. His eyes are glistening in the dusk as if with unshed tears.

Roy insisted on paying child support, even though I initially refused. I still could not forgive the first question out of his mouth when I told him about my pregnancy.

"Are you having an abortion?"

I should have known, of course, that Roy never reacted like ordinary people. The subtleties and nuances of human communication, the welter of the unspoken bubbling under the surface of every conversation, were invisible to him. He did not imply that he wanted me to get rid of the baby. He simply wanted to know whether I did. The only way to understand Roy was to take everything he said literally, so when he said he would take care of his son the best he could, he meant it. And he did, even though "the best" included trying to teach Michael algebra at the age of three.

"I'm sure your dad is alive and well," I say. It's bad to lie to your kids but it's much worse not to know whether you are lying or not.

There is a chittering sound outside, so loud that it seems to pierce the insubstantial shelter of the curtain. The garden must be totally consumed by darkness already.

"You need to sleep," I say sternly and pull the blanket over his head.

## Roy – Before

He sought refuge where he always did – in his work – but as he brought up a rotating, multi-petaled shape on the monitor, his phone trilled. The farmhouse never had any cellphone signal, so he used WhatsApp to communicate with the outside world and only few people were in his group. He knew it was Anika without looking at the screen.

They exchanged awkward greetings. He always expected Anika to start a conversation by telling him she had found somebody. Why not? She was only twenty-five, young and beautiful. It was not like they had anything going on.

Except their son, of course. Always Michael. An unbreakable bond between people with nothing in common.

Instead of announcing her engagement to another man, Anika stumped him by asking a question out of the blue, as she often did. Their minds worked in very different ways. He had no insight into Anika, even during their brief affair. He did not know whether she had ever loved or even liked him, and he had given up wondering. At the beginning, Roy had tried to create a topological model of her inner space until he realized it could not be done. Anika's mind was attuned to flow rather than shape. She was a storyteller. She still believed time was real, while he knew it was not.

Her smooth voice, spiced with her mother's Bengali music even though Anika was born in Des Moines, dripped into his ear like honey.

"What is embedding?"

"It's homeomorphism," Roy responded automatically, "a mathematical structure contained within another structure…"

"I am not asking for a lecture!" Anika interrupted. "I'm asking whether it's appropriate to tell Michael about topological shapes that give him nightmares. He is only five, Roy!"

"I never told Michael about embedding!" Roy defended himself. "You know what we did over the weekend: watched Disney, had ice cream, and played with Ada. He saw my manifold, true, but I'm not doing homeomorphism specifically, and I don't think I used the term. He asked what I was doing, so I told him."

"He woke up in the middle of the night!" Anika said. "He cried and wanted to sleep in my bed. And when I asked what he was afraid of, he said 'embedding'. It's not the kind of word he would hear in daycare."

"Maybe it was something from your stories," Roy countered, feeling unjustly put upon. "You know, from one of those fairy tales you read to him every night."

Anika was still taking night classes in creative writing, even though she worked as a pharmacist nowadays. She believed that children's imagination needed nourishment and read stories to Michael since he was a toddler, favouring the original Grimm Brothers' tales. Roy's personal opinion was that some of these tales were grim indeed, but he deferred to Anika's expertise in all matters narrative. Math was not storytelling. It had no beginning, middle, and end. It bred no monsters. It permeated everything, outside space and time, eternal and immutable. The language of God.

"Embedding? In a fairy tale?"

"Whatever. Maybe he picked it up on TV."

That was possible: Michael was extraordinarily bright, though to Roy's relief he had not inherited his father's social awkwardness.

"In any case," Roy continued, "there is nothing to be afraid of. Let me talk to him."

Anika hesitated, and Roy's heart lurched. His greatest fear was that the fragile balance of their co-parenting would be broken by one of those incomprehensible surges of emotions that happened to other people. At his insistence they had joint custody, but he knew that Anika could sue for sole custody and probably win. He did not want to lose his son.

"All right," she said, and Roy breathed a sigh of relief that turned to joy when he heard Michael's voice.

"Daddy!"

"Hi, buddy. What is that your mother is telling me about you being afraid of monsters under the bed?"

"Not under the bed, Daddy," Michael corrected him. "Embed. They are trying to embed us."

"Who?"

"The monsters."

## Anika – Now

The next morning is bright and sunny, and I exhale with relief. I know the nights are getting longer. I see the leaves on my apple trees gilded with autumnal gold. But we still have some time before the dark season is upon us. Some time. This is all I can ask for. Time has become infinitely divisible; its shreds – our currency.

Ruth comes for a visit, and Michael's solemn face breaks into a smile. I now see how important it is for kids to have a granny presence in their lives. I bitterly regret the rift between my mother and myself. She wanted me to give the baby up for adoption. She wanted me to continue with my studies. She even wanted me to marry Roy. Though she had rebelled against her traditional Hindu upbringing, she abhorred abortion and single motherhood alike. It was suddenly as if old stories and ancient taboos floated up to the surface of her modern life from some deep dark reservoir of time. Of course I refused to do any of this and walked out, slamming the door. It was only in the last year before the Wall that she and I tentatively reconnected and she saw her grandson.

Ruth is not your stereotypical grandmother with kindly smiles and home-baked cookies – that was Kathy. Ruth is a stern middle-aged woman, thin as a rake, with a deep voice and martinet manner. She used to be a school librarian Before. This is great because my storytelling inspiration is running dry, something I would have never believed Before, when tales jostled in my brain, begging to be released onto paper. But now I am sometimes at loose ends when Michael asks for a story at bedtime. Children's minds need stories like their bodies need food, and while our unknown masters provide the latter, they assiduously avoid giving us the former. No books, no paper or writing utensils, and of course no electronic media.

Ruth is well-read and has a memory like a steel trap. Unfortunately, this memory has snared too many Biblical narratives, which she persists in unloading onto her fellow inmates. I don't know if she was devout Before or developed her faith due to our extraordinary circumstances, but her apocalyptic zeal is getting on my nerves. Still, Michael welcomes her stories, and I let him spend time with her, only asking that she stick to the more acceptable parts of the Bible like the Nativity. Certainly no Revelation, we don't need more monsters in our lives.

I offer her a plum tart. On the last Boxing Day, I received a packet of flour and some eggs. I wonder what Ruth received.

I don't have to wonder for long.

She pulls a piece of lined paper out of her pocket. Written across the lines in a clumsy, childish hand are three words: "You will burn".

I stare at it and shiver in the bright warmth of my breakfast nook. I hiss at Michael to go play outside. He promptly disappears into the garden, and I hear the snick of the wicket gate. I hope he has gone to Melissa's but what if he has sneaked out to Kathy's?

Well, it's still mid-morning and the sun is high in the sky, burning away the residue of night terrors. He'll be safe. And opening the Box…he knows not to do it. Anyway, nothing could be worse than soaking up the fear that seems to pass like an electric current between Ruth and me.

"He will burn the chaff with unquenchable fire," Ruth says. "Luke 3:17".

My atheism kicks in, supplanting fear with indignation.

"Come on, Ruth! Cut it out, will you? You and Melissa are driving each other nuts. We are not dead. We are not in hell. This is important: somebody is trying to communicate with us."

Her lips squeeze tighter, the vertical wrinkles like knife slashes.

"Communication? You still believe that this is some kind of experiment?"

"At least I'm trying to be rational. You pray every day, don't you? Any answers? Any heavenly visitations? This doesn't look like a message from Lucifer, more like a first-grader's scribble."

"If what comes at night are not demons…"

"We don't know what comes at night. We have never seen them. For all we know there is a noise machine that is turned on every nightfall. I heard better audio effects in a horror movie!"

Ruth shakes her head pityingly.

"I'm sorry for you, Anika," she says with a very discernible whiff of condescension. "I am afraid it may be too late for you, but I am concerned about Michael's soul. Will you let him pray with me?"

I open my mouth to say something evasive but what comes out is: "Go to hell!"

"We are already in it," Ruth says composedly and gets up to leave, but not without throwing a parting shot over her shoulder: "You say that we have not seen them? Not true. Kathy and Buddy have. I hope you are not the next."

I drop my head into my hands as she exits my kitchen, trying to keep my thoughts from scattering like frightened mice.

The morning after Kathy disappeared, I went to her cottage with some early apples. Among my fellow experimental subjects – or damned souls as Ruth would have it – I felt closest to her. She was like the kindly mother I would like to have instead of my own tiger mom.

The door to her cottage stood open. I remember the metallic taste of fear in my mouth as I peered into the murk inside. I expected horrors: blood spatters, broken furniture, body parts. But when I finally screwed up my courage and stepped inside, everything looked normal in the empty rooms.

Was she somewhere in the garden? Our plots are not particularly big but not impossible to hide in. I went out looking for her.

The garden was in pristine condition – Kathy was the only one among us who used to live on the farm and knew how to take care of plants. There were no signs of any disturbance but there never were. No matter how noisily the Rat-Wolves, Canaries, Yakkers, and Walkers rampaged through the night, we never found footprints, scat, or trampled vegetation in the morning to give us any clue to the nature of the monsters. This was why my idea of a noise machine made sense.

Until, after searching the garden, I decided on a whim to look in Kathy's Box.

At first, I did not even realize that what lay there had been a human being. It looked like a pile of charred sticks, like firewood pulled out of a conflagration just before it was consumed. I thought it was firewood until I saw the round object among the sticks and the soot-covered claws held above the xylophone of the ribs. But the worst part was that arms and legs bones were wrenched off the skeleton and lay around, splintered. As if somebody had tried to get at the marrow.

I stood there, in the chiaroscuro of shadows on the untrodden path, and then I dropped the cover of the Box and rushed back to my own cottage to hug Michael so tight that he cried.

## Roy- Before

He got up from the computer and stretched, his vertebrae cracking.

He did something which he had never done before. Surprised and vaguely disturbed by Michael's use of a topological term which, he was sure, he had never explained to his son, Roy decided to do a mundane Google search. He wanted to know what embedding would mean to somebody who, unlike him, did not understand the language of God.

Google threw pages and pages of garbage at him, making his head swim with the chatter of human irrelevance, but two definitions stood out. Embedding in linguistics meant recursion, clauses included within other clauses, and in literature, embedding meant stories-within-stories.

Roy tried to reconcile these two with topology. It was hard for him to do: his mind resisted shifting from the purity of math to the fogginess of natural language. He had always known that math involved a very different kind of cognition from ordinary thinking, so much so that it was as if his brain contained a whole set of subroutines which other people's brains did not. Math was like music or poetry: you either got it or did not. He had done nothing to deserve the talent that had made him a rich man at thirty-five and consumed his existence since he was a toddler. He was born with it, and he accepted it with humility.

He remembered Anika's liquid dark eyes as they had sat in the college cafeteria, drinking coffee that tasted like dishwater. She seemed to him a creature of a different species, beautiful and exotic. They were like oil and water. And yet somehow they had managed to mix, producing harmony out of discord. Michael was a living proof that opposites could coexist.

For Anika the universe was composed of stories; for him, it was composed of numbers. She believed in free will and choice, he did not. She thought the future was open-ended and unpredictable, he knew it was not.

She asked – no, demanded – that he explain his remark about the language of God at their first meeting. Anika had the courage of a child who asks questions out of sheer curiosity.

"It's a saying attributed to Galileo Galilei," he said. "'Mathematics is the language in which God has written the universe'."

"But you said you did not believe in God."

"I don't. At least not in any personal god. My parents were Methodists, but I hated going to church. It was boring, and the stories were absurd. But math underlies the structure of physical reality. What we see is just froth on the surface of the topological sea. So, if you want to believe that there is a mind behind it, then yes, math is the language of God. Or maybe math is God."

"But language can be used to wound, lie, and deceive," Anika said. "Stories can breed monsters in people's minds."

"Math does not lie," Roy had said then.

But now he was not so sure. Something troubled him deeply, things piling up and falling into a pattern he did not recognize. Ada still did not come back; Michael was upset, and his project was stuck.

Roy had used topology to model the stock market – something that had been attempted previously and always resulted in failure. His method, on the other hand, was spectacularly successful. He had made enough money by day trading to last him a lifetime.

He published bits and pieces of his research in abstruse scientific journals, but he did not strive for a Nobel Prize. He only valued money as a means to gain independence. What he really wanted was to capture time itself in a multidimensional shape. In topology, past and future were the same. The universe was like a flower of many petals, blooming across the four dimensions of spacetime, frozen in its own perfection. Roy wanted to see it. The manifold he was creating was supposed to be a visual representation of the universe's eternal and unchanging harmony.

But now his manifold was throwing off distorted and ugly splinters of itself, curling inward like a wounded hedgehog. Some unexpected variant was forcing parts of it to project upon other parts, creating folds and bubbles.

Embedding.

Anika once told him that it was hard to be a writer nowadays because so many stories were created, proliferating online like viruses, splicing and interbreeding, insinuating themselves into other stories…

Embedding.

Roy came to the window, realizing with some surprise that it was already night outside. The lights came on automatically in his office, turning the window into an unflattering mirror that deepened the creases in the corners of his eyes into crevasses and made him look far older than his forty-three years. The rest of the farmstead was dark. When Michael stayed with him he wanted the porchlight on and Roy complied, but for himself he liked the absence of light pollution and the scatter of stars in the sky. Unlike his son, he had never been afraid of darkness.

They are trying to embed us. The monsters.

Most kids believe in monsters. Then they grow out of it. Would he have to grow into such a belief?

Something seemed to move in the woods at the edge of the property. Cupping his hand around his eyes to cut out the light, Roy peered into the tangle of shadows.

A vague whitish shape loomed over the ragged fringe of the treetops. No matter how much Roy squinted, he could not make out what it was. It was not just the lack of light. His eyes swam and burned, as if refusing to focus. His brain hurt, unable to make sense of what he was seeing.

He mashed his fists into his eyes, tears running down his cheeks. The perspective was all wrong. The night itself was swirling like water going down the drain. Then it folded into a funnel, but instead of leading away from him the funnel stuck out, protruding like a nail driven into a picture. Roy was used to modelling multidimensional shapes in two or three dimensions, but this was no model. It was as if reality rebelled against the structure of human perception. Whatever he was seeing could not – or should not – be seen.

He staggered away from the window and clicked off the light in the office. He was not sure whether he wanted to see the outside better or not at all, but darkness gave a respite to his strained eyes. He peered cautiously through his burning lids.

The impossible funnel was gone; the dark was, once again, a flat sheet of nothingness behind the glass. Or...was it?

The whitish shape he had glimpsed before moved again, before dissolving like sugar in water.

Roy realized he needed a drink. Or maybe more than one. Abstemious to a fault, Roy now wanted nothing better than to shut down his overheated brain. Clearly, he was hallucinating. For what else could it be but a hallucination?

A leg the size of a construction crane towering above the woods, its ragged end dissolving into a swirl of unclean air.

## Anika – Now

I sit with Michael again in the evening, but I can see he doesn't want me here. He is fidgeting, pulling on his blanket so hard that a seam rips. I catch his hot little hand – who knows when and whether there will be more blankets in the Box, and winter is coming – but he pushes me away fretfully. I finally give up and leave him alone, only to realize it is still early. The sun has slid behind the Wall, but the sky is of that pearly transparent pink that separates full light and darkness like a long indrawn breath. I promise myself not to send Michael to bed so early in the future. He is not a baby anymore. To make up for what might seem like a punishment to him, I go into the kitchen and set up a plate of cookies and a jam jar on the table, so he can have a treat first thing in the morning.

I step into the shadowy garden against my better judgement, breathing in the cool, earthy evening air. The berry bushes have been cemented into a tangled mass by the dimming light. The gnarly apple and plum trees stand out in spiky silhouettes against the sky. The twilight is full of unspoken menace, waiting for me to turn my back so the monsters can crawl out of their hidey-holes and spring at me.

The monsters are real, but haven't they always been? Haven't people always been afraid of the dark?

I lock the door, go back into the kitchen, make myself a cup of tea, and sit at the table, staring at the fading rectangle of the window. I know I need to draw the curtains, but I procrastinate, challenging the night.

Are Ruth and Melissa right? Are we in Purgatory, being punished for our sins by some perverse deity?

No, I won't accept this. Every beat of my heart tells me I am alive. Locked up in some unfathomable prison, beset by invisible monsters, fed and watered like an animal in a zoo – but alive.

For how long?

# Roy-Before

There were three options. He wrote them down on a piece of paper laid out neatly beside his computer. Roy seldom wrote by hand, but for some reason he now felt more reliant on old-fashioned physical interactions than on the digital dance of information in cyberspace. Black traces of synthetic ink on a white sheet of interwoven fibers. The language of man. It could still betray him, but the physical world now felt like a shelter from the insidious rot of the language of God.

Option number one: He was suffering from a mental illness. Perhaps he had always suffered from a mental illness and only now was becoming aware of it. His school counselors had certainly believed he could do with therapy and medication, and pestered his father when Roy refused their help in "connecting with his peers in meaningful interactions".

Option number two: The woods on his property were haunted.

Option number three: The underlying topology of reality was breaking down.

Roy instantly rejected option number one. He knew he was not insane. His difference from the common run of humanity was not a pathology but a gift. And he had never had hallucinations of any kind, nor had he taken drugs that could produce flashbacks.

He lingered over option number two. While he did not believe in the demons of horror movies, he did not reject the possibility of the supernatural out of hand. His research had led him to believe that what people call reality was just a froth of the deep sea of shapes and numbers. Who knew whether this froth could contain some manifestations corresponding to what people called ghosts? But eventually he decided against it. He had played in those woods as a child and knew them like the back of his hand. He had never felt anything but sheltered and protected in their cool, whispering green.

That only left option number three.

Roy turned on his computer and considered the fractal shape of the manifold slowly revolving on the screen. It was a projection into the three dimensions of a four-dimensional structure that he had developed to represent the hidden topology of the universe. It used to be as beautiful and beguiling as an infinitely complex orchid. The flower of the real.

Now it was visibly rotting, its petals curling and blackening, small vortices of chaos dotting it like plague buboes, eating through its self-nesting shape. Roy did not understand how it was possible, but as a farmer's son he knew a blight when he saw it. Reality was infected.

But what to do about it? What could be done? Even the question sounded presumptuous, if not altogether ridiculous. Roy loved science fiction, but the notion of a lone superhero turning back the horde of ravening monsters always struck him as ridiculous. There was only so much an individual could do against a universal calamity. And Roy was no superhero. He had money but no special skills that could be of use in the physical world.

And anyway, why should he bother? He owed nothing to humanity which had always treated him with suspicion and distrust. He had no close friends, no siblings, no parents.

But he had a son.

The back door slammed. Roy had not locked it; in fact, he seldom locked any door in the farmhouse. Who would bother him here? But he was not defenseless. His father had left him his shotgun, and Roy liked having it around as if the wisp of his old man's presence still clung to the oiled metal. Now he reached for it.

A patter of clawed feet on the stairs. Roy exhaled. His dog came back! Perhaps reality was beginning to heal itself.

"Ada!" he called out, throwing the door of the office open.

Nothing showed over the curve of the staircase, but the patter continued. In fact it multiplied, echoing through the farmhouse, as if a whole pack of dogs were climbing the creaky stairs to his second-floor office. Roy peered into the gloom. He had not bothered to turn on the light downstairs, and a puddle of buttery illumination from the office's corner lamp petered out on the landing.

"Ada!"

There was no barking, but instead a sort of asthmatic wheezing.

This made no sense. Even if Ada came back injured, how long did it take for a dog to run up two flights of stairs?

Roy stepped out of the office and fumbled for the light-switch on the wall. It clicked but no light came on, even though he knew the electric wiring in the farmhouse was sound.

A bulky shadow rose from the murk pooling in the stairwell, and then a familiar beige muzzle was illuminated by the light from the office: the black wet nose, the hanging tongue, the shaggy mane.

"Ada! Come on, girl!"

The head was too close to the floor. She was crawling. She must be injured. Perhaps she had had a fight with another dog or was shot by a hunter.

But hadn't he heard the sound of running dog-feet?

Roy dropped to his knees and reached out to his dog who panted, her tongue out. She licked his hand. He tried to pat her back and froze with his hand in the air.

Ada's head was perched at the end of a flexible pink tube like a giant earthworm. And behind it was another head, identical to the first one, also threaded on the same tube, and behind it was another and another…a necklace of dog-heads strung on a bleeding gut, a chain of Adas, crawling up the stairs. An endless canine centipede whose multiple doglike paws clicked and clacked on the hardwood as it hauled the rest of its seemingly interminable body up the stairs.

Roy backed off. The Ada-heads whined, reaching for him, the pink rags of their tongues dripping saliva. The wormlike tube convulsed. It was as if somebody arbitrarily spliced together bits and pieces of discordant creatures, sniping through the fabric of reality like a child with scissors, and then multiplied the resulting chimera indefinitely like a string of prime numbers.

Roy lifted the shotgun and pulled the trigger.

## Anika – Now

I go to see the Carters first thing in the morning.

At the beginning, I was glad to have this academic couple in our surreal jail. Surely if anybody was able to offer a rational explanation, be steadfast and level-headed, and disentangle the strands of absurdity that were wrapping Michael and me in this suffocating nightmare, it would be them: two college professors. From my interrupted stint of higher education, I learned to look up to those who had scaled the academic heights. Marvin and Emily Carter both used to lecture at the University of Iowa, he in the Anthropology department, she in Psychology. They seemed old to me at first until I realized they were no older than my son's father. Marvin, a stocky mid-western guy with a nervous laugh, and Emily, a slender brunette with the long fingers of a pianist, from somewhere on the East Coast. No kids. I hoped they would be my friends.

Unfortunately, this was not what happened. The Carters handled our imprisonment worse than anybody else, with the possible exception of Buddy. Well, at least Buddy learned to make moonshine, while Marvin only learned to consume it in inordinate quantities. No explanations or plans for escape were forthcoming from these two academics. I had to cope on my own.

That first morning when I woke up in an unfamiliar bed, I had a panic attack because I did not remember whether Michael was supposed to be with me or with Roy. Our custody arrangements were the armature of my life, giving shape to the passage of time, so much so that in my mind these different chunks of my existence had different colors: red for my days with Michael, blue for Roy's. At first he insisted on keeping him for several days at a time to let me study for my pharmacist's license, but now Michael was going to daycare and the blue squares on my internal calendar shrunk to alternate weekends. That was the first thing every morning, even before I opened my eyes: the wash of imaginary color telling me I should jump out of bed to make breakfast for my son or could lie in a little longer. But all I could see in my mind now was murky gray.

I sat up and stared uncomprehendingly at the drab curtains and a rickety bedside table. Neither were mine. Pale dawn light seeped through the crack in the curtains, but the room was inhabited by shadows. I automatically reached for the bedside lamp and my fingers slipped off the wood of the table. There was no lamp. I got up and staggered to the wall, searching for the switch. No switch. I bumped into a chair, bruising my knee, but the pain was drowning in the horrified realization that I did not know where my son was. The fact that I did not know where I was either was secondary to the horror.

I yanked at the curtain and blinked at the bright foliage of a garden that must have miraculously grown in a single night on the asphalt forecourt of my rental apartment. Behind the nodding feathery tops of the trees, I caught a glimpse of a towering gray wall…but none of that mattered now. I had to find my son!

I let go of the curtain and tried to open the door of the smallish bedroom I was in, but it was locked and I panicked, hammering on the door with both hands. Only later did I realize the door opened in and I was so muzzy I was trying to push instead of pulling. But my hammering did produce a result: a voice, coming from somewhere on the other side of the wall:

"Mummy!"

After that, everything was done because it had to be done for Michael's sake. Learning the laws of our new existence, getting acquainted with my fellow inmates, discovering the Boxing Day. I did try to engage Marvin and Emily in discussions about the nature of our jail or the possible means of getting over the Wall, but it was useless. I had better luck with Ruth and her Bible-quoting sermons. At least she had a story she could live with, even if I could not. Marvin and Emily just fell apart.

But today I need to talk to them again. I have a feeling that there is some piece of the puzzle that I am missing, a random sliver of knowledge that will fit in to make all the difference. If anybody has this piece, it would be the most knowledgeable people among us. And I have to try. Michael is growing up, and my son is not going to become a farmyard animal, prodded into obedience by spooky noises. The rest of them may have accepted their lot. I won't.

I ask Michael if he wants to come with me. It's no surprise that he pouts and shakes his head. If I had any illusions that Marvin Carter could step into Roy's shoes and play a father figure to Michael, they have been dashed. Marvin with his nervous laughter and awkward talking-down to a child is the opposite of Roy, who was natural with Michael because he treated him as his equal. And

Emily's depression is not something I want Michael to witness, so I don't object when he says he is going to play with Carol. I trust Melissa will keep it together for the sake of her daughters.

I am stunned by how neglected the Carters' cottage looks. Clearly, they have not done any work on the garden that is turning into wilderness. The vegetable plot is smothered by a tangle of weeds, and the fruit drop litters the ground under the trees like a scatter of green golf balls. What are they going to eat when winter comes? Will they rely on the unpredictable bounty of the Boxing Day only?

Or do they believe that winter will never come – at least, not for them?

As I come closer, I see that the porch of the cottage is trashed, the boards splintered as if somebody hacked them with an ax. With my heart in my throat, I creep closer, looking for traces of blood.

There is none that I can see, but something is lying by the steps: a dark bundle, too small to be a body, too large to be anything else.

It is a bird.

There are no birds in our jail. For a long time I watched the sky, hoping for a glimpse of a plane or a white smudge of contrails. There was none, and after several weeks of staring into the blue or grey void I realized something else was missing: birds. Since that morning when I woke up in an unfamiliar bed, I have not seen a single finch or jay or crow.

The dead bird that is lying by the Carters' porch, its bony legs sticking into the air, is too big for any of these. There are bald eagles in Iowa, but it doesn't look like one.

And we are not in Iowa anymore.

The pungent reek of decomposition wafts into my face as I bend down, studying the bird. It has a bald head like a vulture but the rest of it is covered by...fur? No, a strange mixture of fur and feathers, a patchwork of grey and brown that seems to be clumsily sewn together. Its wings are tiny. How could it possibly fly?

The creature is unnatural. It is a poor sketch of a bird made by somebody with no knowledge of biology. It is a jumble of discordant elements roughly glued together. It has no business being alive – or dead.

But it was alive, the sweetish stink of rot is a testimony to that. And it is boiling with maggots. I draw away, disgusted.

A maggot squirms out of the carrion and crawls away. It is as long as my middle finger. Are there maggots that big? Despite my revulsion, I pick up a stick and poke at the dead bird. A veritable maggot rain drums upon the ground. They are much bigger than anything of the vermicular kind I have ever seen. They are paper-white, with fat segmented bodies. I turn one over with a stick and stifle a scream.

On the underside of the creature is a human face. It is tiny, like a porcelain doll's, but recognizable. Two unblinking round eyes, a cupid-bow mouth, a miniature nose. It seems to grow out of the maggot's squirming belly.

And now I see that the dead bird has no eyes.

I back off. I should be used to madness by now. The most important aspect of our existence is that it makes no sense. The enclosure has rules but no rhyme or reason, nothing like the tidy equations that Roy believed ruled the Universe. Once I accepted this rule of chaos, I learned to survive.

But this…this is worse than anything we have experienced so far. Madness within madness, the breakdown of the basic categories we use to navigate the world. Bird and beast, human and animal, life and death; they are all jumbled together in this unexpected carrion.

And what happens next?

I look up and realize that the windows of the cottage are scribbled over. It looks like the Carters have used soap to write on the glass – over and over again, the same phrase.

"You will burn."

I want to leave, to run away. But there is nowhere to run. We are caught up in this miniature hell, imprisoned in its nonsensical horror. We are embedded.

If the Carters went out at night, they are dead, but I need to make sure. And if one – or both – of them went completely bonkers, I have to find a way to render them harmless. With Buddy gone, Marvin Carter is the only adult male remaining. He is strong. He has knives in his kitchen, as we all do. He can be a danger to the rest of us.

I climb the steps to the porch, casting an unwilling glance at the dead bird. The roiling of the maggots feasting on its dead flesh is going on but most of them are hidden, just an occasional white flash that, fortunately, does not show the human face on a carrion-eater. But the bird itself looks even more monstrous than before: an offensive mosaic of mismatched features, a ragdoll of creation. I am reminded of Frankenstein's creature.

Could it be one of the monsters that come at night? Does it mean they can be killed?

The door swings open before I can knock, and Marvin Carter confronts me. Even though I expect it, I am still shocked by how bad he looks. He is unshaven; his t-shirt is stained, and I can only hope the stains are food.

"What do you want?" he barks.

"Where is Emily?"

"I don't know," he replies indifferently.

"Did she go out at night?"

Before he can answer, I hear a weak call from inside the house. Thank God, Emily still shelters behind the closed curtains and locked doors!

But what do I care if she chooses the same way out as Kathy and Buddy?

Because if they all succumb to the inexorable calculus of despair, one by one, at the end it will only be Michael and myself. And I can't let it happen. In order for my son to survive, he needs other people beside me. He needs a community.

Even though another glance at Marvin's stubbled dirty face makes me doubt it's true. Maybe we are better off on our own.

"What is this bird?" I point to the carrion. "Where did it come from?"

Emily staggers into the hallway. She is wrapped in a filthy blanket, her hair a mess.

"Anika!" Her face dissolves in a lopsided smile that makes me realize she is either drunk or high – and since there are no drugs available to us, this leaves the first option. Did Buddy unload his entire homebrew supply on the Carters before he walked out after the sundown?

Marvin steps away from his wife, as if from a pile of stinking garbage. Emily, oblivious, urges me to come in. I hesitate. Marvin stares at the dead bird as if finally made aware of its existence.

"Did it fly over the Wall?" I ask.

We don't know what's on the other side. We did try to get over the Wall at first, but it is fifty feet high, as smooth as glass, with no gateway or exit. Buddy's attempt to build a scaffolding…well, let's just say it taught us a lesson.

But my question now is not rhetorical; it comes out of a sudden suspicion. I took it for granted that all of us shared the same knowledge about our prison's origin and purpose: none.

But what if I was wrong? What if some of us know more than they say?

That first morning, after making sure Michael was okay, I staggered into the garden and ran into bewildered Kathy peering over the hedge that separated her domicile from ours. Reassured by her grandmotherly presence, I peppered her with questions. It turned out she knew nothing. She had woken up in an unfamiliar bedroom, just as I had. Kathy lived alone, so she went out looking for her cat who was not there. Neither was Melissa's golden retriever, as I found out later. No pets. No phones or computers. No personal possessions.

Kathy and I went exploring, zooming in on other voices coming through the trees. We discovered that our world consisted of five garden cottages, laid out in a circular pattern, and surrounded by a towering Wall. That was it. No streets, squares, or public spaces. No lawns. The gardens had paths but in order to move from one garden to another we had to hack makeshift gates through the hedges. Everything was utilitarian, stark, and unfamiliar. Everything was designed to keep us in and to make it possible for us to survive on the bare minimum of necessities. The gardens bore fruit. There were water pumps in the kitchens, the likes of which I had only seen in historical movies. There was indoor plumbing of sorts. And as we found out later, there were the Boxes.

On that first chaotic day, exchanging hysterical exclamations and sharing ignorance, I realized that nobody had any memory of going to bed the previous night. I racked my brain but all I could bring back was the recollection of talking with Roy on the phone about Michael's night terrors. This was sometime in the early afternoon. Roy reassured me he had not told Michael anything about embedding. And after that…I drew a total blank. They all said the same: no memory of the night before we all woke up in our respective cottages. But was one of them lying?

Because it turned out that while we had inexplicably lost some knowledge, we had also gained some. As the sun slipped behind the Wall, uneasy silence settled on our small group. We were crowding on Melissa's porch while she was trying to calm down hysterically crying Carol, and I cuddled Michael. Safety in numbers. The air was balmy outside, and there was no reason to go indoors, to scatter to our respective cottages. Except that an inner voice positively screamed at me to do so.

We exchanged puzzled glances. And then Michael tugged on my hand.

"We need to go home, Mummy," he said. "We need to lock the door. Monsters are coming."

We scattered as quickly as a group of frightened preschoolers, each family or individual following my five-year-old's instructions.

That first night, hearing the noises from outside – the chewed-up incomprehensible gabbling of the Yakkers, the long, sweet trills of the Canaries that felt like boiling syrup poured into my ears, and the thunderous shuffle of the Walkers – Michael and I huddled on the bed together, my arms around him, his head tucked under my shoulder. Eventually he fell asleep and I remained by his side, paralyzed, chills running up and down my arms. It was as if his instinctive knowledge of danger in the dark was transferred to me by some sort of bodily osmosis. I knew that there were monsters in my garden. I knew they were real. And I knew that even looking at them was death.

The next day we had a community meeting of sorts, the first one in the increasingly dwindling series, and it turned out that everybody had the same knowledge. Melissa, Buddy, and their kids barricaded themselves in the parents' bedroom. Kathy and Ruth, each in her respective cottage, spent the night in prayer (Ruth) and weeping (Kathy). Marvin and Emily held each other and conversed in hushed whispers. The knowledge of the night danger had been planted in our heads by the same forces that had imprisoned us in this leafy cage embedded in the unknown terrain outside the Wall. We knew that nights were deadly. We knew that once the gardens were beginning to fill with dusk, we needed to be indoors, curtains drawn, doors and windows locked. The thing was, we did not know how we knew.

About two weeks after that awakening, Buddy decided to build scaffolding next to the Wall. He cut down a couple of trees, sawing through the trunks with a kitchen knife. He was a true handyman, Buddy was, and the reason the scaffolding or a ladder had never been built was not his lack of skills.

I saw him hauling pieces of timber toward the Wall, and I had an immediate and instinctive reaction that I can only compare to the nausea one feels when seeing a roadkill rotting in the sun. It was as incontrovertible as the bubble of acid in your stomach; not an emotion but a bodily reflex. My head swum so badly I had to clutch a tree for support.

When Buddy touched the Wall, he fell down to his knees and threw up. And then Melissa ran out of the cottage and dragged him away.

We are not held inside this prison by the Wall but by our own fear of the unknown on the other side. We do not know what we are afraid of. We only know that we are afraid. And this fear did not come from experience. It was implanted in our head by the same force that made us resurrect our childish terror of the dark and the monsters that roam within it.

And now, looking at the Carters, I feel suspicions bubble to the surface. How stupid I was, to believe that we would all pool our resources, share our skills and knowledge, and learn to survive together. We have nothing in common: a random selection of people plucked out of our ordinary lives by some accidental stroke of ill luck, some malevolent glitch in the Universe! Roy believed the world was as logical and precise as one of his topological shapes; I knew better. The world is filled with accidents. The future is open-ended. Chaos rules.

The Carters know something. Judging by how badly they are coping, they are on the verge of taking the final step into the dark. If I don't force the truth out of them now, I will lose my chance.

I turn to Emily, the more sympathetic one of the two.

"You know what's outside the Wall, don't you?" I ask.

"Yes," Emily says.

"You don't," Marvin interrupts contemptuously. "You are just making up stuff to look important. But I do. I know what's outside the Wall."

## Roy-Before

He tried to call Anika several times on the drive to her apartment on the outskirts of Des Moines but was not surprised to hear, "Leave a message". It was very late, and he knew Anika slept with the phone by her side only on the nights when he had Michael. It was not because she distrusted him, she explained, but what if…

He understood the fear-infested "what ifs" of the maternal imagination, but when Michael was at home with her, she was not worried. She would turn off her phone and they would sleep through the night, nested together in the perfect self-sufficiency of mother and child.

The image of their warm bubble of domesticity embedded in the unrelenting darkness made him shiver.

He was not sure what he would say even if she did pick up the phone. Roy did not envision her disbelieving him. Since the situation was so clear in his mind, he expected it to be clear to others with the same knowledge. But there was nothing that could be done. No apocalyptic scenarios ever involved anything like that. You could hide from a meteor strike, you could shelter from a nuclear war, you could survive a plague or a zombie invasion, but how could you escape when the fabric of reality unravelled around you?

So why was he driving through the night? Soon enough, Google maps would be as irrelevant as medieval grimoires. Distance would be a meaningless term, and so would be "early" and "late". Space and time were falling apart. The manifold was crumbling.

Roy remembered looking at the orchid shape on his monitor and seeing it gather in like a flower closing at night. The black spots on its petals, the zigzags of disintegration running through its perfection. And then the monitor blinked out. It did not turn off. It simply blinked out of existence.

Who else could he call? To give them a fair warning, no matter how unnecessary. Roy realized how pitifully small his circle of acquaintances was. He had never cared before. Michael and Anika provided all the companionship he wanted, but now the need to hear a human voice was overwhelming.

He remembered a face he had not seen since his father's funeral. Kathy Rasmussen had been a friend of his father. Perhaps more than a friend – Roy did not know the details of their relationship and did not much care. Had his father decided to embark on a second marriage, he would have been on board with it. It had not happened; the old man had remained faithful to the memories of Roy's mother, but Kathy had been a frequent visitor to the farmhouse. Roy had genuinely liked her: a sweet lady with a shy smile who never judged him, never asked pointed questions, never hinted he should get a job or a wife. Unfortunately, he had lost touch with her after his father's death. He realized, belatedly, that Kathy did not even know he had a son, but her number was still in his Contacts.

He speed-dialed her as his pickup sped through the dull darkness. The headlights illuminated the pockmarked tarmac, but he could not see the reddish glow of the city lights in the distance. The flat land lay all around him, swathed in the impenetrable night, and Roy thought how ironic it was that he who loved the clear prairie sky was now pining for the harshness of artificial illumination.

Kathy picked up after a couple of rings. She recognized him immediately and did not even sound particularly surprised to receive a call from her boyfriend's son in the middle of the night.

"Roy? How are you doing?"

"I'm okay, Kathy. Sort of. Listen, the reason I'm calling is that something bad is going on, and I want people to know about it. Just in case something happens to me."

"Goodness! What is it? Don't tell me you are mixed up with a bad crowd!"

"No, nothing like that. I'm fine. It's the world that is falling apart."

"It's been doing this for a while now."

"It's bigger than that. The end of all."

"You mean, like in the Book of Revelation? Never took you for a religious kind."

"I'm not. It's knowledge, not faith. Anyway, Kathy, I just wanted to tell you I really liked having you around. And so did my dad. I know, we are not a demonstrative kind, but it's just…I wanted you to know."

Kathy chuckled.

"I did know, Roy, but thank you for telling me. Anyway, you can always come to me if you need anything. I'm sorry we lost touch after your dad died. Maybe it's not too late."

It was too late, Roy thought, after they had ended the conversation. It had always been too late. It had been part of the manifold from its very inception, from the moment of the Big Bang. Nothing that he or his father could have done would have changed it. Time did not exist. Past, present, future – they were all the same, and now the illusion of time was coming to an end.

Still, he felt better having spoken to Kathy. The spark of human warmth their conversation had ignited glowed in the night surrounding him. He realized why he was speeding toward Anika's apartment as spacetime was falling apart around him. To be in the same bubble with his son and his son's mother.

## Anika-Now

"So, what is outside the Wall?" I ask Emily.

"Fire."

"Fire and brimstone?" I can't keep skepticism out of my voice. I have had enough apocalyptic verbiage from Ruth. If this is all the Carters know, I am wasting my time.

Marvin barges in, unexpectedly supporting his wife whom he had put down a minute ago.

"I saw it, Anika. The world has been destroyed. There is a raging inferno outside the Wall."

"You saw it? How"

He sighs and motions at me to join him on the porch. Emily also sits down, still huddled into her blanket.

"The night before, I got a call from an acquaintance. He was ranting and raving, telling me that reality was crumbling. 'Manifold collapse', he called it. Something was eating up the fabric of the universe itself. I barely knew the guy. Of course, I was sure he just flipped or was on drugs. I slammed down the phone. But as I went back to the bedroom, I saw…"

He falls silent.

"Saw what?"

"The fire," he whispers. "Buildings melting down. Human torches staggering down the street. It was falling down from the sky, long streamers of pink, orange, scarlet. The rainstorm of embers and ashes. The sky was blazing but there was no sun. It was as if the darkness itself caught fire, and pieces of it were curling up and fluttering down. And beyond the burning sky…I saw…figures. Giants. Monsters. Heads of snakes, bodies of women. A dog braying at the moon, and the moon laughing back at him."

This is madness. I look at Emily, who is nodding enthusiastically.

"Did you see it too?" I ask.

"Yes," she says. "I told Marv what it was, but he would not listen to me."

"And what was it?"

"Archetypes."

"What?"

"Nonsense!" Marvin interrupts, slamming his fist on the wood. "It was an invasion!"

"That's what I said!"

"Wait, wait!" I am trying to stop this marital fight before it gets totally out of control. The fact that both of them are drunk is not helping. And something that Marvin has just said niggles at me, but I can't figure out what it is. I turn to Emily.

"Did you say archetypes? Isn't that…like stories?"

She nods enthusiastically, and it comes back to me. My interrupted liberal arts education may be good for something after all.

Archetypes are images from the deepest part of humanity's collective unconscious. Our oldest fears, our collective dreams, our shared narratives. Archaic stories from the dawn of history, sedimented into images that are still haunting us today. The hero, the monster, the dragon. Mother and child. Lovers, separated and reunited. In college I studied Carl Jung, the psychologist who developed the theory of archetypes. I thought at the time it might be useful for my future writing career.

"We have been invaded by our own nightmares," Emily says.

It's a good line. I look to Marvin, who is scoffing.

"You don't agree?" I ask.

"I worked with indigenous tribes to study their mythology," he says, his voice dripping with scorn, "and I can tell you that stories can help you make sense of things, but they can't take a bite out of you. Those creatures that cavort outside every night, they are real. Not to mention the fact that there is no archetype of Yakkers."

"Tell that to my patients," Emily throws back. "Their stories are just as real to them as this table. And they can take a bite out of you. I saw them self-harm, leaving scars that a shark would be proud of."

"That was then, and this is now!" Marvin bellows. "Don't you get it? This is all over and done with. We are imprisoned by something that's not human! Something more dangerous than your snivelling neurotic housewives! This is no fucking archetype rotting just under your nose!"

He jumps up and saunters away, kicking the dead bird as he leaves. Another clutch of giant maggots spill out. I can definitely see tiny human faces plastered to the underside of their bellies.

I glance at Emily, but she is smiling beatifically, lost in her alcoholic haze.

"He thinks it's aliens," she says.

I can't say that the idea hasn't occurred to me.

"But you don't think so?"

"Why would aliens keep us in this cage and provide for us?"

"An experiment, maybe," I say, but I sound unconvincing even to myself. What kind of experiment would run for three years with no variables? Even rats in a maze have more stimulation than we do.

Emily's dilated pupils follow the path of her husband as he stumbles toward the Wall.

"He wants to go out tonight," she says. "To make contact."

The ice that flows through my veins makes me shiver. The idea alone is enough to darken the sunlight.

"But this is death!"

She shrugs.

"Everybody wants to be the hero of their own story," she says, unconcerned, and I realize that Emily no longer cares if Marvin lives or dies. Maybe she no longer believes her husband is even real. Maybe she thinks we are all archetypes now, cardboard figures in some dusty museum of forgotten apocalypses.

A whiff of decay from the bird reaches my nostrils. Well, archetypes don't rot, do they? It's easy for Emily to slap an important-sounding label on our jail, but it actually explains nothing. No matter how hallucinatory our experiences are, they are real. Pain is real, hunger is real, Michael's cough last winter when he got cold and shivered in my arms, his forehead beaded with sweat, that was real. And if Marvin's burned body is found in his Box, this will be real and forever. The dead don't come back. Time only moves in one direction.

Another pale wormlike shape rises from the swarming mess of mangy feathers and slimy flesh of the monster as it lies in the sun. Breeding maggots.

Something tugs at the edge of my memory.

"So what is it?" I point to the bird. "What kind of an archetype is that?"

A vertical wrinkle cuts through Emily's forehead as she stares at the bird, perplexed.

"Maybe…" she begins uncertainly.

A scream cuts through the afternoon hush.

It is my son's voice.

# Roy-Before

He made several more phone calls as he sped through the goo of darkness. Reality folded and tore around him, and unravelled like a piece of scrunched-up fabric.

There were no lights on the highway, even though according to the maps on his phone he was within a short distance from the suburbia of Des Moines where Anika and Michael lived. But there were brief flashes of white in the black sky; not like lightning but rather like cracks, as if the dome of heaven splintered and then reluctantly glued itself together. These flashes were so quick that for a while Roy thought they were optical illusions, induced by fatigue and tension. But gradually they began to last longer, and Roy realized he was not hallucinating. It was the world that was out of joint, not him.

The phrase triggered some vague memory he tried to fish out of the depths of his tired brain as the pickup flew through the empty highway. It was midnight according to the dashboard clock, so no commuting traffic, but where were the trucks and the interstate travelers?

Probably in the same place where the lights had disappeared. He had passed several small towns where streetlights and billboards used to shed their ghostly illumination throughout the night, but now there was not even a flicker. The darkness reigned supreme. It was no longer a mere absence of light but a palpable presence. It was thick, swirling, and gluey like polluted water. If the towns were still there, all the lights were off. Roy did not want to slow down to find out if they still existed. He kept calling Anika every ten minutes, leaving increasingly long and detailed messages.

His headlights illuminated a billboard. Roy involuntarily slowed down.

It should have been an ad for a personal-injury lawyer or a real-estate agent. Instead, a face leered at him from the pool of lifeless illumination: a broad, grinning, yellow face spotted with black rosettes like a hyena's skin. Its lips were also black and stretched by protruding broken teeth. The squashed nose gaped with its torn nostrils.

Roy sped on, refusing to look back. In the corner of his eye he caught a ponderous movement, as if the face on the billboard turned around to follow his progress with its small, savage eyes.

No need to think about it. Think something, anything, else.

The world is out of joint…where did this come from?

He remembered. It was something Anika had once quoted to him. The quote came back to him in its entirety:

The time is out of joint; O cursed spite!/That ever I was born to set it right.

It was from a play by Shakespeare, wasn't it? He could not remember which one.

One of the many discussions he and Anika used to have in that halcyon period before the birth of Michael had reduced their interactions to the matters of bank transfers, time scheduling, and diaper provisions was about space and time. She believed that time was like a story, fluid and unpredictable. He knew that time did not exist. Spacetime was just one aspect of the topological manifold that was the universe. The past and the future were the same, petals on the multidimensional flower of the eternal now. His life's work was to visualize this flower in all its geometric glory.

'But how can you say that math is the language of God and also that the future is fixed? Language is like a story: beginning, middle, end. Past, present, future.'

'But when you tell a story, you know the end from the beginning. Before you say something, you know what it is.'

'Really? For you, maybe. A lot of people don't know what they are going to say before it comes out of their mouth.'

A not-so-subtle jab at his "difference". Yes, it was true; they had little in common. There had never been anything between them, except for Michael. A couple of middling sex sessions – not too spectacular, not too embarrassing – and then the miracle of their child.

But could there have been something more? Could he have loved Anika? Did he love her?

What a useless, ridiculous question as reality itself was falling apart around him! Shouldn't he be more concerned with the reason for the collapse of the manifold? Should he not use his brain, while it still functioned, to find out what had happened to wrench space and time out of joint, to breed a multitude of monsters out of the breakdown of universal logic?

In using topology to predict the fluctuations of the stock exchange, Roy had reduced time to space. His graphs caught the fluidity of change and froze it in the perfection of geometry. The work he was doing now – the work that could bring him the Nobel or the Fields Medal when completed – was the extension of his method to the entirety of history. He was trying to capture time and imprison it in a single multidimensional shape. He was trying to reduce change to certainty. He was trying to optimize the language of God.

But what if time did not want to be stopped? What if it fought against its topological prison, throwing itself against the bars of geometry like a wild animal in a zoo? What if forced into revealing the end of the story that was the creation, the language of God was sputtering and breaking down like the speech of an Alzheimer patient? What if its garbled words roamed the streets and glared from billboards, manifesting as monsters?

What if he, Roy, was at the center of the topological whirlpool, sucking in reality?

What if he had caused it?

He refused to believe it. His mind, used to the purity and predictability of shapes, rebelled against the randomness of storytelling, in which the teller did not know the end when they started at the beginning.

But he suddenly remembered Anika's face when she had told him about her pregnancy. Remembered his own question about abortion.

She had refused. She had been angry with him for even raising this possibility.

But he had seen the hesitation on her face. There was a moment, a split second, before she opened her mouth when she did not know what would come out of it, and their entire lives hung in the balance on this single moment of choice. He saw a different geometry, an infinity of possible futures radiating from Anika's unspoken word. Michael could have never been born. He and Anika could have gotten married and had other children. They could have gone their separate ways. She would have been a famous writer by now – or had become a real estate agent. He could have finished his project – or gone back to farming. All those stories, waiting to be told; God's words trembling in the void of possibility.

And now God's language was gabbling nonsense, breeding monsters with each syllable. Was it his fault? Could it possibly be that by creating a mathematical model of the manifold he had broken some fundamental law of the universe, wrenched time out of joint?

He should be entering West Des Moines. He had done this route so many times that he knew with precision the time of his arrival, but he had been on the road for at least twenty minutes longer than he should have been and there were no familiar signs. Just the same endlessly unspooling ribbon of the highway in the drab darkness. He pulled over and came out, cradling his shotgun.

When he had shot the many-headed worm that used to be his dog, it was as if reality blinked and creased. When it stabilized, he saw that Ada had tumbled down the stairs and lay on the floor panting, her fur spotted with blood. He rushed down to her. She whined and licked his hand. Four legs, a curving tail, a single head. And a wound in her left flank.

He had shot his dog! Roy felt bile rising in his throat. He was attached to Ada, though he was not sentimental about animals, but she certainly did not deserve being maimed by her master. He lifted her in his arms, deciding to take her to the vet.

And then a small head popped out from the bleeding hole in Ada's flank. It was a miniature of the dog's own elongated muzzle, with the same tawny fur and brown eyes, but one third of its size. It emitted a high-pitched whine and licked Roy's hand. And then another head, and another, emerged from the wound, all identical, all whining, all flapping tiny pink tongues. Ada was blooming with copies of herself, becoming a bouquet of tangled dog-flesh.

Roy backed off and bit hard on the inside of his cheek. He tasted blood. The ballooning pile of dog-heads kept growing.

He had left it on the floor of the farmhouse. By now it might have dwindled to nothing – or consumed his entire property.

Clutching the shotgun, he strained to see anything. The beams of his headlights were swallowed by the soupy murk. Roy realized that the darkness was roiling with restless movement, splitting apart and reconstituting itself. There were no objects hidden in the night anymore. The night itself became an object.

Another of those whitish cracks appeared above his head, but now Roy could see that its sides were composed of multiple overlapping layers like the petals of an orchid. A white luminescent substance was oozing out of the crack, illuminating nothing but itself.

Until it caught fire.

## Anika-Now

I plunge through the raspberries, flattening the canes in my wake, thorns lacerating my skin and catching on my clothes. I am oblivious to the pain. Nothing matters but Michael's cry for help. Is he injured? Has the Wall been breached? Are the rules of our jail suspended, and the monsters now roam in daylight?

Until I emerge into Melissa's garden and come to a stop when I see Michael and Carol on the porch. Carol is crying, and Michael is upset but seems to be unharmed. I rush to him, grab his small sturdy body, and examine him for injuries. Nothing. I turn to Carol and see a bruise on her forearm.

"What happened?"

Melissa has also come out, and our queries overlap and cancel each other out as do the kids' tearful replies. Eventually I make out that Carol accuses Michael of hitting her with a stick, while Michael insists it was not him. A normal playground spat – except I never had any complaints from the daycare about Michael being aggressive or bullying other kids. Is the imprisonment getting to him?

"You must tell the truth and apologize," I say sternly.

"It was not me, Mommy!"

"Don't lie, Michael. There were only the two of you."

"Not true. Carol's dad was here. He told me he wanted me to pull him out, so I reached for him with a stick, but Carol was in the way so it hit her on the arm...I did not mean it, Mommy, I promise!"

Buddy was here? But Buddy is dead!

Melissa and I exchange glances, and I see colour visibly draining from her face.

"What do you mean 'he wanted me to pull him out?' Pull him out from where?"

Michael mutely points at the plum tree next to the porch. It is a gnarly but not particularly tall tree with an untidy canopy. Tiny unripe fruits hang from its branches.

"He was stuck in the tree."

There is no Buddy in the tree, needless to say, and as I reluctantly examine the trunk, there is no fissure or fork where an adult male could be stuck. But no matter how much I want to believe Michael just made up a bizarre story to justify a fight with his friend, I have a sinking feeling that somehow he is telling the truth.

Meanwhile, Melissa has examined Carol and pronounced the bruise to be nothing. The little girl stops sobbing and is eager for the treat of homemade jam her mother promises. I want to ask her whether she saw her father, but I hesitate. What if she does not know he is gone?

I catch Melissa's eyes and beckon her to step outside.

"I'm sorry…" I begin.

"I saw him," she says quietly.

"Buddy?"

She nods.

"Where?"

"In the kitchen. Last evening when I sent the girls to bed and was checking the locks."

"Did you…speak to him?"

"He was…he was on the table. Like he was stuck in a hole in the tabletop or something. Only I could see under the table and there was nothing there. Like it was only half of him."

I shudder, trying to visualize the scene.

"So it was like a mirage?"

She shakes her head.

"No. He was…solid. And he tried to speak. But blood was coming from his mouth, so I could not make it out. I did not scream because of the girls. And then he just…disappeared. But not like in a movie, you know. It was like the tabletop became mud or quicksand and sucked him in. And later I saw it was warped. Like it melted and cooled off. But it's wood. It can't melt."

I stand still.

Blood was coming from his mouth.

This jail, this enclosure, this embedding, it has kept us safe for three years. As long as we obeyed the rules of a child's nightmare: don't look out, hide your head under the blanket, stop your ears.

But the rules have changed. A nightmare but maybe not the same one.

"Where is Holly?" I ask, dreading the answer. What if she has followed in her father's footsteps?

"With Ruth. She is teaching her the Bible."

You shall burn.

Something occurs to me. We haven't had a Boxing Day in a while. Supplies are running low.

We can't survive without Boxing Days. If whoever – or whatever – is keeping us here decides to discontinue feeding us, we will have no choice but to try to scale the Wall.

Normally we know it's a Boxing Day because the lid of the Box would be up. But what if…

I glance at the kids in the kitchen who have apparently forgotten their fight and are now demolishing the rest of Melissa's jam. I sidle over to the Box and lift the lid.

Inside lie the charred remnants of a man, his arms lifted up in the characteristic pugilistic stance of a burn victim. His face is reduced to little more than a blackened skull, but it is still recognizable.

It's Buddy.

## Roy-Before

Reality was folding around him like a flower at night. He thought he could discern the petals of the manifold closing in, the night embedding him in the capsule of unrelieved dark, and the sparks of fire lazily floating down like fireflies, snooping him out.

The manifold was trying to stop the infection. The virus that was destroying spacetime. The virus that was him.

He had hacked the language of God – the algorithm that ran all the possible stories and histories that together create the universe. But by doing so, the algorithm was corrupted. The language stuttered. The stories fell apart into slivers of monstrosity.

Roy soberly considered his options. He had a shotgun. One blast to the head – and it would all be over.

But would it?

He remembered the fractal shape on his computer. For most other people it would be just a pretty visual, a multidimensional mandala that would probably give them a headache instead of enlightenment if they stared too long into its slowly rotating heart. But Roy was different, he could read topology like Anika could read stories. And he could see that the corruption was now set in, running on its own, spreading through the manifold like a fast leprosy. He could kill himself but there was no guarantee that it would be the end of him. He could come back in an unrecognizable shape, distorted into something as monstrous as the many-headed Ada. He could remove himself from this particular iteration of the phrase that was Roy Hunter – and then it would pop up somewhere – or somewhen – else. And most of all, killing himself would not save Michael and Anika.

He suddenly realized why his taciturn father who would not know a Klein manifold from a whisky bottle had stood by his peculiar son, defending him against school counselors and snooping busybodies, why he had slaved on the farm to finance Roy's seemingly useless degree in theoretical math, why he had talked of his son's achievements to anybody who would listen. You did not abandon your flesh and blood. You did not abandon your family.

The time is out of joint; O cursed spite!/That ever I was born to set it right.

Michael and Anika were his family. He had to set time right for their sake.

With a familiar reflexive gesture, Roy took out his phone. No signal.

The screen cracked, and a multitude of scuttling legs fanned out of it as if a large centipede tried to wriggle out. Roy flung it away. A flaming ember landed on his hand. Another one floated so close that it singed his eyebrows.

Reality was trying to cauterize the corruption within itself.

Roy closed his eyes, ignoring the pain of the burn and the soft hissing of spreading fire above his head. He ignored the wet sounds in the distance, as if a giant mouth whispered incomprehensible insults beyond the horizon. He ignored the earth trembling under titanic footfalls.

He called upon the capacity of his unique brain to visualize what others could not even imagine. The language of God was both a story and a picture, both static and dynamic, both time and space. Nobody could decipher it because nobody could hold the two concepts simultaneously in their heads. Until he met Anika he had not been able to either, but now he knew that every picture was a frozen story and every space was a seed of time.

And with an effort so wrenching that it felt as if his entire being was unravelling, Roy forced himself to see the manifold spreading out into the future, spinning out possible paths of history like a busy spider. But every path that he tried to follow ended in the same thing: fire. An apocalypse was raging across the universe – no, across all possible universes. His algorithm has broken the code and infected the manifold with the plague of monstrosity. And so the fire was cauterizing the spreading infection – and failing to stop it.

There was only one option left. He found the nesting shapes of his timeline and forced the petals of probabilities to close around a kernel of existence where his son was. He could not see Michael or Anika, of course, but they appeared as bright oscillating spots in the self-reflexive fractal shape that was filling his brain to the exclusion of everything else. Protect. Shelter.

Embed.

The nested space contained within the larger space closed in, a bubble within a series of bubbles like a mathematical Russian doll. Other oscillating spots seemed to have been caught in it together with the ones that Roy knew to be Anika and Michael, but he could no longer follow them. The visualization in his brain was breaking up, the synapses overloaded and shutting down like overheated computer circuits. He smelled burning, and realized it was himself.

As Roy slumped onto the unsteady ground, the titanic footfalls came closer, shaking the bones in his body, wrenching him apart into a whirlwind of fleshy petals.

## Anika-Now

I don't want to tell Melissa what lies in the Box, but she has seen it too. Our eyes meet.

I realize she needs to bury her husband. But how? We cannot let Holly and Carol see the horror that he has become. The obvious thing would be to do it at night when the kids are asleep. The obvious thing is the equivalent of stepping off a high-rise's roof in what used to be our world. Our reality.

It just brings home what this reality is. The monsters are not just scary noises in the dark. Our choices, our feelings, our actions, all have become equally misshapen. Horror is creeping into us, poisoning and distorting everything. We are all monsters now.

I have left Kathy's burned body in her Box. How could I have done this? In Hinduism, desecration of a corpse is an ultimate wrong, punished by bad karma throughout reincarnations. Was it really me, the Anika that I used to be, so conscientious, so moral, so proud of my rectitude? Always doing the right thing!

I take Melissa's arm and lead her away from the Box. She is shaking. I shoo the kids out of the kitchen and make her a cup of herbal tea.

"We were not getting along," she says in a monotone. "He was drinking. Not making any money. I had to support both of us."

Melissa was a beauty consultant Before. Not much call for beauty treatments in the Now, but she knows some medical basics, and with my pharmacist training we have managed to provide rudimentary care so far with the occasional packet of aspirin and some bandages delivered on a Boxing Day.

"But it got better just before…before all this," she goes on with a sob. I press a tea towel into her hand but let her speak. She needs it. My role is to listen.

"He got a job as a contractor. Working on some guy's farmhouse. A weird guy, Buddy said, living there all alone. But he had loads of money, and he paid well. We were on the upswing. Until…until…"

A bright bulb goes on in my head.

"What was the guy's name? The one Buddy worked for?"

"Hunter, I think. Roy Hunter."

## Anika- Now

I managed to calm Melissa down. We agreed that we would ask Ruth to give the kids a Bible lesson tomorrow, so we would be free to bury Buddy and – belatedly – Kathy. I am not looking forward to it, but it has to be done.

After that, I went and talked to the Carters again. Or rather, I talked to Emily – Marvin was "resting", she told me, which I took to mean he was sleeping off his hangover. Or maybe he really cannot sleep at night. Emily said she made earplugs out of old towels, but Marvin refused to use them. He believed he could decipher the alien language if he listened to the screams, the yells, the trills, and the footsteps outside. I am convinced he will be gone soon – if not tonight, then tomorrow night.

I also talked to Ruth, who was suspicious of my sudden interest in Bible lessons for Michael but went along with a chat. Her face was so gaunt that it seemed to be melting from the inside.

It is all true.

I often wondered what principle of selection was responsible for this unlikely group of strangers thrown together in the prison enclosure, to be tormented by invisible monsters at night. A single mother, a struggling family, an academic couple, a retiree, a former librarian. Eventually I decided it was pure chance.

Not chance. We are all connected, rotating around the invisible center of gravity like a group of planets around a black hole. The black hole called Roy Hunter.

Buddy worked on Roy's farmhouse. The Carters knew him from the time he got his PhD; they even hung out together at some academic watering-hole. He had called Marvin on the night before it all ended. Ruth was the librarian at the school he attended. Kathy…it is too late to ask, but I remember Roy telling me that his father had a lady friend with whom he had been in a long relationship but refused to marry out of loyalty to his dead wife.

And of course, us. Me, the mother of Roy's child, and the child himself. Michael, with his father's intent eyes and thoughtful disposition.

Roy is not a sociable person. His circle of acquaintances is pitifully small. Would the enclosure be much bigger if he had more?

But where is Roy himself? If some alien intelligence has decided to collect people related to him, why skip him? I could understand why an alien race might be interested in Roy: a mathematical genius who has done what most people believed could not be done. He predicted the unpredictable. Calculated what cannot be calculated. Tamed the unruly randomness of the stock market.

Roy pinned down the future.

And maybe the future did not like being pinned down.

My head is swimming, and I realize it's getting late. Michael is not yet back from Ruth, so I go to fetch him. As I cross the Carters' garden, I stop and look at the dead bird. Marvin did not bother to bury it, and it is just lying there in the sun, breeding maggots.

Breeding maggots.

I remember it now. It is a line from Shakespeare. Hamlet.

For if the sun breed maggots in a dead dog, being a good kissing carrion…

Hamlet is supposedly mad when he speaks to Polonius, but there is a method to his madness. He is pointing out that the world is darker, more dangerous, and more disturbing than most people realize. Hamlet is not mad. The world is.

Emily thinks we are beset by archetypes. Well, maybe. Or maybe something is happening to the very fabric of reality. Maybe the monsters infesting our gardens at night are only a manifestation or a symptom of something much deeper. Maybe the logic of the universe is falling apart.

The bird's corpse is roiling with hidden life. A wormy shape rears from the scattered feathers. And then another.

They have puffy baby faces with round eyes and tiny teeth in cupid-shape mouths. Worms? Dolls? Babies?

The categories we used to organize our lives are useless. The language of God is devolving into nonsense.

## Anika - Now

I give Michael his dinner. He is listless and preoccupied. Carol seems to have forgotten today's altercation, but he is still brooding.

I plant a kiss on his silky light-brown hair – so much like his father's.

"Mommy," he asks, "when are we going to go home?"

What is home? A rented apartment in West Des Moines? Roy's farmhouse? Michael's daycare?

Reality?

"Soon," I say, knowing it's a lie.

Michael is fidgeting.

"Embedding is bad," he says after a while, "but dad knew how to end it."

My heart skips a beat.

"How do you know that?" I ask.

Michael does not reply. He has not inherited Roy's spectrum disorder – if this was what it was – but occasionally he lapses into long silences when his eyes seem to stare inwards. I know better than to pester him when it happens.

I clear the table, seeing how low we are running on provisions. Unless another Boxing Day is coming soon, we are not going to survive much longer. The produce from our inexpert gardening won't keep us alive.

He climbs the stairs to his bedroom.

"Do you want a story?" I call after him.

"No."

The door slams, and I wearily go up to my own bedroom to prepare for the night filled with the noise of monsters frolicking outside. Has it gotten worse recently? Will the silent dark cottages no longer offer protection? Will the blanket over the head prove as useless as it was when I was a child?

I had night terrors, then; my mother told me. Eventually, I outgrew my childhood fears, only to acquire a whole set of new ones.

The last dregs of sunlight are bleeding away. The foliage blends into a mass of shadows. We have no clocks, but I guess it is about 8 pm. In my former life, I would laugh at the idea of going to bed so early. It strikes me again how among all the many deprivations of our prison life, the absence of artificial lighting is the worst. What would I not give for a simple candle like the ones my ancestors used to keep darkness away? Diwali, the Indian festival of lights, Christmas' glowing reindeers, Hanukkah menorahs. All humanity's defiant challenges to the rule of the night. And here we are, cowering in our dark homes like animals in their lairs after sundown. In winter when we use our woodstoves to keep warm, we even bank up the fires so no glimmer will give away our wakefulness to the monsters. Implanted prohibitions are keeping us penned in, not the Wall.

But if Roy's work is the reason for our embedding, where is he? Is it fair that we are suffering for what he has done while he is not with us?

Fairness does not come into it. Again, I realize how off-base his vision of the world was. Roy imagined a perfect and complete structure, harmonious and balanced; a poem in God's language where the end coexists with the beginning. But reality is more like an untidy snarls of horror stories, all intertwined with each other for no rhyme or reason. And the end is not written yet.

I go down, lock the front door, and walk into the kitchen to draw the curtains. I pause with my hand in the air.

What if I stay awake, stay by the window? What if I could finally see what's out there?

And what will happen to Michael if I end up like Kathy and Buddy?

The thought of him makes me draw the curtain tightly. It's now pitch-dark in the kitchen but I know the position of every bit of furniture by heart, so I navigate it easily. As I am preparing to climb the staircase back to our bedrooms, I hear soft, measured footsteps outside.

A Walker!

They don't show up every night, but when they do they keep me awake with my head half underneath the pillow, straining to hear and fearing to hear too much. There is a hypnotic quality to the soft, heavy padding that goes around the cottage, never stopping, never pausing: a circling presence that prowls in the night, sniffing for a way in. The heaviness of the footsteps suggests a big creature; their muffled quality – something feline. A giant cat? An oversized tiger? But what predator would just circle around a house for a whole night, as steady as a metronome?

I climb the stairs and enter Michael's bedroom. My eyes have adjusted; I can see the blurry outline of his night table, the blocky shadow of the bed.

The bed is empty.

The next few minutes are swallowed up in a panic so overwhelming that it feels like drowning, like losing my breath in the ocean, being pummeled by wave after wave of disbelief, denial, and despair. I paw through the bedclothes, flinging them on the floor, I throw myself at the furniture, I yell until I am hoarse. I drop onto the floor and crawl about, hoping he has hidden himself under the bed or in the corner.

But I know he is not here. He is nowhere in the house.

My son has been locked out. In the darkness. With the monsters.

He must have sneaked out while I was preparing his morning snack in the kitchen. And I locked the door without checking on him first.

The door of the cottage cannot be opened from the outside without a key. And the key is on the kitchen counter.

I stand up, blood rushing to my head. My vision is stippled with floating patches of light – a false dawn produced by my treacherous brain. The Walker is still circling the cottage but now the footsteps are overlaid with high-pitched sugary trills that set my teeth on edge. A thread of distant howling. And closer, a gabble of many voices in an incomprehensible language, as alien as if cicadas tried to speak English.

I stagger to the window and pull off the curtain.

Silvery radiance floods the room and for a moment I am so overwhelmed by this miracle that I just gape stupidly at the thin crescent floating above the shaggy treetops.

The Moon! I have forgotten it even existed. I have forgotten that night has its own light.

But the illumination is so dim and uncertain that I cannot discern anything in the garden below. Ponderous movement, shaggy shapes, quick fluttering. If there is a little boy lost among them, I can't see him.

I run downstairs, unlock the door, and throw it open.

Fresh cold air, spiced with strange odors, pours down my throat like wine. Cinnamon, crushed leaves, excrement, magnolia. And overlaying all of them – a faint bitter odor of burning.

The night is alive with movement. Something looms ahead of me, something so incomprehensibly big that I have to crane my neck to take it in. Moonlight dapples with silvery reflections on its hard, slick skin like a turtle carapace. A creak as the creature – is it a creature? – bends toward me.

Something careens into me, bowling me over, so I end up on my back in the row of lettuce. The stench of raw meat makes my eyes water. A human face disfigured with horseshoe-shaped markings, its black lips stretched to reveal a row of peg-like teeth.

Human? No. A hyena pretending to be human.

A clawed hand descends upon me, but I roll aside and spring to my feet.

"Where is my son?" I yell into the night.

The enormous turtle-skinned creature makes another creaking step toward me. I can see now that it is shaped like a cone with no obvious legs or arms. Its carapace is composed of embossed plates that crackle as they rub against each other and part to reveal bottomless cracks. Faces peer from the cracks, idiotically cherubic faces with pouting mouths and blinking eyes.

I run through the dark garden toward the Wall.

There is radiance on top of the Wall. Not the gold of sunlight but the sullen feverish glow of a forest fire. I can't see any flames, but the bitter reek of burning is now stronger, overwhelming everything else.

Something bars my way. It is a cluster of naked stick-like figures, all glued together every which way, clumsily hopping on its accidental limbs. Its multiple mouths release an unending stream of idiotic gabble.

I maneuver to avoid the creature, but the hyena-man is behind me, gaining fast. And behind him, in the flood of moonlight, I can see the Walker as it rounds the corner of the cottage. Two enormous barefoot legs, each the size of a full-grown man, joined at the top into a lump of pale flesh. The legs pause and then change direction, padding toward me.

"Where is my son?" I scream into a swarm of monstrosities.

Something rears into the flaming sky above the Wall.

It is a man, nude from the waist up. I can't see below the waist because this is how far up the Wall reaches.

The Wall is fifty feet high.

The fire illuminates his face in dancing scarlet.

It is Roy.

Or is it? The face is pixelating like a bad TV set, the features falling apart and then reforming, seething, surging, and receding. The body is a roiling mass of…bodies?

The figure is made up of a swarm of its own smaller versions, each of them a swarm of even smaller Roys, and so on ad infinitum. My brain hurts as my eyes are drawn into this infinitely recursive giant, trying to focus and failing. A fractal Roy. A self-mirroring topological body.

"Where is Michael?" I scream at him.

His hand reaches above the Wall and stretches toward me. Each finger is the thickness of my waist. But from close up, the hand dissolves into a crush of revolving nude bodies, desperately clutching at each other even as they are drifting apart, tugged away by the centrifugal forces that are pulling the creature to pieces. I back off – and feel a fetid breath at the back of my neck. The hyena-man's teeth clack next to my cheek, his claws raking my arm.

The fractal Roy makes a sound like a thousand overlapping recordings of the same cry. It is so discordant that my eardrums are about to explode.

The cry is my name.

I clutch at the hand of one of the smaller Roys that constitute the main body. It is like trying to hold onto a hurricane. The composite giant is breaking down into a cloud of helplessly floating bodies, each of them undergoing its own progressive disintegration. He is trying to help me, I know, but it is like trying to enter into a story to help a character. We exist on different planes.

The hyena-man's claws close over my shoulder, drawing blood. I kick him off, grasp a branch, and start climbing. The tree is not tall enough to reach the top of the Wall – none of them are – but at least it will lift me above the fray.

Until the Walker stomps toward me. The pair of joined legs towers above the treetop. There is nothing it can grab me with – the juncture is just a blob of sagging flesh – but it kicks the tree I am holding onto for dear life, and it trembles and shakes. Green fruit-drop rains down. I manage to cling to the branch, but I know that after another kick I will plummet down like an unripe apple. Down, where the hyena-man is pacing, his yellow claws fully extended on the tips of his spotted fingers.

Something erupts from the thicket of bushes: a flock of bald chicken-like birds, each the size of an eagle, a nauseatingly sweet trilling coming from their gaping beaks. I recognize them – the same kind as the dead bird in the Carters' garden. I guess my nickname of Canaries was appropriate, after all. In the mingled moonlight and firelight, I see that each bird has a rider: a bleached maggot-like creature, hanging onto the birds' mangy feathers.

My situation is desperate. The Walker lifts his leg to deliver another kick. The Canaries are flapping their pimply wings, ready to pluck me from the tree. Their maggot riders bare their pointed teeth and cry in baby voices.

I strain upward, scrabbling at the glassy surface of the Wall. A couple of centimetres more and I could haul myself over it. I am high enough to almost reach the edge. My life is measured by this "almost".

I lift my face to the giant. By now Roy has become a constellation of revolving bodies, a galaxy of himself, a fractal image of infinity. It is painful to look at him. My brain is not made to see the armature of reality.

"Help me," I say quietly.

"Mummy!"

Somewhere in the cloud of infinitely diminishing identical bodies, an opening is formed. It looks like a tunnel – or a pipe, leading in or leading out. By now I have given up trying to assimilate this space to the familiar grid of three dimensions, and it does not matter because of the small figure that is running toward me.

"Michael!"

I grasp my son's hand just as the Walker delivers another kick. The apple tree breaks with a screech and collapses into a rustling pile of branches, but Michael's small tug is enough to carry me over the top of the Wall.

I am sprawled on a flat surface, clutching Michael's small body. The top of the Wall is a ledge, broad enough to prevent us from tumbling down and narrow enough to make our situation precarious. But never mind! We are together!

Michael wriggles away from me, and I raise myself, peering over onto the other side.

On the other side of the Wall, an inferno is raging.

Something is wrong with my vision. I can make out the complex dance of fire and shadow below me, a puzzle of ruins lit up by the sporadic sprinkle of flames. But the perspective is all wrong. It looks as if the landscape is curling inward, forming into a tube that sucks me toward its impossible narrow end, only to spit me out into another identical black-and-red landscape that is beginning to curl inward like a sheet of paper on fire, drawing me in, and then again and again…

It is impossible to bear. My mind is cracking under the strain. I squeeze my eyes shut and grope for Michael, reassured when I grasp his warm hand – the only certainty in the reality gone mad.

"Look, Mummy," he says. "This is our embedding."

I open my eyes just a crack and look where he is pointing. It is our enclosure. Our shelter. Our jail.

It looks stunningly ordinary after the distorted space on the other side of the Wall. A small piece of suburbia in the midst of a multidimensional storm. Five identical homes surrounded by orchards and vegetable gardens, laid out in a circular pattern. The Wall curves around them, cupping them in its protective embrace, separating them from the furious chaos outside. An island of normalcy in the midst of madness.

I try to remember what Roy told me about embeddings. They are spaces nested within other spaces but separated from them by their topology. Ours is the familiar three-dimensional space within…well, whatever that is. The apocalypse? The end of the world? Or the worlds?

And where is Roy? Still grasping Michael so hard that he makes a sound of protest, I look around for the fractal constellation of Roy, the composite giant that Roy has become. He seems to have disappeared. And then I see a man sitting on the edge of the Wall, facing away from me, his legs dangling over the manifold abyss.

"Roy!" I call.

He turns to face me. With relief, I see that he is an ordinary solid-looking three-dimensional Roy.

Well, maybe not quite ordinary. As I sidle closer, I realize that he looks like a plastic mannikin made in the likeness of my ex-boyfriend, and not even a particularly realistic one. His skin is glossy and lifeless, his eyes are unblinking, and his clothes seem to be of a piece with his body, but it is a definite improvement over the galaxy of rotating Roy eidolons.

"Anika," he says. "I am sorry."

"As well you should be! What is this? What are these creatures?"

"God's stutter."

"Come on! I don't need metaphors anymore."

"It's not a metaphor. Math is the language of creation, but the creation is always in the process of becoming. It is a story, not a picture. I should have listened to you. You said the future does not exist. I tried to predict the future, and my math was so powerful that it infiltrated the structure of spacetime and corrupted it. The more I tried to pin the universe down, the more it struggled against me. And in the process, it broke. I managed to write down one last equation that created the topological embedding within the corrupted space. To protect you and Michael. I don't know why it snagged other people I knew. I must have made some mistake. But I failed even in this. Corruption has started seeping through the Wall. These creatures – the monsters – are broken bits and pieces of the language that underlies reality. Bad words with teeth and claws, meaningless syllables made flesh."

"Why do they only come at night?"

"I don't know," Roy's eidolon says. "Unless…"

He breaks off, but Michael interjects.

"I made it so, Daddy," he says proudly. "I made your embedding better."

His face is lit up by a happy smile. He is unfazed by the fire reflections in the sky, by the cackling and screeching of the monsters, by the plastic face that looks like a nightmare of his father. He wriggles away from me and scoots toward Roy's eidolon.

"I knew they would come," he explains. "But monsters only come at night, everybody knows that. So, I set it up this way."

The eidolon's countenance is not made for human expressions but something like astonishment glimmers in his glassy eyes.

"How?" he asks.

Michael shrugs.

"I just did."

Of course. A child's story: the monsters that roam outside but cannot come in as long as the windows and doors are locked, and the blanket is safely pulled over the head. How did I not recognize it?

Our jail has been designed by a child. A child who is my son. A child with the power to speak God's language of creation.

My eyes meet Roy's over our son's head.

"Can he repair it?" I whisper.

He shakes his head.

"I don't think so. What happened, happened. Unless you can make time run backward, and I can't do it."

He can't because he does not believe in time. But in stories, time is flexible and pliant. The same story can be retold numberless times, and every time it can be given a new ending.

I turn to Michael.

"Why are you crying, Mummy?" he asks.

I hug and kiss him. No, this is impossible. It is too much to ask. No mother should be asked to make a sacrifice like this!

Numberless mothers did.

"I love you, Michael," I say. "Now, let me tell you a story. It is about how your dad and I met."

## Anika-Before

She was bored by the lecture. The man at the podium droned on about the manifold, multidimensional topology, embedded spaces. The latter caught her attention for a second as she visualized a nested enclave surrounded by raging fire…the seed of a story? No, she was not going to write another boring apocalypse-by-numbers. Too many of these already. Anika was not sure what her first novel was going to be about, but she knew it would be great. Her creative writing program was going so well. Her tiger mother wanted her to study pharmacology. Well, no way! Anika knew what she wanted to do and who she wanted to be. A family and a safe job were not on the cards.

A man next to her in the row stirred and muttered something under his breath. Anika stole a glance at him. An older guy with a receding hairline and a pleasant inconspicuous face. Probably not a student. What was he doing here?

He got up, oblivious of the disapproving looks, and made his way to the door. Grateful for the diversion, Anika slipped out after him. They almost collided outside and smiled at each other.

"You did not like the lecture?" she asked.

"He has no idea what he is talking about!"

"Really?"

He was rather good-looking, she noticed, with a graceful physique and fluid movements. Too bad he was so much older!

"He claims topological spaces are imaginary."

"Are they not?"

"No. Topology is the study of the underlying mathematical structure of space and time. How can it be imaginary?"

"I never thought of math as real," Anika said.

"Math is more real than real. It is the language of God."

"I am an atheist," she said.

"Can't a language exist without a speaker?"

Anika frowned.

"No," she said. "A story needs a storyteller, and a protagonist. When you start telling a story, you don't know how it will end. The future is unpredictable."

"I don't think so," the man said. "I think the future and the past both exist in the manifold. The story of the universe is already written."

Anika shook her head.

"You are wrong," she said.

They looked at each other for a long, awkward moment. She felt embarrassed; why was she so rude to this stranger? Surely a philosophical disagreement did not merit biting his head off! What did it matter, after all? He was clearly intelligent, good-looking…and if he was older, so what? Anika preferred older men.

"Can I buy you a drink?" the man asked.

She hesitated. What if they did go out? It would not be the end of the world, would it? They could just hang out, talk about topology. Who knows, maybe she would get an idea for a story out of it!

She opened her mouth and was surprised to hear what came out of it.

"No, I'm sorry. Too busy today. No time."

And she walked away.

As a great fan of Doctor Who and other fantastic time travel stories, when my friend sent me a message giving me the idea that became this novelette, I knew I had to take on the challenge. Soon, "Hey, you should write a book about x and y that do Z" became a fully fleshed out story that was a blast to write. My dad loved history dramas and science fiction (and rom-coms as well), so this story has so much of what I know he'd absolutely love. And I know he'd be tickled pink if he were here now.

The process of combining future tech with history-accurate settings and descriptions resulted in what was probably the most in-depth research I've done for my writing. I also had to ensure that my BIPOC characters felt authentic and were written with the utmost respect while I took them on this wild journey. My dear friend, Nati, was key to helping me with that process and I am so grateful for her.

 I took many historical liberties but overall I believe the settings, tech, and people will feel real enough to immerse you, the reader, into the world I've woven together. Enjoy!

*Kelly D. Holmes*

Kelly D. Holmes is an avid reader of all things scifi, spec fic and fantasy. She's been writing ever since she was ten years old and has worked on everything from comics to songwriting. She lives in London, Canada and can be found curled up by the fireplace with a good cup of tea.

# THE IMPOSSIBLE MAN

## by Kelly D. Holmes

"**C**ome on, Xo, you got this. You got this. Just...a little...further. Yes!"

Xiomara Lopez snatched the small vase off the noblewoman's night table from her outstretched perch on the window ledge. Her blasted stola had nearly tripped her up on her ascent to the second story but now, with the prize in her hands, it had been worth the risk.

The soft blue glow of the moonlight painting its edges, the small, colourful vase looked insignificant. But this worn out piece of pottery held answers to a question historians had been puzzling over for millennia. And now they would have what they'd been searching for, thanks to the efforts of the Canadian Academy of Temporal Travel.

Xiomara turned the vase over, dumping out the dead flowers, and studied the letters engraved on the bottom. "'My Little Lucretia'," she read the inscription aloud, translating from Latin, and ran her thumb over the embossed seal of Julius Caesar with a thrill. Finally, after years of finding only hints and incomplete accounts on crumbling parchment, ancient archives checked at their source had led to this moment. This was proof Cleopatra Philopater and Julius Caesar had a surviving heir - a daughter, stowed away in plain sight.

This heirloom would break open the door for researchers to discover who the modern descents might be, if there were any, invite them to become patrons of the Academy, and of course ask permission to do a study into their family tree. The Historical Accuracy Department of the C.A.T.T. would have a field day with this. Textbooks around the world would have to be updated to reflect this discovery and any others this new rabbit hole led to in the coming years.

Xiomara rummaged through the linen bag she carried slung over her shoulder and pulled her holo scanner free. Holding up the vase, she let the tech do its job, taking 3D holographic imaging of the object and inscription. Since the scanner's invention, the C.A.T.T.'s field agents could not only make fully detailed documents of objects and significant people, but the Academy could now use those scans to make accurate replicas of every ancient object and structure they encountered, eliminating the need to remove artifacts from their countries of origin.

In fact, temporal travel had nearly put archaeologists like her grandmother out of business before the C.A.T.T. created a program to train them for a very different kind of field. Xiomara smiled at the thought of her abuela hearing about this discovery. Nobody would ever get her to stop gushing over her little Xiocita every chance she got. Not that Xiomara minded, of course.

The scan completed, she stuffed the scanner back in her bag and laid the vase gently on its side on the small side table, hoping Cleopatra's potential descendant would think a bird knocked it over while she was away.

Once Xiomara took the scan back to the present and had it properly documented in the archive, a temporal forensic anthropologist would be sent to take DNA samples to compare with those in the database. Then if a genetic match was found, the story would break to the media and it wouldn't be long before everyone with even a possible tie threw themselves at the C.A.T.T. for the chance to be named a descendent of Caesar and Cleopatra. Xiomara rolled her eyes. She'd never find a parking spot at work now.

Positioning herself on the window's ledge, she prepared for descent. But as her foot touched the outcropped stone of the villa's wall, a traitorous crack sounded through the empty night air and her heart lurched for a split moment right before —

She slid.

Down.

Down.

Down.

Gritting her teeth, she found purchase, her arm wrenching in its socket at the sudden catch of her entire body weight. Xiomara exhaled, relief washing over her, though her pulse still crashed over and over in her ears.

She really needed to get back to the gym after this.

Closing her eyes, forehead pressed against the warm stone, Xiomara lifted her other arm to find a second grip. The vine she'd used earlier to climb up was all but shredded from her slide, so anything strong enough to hold her would have to do. If she could just —

"What are you doing up there?" The male voice spoke in accented Latin, likely someone from the Outer Empire. The voice sounded curious rather than stern.

Xiomara froze.

Crap crap crap crap crap crap, she chanted in her head.

If she was lucky, it was only a bored patrol guard. She hadn't stolen anything, but he didn't know that. She inhaled deeply, recalling her training. All she needed to do was get away from him long enough to activate her recall to the temporal lab, then everything would be fine. There were plenty of dark corners for her to scuttle to once she evaded this stranger.

"Are you deaf? I said, what are you doing up there? You look ridiculous."

Xiomara bristled at his tone. Anchoring herself the best she could, she swiveled enough to get a look at the man. In the dark, she saw very little of his features beyond what the moon highlighted of his sharp jaw and large eyes, casting him in hard edges of silvery blue.

She couldn't stop the annoyance from flowing out of her along with all the sweat the strain of holding her grip brought. "If you are a guard, I would appreciate it if you just arrested me now. And if you are not, you could at least help me down instead of gawking and giving unsolicited commentary."

The man put his hands on his hips and tilted his head, like a puppy trying to discern a command. "You speak very strangely. You must not be from the Empire."

"Yes, well, you do not speak like a native either, friend." Her Latin wasn't that bad. "At least I bothered to — oh no…"

With a small yelp, Xiomara lost her hold and it wasn't until she lay face up in the bushes below, branches cracking and snapping under her, that she realized she'd only been hanging six feet from the ground.

She'd absolutely be asking for portable grappling gloves when she got back home.

A shadow appeared over her and then a face came into focus. "Are you always so athletic in the middle of the night? It is a strange time to be scaling walls." The man extended his hand to her.

Now that he was closer, it was clear he wasn't a patrol guard. A toga draped from his broad shoulders, obstructing most of the tunic underneath. Resigned to her necessary encounter with him, Xiomara allowed him to pull her out of the broken foliage and to her feet. In the darkness, he wasn't much to behold — short curls, average build, and skin darker than most Romans as far as she could tell. He wasn't particularly tall for a man of her time, but being short herself, he towered over her.

She brushed dirt from her stola. "What makes you believe this is a stranger's home and not my own? Can a woman not enjoy some recreation?"

He studied her for a moment before reaching casually to pluck a twig from her disheveled coiffure of dark brown hair. He wore an amused curve to his mouth. "Because I know the donna of the house and I would remember if you lived with her."

Xiomara's hands went cold and tingly even as her cheeks flushed with heat. She schooled her emotions. "Fine, I do not live here. Are you planning on calling the guard?"

"That depends. Are you a thief? If so, you are a terrible one."

"How charming of you," she shot, brushing past him. "And in truth, I am certainly not a thief. Quite the opposite, in fact."

Why did she say that? Now he was likely to ask —

"What is the opposite of a thief? Someone who brings things back?"

Xiomara heard the man following after her. Good thing she knew that the owners of the house were on a tour of Dalmatia at the moment or else all this hushed talking would have drawn their attention. She sighed, trying to conjure up an answer that would satisfy him enough to leave her alone. "I was hired by the donna to make sure no one stole from this villa while she and her family were gone. Nothing has been taken so my job is done for the day. Now, if you will excuse me, I need to head back to the inn. I am very tired." She accentuated her statement with a large yawn that wasn't entirely fake.

"Why would she hire a woman to do a job like that?" he asked from several paces behind her, as if he couldn't decide whether to mind his own business or continue following.

Xiomara rolled her eyes. "Perhaps because I am the best at my job and the donna is a smart woman of considerably fine taste. But by all means, please continue to insult your friend's choices strictly on the basis that I am a woman."

Silence filled the air between them and she hoped that maybe he'd become bored and sauntered off. But when his voice came again he was so close behind her that Xiomara nearly jumped out of her skin. "I did not say she was my friend. I said I knew her. She buys from my shop once a week and I deliver her goods myself."

"I truly do not care. It is late, I have fallen, and I want to go to sleep now. Alone," she snapped.

The man chuckled. "You think highly of yourself if you believe I have any intention of wooing you. I have certain standards to maintain."

Xiomara halted so abruptly the man collided with her back. A bubble of misplaced anger rose up in her. She knew she should be relieved, but his tone — cocky and condescending — rubbed every one of her remaining nerves the wrong way. Before she thought better of it, she whirled on him, arching her eyebrow. "Are you saying I am below your standards?"

The man was unfazed. In fact, he was smiling. "If you must know, I do not make lovers of suspicious strangers who climb walls at midnight. After all, I am not entirely convinced you are not a thief."

She bit down on her scathing comeback as the gentle vibration of her recall device buzzed under the skin of her forearm, reminding her she needed to go, and quickly. She sighed. "Well, thank the gods for that. I suppose that is fair. Now, this is where I leave you. Goodnight." She turned back around and headed down the stone street, expecting him to follow after her, but she heard no other foot falls outside of her own.

"Goodnight," he bid after her. "I will be sure to tell Donna Octavia her household is safe."

She grit her teeth and kept moving, refusing to continue this battle of wits. She didn't have time for it. Soon he'd be nothing more than a footnote in her assignment files. Yet, he hadn't sold her out to the guards, or made any untoward advances. The bare minimum as far as encounters went, but still. She stopped and turned back to him. It went against every protocol she knew but she did it anyway. "One more thing. If you are still living here in two years' time, you should consider moving somewhere else. The mountain is a sleeping giant that will not stay asleep forever."

She heard him chuckle as he raised his hand in acknowledgment and then walked away. Mentally scolding herself, she turned and headed for the nearest alley. The shelter of the buildings bathed her in shadows and she tucked her bag closer to her side, then she pressed the subdermal recall in her wrist.

A familiar tingle radiated through her body and in a second the moonlight soaked stones of Pompeii drained away to the black of the time lab's walls. The light slowly came up in the room, allowing her eyes to adjust. Thank God Leon had remembered she'd be returning from a night assignment. Last time, he'd forgotten to dim the lab and Xiomara saw spots in her vision for hours.

"Welcome back, Xoey," came a female voice through the intercom. Layla McDoogal, her temporal operations tech. She was in charge of programming Xiomara's temporal device for the correct dates and ensuring the recall came back home when activated. In cases of emergency or a user being too long in the field, techs would recall the temporal device and its user back to the lab, a failsafe that brought most temporal agents a sense of security.

"You're late and your BPM was elevated. Run into trouble?" Leon's voice sounded distorted over the intercom.

Xiomara sighed as she swung the strap of her bag over her head and deposited it into one of the processing bins. Someone would come collect it and take the scanner back for download while the bag itself would be sanitized and placed with the other first-century Roman apparel in the vault.

When the C.A.T.T. first started, they had commissioned costume designers from Hollywood to make all the field apparel as historically accurate as possible. Over time, the agents were able to accumulate clothing items they bought from vendors in every era they were sent to. Eventually, the apparel vault held more authentic articles than modern recreations, which helped the agents blend in better.

"You could say that, I guess. Some guy caught me trying to leave the donna's villa after I slipped on a window ledge. Fortunately for me, her bushes broke my fall."

"No injuries though, from what I can see on your monitor," Leon said after a pause. "Do you feel okay? Concussed?"

"Other than a sore backside and a bruised ego, I'm fine."

"Bruised ego?"

Xiomara shook her head. "It's a long story. I just want to get through decontamination and go home."

"Gotcha. Well, enjoy your spray-down! Your nose plugs should be on your shelf," he commented before Layla cut in with a crackle of the intercom.

"And don't forget Hazel's baby shower is tomorrow. You're not scheduled for another assignment until Tuesday so you have no excuses to bail on me this time."

Xiomara wrinkled her nose and gazed up at the dark windows of the time lab's observation deck. Leon and Layla were behind it, their headphones over their ears like Princess Leia buns. She could just imagine the smug look on Layla's face. "Fine," she conceded, "but that means you can't opt out of going to Zander's birthday at the Fox and Fiddle. And I'm sure it'll be karaoke night."

A pause and then, "You got me by the throat, Lopez, but deal." The crackle of the intercom came again and Layla's voice fell silent.

A cheeky smirk on her face, Xiomara waved at the dark glass and followed the adjacent corridor to the de-con room. She had already pulled off her clothes before she stepped inside the nearest chamber, swiping her nose plugs off the shelf where Leon said they would be.

As she stood there, hand against the chamber's tiled walls and waiting for the sanitization jets to commence, she couldn't stop replaying her encounter with the man on the streets of Pompeii. She encountered many people during her assignments, but he seemed to stick in her mind more than people usually did. A part of her hoped he had heeded her warning, but she wasn't quite sure why she cared so much.

Xiomara adjusted her bodice while striding through the alley and into the streets of what would become Budapest in about six centuries. This assignment detailed the documentation and cataloging of a lost silver comb from the Árpád Dynasty that turned up at a garage sale in Milwaukee. The appearance of such an artifact in a residential American town had antiquities experts baffled, but they needed confirmation of the carbon dating's accuracy and the experts' opinions before anything further could proceed. With the Mongol invasion a couple decades previous, the complete collapse of the Árpád Dynasty, and the coming outbreak of Bubonic plague, records of items pilfered from Buda Castle and sold for souvenirs were practically non-existent. The only thing linking the silver comb to the Árpád's was a half-faded embossed sigil.

So off she went to use her doctorate to confirm the accuracy of the comb's origins. The C.A.T.T. could then return the artifact back to the Hungarian National Historical Society where it belonged. Xiomara just needed to find the comb in Buda Castle without anyone knowing.

Which was shockingly easy, as it turned out. A small mention from the castle overseer in a written document had survived the Ottoman Occupation for centuries and found its way into the C.A.T.T. archives. Mundane record keepers were history's real MVPs, because without this one her team wouldn't have known a maid had been dismissed for suspicion of stealing on September 22, 1250. A perfect opening for a time traveller disguised as a lowly peasant to ask about employment.

Striding up to one of the castle guards, Xiomara kept her eyes trained on the ground as she curtsied before him. "I was asked to see László about a maid position, sir," she said, the early Hungarian dialect rolling off her tongue thanks to her maternal grandmother's modern fluency of the language. It was a challenge to remember the differences in the dialects though, and when the stakes were so high in the field, she sometimes wished things were like the old days where all an archeologist had to do was dig in the dirt and read dead languages instead of actually having to converse proficiently in them.

The guard hesitated for a moment and she flicked her gaze up to gauge his reaction. His features gave away nothing but he nodded in confirmation and let her pass into the courtyard. Once inside the grounds, she knew enough from the layout diagrams to navigate through the castle. Servants carrying laundry and herding chickens milled about between merchant stands and entertainer wagons. The cacophony of sounds reminded her of a country fair, minus the flashing of carnival rides. But the fair certainly smelled better — unwashed bodies and animal manure were her least favourite things about the Dark Ages, right after women's rights and the plague.

Xiomara passed into a hall leading down into the servants' wing. It looked like the unfinished basement of an old farmhouse, all exposed crumbling stone and dirt floors covered in straw. She got no more than fifteen feet when a man stopped her.

"Woah. You can't be down here. Why are you down here, woman?" The short man wore clothing slightly more expensive than the other servants, pointing to his higher station. László, she presumed.

Showtime.

"I am sorry, sir. My husband heard you were looking for a maid, sir. He sent me to apply." She lowered her gaze and fiddled with the hem of her apron, hoping to look as meek as possible.

He scrunched his brow. "I just sent word to the village not two hours ago. How are you here already? Nevermind. You're here now. Can you read and write?"

She hunched her shoulders. "No, sir."

He sighed, running his fingers through his brown hair. "I see. You know how to build a fire, yes? How to clean?"

Xiomara nodded.

"Good. I will start you off cleaning the bedrooms and starting the fires. It will be your job to make sure they are maintained in the evenings. Here, take this," he said, handing her a bucket of water and a rag. "Theresa will show you the rooms and you can get started when she's finished."

She nodded but didn't move. László eyed her suspiciously and then understanding came over him.

"Over there, girl with a blue dress. That is Theresa. Now go and tell her your name and what I said, understand? Get going."

Xiomara rushed past him to the person he showed her.

"Oh and keep the King's things out of your pockets. He doesn't take kindly to thieves in his house."

After two hours of being given instructions on the various royal members' preferences and individual demands as Theresa took her into each private chamber, they reached the queen's rooms where Xiomara spotted the silver comb winking up at her from Queen Maria's dressing stand. She did her best not to stare as Theresa babbled on about how the queen didn't tolerate being looked at directly and required a fire to be in the hearth at all times.

"Now I have been through the rules, you will start your duties here. The queen is taking her daily walk through the gallery and should be back soon. Make sure that fire is stoked high and wipe up any ashes that fall out. Understand?" The young woman, probably no older than Xiomara herself, had a heavy brow and grey eyes that regarded her intensely, like a cat seeing something odd out a window.

Xiomara nodded, dropping her gaze as a good servant would at the time. Without another word, Theresa turned and left the rooms, presumably to carry on with own duties. The second Xiomara was alone, she let out a deep breath and deposited her bucket and rags at her feet.

Time to do her real job. She hastened over to the gilded vanity and picked up the silver comb. Other than looking polished and not a thousand years old, it looked to be the same one she'd examined before leaving for the assignment. She turned the comb over, the gleaming metal catching the dying fire in its reflection, and saw the embossed sigil of the Árpád Dynasty. The crisp edges of the sigil and its placement in the queen's possession proved the findings without a doubt.

Laying the comb flat in her palm, she fished out the small camera her team had placed inside a hidden pocket in her skirt. She took an image of the sigil but as she replaced the camera where it belonged, a familiar laugh startled her from her focus.

It came from a distance, probably from the courtyard five stories below the queen's narrow window. Still clutching the comb in her hand, she went to the window and looked out over the small patch of courtyard she could see from her view. Only a few seconds passed before she saw the source of the laugh. Her blood ran cold and she swore her limbs went numb.

Impossible. Absolutely impossible.

There, laughing raucously at a child entertaining a small crowd, was the man she'd encountered in Pompeii — nearly a thousand years ago. He wore different clothes and had longer hair, but even from where she stood she knew it was him. And that fact was impossible.

She had to be hallucinating. Maybe her temporal device had malfunctioned and fritzed her brain somehow. Maybe she was simply dehydrated. She had gone straight to work after the gym that morning without stretches or finishing her bottle of water. Yes. That had to be the —

"What are you doing over there, child, and why is my fire not roaring?" came a stern female voice that made Xiomara whirl around in shock. The woman's fine dress, elaborately coiled plaits, and gold jewelry told her exactly who this woman was.

"I…uh…your Majesty, I —"

Queen Maria's eyes darted down to Xiomara's hand and her sharp tone turned low and deadly. "Why are you holding my comb?"

Xiomara's heart pounded like a battering ram behind her ribcage as horror swept over her. For half a second she was paralyzed, helpless to do anything but stare at the queen. When her mind caught up, she dropped the comb like a hot coal and raised her hands, palms out.

"I did not mean to hold it, Majesty. I was simply trying to —"

"Guards! Thief! Guards!" the queen screamed, the long brown plaits of her hair swaying with her intensity.

Crap, Xiomara thought. She squeezed her eyes shut to center herself. This was bad. If they arrested and searched her they might find her camera and she'd be forced to leave twenty-third century tech in medieval Hungary or stay and face having her hand cut off for stealing. Neither option appealed to her.

Instead, she bolted.

She may have knocked the Queen of Hungary off her feet as she shot past her and slammed her own shoulder into the doorframe in the process, she couldn't be sure. It happened in a hyper focused, adrenaline-fuelled blur. Her brain frantically tried to remember the layout of the castle from her assignment documents. Should she run left or right at the end of the corridor? She chose left, hearing raised voices and the heavy footfalls of armoured men coming down the hall behind her. Her calves protested and she cursed her trainer for pushing her a little harder that morning. She knew should have drunk that recovery smoothie instead of leaving it in the fridge for lunch.

An arch ahead of her led straight out into the courtyard. Though a mass of dark rain clouds obscured the sun, the brightness of outside stung her eyes and she staggered until her sight adjusted. She needed to find a place to hide and hit her recall, fast. She turned sharply to duck under a merchant stand and nearly fell backwards when she collided with another person.

"You…" he murmured, catching her arm before she took a tumble. His light brown eyes looked like pale honey in the daylight. And those eyes snapped from his shocked stare at her to the shouting voices of the guards who had just burst through the door.

"Quick. This way," he whispered to her in Latin as he grabbed her hand and whirled them both away from the commotion. He walked briskly behind the merchant stands to a tent displaying fine fabrics of all sorts of patterns and colours. They felt like silk as they brushed against her skin.

He pulled several garments from their perches and shoved them into Xiomara's arms as he released his grasp. "Put these on. Hurry."

She complied, too shocked and adrenaline high to argue. In seconds, she had donned a loose silk dress along with a fine linen headdress secured by a simple circlet. Thankfully the clothes were loose enough to fit over her servant's attire. When the man turned to observe her, something passed across his features she couldn't read.

Perhaps she looked truly as ridiculous as she felt, all flushed and perspiring in a too-big dress. He approached her in one stride of his long legs, a green rope belt and fur cuff in his hands.

The shouting and clanking of armour drew nearer. Xiomara heard the guards demanding to look into wagons and behind merchant stands in a frenzy. She almost startled at the man's touch as he looped the belt around her waist, cinching the fabric layers into an actual feminine form. Her heart thrummed in her chest so vigorously she felt her pulse twitching at her throat like a butterfly.

He had barely secured the fur cuff to her collar when a gruff voice called out to them. "You there! We are checking your tent for a thief. A servant woman. Don't try to stop us. If you are harbouring such a woman, give her up now and the queen may reward you."

The announcement of a reward for aiding in her arrest dropped a ball of acid into Xiomara's gut and she swallowed to keep the bile from escaping. Would he turn her over? Could she trust the impossible man beside her?

He must have seen the panic in her eyes because he softly brushed his hand against hers and laced their fingers together when she didn't protest. He turned to the guards and spoke not in rusty Latin this time but in fluent Hungarian. "It is my honour for you to search my tent and my wares if it will bring justice to the one who trespassed against our queen."

The guards didn't wait for him to finish his sentence before they barged past the two of them and roughly rummaged through the shallow tent of fabric, upending stools and tables and dumping out chests of silk. Had it not been for the patterned rugs covering the ground beneath the tent, the man's wares would have been ruined by the dirt. Xiomara barely lifted her eyes from the guards' pointed shoes, too worried one of them might recognize her.

Almost all the guards had begun moving on to the next stall when one of them stopped, to Xiomara's terror, in front of her. He roughly gripped her chin and lifted her face to look at him. She saw instant suspicion in his cold stare. "You," he said. "I have seen you."

"I would kindly ask you to unhand my wife, sir," the man from Pompeii said with more protective grit than she thought possible for a mere ruse. The guard washed his scrutinizing gaze over the man and then released his hold.

"You did not have a wife last week when you were here with your wares," he said, cold and threatening.

The man took in the guard with a calm focus before lifting their entwined hands up to press his lips to the back of her hand. He smiled into it, like a man in love, and the action sent a shiver up Xiomara's arm.

"We were married just four days ago," he lied and even Xiomara almost believed him — if she hadn't been the one he was talking about. "After our business is done here, we travel to the sea to celebrate our union."

The guard crossed his arms, clearly unconvinced. He turned his scrutiny on Xiomara. "Is this true?"

Xiomara lifted her eyes and nodded. "Yes, it is true." Gripping the man's hand tighter, she forced as natural a smile as she could conjure while every piece of her screamed to bolt.

This situation was not covered in her job description. Those good ol' days of archeology were looking really attractive right then. She'd rather face a mummy's curse than this.

The guard didn't drop his daggared glare. "Well then, let us all see the happy couple show us how happy they truly are. Come now, give your new bride a kiss."

Xiomara's blood froze and feeling left her face in a quick flash before returning hotly. She barely kept hold of her pinned smile.

Then, a squeeze at her hand. Then another. The sensation pulled her attention away from the guard and toward the impossible man. His gaze fell on her surprisingly softly, though she supposed it was all part of his act. Two squeezes at her hand this time. It took her a moment before she realized why he was doing it. His eyes dipped down to her lips and then two more squeezes.

He was asking to kiss her.

She darted her eyes sidelong at the guard and back again. The easy way to get through this was literally staring her in the face. Xiomara squeezed his hand back and swallowed.

She'd figure things out after she was out of danger.

One thing the man from Pompeii had going for him — his smile was beautiful. It lit up his eyes and sent small crows feet to their corners. His teeth were remarkably well kept for the Middle Ages. It had been dark the night she first met him, but he didn't look much different than he had then, well over a millennia ago. His long, dark lashes shadowed his cheeks as his gaze dipped back to her lips.

He leaned in and gently tipped her chin with his finger, so gentle in comparison to the rough handling of the guard. She closed her eyes, exhaling a nervous, shuddering breath.

Then his lips pressed against hers.

At first it was merely contact, soft but not intimate, but as he held onto the moment, she felt herself leaning in, melting the kiss she shared with this impossible acquaintance. Her heart stilled and her lips tingled. A wash of warmth flooded her body.

With a twinge of disappointment that she'd admit to exactly no one, the man pulled from their kiss and rubbed his thumb soothingly over the dimple in her chin before leaning away. He turned to the guard, wrapping his arm around her waist.

"If you do not mind, sir, my wife and I have some tidying up to do. I wish you wisdom in finding the queen's thief." He smiled again, this time tight and without his eyes. He was annoyed.

The guard uncrossed his arms but said nothing as he turned on his heels and stalked back to the rest of the castle guard, who were ransacking a fruit stand on the other side of the courtyard.

As soon as the attention was off Xiomara, she took a deep breath, chasing away the stifling anxiety that edged her vision in black. Frankly, she was shocked Leon hadn't told Layla to recall her based on her vitals alone. She'd have to have a talk with him when she got back to the lab. However, for now she was safe. All she had left to do was hit her recall.

The man cleared his throat and she realized with a wash of heat that they still held hands. "I suppose you are going to tell me the queen hired you to be the opposite of a thief," he said, an amused smile curling the edges of his mouth. This time, he didn't speak to her in Latin, but Hungarian.

Xiomara pulled her hand free and rubbed it as if he were a snake that had tried to bite her instead of the man who just kept her from causing a temporal fiasco. "Who are you? Are you working for the American Academy? If I had known you were another agent I would never have treated you the way I did."

His amusement turned to confusion and strangely she caught disappointment in his eyes. "What is American? What is an agent?"

She couldn't tell if he was joking or being serious at first, but the look on his face made her curiosity deepen. He had no idea what she was talking about.

Impossible. How was this possible?

As far as she knew, no science other than time travel could explain how a man she met in Pompeii twelve hundred years ago could still be alive and visibly unchanged in thirteenth-century Hungary.

Sweat dripped down her temples and the back of her neck, though it was late October and crisp enough to raise gooseflesh. Her hands trembled. She felt numb. She realized, later, she could have easily hit her recall, witnesses be damned, but in the moment curiosity and excitement wiped away all semblance of wise thought.

"I…are you a vampire?" she asked, backing away from him. Of course she knew they weren't real, but when faced with an impossible anomaly within known history, she had to consider the fantastical.

She didn't expect his reaction, though.

The man looked taken aback for a moment, a skein of red cashmere in his hands, then he threw his head back and laughed, light dancing in his gaze when he finally looked at her again. "Me, a dhampir?" he said, correcting her pronunciation. "I am more than certain my father was a goat herder and not a blood-drinking demon. Too bad my mother has long passed, or else I would ask her. Just to make sure." His tone hit light and teasing, but she didn't feel reassured.

"Then what are you? The last time I saw you, Vesuvius had not yet destroyed Pompeii, but here you stand."

He took a step closer to her and then retreated back to his original spot when he saw her shrink away from him. "Well, I am a man. I do not know what else I could be." He gave a shrug to emphasize his words as he picked up fabric off the rugs and tossed them back into their trunks. "Thank you for that warning you gave me. I almost decided not to leave Pompeii but it seems you saved me from a horrible fate." The teasing in his features faded and he turned somber. "Though, I often wonder what would have happened if I had stayed. Perhaps I would finally be with my family now."

Xiomara braved coming closer. She slowly bent and picked up a skein of white silk. "Tell me. What are you? How have you lived so long?"

The man took the skein from her and darted glances out at the courtyard. He gestured for her to come further inside the tent and once she had, he pulled the ties keeping the mouth of the tent open. The flaps closed and the only light seeped in through the seams. She heard a flicking sound and suddenly a light flared up from an oil lamp the man held in his hand. He gave the lamp to her as he turned over three stools and motioned for her to sit across from him.

When she hesitated, he sighed. "I am not going to bite you, if that is what you are thinking. Sit, please. It seems we have much to talk about and I do not wish to stand anymore."

Every bit of training in her said she needed to get back to the time lab and write a formal report about what she'd discovered, but when would she ever get this opportunity again? Thirteen-hundred-year-old men — living thirteen-hundred-year-old men — didn't pop up every day. The chance to have a real conversation with one was too good a temptation to pass on in favour of protocol. If she went back now, she may never find him again. All her questions and curiosity would eat her from the inside.

She sat slowly.

"Good," he murmured, also sitting. He took the lamp from her hands and placed it on the empty stool beside them. He searched her face, focusing so intently she felt like she was under a microscope. Now that the danger of the moment had passed, she took in all the features she hadn't yet noticed. Tanned olive skin clung to his lean frame, much lighter than it had seemed under the Pompeii moon, and the same dark curls crowned his head as before, only this time long enough to cover the tops of his ears.

Objectively, he looked better with the longer curls.

In the dimness of the lamp light his irises deepened from honey to dark sepia and the shadows cast over his face made his features sharper, as he had looked when they first met. He focused his eyes on the rug underneath them and she let her gaze slip down to this mouth.

She still felt his lips pressed against hers like an impression.

Her focus broke when he cleared his throat. He'd been saying something. That infuriating amusement in his expression returned. "I said we should introduce ourselves."

"Our names?" she asked, feeling heat rise to her face at being caught looking at him.

"Unless you prefer I call you Trouble? Or perhaps False Wife?" Despite keeping his tone light, something heavy edged it. He sounded a little afraid.

At least that made two of them.

"Xiomara," she said, holding out her hand. "My name is Xiomara Lopez. But you can call me Xoey if that is easier."

He hesitated, staring at her hand. Instead of shaking it, he took hold and dipped his head to it, a reverent greeting she hadn't expected. "I am Yedder. Currently Yedder Munatas, but I've gone by other surnames."

She blinked, recognizing the name. "Imazighen?" she said in horrible Tuareg. She didn't know much of the North African languages except a few sentences and the names of the indigenous people, which was why she rarely got assigned there, but she couldn't think of the right word for it in Hungarian.

He grinned. "You know my people? Since the Caliphates took over, very few know us. I have not seen my home in so long it makes me happy to hear you say that name."

"Where is your home?" She leaned forward.

"We call it 'mur n akush' but most of the world knows it as Marrakesh now," he replied, also leaning forward, placing his elbows on his knees.

"It is called 'Morocco' where I come from. Much has changed."

He furrowed his brows, a deep crease forming between them. "And where do you come from that so much has changed in Marrakesh?"

Xiomara swallowed. "It is...a harder question than you think." She paused, fiddling with the hem of her sleeve. If she told him, he might not believe her and think she was a liar. At worst, he'd get angry and she could recall herself immediately back home. He might tell other people and they would then think him a madman. However, nothing would harm the future by telling him, she consoled herself. "I am from a country called Canada that lies across the ocean. You have never heard of it, I assure you, because it will not be officially discovered for another two hundred years and will not become a nation for over six hundred years from now."

Yedder's mouth twitched, then he laughed to himself. Then he became so still she wondered if he were about to fall over dead, which would be just her luck.

Finally, he took a slow deep breath. "I do not understand."

Of course you don't, she thought. The idea of time travel wouldn't be seriously imagined for centuries yet.

"I come from the year AD 2239. We use...mathematics and the laws that govern the world to send us back through time so we can record and confirm what truly happened. To ensure history is accurately written, free of biased interpretation." She swallowed, knowing he might still be lost.

Yedder went quiet for a long moment. She watched the proverbial cogs turn as he blinked silently at her. His posture never changed, though. He never straightened or tried to move away from her, which was a good sign.

Then, he softly said, "So you truly are not like me, then." The somber tone of his words struck her squarely in the chest. He blinked rapidly and added, "I am the only one."

"The only one of what?" This was the question she'd wanted answered from the moment she had spotted him from the queen's window.

Pain touched the slight smile he gave her as he nodded absently. "I do not know what I am." His gaze fell to her feet. "I was born when Alexander of Macedonia set his mind to conquer the world. My family grew old and I, alone, remained as I am now. I took a wife and had children. When they all passed, I could not hide what I am any longer and I fled my home, a feared man. I lived and I lived, never changing. I married and had more children and watched them, too, die of age and disease. Still, I remained. And again I moved on. I have changed my name so often, I sometimes forget what my family was called. But I always keep some piece of the name my mother gave me, so she can still watch over me.

"Then, I saw you today and I thought…I hoped for the first time in centuries that…"

"You were not alone," she finished for him.

He nodded, running his fingers through his hair. "But if what you say is true and knowledge in your time brought you here instead, I must be the only one like me in all the world."

He peered at her from under his brows, and she saw it — the weight of fifteen hundred years and all the sorrow that came with it.

Before this moment, if you had asked Xiomara if she wanted to live forever, she would have said yes. But now, seeing ancient eyes behind a face no older than thirty, she realized the toll of immortality. She could never carry that.

"I am sorry." Her words came out in a near whisper but she knew he heard them. "I did not mean to bring you false hope. I was just doing my job."

"It is not your fault, Xoey. Just the foolish dreams of a very old man," he said with a half-hearted chuckle.

You certainly don't kiss like a very old man, she thought.

Yedder suddenly perked up with his usual look of curious amusement and stared at her strangely. A split moment later, she realized she'd said her thoughts out loud. She wanted to retreat into her dress and disappear entirely. Of course she could do that if she recalled to the time lab. She was tempted.

"I mean…you seem…you just…" she began

"It is fine. I know what you meant," he said, his grin completely insufferable. His eyes danced with thrill. "One advantage of my endless life is that my youth never wanes. I am free to explore the world without the limitations of a weakened body."

She didn't know what that had to do with kissing, but she didn't ask.

Xiomara avoided noticing that his impossibly youthful face also just so happened to be quite handsome. She pressed her lips together, conjuring up a teasing laugh. "Well, I am certain it has been popular with the ladies…or gentlemen, whichever."

He sobered. "It has. I know it may be hard to fathom for young ones like you, but I remember them all. I have loved deeply more times than the years most people contain in their entire lives. I watched them all fade away to time while I remained stuck in it. And every one of them I carry with me." Yedder patted his chest. "I will never — could never — forget their faces, their smiles, their laughs, their dreams. They live while I live."

In novels and in cinema, immortals had often been portrayed as careless lovers and cold companions. Rarely were tales told of serial monogamists who lived forever. It was a shame. Her own experience told her they were more interesting, though until now she had never fathomed an actual immortal being real.

"Then they will live long and happy," she affirmed. A muscle flexed in his jaw as he nodded.

Xiomara shifted in her seat. "Do you know why you are like this?"

"No. I have wondered myself but I have never come up with any reasonable answers. I suppose, simply, I was blessed. Or cursed. I do not know which is more appropriate."

"If I were allowed to, I would take you back to my time and see if our advancements in knowledge could figure it out, but my means of moving through time can only transport one person." She absently rubbed her wrist. She'd also be violating about a hundred temporal mandates and twelve international laws, but she didn't feel the need to tell him that.

"Do not worry over me, Xoey. I may not understand everything you have told me, but I know I will in time. I do have an abundance of it." He flashed a half-hearted smile. "Perhaps a thousand years from now — maybe two — I will finally know why I still live. And maybe then I will find my peace."

Xiomara swallowed, knowing what he meant by 'peace', but how could she blame him for wanting a way to grow old as everyone else did? On an impulse, she reached out and squeezed his hand, hoping all the words she didn't know how to say would somehow be communicated in the gesture.

He gently squeezed back.

"I hope it will be much sooner than that," she said. "And…thank you for saving me from being arrested. You do not know the trouble I would have been in if you had not."

He laughed at this, the gleeful sound in such contrast to the heaviness of their conversation. "It seems every instance I meet you, you are getting yourself into trouble."

The statement pulled a grin from her. "That is not fair. For one, you have only met me twice, and two, I am not getting into trouble on purpose."

"I shall take your word for it," he conceded. "Why then were you being chased for theft?"

"Well…people that I work for found a comb and they needed me to confirm it belonged to who they thought it did. If I had not become distracted by seeing you from the queen's window, she would not have thought me a thief."

At this he leaned further towards her and said in a conspiratorial tone, "You were distracted by my face? I shall take that as the highest compliment."

She rolled her eyes but she was grinning nonetheless. "Do not let that go straight to your ego. You might fall over from the weight of it."

His eyes grew dark and his smile turned devilish. He leaned in and —

"Crap!" she blurted in English as her temporal device vibrated at her wrist, the red light starting to flash its countdown of the forced recall. She'd been here too long. She remembered how scared she'd been earlier and how her vitals must have gone berserk. She imagined Leon arguing with Layla about which protocol to use and how long to wait. "I have to leave now. Thank you so much for helping me."

She rose to her feet and Yedder stood as well, holding his features tight.

She suddenly remembered. "Oh! The clothes! Quickly, help me to take them off so they do not come with me. I would hate to —
"

He caught her fingers. "Keep them," he said, dipping his head to the top of her hand like he had before. "They are my gift to you. To remember me by."

She smiled, moisture stinging her eyes. "In case I never see you again, it was a pleasure meeting you. You are truly unforgettable."

Then the spicy, masculine aroma of the tent melted away to the blinding lights of the sterile time lab.

"Outta my way!" a robust man shouted as he barrelled his way passed Xiomara to flag down a handsom on Upper Grosvenor Street. 1891 London bustled with a chatter of activity and reminded her of a busy beehive. News cryers stood on every corner peddling papers and between them, flower girls offered roses for a pence, likely the first crop of the season as it was early June. Cabs and hansoms littered the cobbled streets, the constant clopping of hooves a drone under the other noises. The sky blanketed Hyde Park in an oppressive grey, as it seemed to always be every time she came to London, a steely barrier separating her from the sun. It probably wouldn't rain but she couldn't be certain.

She shook her head at the man's rudeness as she crossed to the park where nannies and mothers alike pushed prams all along the paths between hyacinths and lavender. Children ran gleefully through the grass playing Blind Man's Bluff and other such games while young ladies sat on blankets in their finery, reading.

It had been a long week and once Xiomara dropped her bag off for Carl — a temporal forensic investigator currently assigned to this time and place — she would be free to go back to the time lab and enjoy her weekend off. Rosé and Brioche were calling her name.

She found Carl much faster than she thought. He sat on a wrought iron bench, chatting up a couple of pretty ladies in posh hats, one with a pale pink feather and the other a bouquet of yellow silk daisies rimmed around the hat's crown. Both women seemed enraptured at whatever her co-worker was saying, their hands covering discrete giggles. When he saw her, Carl turned his attention immediately. He rose to his feet and kissed her hand.

"Miss Lopez, it's wonderful to see you so soon," he said. His accent matched perfectly to the upper crust of London society. "What brings you all the way here?"

She suppressed her smile. He was playing his role to the letter, but she supposed that was part of his job as a long-term agent. "You forgot your bag at the office, Dr. Carl. I'm simply returning it."

"Heavens! Where is my mind these days, hmmm? Thank you, my dear, for bringing it to me. I'd be lost without you. Remind me to give you a raise on Monday." With that he gave her hand a gentle pat.

Xiomara arched an eyebrow and flashed a cheeky grin. "Keep that up, Doctor, and you'll positively not be able to afford me," she teased. Carl beamed at her remark and her ability to play along.

"You're worth every penny, Miss Lopez. I'll see you on Monday."

"Good day, Dr. Carl," she replied as she turned from him.

Her mood soured a bit however when she heard one of the ladies say, "Lopez. How exotic! She must be from America." Xiomara rolled her eyes and groaned inwardly. Willfully ignoring the comment, she kept her pace and headed back towards Park Lane.

"Off to go rummaging through the Crown Jewels this time?" his voice said from behind her. English, with an almost perfect West London accent.

Xiomara halted in her place. There was no way. Absolutely no way. Twice was a coincidence but three times was highly improbable. She turned and there he was, dressed in a cream suit with, a pocket watch chain arched across his grey vest and a navy blue top hat perched on his head. The colours were bold for the time but somehow they suited him quite well.

"Yedder?" She couldn't help but grin.

He approached her, his hands casually in his pockets and his signature amused expression on his face. "It's Ed these days," he said coolly. "But my special, time-hopping friends can call me Yedder."

She lifted a brow. "Oh, we're friends now, are we?"

He beamed. "Well, I don't go around hiding just any strangers charged with stealing the queen's belongings. What was it again? A mirror?"

"A comb, actually," she corrected. "And do you also make it a habit to run into all your time-hopping friends or is it just me?"

Though she jested, the look in his golden brown eyes was anything but. He stepped closer, his gaze never leaving hers. She swallowed.

"Only you," he replied.

She had to step back from him to keep her knees stable. She cleared her throat. "You must have come across more of us by now. There's two hundred of us in seven countries and you're what…two thousand or so years old now?" She couldn't believe those words came out of her mouth but then again, nothing about his unusual friendship was believable. Which was probably why she had decided not to inform the C.A.T.T. about his anomalous existence just yet. Or maybe, she admitted to herself, she just liked having an impossible secret friend.

Yedder…Ed offered his arm to Xiomara and she happily grasped it as they strolled across the park. "I haven't. Not that I'm aware, of course. I keep looking out every few centuries for people I recognize but…nothing. Just new faces. Your people must be very good at their jobs," he said.

"You noticed me."

"I did."

"Are you implying I'm bad at my job?" She raised an eyebrow, tilting her head and daring him to say yes.

He looked at her sidelong, that teasing smirk turning up the edges of his mouth. "You fell from a window in the middle of the night and then you crashed into me while fleeing on suspicion of theft."

She shrugged. "Alright, so you happened to catch me on a couple of my bad days."

He chuckled and looked at her with a sultry expression that made her sweat.

"Anyway," she added to fill the gap of silence between them, "why do you think we keep running into each other? Statistically, it shouldn't be possible."

He wet his lips. "I don't know, but I'd be lying if I said I haven't been thinking of you all these years."

For her, she had last seen him three weeks ago. For him, six centuries had come and gone since Budapest. It flattered her immensely to hear and she wanted to admit out loud that she'd thought about him too, though it seemed hardly as impressive. But she knew nothing could come of it, if she did. It would mean everything and nothing. In her line of work, she could run into him at any point in time. The notion she could meet much younger and older versions of him who would have vastly different relationships to her didn't sit well with Xiomara. She acknowledged her attraction to him, the spark she felt between them like a low voltage constantly pulling her toward him, but for an immortal and temporal traveler to have a lasting romance would be far too complicated for her to fathom. And far too much to gamble if the mysterious reason for his everlasting life suddenly disappeared. She knew herself enough to know the depths in which she'd dive to find out what happened to him. It would break her heart.

Still, she caught herself thinking about their kiss six hundred years ago.

He must have sensed it because he stopped and turned to her, his gaze dropping to her lips. She realized with a flush of heat how close they were standing to each other, so close it was practically scandalous for Victorian England.

"It's time for me to go, Ed," she said quietly. "It was good to see you again." She turned to leave, but he caught her wrist in a gentle grasp.

"Wait. Please." His voice was achingly soft. "Stay. Just for a little longer. When you go, I have no way of knowing if it'll be for the last time."

The hint of fear beneath his tone broke her. She faced him and saw something in his expression that she couldn't acknowledge. He pointed to a park bench. "Please. For just a few more moments."

Xiomara nodded, knowing she was cutting it close, but she didn't care.

A relieved smile curved his lips and they sat on the bench. A moment of silence passed between them and then he leaned sideways and said, "So, the Crown Jewels?"

She frowned at him and then suddenly remembered what he'd said earlier. "Oh! No, I'm not here to mess with the matters of the monarchy. Contrary to the popular opinions of immortals, I'm capable of going on assignment without completely mucking it up. I'm just a modern archeologist trying to do her job with as little fuss as possible. Sometimes it doesn't go to plan."

He laughed. "And what archeological discovery are you confirming this time?"

She leaned in, conspiratorially. "You promise not to say anything to anyone?"

He mirrored her posture. "I swear on pain of death."

She gave him a pointed look. "Very funny. I'm here to drop off some equipment for my colleague. He's investigating the Ripper murders. He's one of our long-term agents, meaning he lives in the past for a period of time until his assignment is over. Most of us do single day or night trips. He's been here the last two months solving the case with our technology and then he'll report back his findings for documentation. Scotland Yard can never know the outcome so that the timeline can remain unmarred, but future history will know the truth and those girls can rest in peace."

Ed remained quiet for a moment and she saw he was processing again, though not nearly as hard or long as he once had when the things she said were entirely inconceivable at the time. Finally, he said, "Couldn't you save them? The victims."

This question she'd struggled with her whole career, despite knowing the logic of the answer. She shifted in her seat, the boning of her corset digging into her hip. "To put it simply, no. We are here to observe and document history as it is. If we were to change the injustices we know about, it could cause chaos in the future. The new changes might make history worse than the way it was before. Lessons learned and laws formed out of tragedy would be undone. And though we've learned them the hard way for a very long time, we have finally learned them."

"You can only move forward by acknowledging and accepting the past," he said.

"Exactly. It breaks my heart to only watch history repeat itself and not be able to change the outcome. There are a good many injustices I would personally like to change if I could. But we have to preserve our present and everything we've been through to get there."

He nodded and she felt he truly did understand. After all, he'd lived through so much and seen the outcome of humanity's victories and failures. And so much more was yet to come at the turn of the next century.

Almost in a whisper he said, "You saved me."

Xiomara stiffened. "I…I suppose I did. I shouldn't have. It was very foolish of me."

"Then why did you?"

"I…don't know. But nothing in my present changed, so either you were going to leave on your own anyway, or your immortality would have saved you from destruction."

He went silent and then nodded. "I see," he said tightly.

"What about you? What are you up to these days?" she asked, hoping the change of subject would leave temporal ethics and laws behind.

He smiled, slow and broad. "The same old thing, really. I won a fleet of merchant ships that trade all over the globe. Everything from spices and tea to silks and silvers."

Her eyebrows shot up. "Wow…you've been busy. I'm glad to hear it."

"Well, there was that century where I had to flee Hungary for the Orient because I was the only merchant who'd traveled to plague cities and not gotten sick. I was either venerated as an angel or hunted as a devil and neither of those were the least bit appealing." He shot her a sideways glance. "Oh, and thank you for warning me about that whole Bubonic fiasco. It was fun."

She noted his sarcasm and winced. "Sorry," she offered, knowing it wasn't quite enough to make up for the Black Death, "but in my defense, you're an immortal and you got through it just fine."

"I did, I suppose," he said. His smile beamed. Then he sobered. "Xoey, I have a confession —"

Vibration tingled at her wrist and she straightened her posture. She'd been here too long, again. "I really have to go now, Ed." She stood and darted glances all over the park for some sort of cover, a small copse of low-growing trees stood only a few metres away. She could make it if she sprinted.

He got to his feet as well. "Wait, I need to tell you —"

"I know this is abrupt but I have to go. I can't be recalled with so many witnesses. I'm sorry." The red light began flashing under her skin and she swore, drawing the attention of a scowling governess.

But there was one last thing she had to do before she left. Throwing protocol, propriety and wisdom out the window, she leaned up, fisted Ed's lapel in her hands and kissed him. Hard and brief and little askew, but even then, he still followed her mouth when she pulled away, a pained look on his face as their lips parted.

She scolded herself silently, dashing towards the copse. It lacked complete cover but the flashing of the warning light pulsed faster and it would have to do. Clutching her skirts and not caring that her hat went flying, Xiomara ran as fast as she could, not daring to look back at her impossible man. She barely made it into the safety of the trees when the familiar tingling began and everything melted away.

Xiomara's heart drummed inside her ribcage as she rounded the corner of 18th and State, thinking about what she'd say. The beads on her knee-length dress rustled as she walked down the dark street towards the bakery she knew was also a speakeasy. She shrugged her coat up around her ears as a blast of cold Chicago wind blew through her.

I met him on a night like this, she thought, though the air had been warm and humid then. The sky was so clear the moon highlighted everything in blue and silver. She still remembered what he'd looked like, staring down at her in the bushes, that infernal amusement on his face.

Against her better judgment, she'd search for him in the C.A.T.T database and archives, under every name variation she could think of. A man named Yedder Wararni was recorded as being the owner of a chain of bakeries in Chicago 1926, but all mention of him — and every other person with that name who could possibly be him — vanished with the crash of 1929.

She twisted a handkerchief in her grip, the cotton catching on her satin gloves. She knew she'd only have a few moments. She was late already but she had to see him. All the records said this bakery was the head office for the chain, and she hoped that meant he ran the speakeasy himself. She took a gamble when she asked for this assignment but if it paid off, it was worth it.

She had to take the chance to say goodbye.

The plump man at the counter eyed her suspiciously as she entered the bakery. "Hi, there. I'm here for the special order of dark rye and soda biscuits," she said, trying her best to sound like a confident socialite. She mustered a coy smile.

The man nodded and led her through a curtain, a sign posted above it saying "Employees Only". "Down the hall to the left," he said, pushing open a hidden panel in the wall. "The boss will show you the way out when you're ready, sweetheart."

"Thanks," she said and brushed past him. Once she entered the hidden room, music burst forth, piano and saxophone. The air laid thick with a cigarette and perfume haze and she blinked away the sting in her eyes. Murmured conversation and laughter surrounded her as she made her way to the bar.

"What are we having tonight, miss?" the bartender asked.

"Gin and tonic, please."

The bartender nodded and got to work immediately. Another man walked behind the bar, his back turned to Xiomara, but she'd know his voice anywhere. "Hey, Harry, are we running out of whiskey yet? My guy wants to know what to put us down for."

Xiomara sucked in a quiet breath, preparing to get his attention, but it seemed she didn't need to bother. He turned around. "And don't forget we need to hire someone to si—"

She'd found his eyes from across the bar and the look on his face bordered between shock and adoration. Thankfully the style of the time period called for outrageous amounts of rouge because her cheeks flushed.

His usual dark curls were slicked back against his head with some sort of hair product and he wore a pin-striped suit that had obviously been tailored to him.

He looked good. Really good. And it made her heart ache traitorously.

Slowly, as if he walked in a daze, he came near her. "Are you real?"

Xiomara grinned. "Quite."

He took hold of her hand and kissed it, lightly rubbing his fingers over her knuckles. Ed grabbed an extra glass from behind him and poured himself a drink before taking both glasses around the bar. He sat beside her and slid over her drink. "It's only been thirty or so years. To be honest, I wasn't expecting to see you again for another two hundred at least." His lips quirked up at the corners. His English accent was nearly gone now, Americanized except for a few words.

A flash of something painful streaked through her body as she remembered, then, why she had come. And she couldn't bear the way he was looking at her.

Her smile faded. "Yes, well. About that…" The words stuck to her tongue even as he frowned.

"What's going on? Are you alright?"

His concern rattled through her like a gong, echoing deep in her bones. She knew by his expression that if she didn't answer him now, he'd assume the worst.

She pressed her lips together, trying not to smear her lipstick. "I'm fine, Ed. There's nothing wrong with me. I —"

"If you need anything, all you have to do is say the word and it's yours. No questions asked."

Xiomara gave a patient sigh and placed her fingers against his mouth in a shushing gesture. "I appreciate that very much, but I need you to let me speak."

He simply nodded and she removed her hand. "Like I said, I'm fine. More than fine, actually. I just got word from my department head that they're retiring — and they want me to take their place." When he didn't react, she said, "I'm being promoted at work!"

This he understood. He grinned, his eyes lighting up. "Congratulations, Xoey. After all the trouble you've gotten yourself into for your career, I'm sure you deserve the honour."

She narrowed her sight at him but the edges of her mouth curved up in a smile, which defeated the effect she had intended. "Yes, very funny. Did you learn that from a court jester?" she deadpanned.

"Chaucer, if you must know, though I don't think he'd be all that happy you called him a court jester. Writers, always a bit sensitive." But Ed's playful expression slowly turned pensive. "If this is good news, why do you look like someone died?"

She looked away from him. She swirled her gin around the glass, studying it intently to stall. "I asked to take this current assignment so I might have a chance to find you. So I can say goodbye."

She'd said goodbye to him several times before not thinking she'd see him again, and yet this time was different. Permanent. He must have sensed it too, as he went so still he looked like a wax figure.

"Since I'll be the new department head, I'll be the one doling out assignments and coordinating teams, among other things. I won't be in the field anymore. This is my last assignment."

He stared at her so long, she wondered if he was having a seizure. To her relief, he reached for his drink and downed it in one shot. "So this really is goodbye."

She nodded. "I looked you up, you know. In our archives. The last time your name comes up is here. After that…I don't know what happens. I don't know if you're still around Earth or if you go to the moon colony. Or if you…"

"Die?"

She nodded. "I don't know if you finally find your peace. Right here, right now, is all I may have. And I wanted to say a proper farewell. Because…well because…"

"I know," he said softly, sliding his hand into hers. His warmth seeped through her gloves. "I feel it too. I wish we had more time. I've always wished we had more time. Ever since I helped you out of Donna Octavia's bushes, I've wished for it. And then I'd see you like some beautiful ghost and I wouldn't feel so alone. I found myself hoping to see you, like a long lost friend. Now I…" He cleared his throat and shifted in his seat. "I don't know how to feel."

Xiomara blinked back the sting of tears, knowing that for him everything was different. That he'd known her for nearly two millennia, when she'd only met him just three months ago. He'd harboured his feelings for her while empires rose and fell and rose again. For him, this was different. And she couldn't make it hurt any less.

"I'm sorry," she whispered, letting a tear stream down her face.

Silently, Ed reached up and wiped it away. He lifted her chin and gave it an affectionate squeeze at the dimple there. "It's alright, doll face," he teased, though his usual bravado was gone. "No one in my life has been around as long as you have. I've been honoured to consider you a friend, but I knew it couldn't last forever. Nothing in this life lasts forever. Well, except me, apparently." He gave a sardonic chuckle.

More tears trickled down her face. "I will miss you dearly, Ed. I hope whatever force that keeps you alive will be kind and we'll see each other again."

"Me too." His words were thick with emotion.

Her temporal device vibrated and she squeezed her eyes tightly, knowing the red warning light was already flashing. She stood and took his hand as he swiveled on his stool.

"You have to go," he said.

"I have to go," she whispered back.

Ed pulled her to him and wrapped his arms around her. "Stay out of trouble, alright? I want you to live a long and happy life."

She nodded into his shoulder. "You're not the boss of me but I'll concede if you will."

"As long as illegal liquor operations don't count as trouble, it's a deal."

She grinned, squeezing him tighter. She didn't want to let him go, but she had to in order to live her life in her own time. As she pulled away from him, he kissed her forehead so tenderly it nearly broke whatever semblance of composure she still had.

"See you around, Xiomara," he said, his smile lopsided and adorable.

"Goodbye, Yedder." With that, she turned and rushed to the speakeasy's powder room, already feeling the recall activate.

Two weeks passed and Xiomara found herself so busy preparing for her new position, she barely had the time to think about Chicago. She'd had the odd warped dream of Pompeii and Hungary, but other than that, paperwork demanded all of her waking hours. Finally, she had made it to the end of the insanity, or to the beginning as some had said, and now could enjoy her promotion party.

She sat at a table in the banquet hall, sandwiched between Leon and a very weepy, tipsy Layla who hadn't let go of Xiomara's hand in over an hour.

"Hunny, you know I'm still going to see you at work every day, right?" she'd said to Layla earlier when the tears had started.

"I know, but it won't be the same," Layla protested. "You'll be our boss and then we'll actually have to do our jobs properly."

Xiomara smiled while thinking of her friend's words because she knew Layla would remember them in the morning and send a frantic apology message, even though there wasn't anything she needed to be sorry for.

Leon was the opposite of Layla. He became extra chatty and silly when plied with booze and he hadn't stopped for a break in a concerning amount of time. Xiomara was about to demand he take a bathroom break, when someone tapped her on the shoulder.

Her boss, the Director of the C.A.T.T., stood behind her. "Congratulations again, Dr. Lopez. We're very excited to have you take over for Dr. Shawani. They will be missed around here but I'm looking forward to seeing where you take the Accuracy Department. I know it's in good hands."

Xiomara stood, prying Layla's death grip off her arm. "Thank you, sir. I'm sad to be leaving the field, but now I get to break in some newbies, which is always exciting. I won't let you down."

"I have no doubt of that," he replied, lifting his glass to offer her a toast. She swiped her own drink off the table and clinked it with his. "To new beginnings."

"To new beginnings," she echoed and took a sip of champagne.

"May I steal you for a moment?" he asked. "Some of our patrons came out for the celebration and they wanted to congratulate you in person. And to see who Dr. Shawani chose as their successor."

"Of course you may!" Xiomara beamed. She deposited her glass back to the table and followed Director Galos across the room to where a group of people had gathered in a circle, chatting.

"Pardon the interruption but I believe you wanted to meet the woman of the hour." The group slowly turned around. "Dr. Lopez, this is Sheridan Murray, Parminder Rai, Kacey Connick, and Nednir Warni."

Xiomara was very glad she'd left her glass on the table because if she hadn't, it would have shattered on the floor just then.

Honey-coloured eyes met hers and she nearly turned to soup in shock. "Hey, Trouble," he greeted when it was his turn. His hands were in his pockets and he exuded that cheeky swagger of his. "It's good to see you again. It feels like it's been forever."

Xiomara struggled to keep her jaw from falling to the floor.

"You two know each other already? Excellent!" Director Galos said.

She swallowed, forgetting how to speak for a moment. "I...uh...yeah. Yeah we do."

Ed's eyes were dancing in mischief. "We go way back."

Xiomara knew people were talking to her and asking her questions, and by some miracle she managed to reply coherently despite not really paying attention to what they said. All her attention was on Ed.

He was there. There in her present. Real and so tangible she wanted to touch him. And hug him. And hit him for not revealing himself sooner. And kiss him just for being there.

But she waited until the rest of the group had moved on to other conversations before pulling him aside.

"You're here," she said.

"I'm here." His smile turned wicked. "Did you miss me?"

"Miss you? I only saw you just two weeks ago. I haven't had time to —"

"You said you'd miss me. I'm a little offended right now. It has been three hundred years, you know." He feigned chest pain.

"Yeah well, join the club. Where were you all this time? I couldn't find you in the archives anywhere."

He shrugged. "Changed my name. Moved to the moon colony for a while." When he saw her unimpressed expression he added, "You said moon colony to someone in 1926. Obviously, I'm going to look forward to the moon colony."

She smacked him half-heartedly in the arm. "And you've been partly funding the C.A.T.T this entire time and you said nothing! Why?"

"Because every encounter we had brought us here, to this moment. I couldn't risk that changing. Not for anything." He stepped closer to her and she could feel the warmth of his skin as he brushed a lock of her dark brown hair behind her ear. "I've been waiting since 1892 to ask if you'd let me court you."

She gazed up at him from under her eyebrows, her annoyance disappearing. "It was 1891, actually," she corrected. "And you want to court me, huh? That sounds awfully antiquated for 2239."

He shrugged, noting her grin. "Well, what can I say? I'm an antiquated kind of guy."

"Wait a minute." Xiomara frowned and reached up to run her fingers over a light streak of his hair curling just above his ears. It was silver. "Is that dyed?"

"No, it's real. Other guys would probably cover it up or use gene therapy but I can't bring myself to hide something I've longed for since the fall of the Roman Empire." He emphasized his words by also running his fingers over the silver streaks.

Xiomara went hot and cold at the same time. "But…how? When? Does this mean…?"

"Oh yes! That. I'm finally losing my immortality. And all thanks to a little poison cooked up by a scientist friend of mine I met this century. I take a daily dose, like a vitamin but opposite, and it weakens my superpowered immune system enough to allow my cells to degrade naturally, like they're supposed to. It's fantastic!" His giddiness didn't match up with a man who just started dying, but considering all he lived through, how many loved ones he'd lost, she understood why.

"So, how long do you have?" she asked, trying to suppress her disappointment. She didn't want to lose him just as they were finally living in the same century.

He beamed. "Luckily, only about another sixty or seventy years. I mean, I've waited two millennia, what's another handful of decades, right?"

She laughed and tears welled in her eyes as relief rushed through her. "So you're saying we have time to fit some dates in there. I can work with that." She gazed up at Ed. She so badly wanted to kiss him.

As if he were thinking the exact same thing, he darted his sight around the room and entwined their fingers. He led her onto the balcony, stars winking down from the night sky. He enfolded her in his arms, molding her to his body.

"I've waited three centuries to do this," he murmured against her mouth. And then he kissed her. He kissed her the way every woman deserved to be kissed.

When he pulled away, Xiomara felt deliciously hazy. "Worth the wait?"

His grin would have made the devil blush. "Absolutely."

The tale that would eventually become The Repositioning March started out as tales (and writers) typically do: as a failure. But that early draft was a necessary failure. Originally, the story of defeated soldiers trying to survive upon a foreign and hostile island merely advanced themes asserting that war was a harrowing odyssey destructive to the individual. I believed in these themes and in the story's setting, plot, and characters, yet that draft went straight into a dark drawer because I felt that the world did not need another story about what war is.

But in the way of writing, the story that was hidden in a dark drawer remained bright in my mind.

Eventually, it occurred to me that the tale should not be about the what of war, but rather the why. That made the difference. The everyman soldiers in the original draft suddenly had faces. And these faces were masks.

*Buddy Young*

Buddy Young is a staff writer and a writing educator living in London, Ontario, and the long-time president of the London Writers Society.

# THE REPOSITIONING MARCH

by Buddy Young

A little man hunched beneath the grey pounding of the monsoon rains, struggling up a mountain ridge toward fire in the sky: Doctor Morita saw himself this way as though from above the jungle canopy, his fatigue so deep that reality itself seemed a disembodied hallucination. The red clay of the ridge was as slippery as grease rendered from blood, and he managed the worst spots only by using a rusty bayonet as a climbing axe. He was puffing so hard that pulsing sprays of breath droplets emerged from the mouth slit of his army-issue aluminum mask, to be immediately lost in the torrents. It took him an hour to climb the ridge, which a man not ravaged by starvation could have ascended in fifteen minutes. But finally, the distant firelight along the ridge's crest that had been mere spark-streaks in the rainy sky now outlined the trees immediately above him, blurring them into the silhouettes of gigantic crones hunched before a summoning fire.

Crouching in the lee shadow of the ridge crest, he paused for breath. A breeze from the valley beyond the crest suddenly drove away the jungle's omnipresent stink of organic rot, and he instead smelled hot oil, burning rubber, and pulverized stone. Along with the stink of this mechanical miasma came the mighty crackling of granite being crushed. His heart already lead, he adjusted his mask so that its slits were directly before his eyes, then he rose from his crouch and gazed over the firelit crest.

Far off in the midst of the valley beyond, a leviathan titanic beyond comprehension was moving through the jungle, its sinuous body a mountain range of machinery. The beast's scales were overlapping armour plates redeployed from the flanks of battleships from the invasion fleet that had landed on the coast a month earlier, and these plates screeched against each other in showers of sparks as gears ground within the depths of the beast, inching its body forward segment by segment in the way of a colossal worm. Each time one such segment extended to its utmost, fields of hydraulic hoses and electrical cabling became briefly visible between the steel plates. The heat of the grand machine caused the rain to evaporate the moment the drops touched the plates, so that the beast moved perpetually in storms of steam. Each segment of the monster of war was topped by forecastles bristling with antennae, radar dishes, sirens, signal lamps, observer cupolas, gun positions, pennants, smoke stacks.... Within the high windows of command decks, officers and their staff moved among map tables and consulted scopes that made their faces glow green. Uniforms pressed, coffee cups in hand. Rows of portholes lower on the vast machine glowed with the warm crimson light of watch lamps and furnaces, the portholes winking as legions of crewmen tending to the gears, furnaces, and generators passed before them.

None of these officers or crew wore masks. They were the Soulless. They did not call themselves that of course, but the citizens of the Empire of Gestalth were forbidden to call the maskless citizens of other nations anything but 'the Soulless'.

Holding his hand over the eye slits of his Gestalthian Army mask so the rain didn't dribble into his eyes, Doctor Morita noticed that he had instinctually taken refuge behind the fibrous trunk of a tree. Intellectually, he knew that the leviathan assault platform's spotters would never see one small man in the tangled jungle across leagues of steam and rain. Yet, an instinct surely born in the primordial times when mammals had been mere rodents in a land of dinosaurs still demanded that he hide, hold still, maybe even burrow into the earth. But an equally primitive survival instinct to preserve hope forced him to keep watching as the enemy assault platform reached the river that ran across the valley floor.

The mechanical juggernaut had a breast prow that cut through the jungle's ancient trees and lesser ridges, cleaving them aside like so much torpid green and brown foam. When the beast reached the river at a place where a flimsy bridge of vines and floating logs had been hobbled together by remnants of the retreating Gestalthian army, it ignored this tiny thread and instead plunged directly onward—into the deepest, swiftest stretch of the river. The rushing water rose halfway up the flank of the gargantuan machine, a muddy surge of thousands of tons, but was turned aside, diverting from its natural course into the jungle to sweep away trees by the acres. The riverbed on the other side of the leviathan ran dry within moments. Indifferent to both the forest that it was killing with a flood and the river it was slaying with a flash drought, the leviathan rumbled ever onward.

Within his rain-drumming mask of chilled metal, Doctor Morita wept soft, warm tears.

To one side of the beast, something twinkled in the forested slope of the valley. A mere pinprick of yellow light. A shot fired from a Gestalthian field gun hidden in the jungle, Doctor Morita recognized. Too puny to have any meaningful effect on the enemy machine, the shot was merely the gun crew's plaintive cry, We have not surrendered. We still fight. We still exist.

The detonation of the shell against the enemy's flank prompted merely a repositioning of the armour plates in that localized spot, the way a flea bite causes a small patch of fur on a dog's flank to twitch. But even as the leviathan continued its advance, several turrets on its crest rotated inexorably in the direction of the Gestalthian field gun, a dozen nimbler searchlights already converging on its hidden position. When the turrets—each fifty tons or more—fired on the Gestalthian gun position, acres of ancient trees hundreds of feet high were flung blazing into the sky like blades of grass rising from a meadow fire.

No, this destruction declared. You do not exist.

As this thunder rumbled across the valley to his position, Doctor Morita turned his masked face away and started sliding back down the slope of blood-red clay.

Sergeant Teneke and Private Bahp were, of course, on the trail at the base of the ridge where Doctor Morita had left them. If they had moved so much as twenty paces off the trail, the blinding monsoon and the dense jungle foliage might have made it impossible for him to ever find them again. Or for them to find any other trail in this wilderness.

The entire Gestalthian garrison on the island had lost track of itself this way, units becoming separated in the unfamiliar jungle of this wretched foreign island. After all, they really had no idea where they were. Before the war started, almost nobody in the Empire had ever left the insular home archipelago, let alone come to this island at the end of the world. Forbidden to consort with the few natives who dwelled in fishing villages on the coast, the garrison's soldiers had learned nothing of the island's interior except that its jungles and mountains were so hostile that not even the natives ventured there. And no maps of the interior had been issued—or even existed. The reasoning for this had been that that the bauxite mines, which were the only reason that the Empire had occupied the island in the early stages of the war, were located solely in one stretch of coast, and since these were vital to the war effort, the very idea of defeat and hence retreat inland was treasonous. Even scouting the interior had been proscribed. So when the Gestalthian garrison defending the coast fractured under the massed fire of the enemy invasion fleet and had been driven away from the coast into the jungle interior by assault leviathans rising dripping from the depths of the sea, nobody had known exactly where to go.

The resulting long retreat had been deemed a 'repositioning march'. To call it a 'retreat' brought instant execution. Retreats were for defeated armies, and it was a core cultural truism that Gestalthians could never be defeated by the Soulless. By the maskless.

Reaching the trail at the bottom of the ridge, Doctor Morita spotted the rain-blur of the heavily loaded wagon first, the image prompting a memory of a storybook illustration from his childhood: a woodblock print depicting a cart heaped with the bodies of the enemies of Gestalth after a victorious battle in the bygone eras of swords and bows, when the island nation had been unified into the Empire. Such victories had been inevitable, the storybook logic had insisted, because only Gestalthians truly had souls that survived the end of life. Since their enemies did not have immortal souls, they fought merely to aggrandize their bodies' appetites and to preserve their flesh a short time longer, whereas the Gestalthians fought to preserve an honourable place in eternity for their souls, enduring all physical suffering in the faith that the body did not matter.

This particular wagon was not filled with carrion bodies: it was filled with souls. Masks. In the wake of the invasion battle, when the field hospital in which he had been a surgeon had been only minutes from being overrun by the enemy, Doctor Morita had piled the first few score of the masks of the honoured dead into a commandeered ammunition cart and then fled into the jungle. The bodies of the soldiers who had worn those masks were left behind in careless heaps. Bodies did not matter, only souls, which had transmigrated into the masks at the moment of the wearer's death. At the start of the repositioning march, the remains of three mangled platoons had walked with Doctor Morita, the men taking turns pulling the two-wheeled cart through the muddy trails of the jungle. It was not so hard a task, and an honourable one, the cargo of soul masks destined to be repatriated to the mother country and enshrined as befit the souls of war heroes.

But the repositioning march had stretched onward into two wearisome days of trudging along the muddy tracks of the wild jungle. By the third day, men had started to die from wounds. When each died, the soldier's mask was added to the cart. By the fourth day, hypothermia from the inescapable rain started to carry off the weak. By the fifth day, even the strong started to falter. By the seventh day, rations gave out and starvation began. And still, the march went on and on.

The repositioning march had now lasted thirty-two days.

Now, the cart was heaped high with the masks of the dead who had served it, and there were only three living men left to push it through the mud. Three grey meat scarecrows. The constant monsoon rains and the inescapable heat had rotted their imperial army uniforms into tatters. Their web belts could no longer be cinched tightly enough to remain around the starved-thin waists and instead hung slanted over the jutting hook of a hip bone. These web belts served only to hold their meagre ammunition and what few tools they had not cast away to save weight, since none of the three wore pants any longer. Their diet of jungle grubs and roots had afflicted them all with diarrhoea that made pants impractical, and now they wore the shredded remains of their uniform pants as loincloths whose filthy folds drooped like wet bandages. They had eaten their leather boots. Only the laces remained, holding in place leaves wrapped around their feet.

Private Bahp, lashed into the cart's traces, had lapsed into unconsciousness but had not been allowed to fall into the soft mud: the twin yokes of the cart and its hemp traces held him up, his gaunt body easily outweighed by the cargo of heaped masks. Doctor Morita spoke his name three times, without a response. This was not surprising. During the weeks of monsoon, the soldiers had become acoustically numbed, since the constant drumming of the rain on their masks drove men insane if they could not learn a certain deafness. Private Bahp wore the cheap wartime mask of a conscript, and the high command had decreed that conscripts could not wear masks with the same stern warrior visage as those patriots who had volunteered. Thus, the features of his standard-issue conscript mask had a mouth slit pursed in infinite patience and rounded eye slits that suggested a lack of intelligence. The placid face of a mule. Steel now rationed, conscript masks were formed of mere iron, welded along seams and bolted here and there with a dispiriting crudeness. The Private's mask did not have the crescent moon image denoting a full year of military service stamped on the forehead. But his serial number was stamped deeply, permanently, on the cheek.

Doctor Morita retrieved one of several canteens affixed to the side of the wagon with crude makeshift funnels of jungle leaves set into their neck to collect rainwater. Like all Gestalthian drinking vessels, the canteen had a spout designed to fit through a mask's mouth slit. When the Doctor started to trickle water into the mouth slit of the Private's mask, most just drained out of the bottom of the mask. This was worrisome because he knew the poor fellow desperately needed hydration. The jungle's inescapable heat had plagued the soldier so much that he had ignored Doctor Morita's warning to only drink rainwater and had slaked his thirst from jungle streams. This had given Private Bahp dysentery so chronic he lacked the strength even to clean himself properly. Excreted filth on the back of his legs made it clear that his diet had been solely worms, grubs, and snails for days. If he did not drink, the diarrhoea would kill him with dehydration.

"Wake up," Morita said, nudging the Private gently. He knew he should roar the command and slap him hard like a proper officer would, but he did not have that sort of iron in his soul. He just shook the Private instead. "Wake up, please."

Eventually, Private Bahp coughed and stirred. His legs still rubbery beneath him as he hung in his traces, the Private invested some of his strength in raising his mask-heavy head. He croaked, "Are we stopping now?"

Doctor Morita hesitated, aware that the soldier was actually asking, Is it the honoured officer's opinion that I can now die? It was, of course, quite permissible to die in service to the Empire. It guaranteed a honourable place in the afterlife. However, after the debacle of the battle on the coast, all the members of the garrison had been specifically commanded to strive to their utmost to reach the regrouping area, from which a counterattack would be launched. To die on the march to the regrouping area was regrettable, but acceptable; to choose to lay down and die was to disobey orders, and traitors had no place in the afterlife. Yet, the mercy in his soul that had driven him to become a doctor in the first place now whispered, Tell him yes. Let him rest.

Instead, Doctor Morita said, "The sun has not yet gone down, farm boy. Everyone works until it does." This cruelty was the only form of care he had left to keep the Private alive, since his stocks of medicine had long given out. Private Bahp was proud of his peasant heritage—proud of the way his people worked hard in the fields all day long. This emaciated semi-corpse had once been the stoutest, sturdiest soldier in an entire regiment, a plough boy who had volunteered to pull the cart to show everyone that the folk of his small corner of the Empire never shirked. "When we finish our work, we can go home," Doctor Morita promised the poor lad, as he had hour after hour for weeks now. "How can we go home if our labours are not complete?"

The Private nodded, his semi-conscious head lolling with the difficulty of holding itself up, burdened as it was by his iron mask.

Sergeant Teneke returned, materializing from the rain only five paces farther up the trail. As the only career soldier among the surviving trio, Sergeant Teneke wore a mask of the same alloy of fine steel now only rationed for use in the armour plating of tanks and artillery barrels. The army mask's features—literally and figuratively hard—had a pebbling texture, and the inflexible nose, cheeks, and mouth were forever fixed in an expression of resolve. Along the brow, just below where the mask ended at the beginning of his grey-flecked short-cut hair, were stamped a row of sixteen crescent moon symbols, one for each of the sergeant's years in the service of his country. On the left cheek were welded three slightly brighter steel curlicues suggesting ancient sabres, the mark of his rank. His serial number was stamped on the right cheek. Below this had been welded a moon haloed with splendid rays: a medal of bravery. The mask bore uncountable nicks and scratches from years of war, including a bullet gouge that bulged the steel down into the left eye slit, giving him a slightly hangdog look. But the Sergeant took a patriotic satisfaction from this gouge: the bullet would have killed any soldier of the Soulless, since none of their alliance's member nations wore masks. The bullet would have also killed Private Bahp, passing through the conscript's cheap iron mask.

The Sergeant spared Private Bahp a brief, "Be ready to move out, soldier," then he drew Doctor Morita aside. They stood with heads bent and their masks touching so that the faltering Private would not overhear their whispers. The Sergeant asked, "Did you see the enemy when you climbed the ridge?"

Doctor Morita shrugged. "A man with eyes too weak to see his own hand in front of his face could still have seen that thing."

"But how far behind are they?"

In answer, Doctor Morita merely gestured to a puddle protected from rain drops by the canopy of a wide-leafed tree. Its surface, which should have been placid in the windless monsoon, was quivering with ripples. These ripples had the same rhythm as the inch-worm contractions of the pursuing mechanical leviathan's body. If the constant rain and trench foot had not numbed their feet, the two of them would likely have felt the tremors of the enemy's machine.

The Sergeant hissed, rivulets streaking toward his mouth slit as he drew in air sharply. "Definitely still coming our way?"

"Our way, our way—there's only one way!" Doctor Morita snapped, gesturing with hopelessness to the unseen by raising his empty hands upward toward the clouds on either the side of the trail. These low monsoon clouds hid ranges of mountains so steep, so tangled with jungle, and so slick with red mud that the desperate repositioning soldiers who had attempted to climb over them had all either died or returned with spirits and bodies further broken. Only this single narrow valley system led through the mountains. This made it simplicity itself for the enemy assault leviathan to pursue the fleeing remains of the army. "We're lambs herded down a slaughterhouse chute, chased by a wolf."

"And the river didn't stop it?" asked Sergeant Teneke. "Or at least slow the damned thing?"

"As much as this," Doctor Morita said, placing his leaf-wrapped foot down in one of the hundred shallow rivulets of rainwater trickling along the trail.

The Sergeant hung his head, the angle of his face making the rain flow down his mask like tears. Doctor Morita had noticed this effect before, and if he had still been a daydreaming undergrad who wrote snatches of secret poetry during boring medical lectures, he would have written in the journal he always used to carry, In the monsoon, all faces flow with tears unending. Forcing himself out of his funk, the Sergeant stood up straight and beckoned for Doctor Morita to follow him down the trail, announcing with a bit of unintentional poetry of his own, "Pursued by a dragon, we have a problem ahead, honoured officer."

Doctor Morita followed him into the rain, both of them moving with jerky start-and-stop steps as the mud sucked at their feet. The Sergeant leaned on his rusted rifle to ease the strain on his leaf-wrapped left foot, where trench foot had escalated into a purple pulpiness now rising past the ankle. Doctor Morita assumed that the Sergeant grimaced in pain with every step, but he could not, of course, see the man's expression.

They came to the 'problem' within moments. A crossroads, where the path split into two. There were no signposts of course, since all the trails they followed were actually only muddy gullies that had never known a human footfall before the fleeing soldiers had taken to them.

Doctor Morita scratched at the heat rash along the top edge of his mask as he contemplated the dilemma of the crossroads.

When the ten thousand soldiers who had survived the battle at the coast began the repositioning march, there had initially had a sense of purpose and direction. Their commanders had ordered them to withdraw from the coastal plain into the interior out of the range of the enemy's naval bombardment. They would, the commanders ordered, gather at a regrouping point and then launch a counterattack. Military police with silver masks that shone even in the moonless jungle night had been stationed at the main crossroads, directing the drivers of the trucks and fighting vehicles with clockwork gestures of white-gloved hands After two days of marching into the interior, the military police at the crossroads gave way to hastily painted signs. By the time that the trucks had run out of fuel two more days later, the painted signs had turned to mere branches lashed with vines into the shape of arrows pointing deeper into the jungle highlands. Even these ended eventually, and the marching soldiers had doggedly followed whichever path through the mountains had been chewed up by the treads of command vehicles that had gone before them. Eventually, they'd come upon these vehicles, also abandoned for lack of fuel, and the troops had then simply followed the boot prints on the ground.

Then the monsoon had started, washing away all footprints.

Bereft of direction and out of provisions, units separated into smaller and smaller groups to make foraging in the jungle easier. As much as the narrow valley system they travelled would allow, they also took different trails that they hoped would all eventually lead to the same place. "We will meet again at the regrouping area" had become both the order of the day and a traditional farewell.

Doctor Morita and Sergeant Teneke stared at the fork in the trail. Hard to see far in the rain. Both trails were only red-mud seams in the emerald foliage, mere chance products of erosion. The Sergeant wearily half-raised a pale wrinkled hand toward the leftmost of the path forks. "Also, there's two on the trail for you."

Doctor Morita didn't have to ask what he meant, not at this stage of the march. With a sigh of resignation, he held out his hands. Sergeant Teneke took from a much-patched khaki rucksack a hammer with the imperial moon crest stamped into its brutal steel, and two ceremonial nails with wickedly barbed shafts. He offered these to Doctor Morita with a bow. Morita returned the bow as he accepted them, then walked down the left fork alone while the Sergeant punctiliously remained behind. What waited on the trail was for an officer alone.

The two soldiers were easy to find, since they had positioned themselves on the trail specifically so that they would be discovered. They had seated themselves face-to-face and so close that the knees of their crossed legs had been touching. A companionable tableau of two grisly corpses. A steel-masked veteran and an iron-masked conscript, they had seated themselves in this way so that they could share a single grenade held between them.

Doctor Morita had a decision to make. A judgement. Whereas dead soldiers who had fulfilled their duties had their soul masks returned to the homeland in honour, those who failed in their duties had their masks nailed to their faces so that their souls would be trapped within their rotting bodies for eternity. Normally, such judgement fell to combat officers, but their last such officer had died six days ago, leaving only him as an officer of any kind. Suicides could be tricky judgements. Soldiers who committed suicide rather than be captured were fine, of course. (If a soldier surrendered, all his living relatives would be buried alive with their masks nailed to their faces.) But soldiers who committed suicide to escape suffering were a focus of officers' outrage, and Doctor Morita believed that this was so because the officers themselves were often the indirect or direct source of such suffering. The officers, the army, the war, the country—suicides could accuse them all. Many combat officers who came upon these two men would have declared that if the pair had possessed the strength to pull the pin on the grenade, they should have invested that strength in walking a few more steps down the trail in search of the regrouping area per their orders, and then these officers would have nailed the masks to the dead. In this way, the army consigned souls to eternal damnation out of a concern for maintaining discipline among the living, which Doctor Morita considered a bitter hypocrisy.

For him, a doctor with only a non-combat officer rank, the decision was an easy one. Despite the terrible destruction wrought by the grenade, he could see that the two soldiers had been emaciated beyond hope of survival. He set the hammer and two nails into his meagre pouch of medical supplies, took out his scalpel, and sliced away the straps of the two shrapnel-mutilated masks. The jungle's ruinous heat and moisture had rotted the faces beneath into soft, shining blackness like a banana peel left in the sun. A shame, he thought. Nobody in the world had ever seen the men's faces since their coming of age, except for a wife, if either had one, and doctors, if their medical maladies had ever involved the face. Now, they would never be properly seen. War.

As he carefully cleaned the two retrieved soul masks in rivulets of fresh rain streaming off the jungle's nodding leaves, Doctor Morita thought of his own mask. Or rather, his masks. His childhood mask had been traditional cherry wood from his home prefecture, carved into an expression of happiness and innocence, dented from falls from trees and sports and other misadventures, and his mother still kept it in what had been her hope chest before marriage. His adulthood mask, donned at his coming of age, was a light, airy mask of thin cypress painted a lively red and yellow, and it bore the garland insignia of his clan and a pleasant butterfly sigil on the right cheek that he had selected for himself. The veins of its wings suggested the fishing nets of his ancestors, but the rainbows in those wings were all his own. This bright mask waited for him in a sealed underground vault of the Ministry of the Defence of the Homeland back in Gestalth, safe from enemy bombers. If he survived the war, it would be his again. Oh, how he wanted to wear that light, lively face again.

He loathed his present metal mask. It was hot and smothering. Since being conscripted into the army immediately upon finishing medical school, he had worn the aluminum mask, which resisted germs and facilitated disinfection. It was shaped into a benevolently smiling face with a scholarly forehead and fatherly features that didn't fit a man only twenty-three years old. If he died in battle, his companions would bear his soul in this mask back to the homeland, where it would be added to the soul masks in the Shrine of Heroes in the capital. He hoped not, though. He wanted to live long enough to once again wear his mask of butterfly wings. And when he died, he wanted his soul mask to hang with the smiling, mild masks of his ancestors in their warm and sunny ancestral shrine where the living of all ages gathered one afternoon each week to sweep and eat a potluck lunch and chatter happily.

The worst of the rot had been rinsed out of the shrapnel-mangled masks of the two dead soldiers now. He dragged the bodies of the two dead soldiers off the trail, unceremoniously consigning the slabs of dead meat to a flooded ditch in an intentional, even theatrical, show of contempt for the meat. A contempt he did not actually feel. A man or woman who became a surgeon could not help falling in wonderstruck love with the intricate miracles of the human body. Consigning the bodies to the ditch sickened him. But since Gestalthians were the only people who believed that souls resided in masks, any sign of respect for corpses was a disloyalty. And in the army, during war—and particularly, during a war going badly—any hints of disloyalty would consign his own body to a ditch quite quickly, surgeon or not.

When Doctor Morita carried the two masks back to Sergeant Teneke at the fork, the Sergeant reacted to the sight of the masks—retrieved in honour—with a sharp nod. "Very good. Good soldiers to have made it this far at all." This he said in part for the benefit of the masks themselves, which had become living things now that they contained souls. But as he accepted the metal masks from the Doctor and bounced them in his hands, feeling their heft, he whispered, "More weight for the cart."

"The burdens of the living, eh?" Doctor Morita held up the hammer and nails. "If we needed to jettison something, perhaps...?"

Scandalized, the Sergeant snatched the hammer and nails from him and packed them away. "I always march better knowing that they're close at hand." The hammer and nails sealed away, he gestured to the crossroads. "Which direction, honoured officer?"

Doctor Morita considered the two trails. "One could lead to the regrouping area just a hundred steps away in this rain."

"While the either could go onward a hundred leagues before ending in a swamp of bones," Sergeant Teneke agreed. "For that matter, any of the other trail forks we passed may have been the right one, and both of these trails might lead only to death."

All trails lead to death, Doctor Morita thought, but he did not say this out loud of course. "Perhaps you should pick the path."

"That's the only way for me to take the wrong path," the Sergeant replied.

Doctor Morita cocked his head quizzically.

Sergeant Teneke explained, "If we take the wrong path, we die like fools. But what of it? If paradise barred entry to souls for their foolishness in life, the righteous would be lonely indeed." They both chuckled at that. "But if we take neither path—if we simply sit down and wait—then we are disloyal to our orders, to our army, and to our country. There are no disloyal souls in the afterlife's paradises. Yes?"

"Yes," agreed Doctor Morita, trying to sound confident. "Paradise is reserved for patriots."

"So for my part, I march ever onward and do not choose my paths at all," the Sergeant said with satisfaction. "The last time I had to choose a path was when I chose to join the army. After that, I have only had to obey directions. If my officers choose the wrong path—or the wrong time to attack, or the wrong time, or the wrong strategy—what is that to me? I'll still end up in paradise, as long as I obey." Tucking the butt of his rifle-crutch against his gaunt ribs for a moment, he crossed his hands before himself in a show of placid acceptance. "So, honoured officer, kindly pick your path to follow. My path will be to follow you."

Contemplating which path would be the most likely to lead to the army's regrouping area, Doctor Morita pointed at the right-hand path that he had not yet seen. "When you scouted ahead, were there any dead soldiers on that road?"

"No, sir"

"Then that must not have been the path of the army." He pointed to the left-hand path where the two mangled soldiers had been found. "If that is the path taken by the dead, then that is the road we must travel."

Sergeant Teneke saluted and then went back to fetch the cart of souls.

On the thirty-third day of the repositioning march, Doctor Morita and his two companions were confronted by demons. In the way of demons, the trio of creatures haunting the jungle shadows beside the trail had the semblance of humans but were terrible in aspect.

"Comrades!" the leader of the demon trio called out over the thrumming of the monsoon. "Where are you marching?"

Doctor Morita and his two companions came to halt on the trail only slowly, pulling themselves out of the fugue of their numb march with an effort. When Private Bahp loosened the ammunition cart's traces, their rough hemp was stained with blood from raw patches of sores on his shoulders. Doctor Morita had been marching beside the cart, pulling on it, while Sergeant Teneke had pushed from behind. Hands over their eye slits against the rain, they peered into the jungle.

The three demons wore imperial uniforms that had rotted to rags in the same way as those of Doctor Morita and his companions. But whereas Sergeant Teneke and Private Bahp had retreated into privacy within the jungle now and again to scour incipient corrosion off their masks with sand, these three soldiers had allowed their iron masks to rust like the anchors of shipwrecks. The metallic scabbing transformed the docile and solicitous expression of their conscript masks into demonic visages of delight and contempt. They sat in dryness under a lean-to they had constructed and even had a small fire burning before them. The demons had energy in their movements as they gestured up and down the trail with spears crafted of bayonets affixed to long branches.

"Where are you marching, comrades?" their leader asked again. Whatever curlicues of rank his mask had once possessed were now completely hidden by a russet fur of rust. "Why are you still marching?"

"Why stop here?" retorted Sergeant Teneke.

"Why not stop here?" mocked the demon leader, eliciting laughter from his two companions. "Everything you could ever find on your march is right here," the demon leader continued, beckoning Morita and his companions toward the fire and the dry lean-to.

Private Bahp stirred out of his fog of suffering and spoke for the first time that day. "Is the regrouping area near? Or at least a medical aid station?"

"There is nothing like that in this hell," the demon leader said, gesturing with a bony hand to the jungle, the rain, the cloud-wrapped mountains.

"But you just said that everything we could hope to find is right here," insisted Private Bahp.

"I did not say everything you could hope to find," corrected the demon leader. "I only said, 'Everything you could ever find is right here'." With this, the demon leader turned something over the fire: a spit, made of a stick resting on two Y-shaped branches planted into the ground. On this spit was roasting a hunk of meat, red with juice and black where drops of fat hissed.

Private Bahp groaned and started to unfasten his hemp traces with shaking hands.

But Doctor Morita put a restraining hand on the Private's raw-rubbed shoulder and asked the demons, "Where did you get real meat?"

"It's a jungle. Life is everywhere."

"It's a jungle," Doctor Morita agreed, but then pointed out, "Insects are everywhere. Insects, slugs, snails, and worms." He and the two others had eaten no other protein but these for weeks now.

One of the demons shook a bayonet-tipped bamboo spear. "We killed an alligator."

"An alligator? In the mountains?"

"Did I say alligator? My mind dreams of food and my mouth waters words—if only we had killed something so big! I meant that we have meat from a snake."

"Or from a wild boar," suggested Sergeant Teneke.

"Or from a wild boar," agreed one of the demons equitably, all three of them nodding in eagerness as though accepting a proposal. "Meat is meat."

Puzzled by the strange exchange, Private Bahp looked to Doctor Morita.

Doctor Morita crouched so that he could better see into the shadows under the trees. As the leaves of the jungle bobbed in the rain, a small clearing behind the camp of the demons was periodically visible. There dangled a body on vines, strung up in the way of a game animal. The body wore nothing but a steel mask. The legs of the corpse were scraped-bare bones from the intact feet to the groin. As his eyes further searched the green shadows, the Doctor spotted two more bodies similarly strung up.

When they saw the Doctor's mask oriented toward their charnel pantry, the demons tittered. Their leader lifted the spit from the fire, the stick bending under the weight of the fat-popping hunk of meat. "Come! Come, let us feast together, as countrymen newly met in a foreign land should." Waving the meat in the air, he fanned its smoke toward the trail.

Even through the rain, the scent of roasting meat reached Doctor Morita and his companions, lacerating them with the cruelty of a silk-wrapped scythe. Private Bahp groaned and tried to stumble toward the fire again, but Sergeant Teneke clutched the cart's hemp traces tighter around the youth's bleeding shoulders as bindings. "There's nothing here for us, boy. They're mad."

"Mad?" said the demon leader. "Nonsense! Suffering is good for the soul." This, he said with a gesture at his rusting mask. "During the long pilgrimage of woe that brought my companions and I to this place, we transfigured into avatars of reason. We sit here before you as logic incarnate."

"'Incarnate,'" giggled one of his companions for some reason.

"You're not angels," Doctor Morita declared. "You're cannibals."

The demon leader splayed his fingers on his bony chest in the gesture of a man wounded by slander. "You speak in ignorance—but you speak the truth, so I forgive you." He then asked in the raised voice of a teacher posing a question in a garden, "Of what purpose is the soul?"

"The purpose of the soul is to serve the nation," answered one of his followers.

"And of what use is the body to a soul?" asked the demon leader.

"The transitory body serves the eternal soul," answered the second of his followers.

"Where do souls go after death?" asked the demon leader.

"Into our masks," answered the first follower again.

The demon leader nodded. "The body serves the soul, and the soul serves the nation. Very good!" The demon leader pulled a pinch of tender meat from the spit and held the smoking, succulent pearl in front of his eye slits, considering it. "But of what use is the body when it can no longer labour or fight in the service of his country? When a body dies, is it of no use at all?"

"It can still serve the bodies of his comrades, so that their bodies may continue to succour their souls and serve the nation!" answered both of his companions. "Body, soul, nation!"

"Just so!" The demon leader popped the meat through the mouth slit of his mask and chewed with audible satisfaction, the awful sound hollow behind the mask. Then he wagged a juice-glistening finger at Doctor Morita and his companions. "So how dare you stand there starving? Traitors."

"Traitors!" the two other demons giggled, turning the accusation into a madhouse chant. "Traitors! Traitors! Traitors!"

Doctor Morita considered the three demons, shaking his head at the horror of them. He silently gestured his two companions toward the sheet of grey rain waiting for them down the trail.

"Not yet," Sergeant Teneke said. He pointed at the bodies hanging in the trees and said to the demons, "Before we go, give us their masks."

The two lesser demons looked to their leader. His voice sounding almost normal for a moment, the man in the rusted mask asked the Sergeant in a tone of wonder, "You would bear even more weight along that muddy track leading to nowhere?"

"It is my duty. And the trail does not lead to nowhere, it leads to... to everywhere, eventually. We will bear the masks of the honourable dead back to the homeland." He stressed honourable. "There, their souls will feast for eternity."

The demons hesitated.

At that moment, Private Bahp tottered and then lost consciousness, sagging against Doctor Morita. The Doctor recognized the signs of the incipient faint and caught him deftly, having done so several times over the past few days. He barely even noticed this latest flight of the poor lad's consciousness.

But the sight of the Private's weakness tensed the three demons into rigidity. Their leader pointed a finger glistening with grease at the Private. "Give us him. Keep his mask and give us his body, and you can have all the masks of the others."

Doctor Morita considered pointing out that the Private was not dead, but then decided this was not the point. "No. Just give us the masks of the dead you have eaten. Be reasonable, you cannot eat their masks."

"But we can eat his flesh," the demon leader said, still pointing at the Private. "And he's too far gone for you to save him, so you be reasonable."

"Reasonable?" Sergeant Teneke spat. "You demons talk of reason?"

The cannibal leader nodded so vigorously that flakes of rust fell from his mask like dry scabs. "We do. It is basic reason to use the flesh of the dead to save life."

"That's madness."

"It's not madness, Sergeant—it's merely a logic opposite to the logic of war." The demon held up two empty cupped palms in the symbol for a merchant's scales. "Give us flesh, and we'll give you souls."

"No!" said Doctor Morita.

"Pacifists." With this, the cannibal returned to tending the spit of meat roasting on the fire. "Such waste."

Sergeant Teneke grunted, then started to dig in his pack, muttering, "This is why the world needs soldiers." He drew forth the hammer and three nails.

Doctor Morita tugged on the straps of the Sergeant's pack to hold him back. Emaciated though the demons were, the warm and fed cannibals still had more strength in them than did he and his companions. "We need to leave—now."

"No, we need to do our duty—always." Sergeant Teneke handed him the hammer and nails, then started to tend to the rifle he had been using as a crutch. He wiped the mud from the stock of the rifle; blew down the rifle's barrel by cupping his hands around his mask's mouth slit and the chamber, a plug of muck popping out of the muzzle; then inserted a clip of cartridges whose brass had gone green.

"Your rifle is rusted and its bullets are wet," the demon leader noted. "It can't possibly work."

"A reasonable assumption," the Sergeant admitted. Then he levelled the gun at the demon leader and pulled the trigger. The retort of the rifle, the first gunshot that any of them had heard in weeks, seemed all the more loud for its unexpectedness.

A precise hole appeared in the inadequate iron of the demon leader's forehead. He remained seated on his haunches for a few moments, then blood flowed out of his eye slits and down the mask's rusted cheeks, invigorating the corrosion's crimson. He toppled backward. His two companions looked at him with consternation, but did not try to rise from the fire and run. Their lean-to, their cook fire, the grisly meat on the spit—these had become their world specifically because they could run no longer. So they sat at the fire a final few seconds as Sergeant Teneke calmly took aim, then he shot them in the faces too.

After the three shots, Doctor Morita and his companions stood unspeaking for a time, then they silently went about their duties. Having been shocked back to consciousness by the gunshots, Private Bahp began to unfasten the lacings of the ammunition cart's tarp. Doctor Morita gave Sergeant Teneke the hammer and nails, and the Sergeant set about the chore of nailing the masks of the demons to their faces. Doctor Morita limped into the jungle, retrieved the masks of the dead soldiers hanging in the trees, and cleaned them in the rain.

When Doctor Morita emerged from the jungle shadows with the masks, his shoulders were slumped in gloom. With an apologetic bob of the head, he showed the other two his burden, which he needed both arms to lug.

Twenty masks. Twenty more lumps of metal for the cart.

Private Bahp whimpered with the despair of the dead, recoiling from the cart as though already feeling the new masks' added weight. "It's too much," he moaned. "It's too much."

"It's too much," Doctor Morita agreed.

Sergeant Teneke, the hammer stamped with the imperial moon in one hand and his rifle in the either, hesitated on the verge of some diatribe about duty and willpower conquering all, but then just waved his hammer in a gesture of dismissal. "He's right, it's too much. Far too much."

Finding themselves united in this agreement, they all stood in the rain.

Doctor Morita even looked down at the ground, seeing himself lying there in the deep red mud. If he just laid down to die, Private Bahp would join him. Perhaps even Sergeant Teneke. But he couldn't leave behind even one mask. Abandon just one soul and you're as damned as a person could be, and then you might as well forsake everyone—he might as well just crawl into the demons' lean-to and start carving up their bodies to furnish the spit.

Oh, how he wished he knew if there truly was such a thing as a soul.

But he didn't.

So Doctor Morita put the twenty new masks onto the cart and reaffixed the tarp carefully so that the masks wouldn't spill out. Imagine losing someone's soul in the mud?

Sobbing audibly inside his mask, Private Bahp tightened the traces around his raw shoulders.

Sergeant Teneke hung his rifle on a loop of vines on the flank of the cart, put his shoulder to its rear, and muttered, "On three, two, one... march."

The three of them could not march at night even if they had possessed the strength, for the monsoon clouds hid the stars and moon completely, rendering them utterly blind. So when evening approached, the three of them moved into the jungle and patiently harvested half a handful of worms, grubs, and snails from rotting trunks and beneath stones. These they ate raw. Their tent and other gear had long ago been discarded as too heavy, so they crawled into a niche between the giant roots of a tree where the rain would only spatter them rather than fall on them directly, then they curled up together for warmth and subsided into sleep.

When dreams came to Morita, the rain had stopped. And the sun....

Oh, the sun.

In the dream, he was walking the eternal jungle trail, but the rain had ended and golden sunlight transformed the jungle into a land of emerald so vibrant that he forgave the jungle for its trespasses against him with all his heart. Grey and wrinkled and chilled from weeks of being soaked by constant rain, he rose and stood naked in the warm sunlight with his arms outstretched, swaying in peace like clean linen on a line. A gentle breeze swirled white leaves around him. These leaves had slits for eyes and calmly smiling mouths, he noticed. Masks. With a bloom of joy, he realized the rusting metal soul masks of the fallen had been transmuted into delicate white rice paper. Another miracle of the sun, the wondrous sun. He gathered these weightless masks here and there as he journeyed down the trail, which had turned from a muddy russet morass to a warm white chalk that healed his cold and blistered feet. Covering leagues effortlessly, he finally arrived at the glittering blue coast with every soul mask safely retrieved, and there he simply flung them into the air. The salt winds carried the soul masks high into the sky above the cerulean waves. This soul-fall of thousands tumbled merrily over the sunlit sea back toward the homeland. Safe now. His duty done, he spread his arms to the sun and his soul rose from his body, smiling and free, to join the sky-dancing migration home....

With a twitch, Doctor Morita awoke to find his body as wet and cold as a corpse enclosed in clay. But he was smiling, his cheeks dimpling just enough to touch the inner surface of his army mask. A good moment to die, this, and he waited in anticipation of a long slide into whatever dreams death held. But death did not come. With a sigh, he forced open his gummy eyelids.

He was still curled up between the roots of the tree, and the monsoon clouds had barely started allowing grey morning light to leak down through the jungle's canopy. He drew his hands from the warm place between his concave thighs to shake awake Sergeant Teneke, who was lying in front of him. The Sergeant awoke, hacking against a dampness in his lungs. Next, Doctor Morita reached back and elbowed Private Bahp, and the young man let out the slurping hiss of a waker drawing the first full breath of the day.

Doctor Morita began the ritual that had replaced breakfast over the past weeks. "I dreamed of the sun," he croaked. "I dreamed the sun came out and that all the world became warm and dry and gentle and...and everything else that the word is when the sun shines. And that we all became white paper masks and floated on the wind, home."

Behind his mask, Sergeant Teneke let out a soft grunt as his thanks for the sharing of so fine a dream. Then he reported, "I dreamed of a barracks I once lived in." Aware of how this would sound to conscripted civilians, the Sergeant shrugged sheepishly. "I have been in good barracks in my life. In peacetime. They are full of order, everything in its place."

For a time, the only sound was the eternal sizzle of the rain on the leaves as they waited for Private Bahp to take his turn. He would have dreamt of his farm, Doctor Morita knew—the young man always dreamt of the family farm that had been his world before the Empire had summoned him to war. But as he and the Sergeant waited to hear the Private again share his old, precious, dream, the only sound was the hissing of the monsoon. Eventually, Doctor Morita and Sergeant Teneke forced their aching bodies to uncurl and turned to Private Bahp.

Private Bahp remained where he was, a shadow sitting in the gloomy hollow of the tree roots with his head bent over his drawn-up knees. He had fallen back into sleep, apparently. The hiss of a weak snore came from within his mask. Coughing intentionally loudly, the Sergeant reached out to shove the enlisted man awake. But Doctor Morita grabbed Teneke's wrist and held it back. He commanded, "Wait. Listen."

The Sergeant stifled his cough and held still.

The hissing in the air was becoming louder, waxing into a susurration. Sergeant Teneke snatched up his rifle, his head snapping in the direction that the mechanical leviathan of the enemy would come, afraid that somehow the inexorable beast had made up all the leagues between them in the night. But Doctor Morita shook his head and pointed a shaking finger at Private Bahp.

It was the young man who was the source of the sibilant hissing—he and the trunk of the tree against which he rested. The sun, so merciful in Doctor Morita's dreams, now reached wan grey fingers through the rain onto Private Bahp.

Utterly motionless, Private Bahp was nevertheless in constant motion. The shredded remains of his uniform shifted, his very skin seemed to crawl in the bad light. Another wandering ray of dead sunlight fell upon the trunk of the tree, revealing the source of the susurration: a slow cascade of maggots. Tens of thousands of maggots of a kind that lived high in the branches until they scented carrion. In the night, they had flowed down the trunk, forming a rippling pallid sheen, to envelop the Private. His uniform tunic and loin cloth rippled from within. From within his mask's eye slits, maggots fell like pale wriggling tears; from within the mouth slit trickled a drool of tiny bloated bodies.

Sergeant Teneke, a veteran of a hundred battles and a hero in more than a few, let out a scream of terror. Still holding the rusted rifle he had snatched up with every intention of fighting against a mechanical leviathan of a size to crush hills, he fled from the sight of the maggots.

Later, when Doctor Morita emerged from the trees carrying Private Bahp's soul mask, he found Sergeant Teneke waiting for him on the trail. Morita would not have thought badly of the man if the Sergeant had fled in madness into the monsoon never to be seen again, but instead the old soldier had unfastened a flap of the canvas covering the soul masks and was now standing at attention in front of the cart. He had his rifle under one arm, leaning on it discreetly to ease the pressure on his gangrenous foot. The hemp traces, still stiff with the Private's blood that the monsoon could not seem to wash away, were now around the Sergeant's shoulders.

Doctor Morita held up the mask and turned it both ways, to demonstrate that he had completely cleaned it of maggots. Voice quavering with weakness, he announced in the best officer's tone he could manage, "Rarely has so good a death had so ill an appearance. But a good death it was."

"A f-fine death," Sergeant Teneke agreed through chattering teeth. "He did not die of bullets or bombs that kill in a single merciful moment. He faced death every minute of every day in our long march, yet he endured in his duties until death despaired and had to assassinate him in his sleep."

Doctor Morita clapped his hand on the Sergeant's bony shoulder, too overcome with emotion to speak, then he added the Private's mask to the collection of honoured dead in the cart and refastened the tarp. Then he settled himself into the traces of the cart beside the Sergeant and began to fasten a strand of the hemp around his own bony shoulders.

The Sergeant whispered to him too quietly for the soul masks in the cart to overhear, "The maggots, they... they would not come for a living man, yes? Only for a man already dead?"

"Of course! Of course!" Doctor Morita leaned into the traces, the hemp abrading his rain-soft flesh. "We will not speak of that again. We will not even dream of it. That is an order."

The two of them could not force the cart back into motion by themselves at first. So they tore strips of cloth from their already ragged uniform tunics, wrapped these rags around their hands and knees, and started to crawl. Even after the cart's wheels slowly sucked free of the mud into which it had deeply settled in the night, Doctor Morita realized that he would not have the strength to pull the mask-laden cart—not when he was standing. In the traces beside him, Sergeant Teneke must have realized the same thing, for he did not try to rise to his feet either.

Instead, they pulled the cart of souls along the trail by crawling on their hands and knees.

Hours passed in hellish numbness, both of them staring at their hands forever emerging from the mud only to sink back down with the next tortuous crawl-step forward. Doctor Morita noticed that the Sergeant's breathing was laboured. A bad sign.

An even worse sign: at one point, the Sergeant gasped out, "It has just occurred to me that I am now the lowest rank in the unit. Maybe in the whole garrison."

And then, the worst sign of all. Near midday, Sergeant Teneke asked if the rain had just turned oddly warm. Deep in his own misery, Doctor Morita just kept his eyes upon the muddy ground close below his bent face and said nothing. A time later, Sergeant Teneke said in a tone of wonder that the rain had just turned cold. This time, the implications of his words filtered into the Doctor's numbed consciousness. He called a halt, slipped his fingers under the top edge of the Sergeant's mask, and traced them along the damp forehead underneath. Rubbing his thumb across these fingers, he found that the moisture they had gathered from the skin of the veteran was not merely rain, it had slimier texture, like the trail left by a slug.

"The sweats?" Sergeant Teneke said.

Doctor Morita nodded. "Malaria, probably. I can confirm the diagnosis by checking your face and eyes for yellow discoloration. May I remove your mask? We are alone and I am a doctor, so it is permissible."

"Permissible, but not seemly. Besides...." The Sergeant back-nodded toward the cart's burden of masks looming over them. "We are not alone. The dead watch. It would be bad for discipline."

They knelt that way for a time, face to masked face in the rain and the mud, attached by ropes to the cart and its killing weight.

"How would you like to go about it?" Doctor Morita finally prodded.

"You're the officer," the Sergeant said. "It's your decision."

"It's your death, so it's your decision. How do you want it to be?"

Sergeant Teneke nodded and considered. "You cannot pull the cart at all without me."

"No, we'll have to stop," Doctor Morita agreed. "Doctors and soldiers—we fight death all our lives, but we're both bound to obey its orders at the last."

Sergeant Teneke grunted a sour agreement. He looked around at the place in which they found themselves. Just another patch of trail, the world all mud and rain and trees. "Well, this is no place to die. The dead we've borne so far would be forgotten here—we'd be forgotten here." He settled into the traces and nodded for the Doctor to do the same. "A bit farther, then."

Doctor Morita obeyed this wish, as doctors must.

The looming mountains, the cloud-sealed sky, and the curtains of rain made the evening arrive early, so the two of them had entered the village before they even saw it in the gloaming. His eyes fixed on the muddy ground as he crawled, Doctor Morita only noticed the village because he happened to stretch his aching neck. A collection of native huts surrounded them. Thatched eaves drooped in the rain like the manes of dispirited horses. The village's silence and empty wicker baskets half buried in the mud outside the open doorways testified that it had already been searched and everything of use seized by other passing soldiers long ago. This meant that the natives would all have run off or been killed. A humiliated army is the most dangerous army of all, always hungry for scapegoats.

Doctor Morita grunted and stopped crawling.

Sergeant Teneke tried to crawl onward dumbly for a few moments, hands and knees only clawing deeper into the mud, before realizing they had halted. Raising his face, he saw the village through his bullet-scarred mask, then nodded. "Stop the train, conductor. We have arrived at my stop."

Doctor Morita whimpered with an emotion he could not have put a name to, then said, "I will disembark with you, I think."

"You will not!" Sergeant Teneke snapped, though the effort brought on a bronchial coughing fit. When he recovered, his voice was hoarse. "I just gave an order to an officer for the first and last time. You will not die here with me."

"But I cannot pull the cart alone."

The Sergeant considered. "No, that's true, but you can hide the masks. Bury them. Not forever—bury them somewhere safe, then continue onward. If there is a village, we must finally be nearing a coast. You must find the regrouping area and bring back help to retrieve the masks."

"Very well! Your first order is a good one." Doctor Morita saluted the Sergeant, and the act made them both giggle and sob a little. Then he grew solemn. "Honoured Sergeant, in recognition of your unwavering service to the Empire, I desire to award you a field commission. Will you accept?"

Sergeant Teneke made a pleased sound inside his mask—a heartfelt peep of a grunt, such as a person makes when a neighbour notices and admires how well they have kept their home and garden. But he said, "Thank you, sir, but no. I wish to die as a sergeant with a record of duty as thick as a scripture, not as a lieutenant with a career one page thin. After all, what does rank matter in the afterlife?"

"None at all, if it's paradise."

With a consumptive coughing titter and a nod, Sergeant Teneke again looked around at the silent huts. He had a proprietary air, as though in his dying he had become the lord of the dead village. He pointed to a hut that had a good thatch roof and stood above the water-running ground on stilts. Inside the gaping doorway, they could see kindling stacked beside a fire pit of hardened clay. "There... I would like... to be...." Frustrated by the hoarseness of his throat, the Sergeant tilted his mask to the heavens and sipped the rain leaking through its mouth slit, then continued in a clearer voice, "We are not supposed to care about the body, only the soul, but I would like to be dry and warm one last time. Let me die by a fire. And when my soul is in my mask? Set the hut ablaze. Burn my body. Leave nothing for this damned jungle."

"I will," Doctor Morita promised. "The maggots will go hungry."

"Ha! Our triumph over the maggots and the worms!" The Sergeant touched two white, wrinkled fingers covered in trail mud to the corners of his mouth slit in the sign for a smile. "A last battle and a final victory!"

Laughing again, a touch manically, they shrugged off their hemp traces for the last time. So weak were they that they had to cling to each other in order to rise to their feet, but they managed it. Still leaning against each other, they tottered toward the sanctuary offered by the dry hut, its open door, and the waiting fire pit.

They never reached it.

A ghost materialized in the rainy darkness before them.

Doctor Morita and the Sergeant froze in fear, their tongues jamming against their palates and their bodies locking rigid.

The ghost glowed in the gathering night, and it took the form of an imperial army major. In the way of spirits who descended from a heavenly domain, the ghost was unsullied by the mortal realm: his pale pith helmet was spotless; his imperial purple uniform, dry despite the monsoon; his gloves, white as swan down. Most strikingly of all, the spirit's mask was an antique porcelain masterpiece denoting an aristocrat from an ancient clan. The crimson features were that of divine warrior whose rage transcended any passion a mortal could feel: the eyes were pure circles of rage rendered in glaring gold; the ebony eyebrows were upraised at their outer ends into wings, yet sharply descended to almost meet between the eyes in the mountain ridges of a scowl; and the mouth was set in a teeth-bared snarl that suggested both nature's fury and the resolve of a magistrate pronouncing sentence.

The ghost spoke to them in a cold, cultured voice. "Why do you not salute?"

But Doctor Morita and Sergeant Teneke could not salute. Or speak. Or run. Hunched and shivering in the rain, they could only clutch at each other like children as they stared in terror at the apparition.

"Do you have no tongues?" the apparition pressed.

In the darkness above the ghost, the rain sparkled and became bright silver streaks like threads descending from heaven. And amidst this silver, four dragons soared in a silent circle, forming a celestial laurel for the spirit. His eyes adapting to the gathering night and his frozen mind thawing a single degree, Doctor Morita realized that the spirit was holding a parasol. A fine parasol of oiled paper hand-painted with four plumed and scaled dragons. The ghost held in his other white-gloved hand a military lantern, and its rays created the nimbus of heavenly light around the being and shone upward through the parasol's translucent paper to cast the sinuous images of the painted dragons on the rain above him. The Doctor recognized that the Major was actually a mortal man. Yet, this epiphany set about easing his fear only as slowly and imperfectly as a hand fan empties a room of incense smoke. But he eventually managed to straighten up and salute.

At his side, Sergeant Teneke remained hunched in ignorance and fear.

The Major pointed at the Sergeant with the hand that held the lantern, this movement causing the halo of dragons to gyre wildly above him. "Why does he not salute?"

"Forgive my comrade, honoured Major!" said Doctor Morita, half-shouting in the proper manner of a subordinate addressing a superior. "He has a jungle disease and is not well in the mind."

Shadows shifted in the deep features of the Major's ferocious war mask as he considered Sergeant Teneke from the man's gangrenous foot and his shaking legs to his rain-streaming mask and its bullet dent. The Major began to twirl his parasol first one direction and then the other with the sharp reversals of a cat flicking its tail, making the dragons dart back and forth in the air above him like hunting hawks. "Sergeant, where is your unit?"

Sergeant Teneke gestured vaguely, numbly, back behind himself into the night, into the jungle, across the hundreds of muddy leagues he had journeyed, to the black-blasted battlefield of a month earlier.

"You mean you have abandoned your unit, Sergeant! Disgrace!" As the Major raged, he held his lantern out sideward. A man previously invisible in the rainy darkness took it. He was a soldier with a steel mask smudged dark, jungle leaves affixed to his uniform and helmet as camouflage, and a rifle protected from the rain by a cover of oiled canvas. He had been crouched on one knee beside and behind the officer all this time—he and another such soldier. His hand now free, the Major drew an automatic from an oiled holster and aimed it at Sergeant Teneke. "For a sergeant to be away from his unit in a time of war is shameful! It is a shame for your clan, a shame for your home village, a shame for your country!"

When it became clear that Sergeant Teneke could not summon the wit to defend himself, Doctor Morita said, "Sir, honoured Major, the Sergeant has not left his unit! He has led them here!" With this, he stepped to the side (pulling Teneke out of the way too) so that the light of the Major's lantern illuminated the cart behind them. Full night had fallen now, and the lantern's light shining through cracks and bullet holes in the side of the cart glistened upon the metal masks of the dead. The metallic glints looked like the eyes of prisoners peering out holes in the walls of a dark dungeon.

Even as the ferocious war mask of the Major oriented its snarl toward the cart of soul masks, the Major kept his pistol levelled at Sergeant Teneke's sunken stomach, holding his weapon in a precise arm-back stance that kept the weapon tucked under the shelter of the parasol out of the rain. "And did the Sergeant bring all the masks of his men so?"

Doctor Morita elbowed Sergeant Teneke to life. The Sergeant sputtered, "N-no, of course not, honoured Major." Struggling against the hoarseness of weakness, he forced a stentorian tone into his voice. "No, sir! Whenever any of my men failed to perform their duty to the utmost or spoke of defeatism, I nailed their masks to their traitorous faces and left them to rot in the mud!"

The Major studied Sergeant Teneke, his face inscrutable even by the standards of a nation of mask-wearers. Then, the shadows of the mask's recesses briefly migrated upward as he nodded in the light of the low-held lantern. "Just so. As it should be. As it should be, forever."

This gave Sergeant Teneke the strength to finally stand up at attention. "Sir!"

The Major's mask tilted quizzically as he studied the Sergeant. "Why do you still tremble so?"

"Chills, sir!"

"It will pass, I think," Doctor Morita added quickly.

But Sergeant Teneke hesitated, then admitted, "It is malaria, sir!"

The shadows of the Major's mask deepened upward and then withdrew back into their hollows as he nodded his understanding. "Then, honoured Sergeant, you have fulfilled your duty to our nation in the fullest possible measure."

At this pronouncement, Sergeant Teneke sagged and made a feeble gesture in the direction of the dry hut, its open door, and the waiting fire pit. But in the next moment, he recovered and resumed standing at attention with parade-ground perfection. As the rain trailed down his gaunt body, the skin white with cold, he saluted sharply, the rags wrapping his worn-bloody hand trailing down like a strip of flayed flesh.

The Major's pistol spat, the eight millimetre's retort no louder than the snapping of a branch.

Sergeant Teneke's used-up body collapsed like a marionette whose control sticks had broken. Doctor Morita reflexively caught him in an embrace before he fell into the mud.

"Leave the body, Doctor," the Major ordered, holstering his gun with a smart motion. "Bring his mask."

"Of course, sir!" Doctor Morita said. But when he tried to release the body of the Sergeant, his arms would not obey. Then he fainted, falling into darkness with his body still tangled with the dead.

Doctor Morita was drawn out of blackness by the sounds of life: men giving orders and the click and rattle of weapons. When he opened his gummy eyes, he found himself staring at a canvas roof of military green. Naked except for his mask, he was lying on a cot, dry and warm beneath a wool army blanket.

He could hear his heartbeat, and the sound oddly filled him with a misgiving. This anthem of life somehow suggested that something was missing. Something had gone out of the world. Something immense. He felt the beginnings of a panic stirring. But then he realized what had gone out of the world: the rain had stopped. The eternal and merciless hiss of the monsoon had vanished.

He sat up in wonder. He'd prayed for an end to the rain, so why did it worry him so as though all the world had lost its heartbeat? Just a sick man's disorientation, he told himself. But his anxiety persisted.

Where was he? The air was cool, thin, clean. Mountain air.

A young corporal ducked through the tent fly, carrying a mess tray. He was thin, but not starved, and his uniform was frayed and patched, but otherwise intact. He had pants rather than just a loin cloth. He even had boots. It had also been weeks since Doctor Morita had seen boots, even on corpses, since the leather could be eaten. From beneath his iron conscript's mask came a young man's friendly voice, "Greetings, honoured officer. I am Corporal Hanno."

Doctor Morita tightened his dishevelled blanket over his nakedness. "How long did I sleep?"

"A day. How are you tonight?"

Remembering what had happened to poor sick Sergeant Teneke, Doctor did not trust this solicitousness, not at all. "I can still serve."

"Who doubts it? I'm only asking if you can eat." The Corporal set down the tray on a crate of rifle ammunition beside the cot. The tray had a tin of mutton, a bowl of brown rice, a small cardboard box of candied raisins, and a thermos. "Major Gentaro sends his regards."

Doctor Morita remembered the officer in the ferocious porcelain mask and pristine uniform. "A major shot a sergeant who was travelling with me."

"That was Major Gentaro, truly. He waits in the village at the bottom of these mountains like a tiger at a watering hole." Corporal Hanno poured him a cup of soup from the thermos. "When the first soldiers in our command reached the village, the Major was somehow already there, standing alone in the rain—the only thing alive. Bullet casings everywhere and all the natives dead."

Morita sipped the hot soup carefully. "He killed them all himself?"

"Personally, I would not have believed it possible, if it were anyone other than Major Gentaro." The Corporal opened the mutton tin and poured its juice into the rice, the scent of the salty vitamin-packed liquid agonizingly wonderful, then he started flaking the mutton into the rice with careful strokes of a worn but sharp army knife. "The Major has haunted the village ever since like the Magistrate of the Court of the Underworld, rendering judgement on the soldiers who arrive. Those he deems to have been insufficiently loyal to their duty have nails driven through their masks into their living faces, then are blinded and consigned to the jungle. Those who have upheld their duty but are too weak to fight onward, his pistol dismisses to paradise. The rest of us, the loyal who can still serve, he whisks up here into the clean air of the mountains with a single wave of his white glove."

Doctor Morita accepted the bowl of rice and mutton and ate a few bites very carefully. His teeth ached at the roots at this first experience for weeks of any food harder than grubs, but they did not wobble let alone fall out. There was hope for them yet. "So this is the regrouping area?"

The Corporal nodded. "There was nothing here before Major Gentaro. Everything is Major Gentaro's work. A creation of his will. When he dies, all will be nothing again."

"What does that mean?"

But the Corporal just rose. "Eat slowly, but then clean yourself up quickly. The war continues." He nodded toward a washbasin and a fresh uniform on a crate of rations in the corner. "Major Gentaro wishes you to report to him immediately. And besides...." The Corporal smiled. "You have a date with a goddess."

When Doctor Morita had eaten, cleaned himself, scoured his mask, and shaved (the Corporal standing guard outside the tent fly while his mask was off), he dressed. It felt pleasurably strange to wear a full uniform again, the boots a stiff bliss on his trail-sore feet. Then he stepped out of the tent—and gasped in wonder. He had assumed that the silence of the rain marked only a brief lull in the wretched monsoon, but as he reflexively glanced upward to gauge how long he had before the hateful rain began drumming down on him again, he beheld a wonder: stars. The sky was clear of clouds. He had not glimpsed the sky at all—not the stars, the moon, or the sun—since the monsoon had begun weeks ago. Hunger, cold, and fear could turn a person into an animal, but the march had taught him that the lack of the sight of the sun made a person feel orphaned by heaven.

Eventually lowering his gaze to look about himself, Doctor Morita discovered the reason for the wonder of the clear sky: the camp was positioned so high upon a majestic mountain that it was above the clouds. "You can see the sun rise from up here?" he said with such joy that it sounded like a question.

"Every morning," Corporal Hanno said with a nicety of comedic seriousness. "The sun is as punctual in her inspections of our camp as the Major himself, though only half as thorough: Major Gentaro inspects the camp at both sunrise and sunset."

As Doctor Morita followed Corporal Hanno through the alpine camp, he saw order everywhere. The soldiers' uniforms were complete, their bodies healthy, their weapons functional. Tents and gun emplacements were all snugged in among the mountaintop's boulders and covered in camouflage netting entwined with living branches. No visible lanterns shone and no fires burned. The enemy would never find this camp in a year of searching. Yet, all watch posts were manned. When he and the Corporal visited the latrine, they even had to give a daily password to a sentry.

"How many men in the camp?" he asked the Corporal.

"Including yourself, forty-five."

"Forty-five, out of an army of ten thousand?"

"Some others are surely still alive in the jungle below, but you and your sergeant were the first to reach us here in the regrouping area for several days now."

A strangeness occurred as they moved through the camp. Seeing the Doctor pass, many of the soldiers whispered to him variations of a strange salutation: "Give Koan my greetings."

Koan? The fact that he recognized the name of the ancient Goddess of Mercy did not mean he understood what the soldiers meant. Adding to the mystery, some of the soldiers invoked her name in this strange way in the tone of a friendly jest, but some spoke her name with an affecting wistfulness, and others with a hint of bitterness. But before Doctor Morita could ask any of the soldiers what they meant by Give Koan my greetings, Corporal Hanno motioned them to hush, grinning like a man guarding a great secret, and led Doctor Morita onward.

The regrouping area's command post could be accessed only by a narrow cave that spiralled upward through the raw rock of the mountain's peak. As Corporal Hanno led Doctor Morita through this darkness using a candle set into a holder fashioned from a tin can, he explained that the tunnel mouth had been originally completely hidden by a screen of vines. "But Major Gentaro found it all the same. Nothing escapes his eyes!" When the rising tunnel ended at a moonlit opening, the loquacious Corporal fell silent, saluted, and then withdrew quietly back down the tunnel.

The moonlit cave mouth looked out onto the starry sky, Doctor Morita saw. The forlorn murmur of a high wind that he had always thought so peaceful when hiking in the hills back home here whispered a warning that he had come to a forbidden place, a sacred place, a place not for the living. He moved out of the cave with small, slow steps.

The command post was a hawk's aerie, a triangular plateau only twelve metres across and completely dominated by a facings of granite on two sides that bulged outward, sheltering most of the plateau. On the third side of the plateau, a sharp precipice gave way to nothingness—to nothing but a void of stars and the moon.

Major Gentaro worked by moonlight, leaning over a campaign table covered in military maps. The way he braced himself with white-gloved fists planted on either side of the maps and the ferocious snarl on his porcelain war mask made it seem as though the state of affairs depicted by the campaign maps were an outrage to the gods themselves. The Major appeared as he had in the village below, his uniform flawless, his gloves spotless, his pistol holster gleaming with oil. He spoke with soft confidence to two aides respectfully standing a half pace from the map table, men with steel masks that had come from the forge with the half-moon emblems of lieutenants. Military college officers. In the innermost corner of the plateau, a cot, trunk, and freestanding rack of uniforms apparently served as the Major's open-air quarters. Nearby, a radio operator hunched over a wireless set, listening intently to the whispers of the war-torn world on his headphones.

Doctor Morita stepped toward the campaign table, his arm already halfway raised to salute Sergeant Teneke's executioner, but then he froze as he noticed the dead staring down at him.

The looming dead were seated on the two cliff faces jutting over the plateau. Dozens of them. Gory effigies of life, they had flesh like dried coconut leaves with bone showing through in places, their fingers and toes twisted and tipped with long nails. The bark-like texture of their skin was covered in a florid orange tinting. Some were as intact as mummies, some were barely more than skeletons. Most were hunched over in primitive stick-frame chairs affixed to the cliff facings' cracks and crevasses, while some were sitting with knees drawn up to chests inside inverted-cone baskets with gaps in the weaving. Coronets of flowering vines desiccated into brittle laurels crowned their heads. But whether rotten or bony, whether seated like kings or curled up like macabre infants, whether possessing eyes like leathery grapes or just empty sockets, all the dead were staring downward at Doctor Morita

At the campaign table, Major Gentaro finally noticed him, his crimson mask rising from the maps. "Good evening, Doctor. Have you eaten?"

Gaping up at the dead, Doctor Morita could neither answer nor move. He considered that he might be suffering from a jungle fever that had rendered him so ill that he did not realize he was having hallucinations. If he did not speak or move, the Major might decide that he was as sick as Sergeant Teneke had been and then shoot him, too—and only hours before he would have seen the sun rise again. As much as this alarmed him, he still could not look away from the dead who stared down at him.

Noticing Morita's grim fascination, Major Gentaro looked over his shoulder upward at the carnal ranks affixed to the cliff walls. "Arresting, aren't they? When I first found this place while scouting, I first assumed they were a jury of the dead. But I have since been told that they are actually guardians. After a native elder dies, their bodies are smoked and then covered in grease—that's what makes them such a striking orange. Then the bodies are placed up here in this sacred place where they can keep watch on the village below."

Listening, Doctor Morita saw that the dead had been positioned so that their implacable faces were oriented beyond the plateau's edge behind him. His legs moved of their own volition, carrying him to the cliff edge. A high breeze plucked at his fresh new uniform, tempting him to walk too far—to take that last step over the drop. But he stopped, leaned cautiously forward, and peered over the cliff, curious to see what the dead saw.

The drop was a sublime plunge into nothingness itself. Below, so very far below, the world was nothing but an ocean of pale mists whose swirling was more formless than mere smoothness would have been. The monsoon clouds, seen from high above. They stretched all the way to the horizons, which were very distant indeed when seen from so high a mountain peak. Lightning flickered in patches here and there, followed by rumbles that sounded subterranean when heard from the sky. The spot below this perch where the eyes of the dead were fixed was nothing more than another smooth patch of nothingness, without even a swirl in the clouds to suggest that there was a village there.

"Yes, the guardians can't even see the village when it rains," Major Gentaro declared. "Pah. Such superstition. Or are you one of those learned men of…of understanding who believe there is wisdom to be learned in foreign faiths?"

"Of course not, sir," Doctor Morita said, easing away from the hypnotic drop. "If the natives of this land believe that the soul resides in the flesh after death, they are no better than all the other misguided races of the world."

"Which is why our Empire must prevail," Major Gentaro declared. "We have a duty to enlighten our brothers and sisters across the world—to uplift them so that they understand the truth of the soul." With this, he stepped away from the campaign maps to a series of crates stencilled Mortar, 81 MM, opened the lid of one, and invited Doctor Morita to inspect the contents with a motion of a white glove that was both courteous and imperious.

Doctor Morita obeyed.

The munitions crate contained soul masks. Hundreds. The topmost mask was that of Sergeant Teneke, recognizable by the bullet gouge above the right eye that had always given the stern Sergeant an ironic hangdog expression. Staring up at him, the forlorn mask seemed to say, Look what has happened to me. Doctor Morita felt a mad impulse to say hello to his comrade. Which, he supposed, was not madness at all—Sergeant Teneke's soul now resided in that mask, after all. But he said nothing.

Major Gentaro opened more munitions crates, revealing more heaps of soul masks. Battered by blows, gouged by bullets, rendered carious as coral by shrapnel blasts, they were nevertheless never rusty—they had all been carefully scoured clean and treated with sweet smelling oil. "We have preserved nearly a thousand masks of our honoured dead here," Major Gentaro explained. "I grieve that we could not redeem all of our comrades' souls from the predations of the Soulless enemy who, I am told, collect the masks of the fallen as souvenirs."

"But that is why we will be victorious!" one of the two lieutenants barked out. "Ignorant, our enemies are maskless. Maskless, our enemies have no home for their souls after death. Possessors of souls only for the blink of an eye that is a mortal life, they fight only for the body. Fighting for the fleeting appetites of the physical, they value life above all and live in fear, so they can never prevail against the bold who care nothing for the flesh as they fight for their soul's honour!"

Doctor Morita nodded emphatically as appropriate, but found himself dizzy. These were nothing more than basic axioms that all Gestalthians learned from childhood. Yet, when he listened to them now, a disorientation came over him and he found himself back in the jungle rains listening to the ravings of demons squatting over a cook fire. Then the moment of vertigo passed. Just the lingering effects of starvation, he told himself.

Thunder rumbled below. All of them grew still. All of them looked toward the cliff edge. Then, without words, the four officers moved toward the precipice and peered down.

Once again, Doctor Morita saw patches of lightning in the sea of monsoon clouds far below, followed eventually by thunder. But this time, he realized that it was not lightning flickering at all. The patches of lightning were cannon fire, and they marked the positions of the Soulless's assault platforms. Not just one, but three…no, six… seven. Seven storms: seven mechanical leviathans. All coming this direction, as far as he could tell. And even as he stared, the nearest of these leviathans, cresting a rise presumably, came so near to breaching free of the cloudscape that the mighty flash of a broadside cast its shadow clearly through the mists—a whale of doom, glimpsed deep in the gloom of the sea.

"The Soulless fire on nothing but suspicious shadows and shifting mists," one of the lieutenants said, his words bold but his voice a mere whisper. "They have not nearly enough courage and far too much ammunition."

All of them were silent for a time. All of them staring down, all of them making the same calculation. The second lieutenant said it out loud, "The nearest will be here by tomorrow night."

"Well then," Major Gentaro said with a decisive clap of his white gloves, "no use saving the good tea."

With chuckles, the two lieutenants fetched stools and served tea, which was indeed true tea from the homeland, not just ground roots. The tea service itself was chased silver with the requisite spouts for drinking while masked. The Major scrupulously ensured that the Doctor's tea cup was never completely empty. There were biscuits too, ones with giant granules of sugar. During the long repositioning march, Doctor Morita had seen platoons of starving soldiers of the Empire engage in firefights with their fellow units over cases of rations. For such biscuits as these, the starving would have slit their closest comrades' throats. The Major and his lieutenants ate just enough of the biscuits to encourage Doctor Morita not to be shy about wolfing them down. As they sipped and ate, the Major made small talk—or at least, what passed for small talk in war. How many enemies had the Doctor seen? When last? And the Major was particularly eager as he asked, "Did you see any potential reinforcements during your march?"

"No, Major. Nothing for days."

"Nobody at all?"

"Well, three cannibals."

Major Gentaro shook his head. "The natives would never fight for us."

The Doctor decided not to correct this misapprehension, keeping his eye slits on a sugary biscuit.

Major Gentaro patted the Doctor's knee. "Well, you finally found the regrouping area, that's the key thing. Now that you have confirmed that we can expect no more reinforcements to arrive, the time has come for us to launch our counterattack."

"Yes, sir! And we will succeed!" This, Doctor Morita shouted in the military way: with a certainty inversely proportional to his confidence. The enemy had been at their most vulnerable on the beach during their amphibious landing, when the Gestalthian island garrison had also been at its strongest—and still the enemy had crushed and scattered them. Now, the enemy had been reinforced and roamed the island in leviathan assault machines. Whereas the garrison? They had very nice tea cups. Doctor Morita could not help adding, "We will attack until the last man!"

"As it should be," the Major agreed. "Which brings me to the special mission I have for you, Doctor."

"I am honoured," Doctor Morita declared, keeping the tears of despair out of his voice—a skill he had learned since being conscripted.

"I am going to have to insist," the Major said in a grave voice, "that you live."

Doctor Morita did not dare answer. Sipping tea to stall, he eyed the two lieutenants for clues about how to react. They were still, watching him intently, a chance alignment of moonlight showing him their eyes within their mask slits. The cliff edge was only a few paces behind him, and he could well imagine that if he thanked the Major for sparing him a death in battle, the Major would fling him to his death as a defeatist traitor. But first would come a nail through his mask. The damned tea cup spout was clicking on his mouth slit as his hand shook.

Mercifully, Major Gentaro did not wait for an answer from his guest. He explained, "The coast is only several hours' journey from here. Tomorrow, my men and I will escort you and our collection of redeemed soul masks to a remote lagoon and leave you there. Then we will counterattack the enemy. Tomorrow night, a cargo submarine will arrive at the lagoon under cover of darkness. You, Doctor, will escort the souls of the honoured dead home."

The sudden rush of hope almost killed the Doctor the way that too much food too quickly could kill a man who had been starving. It felt as though bliss would burst his distended heart. "Truly?"

"Will you do it?"

"Will I escort the souls of the honoured dead home? So that they can rest in our sacred homeland for all eternity? I would die for the privilege of doing so—why, I would even live for it!"

The Major and his lieutenants let out pent breaths of relief. "Then it is settled!" A lieutenant produced a small bottle of supremely precious peach wine from a case—fine wine too, the potent blend reserved for soldiers about to make a particularly desperate attack. The Major poured some into all their tea cups, then proposed a toast. "To the honoured dead, and to the Koan, who shall bear them home."

"The Koan?" Doctor Morita asked. But then he understood. "Oh! 'Koan' is the name of the submarine?"

The other three officers burst into chuckles, having apparently been aware of the Give Koan my regards riddle with which the other soldiers had plied the Doctor. And he laughed with them at the jest, tossing down the toasting wine in a single go and feeling it kindle a pleasurable fire in him. He was going to home. He was going to live.

After the toast, Major Gentaro told his two lieutenants, "I wish to confer private messages to my clan upon the Doctor. Inform the men that they have tonight to compose any letters to home they wish to send with the Doctor." The lieutenants saluted him, bowed to the munitions crates holding the soul masks of the honoured dead, then left the command post by the cave tunnel. The radio operator remained, hunched low over his radio set and log book in deepest concentration, like an eavesdropping prophet attempting to set into words the grand machinations of the gods. But the Major said to him, "You, as well."

At this request, the operator hesitated in momentary surprise, but then switched off the radio and left the plateau on the half trot.

Alone with the Doctor now, Major Gentaro set two campaign stools near the cliff edge and, with a motion of his white gloves, invited the Doctor to have a seat with him and enjoy the night air and the sublime view. Then he refilled their cups with peach wine, and for a time they simply sat side-by-side, gazing down upon the world of clouds. The moon had sunk lower in the starry sky, and now its rays were registering on the cloudscape as a finer silver in the same way that the low rays of morning glisten on the sea as the best gold. Doctor Morita considered expressing his regrets that Major Gentaro and his men would be massacred in their counterattack, but decided not to risk it. You never knew how such an officer would react to sympathy, and he now had much to live for.

Ten thousand men in the island garrison, and I will be the sole survivor. It was hideous. It was wonderful.

"So here we are alone," Major Gentaro said, adding more wine to the Doctor's cup.

"Not so, honoured Major." Doctor Morita back-nodded toward the munitions crates of soul masks. "The souls of the honoured dead remain with us. Always."

"Don't be a child. Of course they don't."

Doctor Morita froze with his cup halfway to his mouth slit. At the Major's words, it was as though all the numbness of the long repositioning march in the cold rain had returned in a single moment. He truly considered that he would jerk awake and find himself back on the trail, huddled with Sergeant Teneke and Private Bahp under a tree after another cold, wet night. Miserably conscious, he would report to them, I dreamed they were sending me home to live. When he did not actually awake, he asked, "Sir?"

Major Gentaro stared at him for a time. Although the gold eyes of his warrior mask were huge with heroic rage, the view slits in their center were actually quite small and hid his eyes well. Eventually, Major Gentaro set his gloved hands to either side of his porcelain face in the traditional gesture for the deepest of dismay— but then, with a sudden movement, his thumbs flicked open the mask's clasps.

Doctor Morita went rigid with fear.

Major Gentaro removed his mask. In the moonlight, his revealed face was handsome and smooth. Pale, of course, but not unhealthy. He was long in the cheekbones and nose in a comely way. Whenever Doctor Morita had looked upon the faces of the living during his duties as a doctor, the patients had been acutely embarrassed and self-conscious at their intimate exposure. But not Major Gentaro. He stared boldly at the Doctor.

Doctor Morita noted in a shaking voice, "I'm supposed to kill you now."

"Try if you like. I won't be insulted." The Major held up his porcelain mask and considered it, turning it this way and that in the moonlight. "As a physician, I expect you studied in foreign countries before the war?"

The Doctor considered his answer carefully. Nobody in the insular Empire completely trusted a countryman who had traveled beyond the home islands, no matter how briefly and for how good a reason. "The government gave me a special mandate to study surgery techniques overseas."

"And you took the chance to tourist around while you were at it, I suspect." The Major held up a gloved hand to forestall the inevitable denial. "I understand, I do. Once one moves beyond the Empire's secret police and the networks of common citizens eager to inform on anyone about anything, travelling becomes so easy—so easy and oh so tempting. When I was sent to study in the military college of a foreign country, I vowed to myself I would never so much as leave the campus grounds. But by the end of my first year, I was bicycling and hitchhiking all over—a dozen countries, I visited. Yourself?"

Doctor Morita hesitated, then hung his head. "Four."

"And did you take your mask off?"

Doctor Morita did not even pretend that he would answer that question, grateful that his face was still hidden behind his mask at this very moment.

Major Gentaro smiled, a pleasant expression that normally would never have been seen. "I've shown you my face, Doctor. Does that not merit a little candour?"

Doctor Morita recognized the truth in this, though it did not remove the danger in the question. But if he didn't answer the question, the Major might fear being denounced for having removed his mask—and the Major was far stronger than he, and the cliff edge only a pace away. "While living overseas, I... I kept my mask on for six months. But it was acutely uncomfortable to intern in a foreign hospital where the patients saw my mask and asked only half in jest if I intended to treat them by sacrificing a chicken. I finally took off my mask."

The Major smiled ruefully, another striking expression that would normally have been wasted. "It was the street-sweepers who broke me, if you can believe that. One strives to be the proudest of soldiers when in a foreign land, but the men and women who sweep cigarette butts from the gutters of the military campus I attended used to shake their heads whenever I passed. Insults I could have endured for a hundred years, but they were shaking their head at the backward foreigner in pity. They would look on this," he said as he held up his aristocratic mask, an artistic masterpiece that manifested his clan's proud heraldic emblem, "and they would see that." He gestured with his other gloved hand to the natives' dead guardians on the cliff walls, rotting in their thrones of sticks.

"They were fools, the street-sweepers," Doctor Morita said. "Like all foreigners."

Major Gentaro sighed. "We are educated men, Doctor. Men who have seen something of the world—a world in which no people but our own hides behind masks. So let us two be honest, at least." He turned and looked directly into the eye slits of Doctor Morita's mask. "When you had your mask off, did you feel you had less of a soul? Or more?"

"More. And less."

"A paradox—and I know exactly what you mean. It is an oxymoron like 'filled with hollowness'." The Major turned his mask around so that he could regard its scowl with a wistful smile. "Without my mask, I felt more of an individual, more intensely myself—a man with a soul, a soul too profound to exist inside a mere thing like a mask. Yet, the idea of living without my mask also filled me with hollowness. How odd. I no longer believed my mask could hold my soul, yet I possessed a conviction that I would fight to the death to defend my mask's honour. How could I reconcile this paradox?"

The Doctor shrugged. "One can't."

"Actually, I could." Holding his mask up at arm's length, the Major aligned its left eye slit with the moon, a slice of silver light bisecting his real eye. "That which we call the soul is identity. It is created. Crafted. Once I accepted this long-known idea, many of the knotted paradoxes of the soul unwound." With this, he twirled the porcelain mask on a fingertip as though the precious antique were a mere child's toy. "This has no soul and could never contain a soul any more than flesh could—until we invest it with identity. We—the creator of the mask, the wearer of the mask, and all those who gaze upon the mask—give it identity. Give it a soul." He stopped twirling his mask and smiled into its snarling countenance. "Our sacred ancestors were only half enlightened when they invented soul masks—they understood only half the truth. A mask is not a receptacle to preserve the soul, it is a tool for creation of one."

"But a soul is not a spirit."

"No. No, I do not believe in spirits. Do you?"

Doctor Morita hesitated. He flashed a guilty glance at the plateau's tunnel entrance. Then, as shy as a bride on a wedding night, he took off his own mask. Major Gentaro studied the Doctor's face. It was, the Doctor knew, a bland one. Then the Major smiled and nodded a greeting, as though they had just met for the first time.

Doctor Morita nodded back, also smiling, but he also lowered his newly exposed face in shyness. Gestalthian literature was replete with tales of comrades and lovers who allowed one another to see their true faces in a passion of friendship and love. Poignant moments, yes, but those tales always ended in tragedy.

Major Gentaro said, "This baring of faces, this candid talk—do you know where I am going with this?"

"I do. You want to leave the garrison's collection of soul masks behind and instead take our survivors home on the submarine. Leave the lifeless lumps of metal and save the living."

Major Gentaro's smile went as rigid as his mask's snarl. "The living...." These words he spoke with all the bitterness in the world. His dark eyes glittered with the stars in the night sky as he studied Doctor Morita. "Isn't it strange and somehow repulsive how easy it is to read faces? That's why they invented masks, I suppose. Nobody can long stomach the sight of human weakness."

"I... I'm sorry, honoured Major."

At this formality, Major Gentaro smoothed out his face and voice. "Please try to understand. If a soul is identity—if it is crafted—then the soul of an individual dies with them. Oh, it lingers onward a bit in the memory of those who knew the person, but it eventually fades as they pass away. The soul of a clan can endure for generations, if its members keep faith with the ideals of their ancestors. But the soul of a nation? Of an entire people? That can be eternal. Must be eternal."

"Of course!" Doctor Morita agreed immediately, while wondering what he was agreeing to.

"The soul of our nation must endure, but...." Major Gentaro's white-gloved hand waved languidly toward the clouds below as a restive roll of artillery thunder rose up to the mountain peak. "But how can our nation endure, when we have crafted for ourselves a soul that cannot endure defeat?"

"We may still—"

"No, the war is lost. We listen to the radio day and night, and all our foreign possessions have been conquered, our fleets sunk, our planes scoured from the sky. The home islands will be invaded in overwhelming force by spring."

"Then instead of dying here in this nowhere place, let us all return to defend the homeland."

"No."

"But... but why not?"

"Because it would not be enough. No reinforcements, no new weapons, no grand exertions of industry—nothing physical can resist the enemy now. We are spiritual, they are materialistic. We are a single nation, they are an alliance." The Major used a painfully white handkerchief to rub at an imperceptible bit of dust on his porcelain mask. "If we are conquered and occupied, they will force us to change our traditions, our laws, our government, our ideologies—everything. Our nation's soul will be mutilated. Losing our masks is only an emblematic thousandth of the changes they will inflict on our way of life. After a generation or two, our craven descendants will look upon our proud history and roll their eyes that we were ever so backward."

Doctor Morita thought this was likely, but did not dare nod. "So... you intend to die on this island instead of living to see such a time?"

"I intend to die here in the counterattack, yes, but I do not intend to allow our national soul to be lost. Saving our nation's soul will be your duty, physician."

"I don't understand."

Major Gentaro patted a uniform pocket and paper crinkled. "I will provide you with written orders commanding you to survive and return home with the masks of the heroes. A hero for this feat, you will give speeches across the homeland in which you will tell the tale of our garrison's supreme courage and flawless sacrifice."

"But why not have all your men return home to tell that tale, not just me?"

Irritation flickered across the Major's naked face. "It is permissible for a doctor to survive a lost battle, but not for soldiers. Besides, one man such as yourself—an educated man—can be entrusted never to reveal the secret of what truly happened here in this battle-scarred island. But what if all our men returned? Two score of simple soldiers? Some of them would eventually tell the truth of this campaign—they'll tell tales about poor training, outdated weapons, men driven mad, executions for defeatism, the dying who screamed for mothers, starvation, disease.... Everything."

"Speaking as a humble physician, I think that perhaps the truth of war should be known."

"Speaking as an officer and an aristocrat, I say no. Never." His gloved hand squeezed Doctor Morita's hand with an urgency. "If we construct our souls as we will, then is surrendering to the truth not defeatism?"

"Respectfully, it is inevitable that the truth will be known once the enemy occupies our homeland."

"Exactly. So your mission is to ensure the inevitable never comes to pass." Major Gentaro stretched out a white-gloved hand across the less perfectly white mists of the world below in the direction that the home islands lay, tens of thousands of leagues distant. "Back in the homeland, the populace is being prepared for the invasion. Armies of civilians are cutting down forests of pines to yield precious litres of fuel that will allow our final pilots to crash their aircraft into the enemy's invasion ships. Old men are being given rifles and mothers with babes on their backs are training with spears to swarm the enemy in mass attacks. School children are learning from their teachers to embrace bombs and throw themselves under tank treads."

Doctor Morita imagined the Soulless's assault platforms rising from the sea on the coast of the homeland. If there were seven of them employed on this forlorn island, there would be hundreds of them deployed in the assault on the homeland. Or thousands. Thousands of leviathans—confronted by spears. "We will still lose."

"Only in body. Don't you see it, yet? Identity is in creative flux all our lives, but death brings the evolution of identity to an end. Glazes it." Major Gentaro softly ran his white-gloved fingertips over his antique mask's fine porcelain finish, still flawless after centuries. "Your return home and your tale of heroic sacrifice will be part of a national effort to convince our people to resist the invasion to the last child."

"To the...?"

The Major nodded, his face a silver mask in the moonlight. "You will help convince our people to perish to the last man, mother, and infant—and in this way, our nation's soul shall become eternal. And then our enemies will look in awe upon our devotion and live in shame of themselves for all time. Who will be the victor then?" He set his mask down on his stool, then held up his white gloves to the moon itself, his hands framing the celestial orb with a clever posturing of the fingers that sculpted the moon into a mask. "There is only one sort of mask that truly is as immutable as the supposedly immortal soul was always imagined to be: the death mask. If our nation cannot live as we always have? Then we must all die to always remain as we have chosen to be."

Doctor Morita wished he had kept on his mask to hide his face. Instead, he made an inscrutable mask of his living face.

"As a soldier, I do not expect a physician not to feel regrets," Major Gentaro assured him. "But as a commander and as a countryman, I expect you to do your duty. Do you understand?"

"I do," Doctor Morita murmured, his voice full of a numb wonder as he grasped the gravity of his task. After a few moments, Doctor Morita repeated, "I do!" in a firmer voice. He jumped up from his stool, stood at attention, and saluted. "My duty is clear!"

Major Gentaro stood to attention and returned the salute smartly. "Very good! You will be a surgeon to our nation's soul, and there is no doctor more honoured than the doctor invited to attend one's death bed." He held out his hand. "Do you have any questions, honoured physician?"

"Just one, honoured Major," Doctor Morita said, shaking the white-gloved hand.

"What is it?"

"If we all live for the truths we create, why should we all die for yours?"

Major Gentaro looked puzzled.

Doctor Morita pushed him off the cliff.

Major Gentaro plunged toward the sublime nothingness of the monsoon clouds far below with arms and legs splayed outward, body slowly swirling. Perhaps bravery kept the officer from screaming, but Doctor Morita did not believe so, for the sudden fall from the mountain peak distended the Major's naked features in horrible ways. The faces of the dying, Doctor Morita reflected, were the most clear of lessons about how life mattered. Another sin of masks.

The falling man dwindled to a speck against the nothingness, then vanished into the clouds.

A time later, an echoing voice called down the cave tunnel from the command post to the sentries on watch below. It ordered them assemble the men in the command post to receive their orders. As the forty-three soldiers filed from the tunnel onto the plateau, they one-by-one jerked in surprise at the sight the single man waiting to address them.

It was Major Gentaro. And yet, it was not.

Doctor Morita had donned the Major's porcelain mask, which had been left behind on the stool, plus a uniform and white gloves he had found among the officer's belongings in the living quarters at the rear of the plateau. This disguise was no real disguise at all, since he was clearly shorter than the real Major and conspicuously emaciated after the long repositioning march, and his attempt to effect the man's effortless aristocratic stance was probably comic. His voice was an additional dead giveaway as he commanded, "Form ranks to receive orders!"

Instead of forming ranks with one line of men kneeling so the others behind could see the officer too, the soldiers just stood in disbelief. Looking around and not seeing the real Major Gentaro, some of them wandered over to the cliff edge and peered over it speculatively. A couple checked the munitions crates, possibly expecting to find his physician's mask there (which they would not, since he had flung it from the cliff). One of the Major's two lieutenants drew his pistol and seized Doctor Morita by the arm so that he would not be tempted to flee, presumably by leaping to his death.

"Physician," the lieutenant said, "you are under arrest for—"

"I have news about the Koan!" Doctor Morita announced, striving for the Major's stentorian tone. "Our orders have been changed."

The mutinous whispers that had broken out among the soldiers eased away, but the soldiers regarded him with crossed arms and insolently casual postures.

"Y-yes, the Koan is a cargo submarine with room enough for us all," he sputtered onward. "Despite our determination that we would fight on this island to the death, we have just received new orders from the radio." He nodded Major Gentaro's mask toward the radio set, cringing a bit behind the privacy of the mask when he realized that he had neglected to turn the radio back on. "We will leave the masks of the honoured dead here in this hidden place in the mountains where their souls will rest inviolate until they can be retrieved after the war. But the rest of us cannot rest yet—we are commanded to return on the Koan to defend the homeland. All of us."

This 'news' did not elicit the cheer that he had hoped. Forty-three silent masks stared at him with steel and iron. The only sound was the distant rumble of artillery from the approaching leviathans below.

Major Gentaro's warrior mask was quite stuffy, Doctor Morita found, sweat trickling down his face. "The Doctor jumped to his death because I informed him that our duty now lies in returning to the homeland to defend our sacred soil from invasion. After the long repositioning march, he could not face the prospect of another mighty campaign. But we soldiers can! We will strive onward and save our people!"

Still no cheer.

"We will go home." He could think of no other way to say it, no orator's soaring technique. He simply repeated. "We will go home. Home."

At this word, a sigh as gentle as a breeze through green spring grass went through the men. Yet, still the soldiers hesitated. They clearly did not believe him—who would? Yet, none had gone to fetch a hammer and nails. They were waiting. They wanted something.

"This is my order." He touched trembling white-gloved fingers to his stolen mask. "After all, must you not obey your commanding officer?" His voice was dwindling. But then he thought of one last thing to say. Even as his voice failed, he declared, "One time when I stood at a strange crossroads in a foreign land with a sergeant, a veteran of many battles, I asked him which path to take. We were lost, I admitted. He disagreed—said he was not lost. He explained that the last time he had ever chosen between trails in his life was when he chose the army. After that, he always knew exactly which path to follow: the trail chosen by his officers. So I might be lost, but he wasn't. He knew the way to paradise. He knew that my foolishness did not matter because his obedience was everything. And I ask you all now: if obedience is everything, how can obedience not be innocence?"

And then his voice dwindled completely away.

For a time, the only sounds were the mountain's whispering breeze and the approaching rumble of leviathan artillery.

Then Corporal Hanno stepped forward. He made a conspicuous show of very carefully examining the features of the crimson-and-gold warrior's mask that Doctor Morita wore, then he nodded. "The mask is unmistakably the mask of Major Gentaro. Who can doubt it?" The corporal stood at attention and saluted. "Sir!"

The others saluted the mask as well. Then they went home.

If you asked me what my favourite book genre is, I wouldn't have an answer for you. Sometimes it's fantasy. Others, it's science fiction. When I stumble across a story that blends both, it feels like I'm eight years old again and it's pizza day at school. Unfortunately, there are precious few stories which combine the genres. The publishing world seems to keep them apart like the Capulets and Montagues. And while I have definitely written stories that are *just* fantasy or *just* science fiction, I wanted to create my own *Romeo and Juliet* for this story and bring the two genres together, albeit in a less melo-dramatic, murder-y, stab-y, poison-y way.

I'm also a sucker for anything with mythology and alternate history, as you may be able to tell. While I write stories based on or influenced by mythology fairly often, the alternate history aspect of *Industrial Honey* is still new to me. Researching events from the past that, if changed, would have dramatic effects on our future is both fascinating and mind-boggling because the possibilities are truly endless. Although only a few different events made it into *Industrial Honey*, I had a list as long as my arm (and I have weirdly long arms). A few honourable mentions that didn't make the cut include:

- Clarence Saunders, an entrepreneur who was credited with developing the first modern supermarkets. I recently read an article in which a Dutch grocer introduced a living herb wall to their store, allowing customers to cut off only what they need, while leaving behind fresh, sustainable, and packaging-free herbs for others. If Clarence Saunders had been introduced to this idea in 1916, supermarkets as we know them today could be more sustainable, working hand-in-hand with farmers to bring fresh ingredients to customers, rather than canned, preserved, and mass-produced goods.

- Ludwig Dürr, the leader of the design team for Zeppelin aircraft. If Ludwig Dürr had been given the idea for a solar sail in place of hydrogen-powered air travel, the Hindenburg disaster in 1937 might never have happened, paving the way for clean air travel and flying cities.

- Ancient Sumer. The Sumerians were the first civilization to develop a system of writing, which they used for accounting. It allowed traders to more easily keep track of the types and quantities of goods being traded. At the time, the Sumerians wrote on clay tablets. However, if they knew how to make paper and a printing press, their ideas and knowledge could have been shared around the world, as could those of literate civilizations that came after them. Imagine how the world might be different if the printing press had been invented thousands of years early!

While I researched the history extensively and agonized over which events to include, knowing that I wanted to include Persephone was a given. What could be more badass than the Greek goddess of spring and nature *and* Queen of the Underworld? I even have a Persephone tattoo. But now it's clear to me that I need to go back and add Glykiá, the tiniest of warriors; the two of them saved the world, after all.

*Rhiannon Lotze*

Rhiannon Lotze is the Canadian science fiction, fantasy, and horror author behind works such as I Am Become Death, Non-Prophet, and Of Gods and Myth. Many of her short stories, including Barrens and Brine, Rattenfänger, and Long May She Reign, have been included in multi-author anthologies. She spends her free time baking, camping, and making puns. If she tells you the pun isn't intended, don't believe her. The pun is always intended.

# INDUSTRIAL HONEY

## by Rhiannon Lotze
*For the Bees*

A jagged rock dug into Persephone's ribs, and the long meadow grasses scratched her bare arms and tickled her cheeks. She wiggled her hand under her stomach and plucked the rock from the ground, chucking it over her shoulder. It landed with a plunk in the pitcher of lemonade set out near a picnic basket behind her. She winced but turned her attention back to the meadow.

"Stop that," she hissed at the grasses that ducked back in to tickle her, trying to stifle a giggle as she batted the fluttering blades aside. "You'll give me away."

She ducked her head when a dark flicker caught her attention.

Hades strolled casually into the meadow from the other side, his hands tucked into his pockets. Persephone pressed herself to the ground and hoped the small hill would keep her hidden from her husband.

She couldn't see him anymore, but could hear the swish of the grass as he made his way closer and closer to the trap she had laid. A small puff of air and a muffled pop, like a shockwave, abruptly blew Persephone's hair back, followed by a wave of buttery pollen and tide of curses and coughs. Unable to stay hidden after that,

Persephone popped upright, her head cresting the hill she sheltered behind.

"Really?" Hades asked as he pinned her with his gaze, eyebrow arching. He waved one hand in the air, dissipating the cloud of pollen that hung around him like an aura, and spread his arms wide, glancing critically down at himself.

"You look dashing," Persephone complimented, an enormous grin pasted to her face. The dark suit he had been wearing when he entered the meadow was now plastered with a vibrant floral pattern. The black tie that hung from his neck had transformed into a bowtie.

"If anyone else sees this, I will never hear the end of it," Hades said, but a matching grin inched across his own face. He strode casually towards the small hill Persephone perched upon, but she caught a predatory gleam in his eyes.

"Oh no you don't!" she shrieked, laughing. She tried to shove to her feet and run away but he was too quick, gently snatching her wrist and pulling her to him. His other hand clamped around her waist and the blush pink gown she wore began to mottle where his fingers touched it.

Black spilled across the fabric like ink. She tried to pull away but only managed to unbalance them both.

Laughing, they tumbled down the hill together and came to rest at the edge of the picnic blanket, Persephone atop her husband. He lifted his head, a self-satisfied smirk upon his lips when he looked down at his wife, now wearing a gown of midnight.

"Now we're even," he said, stealing a quick kiss from her when she pretended to pout.

"Come on, let's eat." Persephone pushed off his chest, and scooted the last two feet towards the picnic blanket. Hades followed, helping Persephone pull food out of the quaint wicker basket.

She passed him two goblets for the lemonade and he grabbed the pitcher, raising it to eye level. His brow arched inquisitively at the rock drifting lazily across the bottom.

"Don't ask," Persephone said. Hades just shrugged and poured two glasses.

With the food served, the duo settled back with plates balanced on their knees, ready to tuck in. Persephone lifted a plump strawberry to her lips and her teeth had just barely broken the skin when a fat bumblebee bobbed by and landed on the ruby fruit.

Persephone frowned at it, her eyes crossing to look at the bee. "Excuse me," she said. "That's my strawberry."

She waved the bee away but it only fluttered a few inches from her face before refusing to go any further. Instead, it flew in weird bobs and zigs and loops.

Her frown deepened as she studied the fluffy, bumbling creature. Something wasn't quite right here. Across the gingham blanket, Hades stiffened.

"Persephone, do you feel that?"

The strange feeling hit home just then. This small bee had a life force, which was odd considering she and Hades were the only two denizens of the Underworld who were traditionally alive. Even the trees and grasses had died in the mortal realm and wound up in the Underworld. Occasionally the other gods visited, or an errant mortal made their way through the border, but she had never encountered a live bee in the realm before.

"I do," she replied. It only took another moment for her to recognize that this little bee was trying to speak to her in the language of the bees. "I believe she's trying to say something."

Persephone frowned. She hadn't ever become fluent in the language of bees. She asked, "Can you move a little slower? I'm having a hard time keeping up."

The bee stopped its dance and nodded, before beginning again but slower.

As it spoke, Persephone translated for her husband. "The mortal realm is sick. Humans have damaged its environment beyond repair since the Exogeny. The coasts are vanishing, the sky is grey, the flowers aren't blooming. People are starving. The bees—" Persephone swallowed hard, fighting back sudden tears. "The bees are dying. She says she's one of the last of her kind and begs for our help."

Centuries ago, the mortal realm had clashed with the two realms of the gods, Olympus and the Underworld. The mortals wanted to control their own world and when they won the war with their guns and their bombs, they banished the gods back to their own realms and banned them from using their magic to interfere with the mortal realm. This event was known as the Exogeny.

Some of the gods shrugged it off and returned to Olympus without fuss but others, like Persephone, had loved the mortal realm and missed it desperately. Especially as they watched the humans run the realm into misery and ruin. The mortals had lost their respect for nature.

Pain was etched into Hades' face. He hadn't particularly cared for the mortal realm—after all, its residents always found their way to him eventually—but he knew Persephone had loved it.

He pulled himself upright and addressed the bobbing bee directly. "I'm so sorry that your people are dying, but we're not at liberty to release them from the Underwo—"

Buzzing burst from the bee and she fluttered up and down, agitated, before turning back to Persephone and twirling around, speaking through a flight pattern.

"She says thank you, but she's not here to ask for her hive to be returned to life."

Hades' brow creased with confusion. Almost all mortals who entered the Underworld and sought an audience with him and Persephone were there to plead for the return of a loved one. It wasn't a stretch to believe the little bee had come for the same reason.

Persephone continued, "She's asking if I'll return to the mortal realm with her to help fix it."

Persephone blew out a breath, tipping her head down so she didn't knock the bee with the tiny gale. Her heart squeezed painfully. She had been watching the demise of the mortal realm for centuries now, ever since they entered the period they had dubbed the "Industrial Revolution". Her pity for the humans only stretched so far, but she had wept openly for the other creatures suffering under their rule.

"I'm sorry," Persephone said, though the lump in her throat made her voice grate. The hopelessness that struck her like a tsunami was sour in her mouth. "The treaty binds my hands. I can't use magic in the mortal realm to fix the damage they have done. The only thing we can do is make our home as comfortable as possible for you one day."

The bee slowly drifted downwards, as if the weight of her sadness pulled her down. Persephone held out her palm for the fluffy creature to land on. "Come to the palace with us for a few days as our guest," she said. "Rest before you return to the mortal realm."

The bee buzzed acquiescently and Hades and Persephone clambered to their feet, picnic forgotten. Persephone perched the bee on her shoulder and Hades laced his fingers with hers as they began the trek back to the city in the distance, where their palace currently resided.

The Underworld was titanic, the biggest of all the realms, constantly expanding to accommodate its new residents. To preside equally over it all, the palace frequently moved. It took the better part of the afternoon to reach the city's border. They could have used magic to reach it quicker, but the bee on Persephone's shoulder would have been injured in the attempt. Mortals and magic didn't mesh.

As they drew closer, the bee began to perk up and buzz excitedly, occasionally launching off Persephone's shoulder to dance exclamations.

Persephone smiled at her. "Amazing, isn't it? The Underworld advances faster than any other realm, since the residents here have, more or less, an eternity to innovate. We have all the best scientists, engineers, and artists from mortal history."

Persephone turned her eyes forward, drinking in the city that sprouted up—quite literally—in front of them. Wood, vines, and grasses twined together in intricate patterns, creating the structure of each building. Flowers sprouted from most of the facades, making the city look like a fairy forest.

Nanobots had been implanted into seeds and programmed to make them sprout into any shape imaginable. Every cottage, school, and high-rise was actually a singular tree, grown in the shape of a building. Leafy branches sprouted from the roofs, wrapped with twinkling lights that looked like stars when they lit up at night.

The glass windows were the only inorganic material in the structures themselves. They shimmered in the sunlight, a faint rainbow of colour undulating so slowly that it was only noticeable if you stared for too long.

"They capture sunlight," Persephone explained, "and we use it for energy."

Right on cue, a glass and steel vehicle whooshed past, shaped like a single-car bullet train. It hovered two feet above the ground and long masts stuck up from the roof at the front and back. Clear sails were affixed to each mast, made of a shimmery material similar to the windows, but which fluttered fluidly in the breeze.

"Solar sails keep the buses running," Persephone said. "The city runs entirely on clean energy."

She sighed to herself. If only humans had achieved solar power before coal and oil.

They didn't need magic to fix their environment—they just needed the right technologies so that they could integrate their societies with nature, rather than steamroll right over it. But mortal innovation was so slow and, so often, destructive.

The bus pulled to a stop at a raised platform on the side of the road and Hades led Persephone up the steps. The palace was on the other side of the city, and a bus was the fastest way to reach it.

A small tide of riders stepped through the doors when they opened and swarmed around the waiting trio. Hades stepped through the door when the clamour had subsided and Persephone moved to follow him, but froze. Her brow crinkled with deep thought.

"The mortal realm doesn't need magic," she murmured. Her head snapped upright and her eyes glowed with excitement. "It needs technology."

The treaty said nothing about technology.

Hades arched a bemused brow. "You're about to do something reckless, aren't you?"

"Without question."

Hades wrapped an arm around Persephone's waist, pulling her close. He kissed her cheek and then her forehead. "Be safe and come home to me soon."

"I'll be back before you know I'm gone."

He released her hand and she stepped back, letting the bus door close between them. When it sailed away, Persephone glanced at the bee on her shoulder. "I have an idea, but first we have to pay a visit to Olympus."

"What are you doing here?"

"Nice to see you too, Chronos."

Chronos grunted and turned away from his door, leaving it open for Persephone and the bee—who, she had learned, was named Glykiá—to follow. She shut the door behind them and followed Chronos into the kitchen.

She said kitchen, but really it was little more than a barren, stone room. If the Underworld was the most advanced of the realms, Olympus was by far the least, stuck back in antiquity. There was no such thing as refrigeration or even electricity. Some of the gods had rudimentary plumbing in their homes, but most did not. Persephone made a note to avoid all restrooms until she was in the mortal realm.

Chronos plunked himself into a sturdy wooden chair drawn up to the only table in the room, and tucked into a breakfast of fruit, bread, and cheese. "What do you want?" he asked, not offering either breakfast or a chair.

Persephone helped herself to the latter, dropping into the seat across from Chronos, but refraining from touching his breakfast.

"I need a favour," she said, and Chronos speared her with a withering gaze.

"The last time you said that, you wanted me to go out with your mother. Worst date of my life."

"How many times do I have to apologize for that? I had no idea she'd spend the whole date crying about Zeus. They broke up three centuries earlier. But I'll give you a favour in return. Whatever you want."

"What do you want?" Chronos repeated, unmoved.

"Time travel."

Chronos, the god of time, could send her back anywhere in time with a snap of his fingers.

"I thought you liked the futuristic glamour of the Underworld."

"I do. My trip is for business rather than pleasure. In the mortal realm."

Chronos laughed harshly. "There's the catch. You know the treaty prevents me from using magic in the mortal realm."

"I thought the time doors operated between realms?"

"They do," Chronos said, aggravation deepening the lines on his face.

"Then you wouldn't be using magic in the mortal realm, technically. Please, Chronos."

"Fine, whatever," Chronos snapped. "If I agree, will you leave me alone to finish my breakfast?"

"I would have been gone five minutes ago," Persephone agreed.

"Then I'll do it. Also, I want a latte."

"A latte?"

"From the mortal realm. We haven't had any coffee in Olympus since the treaty and I despise going to the mortal realm for it."

"Then I'll bring you a latte." Persephone stood and made her way to the kitchen doorway. Just as she passed through, she turned back to Chronos. "Is that why you're always so grumpy?"

"Fuck you," Chronos said, but she caught the slight smile that ghosted across his face.

Back in the bright Olympus sunlight, Persephone held up her palm for Glykiá to rest upon it. "One stop down, two to go."

The second errand went much smoother than the first. Hephaestus didn't ask why she wanted enchanted armour for a bee; he only cared that she had the drachma to pay him. In an hour's time, Glykiá was outfitted in tiny, shiny armour that would prevent her from being harmed by the magic of the time doors. Every time they passed a reflective surface, Persephone caught Glykiá admiring her new adornment and she grinned, pleased with the bee's delight. She looked like a fuzzy, ferocious warrior.

Now they sat in, perhaps, the only modern room in all of Olympus. The room itself was in a classically-Greek home. Pillars led to a rear courtyard, and comfortable couches were dotted throughout the stone space, but a bank of computers, similar to a security room, took up one whole wall. Almost every screen was filled with footage from Olympus, the Underworld, and the mortal realm. Persephone had been studying those of the mortal realm with fascination, shocked at just how bad the world had become since her last visit.

Glykiá hadn't been exaggerating.

Grey smog choked the sky. According to Glykia, humans now used the idiom 'once in a blue sky', rather than a blue moon. There was also very little green to be found. Meadows had become barren patches of dirt and the forests looked like graveyards of jagged bone. Farms had become industrialized and animals were grown on assembly lines in prison-like factories.

It was no wonder the bees were dying—along with the rest of the mortal realm, it seemed.

The door to Persephone's right opened and she stood when a woman in an ivory peplos strode through. "Clotho!"

"Persephone!" Clotho squeaked. The two women collided in a monumental hug. "It's been way too long since you came to visit!"

"Likewise," Persephone agreed, "but I'm not here entirely for a social call."

"I know," Clotho said, pulling a wise face. Being one of the Fates, Clotho knew almost everything. She strode across the room, beckoning Persephone to follow. Glykiá bobbed along just above Persephone's shoulder.

"So," Clotho began, leaning over one of three desks set in front of the wall of screens. She jiggled the mouse and a web browser filled the screen, the top edge crammed with browser tabs.

"Is this all from Wikipedia?" Persephone asked, arching a brow and sitting in the chair Clotho indicated.

Clotho shrugged. "The internet has made being a Fate much easier. We don't have to keep track of nearly as much as we once did. Let me tell you, it's a relief to be able to just look up the names of Zeus' mistresses without having to remember them all."

Persephone laughed. "Hera probably doesn't think so."

"Well, it's a good thing Hera doesn't know about Wikipedia. Anyways, I know what you're planning to do, and I know how you can do it but the rules of being a Fate prevent me from telling you. The rules, however, say nothing about you figuring it out on your own. Isn't it so weird that all of these Wikipedia pages just happen to be open?"

"So weird," Persephone agreed with a knowing grin.

Clotho straightened, ceding the mouse to Persephone. "Are you sure you want to do this? It could be dangerous." She levelled a meaningful look at the duo.

Persephone glanced down at Glykiá, then back at Clotho. "She lost her whole family, Clo. And she's not the only one. We have to fix things."

Glykiá hopped resolutely on Persephone's shoulder, buzzing bravely and proclaiming the same thing. They were determined in their quest.

Clotho nodded. She turned to go, then paused. " I can give you this warning. The farther back in time you go and the more you change, the greater the effect will be. And that's not necessarily a good thing." With her warning delivered, Clotho swept from the room.

Persephone turned to the computer, suddenly sweating, and began studying up on the history of the mortal realm, trying to find the meaning in the tabs Clotho had left open.

"Ugh, that's disgusting." Persephone scoffed at the sloshing liquid in the disposable cup the barista had given her at the cafe. "Why does Chronos like this stuff?"

Glykiá flew from Persephone's shoulder and danced in the air. No more coffee. Only imitation.

"Ugh, go figure," Persephone replied when the bee had resettled on her shoulder. What other crops had humans harvested and chemical-sprayed into oblivion? If all went well, the answer would be none.

Persephone rounded the corner, ducking back into the alley where the door from Olympus had deposited them. Chronos had given her an enchanted doorknob, which would allow her and Glykiá to travel anywhere and any-when. They had come to the mortal realm in its current time so Persephone could see the destruction for herself before they began their journey.

Her first impression of the mortal realm was bleak.

California and New York and dozens of other cities around the world were now under water. Millions of species had gone extinct or were critically endangered. Forests had been paved over to make way for lifeless glass cities made grey by the reflection of polluted skies. People were starving; the soil was dead. They had forsaken nature entirely. In their quest to conquer it, they forgot to love it.

She desperately hoped her second impression would be better.

She chucked the still-full coffee cup into an overflowing dumpster and stripped off her clothes, hoping no one stumbled by at that exact moment. Goosebumps tore across her skin and she shivered in the late-fall air. A canvas bag awaited her, tucked into a derelict doorway. From it, she snatched at voluminous skirts, petticoats, a corset, and the other garments that would allow her to fit into the time period of their first stop.

When she was dressed, she crouched by the pile of discarded mortal clothing and withdrew the time-knob from the pocket of her rumpled woollen peacoat. "Are you ready?" she asked Glykiá, who buzzed excitedly. Persephone blew out a tense breath. "Okay, here we go. Let's go save the bees."

She proffered the door handle at hip height, where it struck an invisible barrier. A faint golden rectangle shimmered into being, growing more solid when Persephone twisted the knob. The centre of the rectangle abruptly darkened before shimmering and revealing a picture on the other side.

Gone was the grimy brick wall of the alley. In its place, lush green filled the doorway. Neatly tended hedgerows unfurled across a meticulous lawn, fencing in straight gravel paths. Tall trees dripped with early autumnal colour and broad lily pads bearing large white flowers shingled a symmetrical pond. In the distance, a wild forest rolled over the hillside. A gently floral aroma perfumed the city-clogged air.

Persephone filled her lungs with it, appreciating the lushness in front of her. Here, nature was appreciated and admired. It was art, not plunder. And, if she played her cards right, nature would become the salvation of the mortal realm.

Glykiá lifted off from her shoulder and danced in the air. Trust. Do not be afraid.

She flitted towards Persephone, gently bonking her in the nose, before resettling on Persephone's shoulder.

"Thank you," Persephone said, trying to infuse some of the small bee's faith in her with her own confidence.

Persephone counted down. Three…

Two…

One…

They stepped through the doorway and into the gardens of Chatsworth House, England, 1823. Glykiá bumbled off her shoulder and Persephone held out her palm for the gold-plated bee, who stumbled dizzily for a moment but seemed otherwise unharmed.

"You okay?" Persephone asked, alarmed.

Glykiá took stock of her magic-rattled body then buzzed with affirmation. The armour had worked.

Persephone grinned broadly at her. "Okay, then let's do this."

She strolled across the lawn, towards the lily pad pond. Shards of glassy water poked through the clustered pads, reflecting the deep blue of the sky back at Persephone. She lowered herself to the ground, stretching out beside it, grimacing as the cheap costume corset pressed tightly into her ribs. She had left it largely unlaced but the stab-happy boning still jabbed her skin.

"Here's hoping our guests are punctual," Persephone murmured to the bee, settling her onto one of the lilies to taste the sweet pollen. "Remember the plan."

Glykiá nodded her tiny head and settled in to wait. The words had no sooner left Persephone's lips than a jaunty whistle carried down one of the pathways. A young man in patched clothing with dirt on the knees strolled through the garden. He carried a basket with pruning tools in one hand and a tin watering can in the other. When he spotted Persephone lounging by the pond, a concerned frown wrinkled the skin between his brows. He diverted from the path and made his way across the lawn towards her.

"Can I help you, miss?" There was an accusation in his eyes. You aren't supposed to be here.

Persephone tilted her head up towards him and beamed her most charming smile at him. "Oh, are you the gardener?" she asked, affecting the appropriate accent.

"Yes, Miss. Joseph Paxton, at your service." He thawed by a degree.

"Can you tell me about these stunning flowers, Mr. Paxton?" Persephone inclined her chin at the lily pads sprayed across the pond.

The thaw became a full spring-melt. "Surely I can. Those are white water-lilies. When they bloom, they produce the largest flower in all of England."

"Fascinating," Persephone murmured. She leaned forward and gently stroked the edge of her pinkie finger along one of the massive floating pads. Its edges dipped into the cool water and the lily pad laughed, ticklish, although Mr. Paxton couldn't hear it.

Persephone shook a few drops of water from her hand before standing gracefully. Her skirts swished around her legs. "I've always had a great deal of admiration for leaves," she said in a conspiratorial whisper. Joseph Paxton blushed at the intimacy in her tone, but he gave her a warm grin.

"I have too, miss. That's why I became a gardener."

Persephone went on, "I find it remarkable that something that looks so simple can be so complicated. Did you know they absorb sunlight and convert it into energy?"

"I have indeed read that, although there aren't many who can say the same," he declared, clearly impressed.

Persephone's smile exuded camaraderie. The science of photosynthesis was still in its infancy, but she knew perfectly well who she was speaking with. As such, she knew what he knew.

"Imagine if we could do that," Persephone gushed. "If we could build homes that made their own energy, we wouldn't need all of that nasty coal, turning everything black."

Mr. Paxton laughed. "You have a wonderful imagination, miss. That would indeed be something."

Persephone spied movement from the pathway behind Mr. Paxton. An elderly gentleman carrying a rumpled letter and looking thoroughly confused slowly plodded along the gravel, his head swivelling like that of a bird. His gaze alighted on the chattering duo and he paced across the grass towards them.

"I have a feeling that such an invention won't remain imaginary for long," Persephone pressed, before the elderly gentleman reached them.

"Excuse me," he said, panting slightly. A thick Italian accent blunted his words. "Is this Chatsworth House?"

"Yes, sir," Mr. Paxton replied promptly.

"Would you happen to know where I might find the Duke of Devonshire? I received a letter in the mail some weeks ago, inviting me to stay with him, but I haven't been able to find a soul on the entire estate."

"I'm very sorry, sir. The duke is away in Scotland. Most of the staff has been allowed to visit family in his absence."

The gentleman's face reddened with surprise and then outrage. Before he could have a fit at being treated so heinously, Persephone interrupted. After all, she was the one who had written him the letter, having posted it some weeks ago. "Excuse me, but you don't happen to be Signor Alessandro Volta, the famed physicist?"

The man's complexion immediately returned to normal and he fixed his attention upon Persephone. "At your service, Miss—?"

"Mrs. Kore," Persephone answered quickly, allowing Signor Volta to take her hand and press a chaste kiss against her knuckles. "I have long been an admirer of your work."

Volta preened under her attention and benevolent smile, which hid the lie. In fact, she thought him a rather odious man, based on the handful of times they had crossed paths in the Underworld, years from now. However, she could not deny his brilliance.

"Sir, you may be interested in the conversation this gentleman, Mr. Joseph Paxton, and I were just having."

"What was the subject of this conversation?"

Mr. Paxton blushed. "Surely he wouldn't be—"

Persephone waved him away. "We were discussing the possibilities of harnessing energy from the sun, much the same way plants do, and using that for power in place of coal."

Volta's eyes lit up ravenously. "Now, that is an interesting topic. You know, I'm somewhat of an expert in the field of electrical energy—"

He was interrupted by a sudden shriek from Persephone, who began batting wildly at the air in front of her.

"A bee!" she yelped. Indeed, a buzzing bee aggressively charged at her face before whirling away in the gales created by her swatting hands only to swarm at her again.

"Miss, stay calm!" Mr. Paxton yelled, but Persephone turned tail and fled into a thick copse of trees, the angry bee following hot on her heels.

Mr. Paxton followed her at a run, only to reemerge from the trees a few moments later, scratching his head. "She has completely vanished," he declared to the waiting Volta.

"How odd," Volta said, though he clearly banished Persephone from his mind immediately, turning fully to Mr. Paxton. "Perhaps you can tell me more about this conversation you were having."

Persephone fell to the ground through a golden doorway, wheezing. Glykiá landed in front of her, buzzing with worry. "I'm sorry, I'm sorry," Persephone gasped, clutching her stomach and wheezing again. "I'm not hurt, I'm laughing." Another volley of giggles escaped, and Persephone swept tears from her eyes. "Their faces when I ran away were priceless. You sold that beautifully."

Glykiá had been given the task of getting Persephone away from Paxton and Volta as soon as possible, lest she give away too much information about the future, and she had done so in spectacular fashion. Broken buzzes wafted from Glykiá and it took Persephone a moment to realize the bee was laughing with her, which made her laugh even harder.

It took five minutes for either of them to get themselves under control.

Finally, Glykiá lifted her armoured body a few feet into the air, examining their new surroundings, which didn't look so different from their old ones. Where? she asked with a little dance.

Persephone clambered to her feet, swiping brown leaves and old grass from her cumbersome dress. She held up her hand and Glykiá immediately landed upon it.

"Hyde Park," Persephone said, heading for the edge of the thick tree line. "May 1st, 1851."

She ducked under a thick branch and the duo found themselves in an excited swell of people from all over the world, all clamouring for a better view of the spectacle towering over the park.

A castle made entirely of glass gleamed in the sun, dazzling the onlookers. If one stared at it for too long, the glass shimmered like a soap bubble. Persephone squealed with excitement, clamping her free hand over her mouth when a group of well-to-do women nearby shot her dirty looks.

She lifted Glykiá up to her face. "We did it!" she whispered. "That's the Crystal Palace, and look at the glass! It's the same as in the Underworld. It's solar glass!"

Glykiá launched off Persephone's palm and flew in a few deliriously excited loops, buzzing the whole time. It worked! I am excited!

Persephone brushed a pearl of anxious sweat from her forehead, letting her relief cool her.

Mr. Joseph Paxton, gardener, was always destined to become an architect. Inspired by the strength of lily pads and the construction of greenhouses, he designed the Crystal Palace, which was showcased at the famed Great Exhibition. Inventors from around the world had gathered to show off their amazing inventions under the roof of a building that was itself a pioneering marvel paving the way for the use of glass as a construction material.

Persephone had only to orchestrate a chance encounter between Mr. Paxton and Signor Volta, a visionary who had invented the first battery, and plant the seed of an idea for solar power in their minds.

The fruits of her labour, with Glykiá as her wing bee, were here for all to see. A quick trip back to the future would prove whether or not the world had fully embraced clean energy, but Persephone couldn't pass up the opportunity to see the first demonstration with her own eyes.

A woman in a luxurious silk dress ascended a raised platform just outside of the palace, escorted on the arm of a man in ceremonial dress. Queen Victoria, and her husband Albert. Persephone had only met him once, when he was helping design a modern sewage system for the Underworld, but she hadn't had the chance to encounter his regal wife. Perhaps when she returned home she'd make it a point to visit them both.

Queen Victoria stepped forward, drawing herself to her full—albeit still miniscule—height and began addressing the crowd. Persephone and Glykiá were too far back to hear her words, but the excitement in the crowd swelled to new heights, like humidity in the air just before a storm. Her short speech came to an end and Queen Victoria gestured to the diamond-esque wonder behind her.

The Great Exhibition had begun.

The excitement burst like a clap of thunder and the crowd surged forward as one, everyone clamouring to rush inside the spectacular building.

Persephone lost herself to the tide, following along with fervent eagerness. In no time at all, the soaring doorway swallowed her and Glykiá whole, transporting them into an entirely new world. Persephone extricated herself from the mob and sheltered by the glass wall to speak to Glykiá.

"Shall we?" she asked.

Glykiá buzzed eagerly before fluttering her wings and bumbling off to see the sights. Persephone followed slowly behind her, ambling through the halls of machinery, manufacturing, fine arts, and exotic raw materials, enraptured. Delegations from around the world proudly showed off their marvels. A new style of fire engine from Canada, an ivory throne from India, gold from Chile. Yet all the treasures brought by other nations were faded and drab to Persephone, whose real focus was on the towering, full-foliage elm trees ensconced under the main dome.

Her heart swelled to bursting at the love and care these trees were afforded; no one could bear the idea of felling them, so they built a palace around them. Perhaps human-kind wasn't doomed after all.

When the light began fading and the spectators slowly trickled away for the evening, Persephone sat on a bench under one of the elm trees, enjoying its company. Glykiá found her there shortly and perched on Persephone's shoulder. Their time in 1851 was nearing an end.

"Ready to go?" Persephone asked Glykiá, who buzzed in agreement.

Persephone tugged the time-knob from a concealed pocket in her dress and twisted it in the air. The doorway shimmered to life, unnoticed by the evening stragglers, and the time travellers stepped through to the other side.

"Oh fuck!" Persephone cried, throwing herself sideways and behind a dumpster. She cupped her hands around Glykiá as she moved, enveloping the armoured bumblebee in her palms.

"Are those laser beams?" Persephone demanded as three more menacing red bolts zinged by. She poked her head around the edge of the dumpster only to jerk it back when a bolt struck the metal, scorching the edge and singeing a lock of her hair.

"Yep, laser beams," Persephone confirmed. "Worse, I'm pretty sure those are robots firing at us."

Glykiá buzzed frantically in the hollow between Persephone's hands, her concern palpable.

"I don't know what we did, my friend, but it's not good," Persephone said.

She swivelled her head, taking in their surroundings. The alley they were in was nearly identical to the one they had started their journey from in the present; dirty and grungy, except…that was a pile of human bones in the doorway across the way.

Glancing up, Persephone was pleased to note crystal blue skies and windows shimmering with solar glass. So where had they gone wrong?

"Kehre zu deiner Arbeit zurück!" A tinny voice exploded from a speaker built into one of the robots' chests.

Persephone gaped. "Is that German?"

Glykiá wormed her way between Persephone's fingers and flew in a frantic pattern.

It said 'Return to your labour'.

Persephone's jaw struck asphalt. "You speak German?" she exclaimed, then shook her head. "Never mind, we can't stay here. We need to figure out what we screwed up so we can fix it."

She stowed Glykiá on her shoulder then angled her head and poked the barest sliver of her face out from behind the dumpster, trying to see what she was up against. Three menacing, claw-handed and footed robots stalked the alley, blocking her exit. The alley ended in a brick wall on the other side.

Her fingers itched to use magic, to turn the robots into flowers or paralyze them with mighty roots around their legs, but she balled them into fists at her sides. If she broke the treaty now, when humans had weaponized robots at their disposal, the ensuing war would be even bloodier than the first.

But no matter what, Persephone was still a goddess. She was stronger than a human and couldn't technically die, though her body could be obliterated by those nasty looking lasers and it would take a long time for her soul to weave a new one.

So, avoid the lasers then, right? Hopefully these weren't fast robots.

Without giving herself time to rethink, Persephone kicked the brake off the dumpster wheel and pushed the metal contraption with all her might. It careened into one of the robots, bowling it over and then crunching violently over it. The robot flailed and pushed, servos whirring desperately as it tried to lift the heavy bin off itself, but one of its arms had been torn off by the front wheel.

At the same time, the dumpster glanced off of a second robot, spinning it around just as it fired at Persephone. Its neon bolt went wide and she charged the silver beast, noting the eagle emblazoned on its chest plate.

The laser gun it wielded was welded directly onto its arm and Persephone yanked with all her considerable might. Metal squealed and wires snapped but she couldn't pry the arm free. The robot turned its head—a rounded, completely blank slab of metal—and backhanded Persephone across the jaw with its free hand. She struck the dumpster and collapsed in a heap, Glykiá flying off her shoulder and tumbling to the ground.

The robot advanced, booming threats in unintelligible German.

Persephone scrabbled under the dumpster, stretching desperately for the severed arm of the crushed robot. Her fingers snagged on a frayed wire, then she jerked the arm and attached weapon to her, swinging it up and squeezing the trigger just as the advancing robot was about to level its own gun at her head.

The trigger locked, the weapon inoperable without a power source.

Persephone swore and swung her arm, walloping the encroaching gun with the severed limb and knocking it aside. In a stroke of good luck, the weapon went off just as it swung towards the robot's leg, piercing a neat hole through the layers of metal and wiring.

The robot crumpled under its useless leg and Persephone scrambled to her feet, only to find herself in the enclosing embrace of the third robot. She planted her feet and squared her fists, preparing to fight her way out when the robot's head and shoulders suddenly drooped. Its whole body sagged and it collapsed thunderously to the pavement.

Persephone jumped back so the machine didn't crush her toes.

From a small hole in the back of its smooth head, Glykiá flew.

"Did you do that?" Persephone asked, delighted. Glykiá buzzed yes.

"I owe you," she said, holding out her palm. Glykiá landed upon it. "Okay, let's try to find a computer and then get the fuck out of here."

The city loomed menacingly above the duo.

Despite the solar glass gleaming jewel-like in all the windows, the architecture could hardly be classified as pretty. Broad brick buildings were hemmed in by narrow shacks, which had seemingly been squeezed in wherever there was room. As the buildings got taller, the materials used to build them changed, flipping fitfully between brick, wood, and plywood, as if new structures had been hastily slapped atop the old ones. Although blue skies shone high above, the ominous buildings were so tall and leaned so precariously over the street that they nearly blotted out the sky entirely. Only small chinks and slivers were visible.

The streets themselves were frighteningly empty. There were signs of life all over the city—shadows in the curtained windows, abandoned sheets of newspaper fluttering in the wind, fat pigeons cooing on the phone wires, cars parked along the road—but the city felt abandoned. She had passed only two other people. The first had hurried by, eyes fixed firmly to the pavement. The second hauled a bucket of glue and a stack of posters. She stopped at every doorway and streetlamp to slap a poster up and slather it with glue, before moving to the next and ignoring Persephone utterly.

Persephone sidled closer to one of the doorways, plastered so thickly with old, faded posters that it looked like a door made of cardboard. She glanced warily around, on high alert for more of those robots. When none jumped out from behind the streetlamps or pigeons, she turned her attention to the signs.

Bright bold letters were emblazoned across them in German, with the English translations printed much smaller below.

Labour makes profit.

Innovation is currency.

Technology is strength.

Spend, spend, spend!

Each poster was painted with rich 50s-inspired designs. One showed young men and women smiling in front of assembly lines. Another was of an older gentleman handing a lightbulb to a corporate drone. A frown shadowed Persephone's face and she turned away from the posters, continuing her trek through the city.

Across the street, a stone banner etched into a building proclaimed it to be the library, according to Glykiá. She darted quickly across the asphalt river, up the steps, and into the building. The full weight of judgment slammed down on Persephone's shoulders like a falling piano the moment she stepped through the library's doors. The hawkish librarian behind the desk raised her brows and surveyed Persephone up and down with a wrinkled nose.

Persephone glanced down at herself. Not only was she still dressed for the 1800s, but her heavy skirt had a wet hem from the nasty garbage puddles of the alleyway, she was covered in grime from her fight with the robots, and a small gash above her eyebrow oozed a drop or two of golden blood, which she noticed too late.

Catching a drip with the tip of her finger and wiping it on her dress, Persephone gave the librarian a sheepish smile. "I'm an actress."

"Should you not be at your labour?" the librarian asked prudishly, thankfully in English.

Persephone's smile faltered. "Er, no. We need some information to work out a historical inaccuracy. I need a computer."

The librarian harrumphed but jerked her chin towards a far corner in the back of the library where a bank of computers circled a table. "Don't get gunk on anything."

Promising that she wouldn't, Persephone hurried across the library and plunked into one of the chairs, immediately getting gunk on it.

The computer she was presented with was leagues more advanced than humans had used in the original timeline. Fortunately for Persephone, the Underworld had advanced faster, so she already knew what she was doing. She pulled up the browser and navigated to Wikipedia, her mouth splitting into a relieved grin.

"Thank Hera Wikipedia is still around," Persephone whispered to Glykiá, who had settled atop the paper thin monitor.

She didn't know exactly what she was looking for, but she knew she didn't want to spend more time in this world than was absolutely necessary. Even though it was technically the present, it wasn't a present she wanted any part of.

Her fingers flew across the keyboard and she pulled up page after page, trying to piece together mortal history after the Great Exhibition. The changes to history leapt off the screen and Persephone gaped, shocked at how one invention had changed the course of history so drastically.

Persephone whispered a summary to Glykiá, who listened attentively. "It's not that much different for the first few years, although the Industrial Revolution happened much faster. World War I still happened, Germany got the stuffing kicked out of them again. But here is where things start to go crazy. Instead of falling into a recession, the Germans started developing an energy source to rival solar power, with the intention of using it to rebuild their wealth. I'll give you three guesses to figure out what the energy source was."

Glykiá did a little dance on the computer monitor.

"Bingo. They developed nuclear energy decades early, under the guidance of the physicist Leo Szilard, but the Nazi Party still came to power. They had it weaponized, nuked the hell out of America and Russia, and essentially took over the world. Herrs Robopricks out there were created to clean up the nuclear fallout, and then they became security robots, forcing people to work, enforcing curfew, basically making life miserable. The Nazis rule through technological might now. Any new invention, no matter how small, eventually falls into their hands and is weaponized in one way or another."

That explained the gunfight, the German-speaking robots, and the nasty looks she had gotten from the librarian for not being at work.

On the bright side, humans had fully embraced clean energy, though it hadn't been enough. The acceleration of the Industrial Revolution, and nuclear power, had still obliterated the environment. From the photos and maps staring her in the face, planet Earth had become one huge, industrial-state. The people had given up apples for Apple—although it was called "Apfel" in this timeline—and they were slowly starving for it. She needed to make them embrace nature, but how?

Persephone leaned back in her seat, pursing her lips and blowing out slowly, trying to absorb the information. In Olympus she had created a list of possible events to influence in the past, which she thought Clotho had been guiding her to. So if that was the case, and changing one event made the world even more dangerous, she clearly needed to change a different event, or perhaps a combination of events.

But which ones?

"I think I know where we need to go next," she said.

Just as she was about to explain, Glykiá began buzzing violently, fluttering off the monitor and grabbing a stray strand of Persephone's hair, using it to tug her head around.

Persephone didn't even have to turn before she heard the familiar robotic voice. "Wo ist der Arbeitslose?"

Where is the un-worker? Glykiá translated.

"Well, no time to second-guess ourselves," Persephone declared, leaping from her chair just as the librarian pointed her way. The clawed robot tore towards them, running on all fours like a jaguar.

Persephone ripped the time-knob from her dress pocket and stabbed the air with it, throwing her and Glykiá through the golden doorway the moment it formed.

They tumbled in free fall for a few moments before landing in a thick mulberry bush. The branches whipped and snapped at Persephone's face while she fell, shattering the delicate limbs behind her. Finally, the ground swelled up and she struck it with an audible thump. A rain shower of broken branches and leaves sprayed her a moment later, followed by a severed, metal claw which landed barely a foot away.

A low, pained groan seeped from Persephone's lips and she was powerless to move for several seconds, stunned. Awareness rushed back in all at once.

Her eyes flew up to where the golden doorway melted away in a shower of sparks. No further robot limbs emerged and Persephone breathed a sigh of relief before jerking upright and scrambling around for Glykiá.

"Glykiá?" she cried. A quiet buzz fluttered against her ear and Glykiá crawled woozily up to her knee. She circled a few times.

I am okay.

"Let's make a pact to avoid deadly authoritarian robots in the future, shall we?" Persephone said, a hollow laugh blowing out of her on her next breath.

Agreed. Where are we?

Persephone clambered to her feet, aching and shaking. She'd be black and blue later, but she pushed the thought aside. "Well, I was rushing to get the door open but, assuming we're in the right place, this should be the English village of Sandgate, 1913."

Persephone shook a few small twigs from her hair and smoothed her hands over her dirtied and torn dress. She had been meaning to change, but being chased by murderous robots tended to cut any shopping spree short. The dress would have to do.

"Okay, we have a lot to fix," Persephone said, waiting for Glykiá to land on her shoulder before strolling into the quaint village beyond the shroud of the mulberry bush. "Let's get it right this time."

A small collection of shops opened onto the cobbled main street and Persephone ducked into the one with the sign "bookseller" in the doorway. She emerged minutes later with a small tome tucked under her arm, which she brought over to a bench where a middle-aged man with a moustache and combover scribbled on a small pad of paper.

"Morning," Persephone muttered as she fluffed her skirt and sat down. The man grunted in acknowledgement, absorbed in his work.

Persephone flipped the cover of the book open and held it up to her face so the title and author could easily be read by her industrious companion. She read patiently, waiting for him to notice. Finally, a scoff came from beside her.

"Henry James?" the man sneered disparagingly. "That hippopotamus wouldn't know how to write a book if the pen did it for him."

"Oh?" Persephone said imperiously, lifting a brow. "I rather enjoy Mr. James' writing. What makes you such an expert to scorn him?"

"Who am I?" Her companion's cheeks purpled as he puffed them up, indignant. "Who am I? Why, don't you know? I'm H.G. Wells!"

Persephone gave him a deliberately blank look.

"H.G. Wells!" he insisted. "The author!"

"Oh, you're an author too? Are you working on a story?" She nodded towards the notepad in his lap, finally showing interest in him.

His chest swelled noticeably and he lifted his notepad. "As a matter of fact, I'm working on a rather good one. I haven't titled it yet, but I'm considering the name 'The World Set Free'. What do you think?"

Persephone twisted her lips, hemming and hawing. "I don't know. Why don't you tell me what the story is about and then I can decide."

"Well, my dear, it's about a weapon. The most destructive weapon in the world! In fact, a bomb made from radioactive material that continuously explodes for days!"

Persephone shrugged her shoulders and leaned back in her seat, feigning boredom. "Do you know, I met Henry James at a dinner party a few months ago and he confided in me that he is writing a science fiction story? His very first!"

"Pah! Henry James can't write a grocery list, much less a science fiction story. What is his harebrained idea about?"

"Well, he envisions a peaceful world. One where scientists use a sort of automaton—no bigger than a germ—to train trees to grow into the shape of houses. Entire cities can be built within days, and when a family needs more space, they simply make the house grow bigger!"

"Foolish nonsense! Utter rot!" H.G. Wells proclaimed. "No one would read such a thing, especially not from Henry James!"

"Well, as I say," Persephone said, "that's what he told me. I had better get on. It was nice meeting you, Mr. Wells."

Persephone stood and strode away, leaving H.G. Wells behind to mutter insults at Henry James under his breath. She meandered down one of the village's many footpaths towards a broad beach dotted with shells and strings of seaweed. A piece of damp driftwood reposed against a shallow dune and Persephone dropped onto it, replaying the conversation in her head.

Had he taken the bait? She was almost positive that he had. Only time would tell.

A soft weight landed on her shoulder and Glykiá buzzed warmly in her ear, clearly asking a question. She didn't even have to look at the bee now to understand what each unique buzz meant. Who was that person?

Persephone laughed. In their escape from the present, she hadn't had the chance to explain the plan to Glykiá. "That was H.G. Wells, the science fiction author. Next year, he publishes a book called 'The World Set Free', which becomes famous for inspiring Leo Szilard and Winston Churchill, among others, to develop the atomic bomb. However, I just told him that his rival, Henry James, is writing a science fiction book of his own. Assuming I pushed the right buttons, Mr. Wells should abandon this book and "steal" the idea for the book he believes Henry James is writing."

Glykiá buzzed again and Persephone nodded. "They'll still invent nuclear power one day. But if they create a peaceful world first, one in harmony with nature and one another, who knows? Maybe they'll never weaponize it. Shall we go find out if the plan worked?"

Persephone unfolded herself from the driftwood log, pulling the time-knob from her pocket. She held it at hip height and the doorway sparked, but before she could twist and open the portal entirely, a searing pain ate through her left hand.

Persephone screamed and dropped the knob, clutching her wounded hand to her chest. Her eyes widened at the damage and bile swelled in her throat. Thin threads of skin and tendon hung from a stump at the end of her wrist.

Panicked buzzes trickled into her ear, asking if she was okay, but she was too shocked to reply. Persephone whipped her head around, looking for what had caused the damage. A one-armed, claw-tipped robot stalked across the beach towards her and Glykiá.

They weren't the only two to make it through the doorway after all.

The robot's remaining arm pointed directly at Persephone, the black barrel of its laser gun honed on her. "Die Technik abgeben," it boomed, jerking the gun at the enchanted doorknob in the sand.

Persephone grasped its meaning through the pain and language barrier. It wanted the time-knob.

The Nazi robot wanted the power to travel anywhere in time. No way in Hades was she about to allow that.

Persephone held up her intact hand in the universal motion for, "Whoa, man, just chill."

The robot did not, in fact, chill. It repeated,"die Technik abgeben," even louder, as Persephone slowly stooped and scooped up the fallen handle.

Her hair fell over her face and she murmured to Glykiá. "When I open the door, get through it as fast as you can."

Small protests filled her ear but Persephone shot her tiny companion a resolute look. "Just do it."

She straightened and faced the robot head on. Although her arm felt like it was on fire and her legs trembled, Persephone's voice was strong and clear when she spat the only German phrase she knew in its face. "Geh, fick dich."

Persephone sprinted towards the robot faster than it could react, and careened past it. When she cleared its shoulder, she jammed the time-knob into the air. The golden doorway shimmered to life immediately.

On the other side of the portal, vivacious trees filled her view. A gleaming, towering city greeted her in the distance. Blue skies shone down on wooden buildings grown from the ground and shimmering with solar glass. Glykiá swarmed through the doorway and turned in midair, waiting for Persephone to follow.

"Wait for me," Persephone yelled at the bee who immediately charged for the doorway again. She wasn't quick enough.

Persephone yanked the knob backwards and the golden doorway collapsed inwards. The robot, finally reoriented, bellowed wordlessly and sprung for her but too late. Her arm reeled back and she heaved the enchanted knob at the fist-sized hole that was all that remained of the doorway.

The time-knob sailed neatly through the hole a blink before it sucked shut. The robot stumbled through open air and sprawled into sand, twisting gracelessly as it tried to right itself. When it sank its claws into the sand, gouging deep rents into it as it regained its feet, it turned to face Persephone.

Weaponless, magic-less, friendless, and down a hand, Persephone stared the robot down.

Her remaining fist curled.

She cracked her knuckles.

And stepped forward.

"That concludes today's lecture. If you have any questions about the principles behind nano-agritecture, don't be shy."

When no one raised their hands, Professor Kore grinned at them. "Then class dismissed. Enjoy your weekend. And remember I'll be on sabbatical starting next week so you'll be working with Professor Agathon for the remainder of the semester. You'll like her."

The students of the Agricultural University of Athens shuffled their papers, zipped their bags, and filed from the lecture hall.

"Excuse me? Professor Kore?"

"Please, call me Persephone," Persephone said, turning from the blackboard she had begun erasing. "What can I do for you, Iris?"

The young woman held out a flyer, which Persephone took.

"I'm organizing a seminar about the history of agriculture," Iris said. "I was wondering if you'd be interested in being our keynote speaker?"

"I'm flattered, but why me?"

"You know more about the topic than some actual agro-historians," Iris said.

Persephone winked, and lowered her voice conspiratorially. "Sometimes, it feels like I was actually there." She folded the flyer, slipping it into her pocket. "I'd love to speak at your seminar. Just email me the details."

"Thanks, Profes— er, Persephone."

Iris followed her peers out of the lecture hall, leaving Persephone alone. Persephone blew out a nervous breath and returned to the blackboard before realizing she had crushed the chalk brush in her robotic hand again.

Apparently gods didn't heal from Nazi robot lasers very well, at least not without a healer around. Fortunately, the timeline for mortal realm cybernetics had leaped forward by decades.

She had destroyed the robot on the beach, more than a century ago now, by the skin of her teeth. But without the time-knob, she had been powerless to return to the present day. She had to take the long way home, avoiding any contact with her past—future?—self, her husband, and any of her old acquaintances until the day she had jumped from the original timeline. Crossing paths with any of them could have unravelled time in ways that made her head hurt to think about. Only Chronos really understood it; she was just following his instructions about what to do if something happened to the time-knob.

Rather than twiddle her thumbs and wait, Persephone had set to work in the mortal realm, disguising herself throughout the decades as an environmental activist, a technological seed fund CEO, a conservationist, and, for the last several decades, a professor at various universities around the world, helping teach mortals to embrace and enhance nature, and keeping watch as she did so.

It was a glorious thing to see unfold. The course of history changed entirely for the better. The technology the humans had created…well, it even surpassed what she had grown used to in the Underworld. Perhaps her favourite thing to witness, however, was the opulent flowers that had bloomed all over the world. She had spent years roaming the globe, studying and admiring them.

When she had commissioned Glykiá's armour, she had Hephaestus add a little chamber to it, which she had filled with pollen from Olympus. The pollen itself wasn't magical, so she wasn't breaking the treaty, but it made any flower it touched stronger and more stunning.

Glykiá had spent the entire afternoon at the Crystal Palace flitting above the heads of the gathering—the first to host visitors from almost every country in the world. Visitors who then travelled home with it, spreading it around the globe.

The evidence of Glykiá's work was everywhere.

But, in one hour's time, her long vigil would come to an end.

Her heart raced as Persephone gathered up her textbooks and notes and strode from the university. She hailed a solar ship, which dipped from the airway to hover in front of her.

The trip to her rendezvous point took only fifteen minutes but it felt like an eternity—especially tedious, considering she had lived almost an eternity. Finally, the solar ship floated down from the sky, its glass door sliding open to let Persephone out. She stepped down at the edge of a lush pomegranate grove. She had planted it herself, before the Exogeny. In this new timeline, it had flourished.

Steeling herself with a fortifying breath of crisp, clean air, Persephone plunged into the grove, dodging branches and low hanging fruit as she made her way to a bench in the heart of it.

She could hear the frantic buzzing from twenty feet away and her heart contracted painfully, even as her feet carried her faster. She burst into the clearing to find a tiny, armoured bee frantically tugging at a doorknob ten times bigger than her fuzzy body.

For her, decades had passed. For Glykiá, it was only seconds. The brave little bee was trying to reopen the door to save her.

"Glykiá," Persephone called and the bee froze solid. Persephone called her name again and Glykiá slowly swivelled to face Persephone.

A burst of joy buzzed from her and she threw herself into the air, speeding towards Persephone so quickly she couldn't pull back in time. She bonked against Persephone's nose and spun away a few feet before righting herself in the air and bobbing back towards Persephone, who held up a palm.

"I'm okay, old friend," she said when Glykiá alit atop her hand. "I made it back safely. I had to take the long way round, but I'm well."

Glykiá peppered her with questions and joyous tears flowed like silver from Persephone's eyes.

"Yes," she answered. "We did it. We fixed the world. It's magnificent, and I can't wait to show you all of it. But, in the meantime, your family is waiting for you. The bees are waiting for you."

Hades' nose was buried so deeply in his book that he didn't hear the rustling of the grasses in the meadow around him. The flowers pounced upon him, and Hades yelped with shock, then groaned as the flowers sneezed pollen all over his dark suit. He jumped to his feet and began brushing the pollen away but it was too late. Dye began bleeding from the dark fabric, and changing colours, until the black had vanished and a floral print took its place.

"I'll get you back for that," Hades vowed darkly, as Persephone crested the hill he reclined against. He grinned at her a split second later, throwing his book aside and opening his arms for her.

She threw herself ecstatically into them, hugging him so tight a quiet "oof" puffed from his lips. "Oh, I missed you," she murmured into his chest.

He dropped a kiss onto the crown of her head. "I missed you too. But it's only been a few days. Did you do what you needed to do?"

"It's been a lot longer than that for me," Persephone said. "But yes, I think I did."

Hades drew back and studied his wife, noticing the robotic hand for the first time. His brows raised with shock. "It seems you have quite the story to tell me," he said.

"How about I tell you about it over coffee? I owe a friend a latte."

"I could go for some tea," Hades said.

Persephone smiled. "Get that with honey."

This story is actually based on true events.

In 2020 the world was celebrating seventy-five years since the end of World War Two.

On a warm September day that year, my mother, our neighbour, myself and our three dogs were walking in our local woods. We have been there many times before and since, but on this particular day something quite extraordinary happened.

As we wandered along chatting as usual, we suddenly heard a sound that seemed completely out of place.

Music from a saxophone being played drifted out from the trees beside the path we were on. We all stopped, even the dogs, and listened to jazzy notes. The dogs ran into the trees twards the music so of course we decided to go and investigate.

We followed the sound along a narrow path, the dogs running ahead, and came to large dip filled with small trees and ferns.

The music was still playing up ahead so we carried on along the path that ran through the middle of the crater. But before we had gone much further the music stopped.

We searched the area but never did find out where it was coming from or who was playing. And we have never heard it again since.

Of course, there was no time travel involved that day, but the story 'Night Music' was born there and then.

The commemorations for the war gave me the idea of sending Anna back to 1942 and the crater we came across may well be from a bomb blast as there are more of them dotted around the woods. The gate house mentioned in the story really exists and is still lived in today.

But whether or not there was ever a mansion in those woods I don't know.

But that music had to have come from somewhere...

*Jane Lupino*

Jane lives in West Sussex on the south coast of England with a neurotic goldendoodle called Stanley.

Since leaving school, she has enjoyed an eclectic career path with jobs involving chemicals, horses, books, more horses, children, learner drivers, and more children with bicycles.

After being diagnosed with Fibromyalgia, she had to make some serious life changes. Writing, always a passion, became a form of therapy.

She writes short stories which tend to become quite long. Her story 'Baby Maker 2065' was published in the Bognor Regis Write Club anthology 'Meet The Winners' in 2019, and she is currently working on two novels, both fantasy stories for young adults.

Her hobbies include art, photography, wildlife and being outdoors.

# NIGHT MUSIC

by Jane Lupino

The woods began to take on a slightly eerie, more sinister feel as the sun began to set. The nights were starting to draw in much earlier now but I wasn't worried because I knew these woods well. The paths were as familiar to me as my home. My feet knew the way.

The sounds of the woodland settling down for the night kept me company as I walked back to the car park and the constant drone of traffic from the nearby dual carriageway hardly intruded.

But still, something seemed…out of place. It was nothing tangible, just a slight prickling at the nape of my neck.

The sun was low and long shadows crossed the paths. When I stepped out of a dark tunnel of overhanging branches another sound seemed to join those of the forest.

I stopped and listened.

There it was again; I hadn't imagined it. Music! Soft in the twilight, drifting on the gentle wind. The trees joined in, a susurration that drowned out the notes for a moment. The breeze dropped and the music was still there, and louder now as I walked on.

The last rays of sunlight blazed through the trees and lit up a small gap in the tall grass at the edge of the path. A smaller, narrower path led off, glowing in the light of the setting sun. The music was louder here, so I followed it, intrigued.

As I carried on the sound became clearer. It was a saxophone! Who on earth would be playing a saxophone in the middle of the woods, and at night?

Other instruments picked up the melody. Slow, low jazz notes that slid across one another in a mournful, mellow wail. The low thump of a bass thudded like a heartbeat as I got nearer.

I rounded a bend and the path dropped down into a large crater. There were plenty around and I often wondered if these woods had been bombed during the war.

I carried on down and climbed up the other side. When I reached the top, I saw lights across a huge empty expanse in front of me. I stepped forward and my boot sank into the soft, springy turf of a well-kept lawn.

Either I was seeing things, or I was definitely lost. I'd walked these woods for years and never in all that time had I seen mown grass, let alone the huge Georgian mansion that stood on the other side of the lawn. Just where the hell was I?

The music stopped and I could hear voices. Laughter filled the air along with the clinking of glasses.

I walked towards the sounds and saw a small group of people on a wide terrace. Two women and two men were seated, and another man was standing and pouring something from a large bottle.

The music started up again, a faster tune this time, something from the Thirties or Forties, I thought. The man who was standing reached out to one of the women and took her hand. He pulled her to her feet and she laughed as she fell into his arms, and then they began to dance.

She was beautiful; tall and slim, with long dark hair styled in keeping with the Forties theme. It flowed down the back of her tight, blood-red evening dress.

The man was taller and darker than the woman, and more handsome than anyone I'd ever seen, like some hero from a classic film.

I stood mesmerized. Did people really do this sort of thing? Themed parties were a bit dated these days, I thought, but who was I to say?

The dancing man glanced up in my direction and stopped.

I froze. I'd been caught.

"I'm sorry," I called and turned to go.

"Wait!" called the man. He was well spoken, his voice rich, deep, and commanding. "Don't leave. You're very welcome here."

As he strode towards me the others watched. They were all smiling, but there was something in those smiles that made me slightly nervous.

"I, I really am sorry," I said. "I didn't mean to gate-crash. I heard the music from back in the woods and followed it."

"Of course you did," said the man. He stopped in front of me and smiled. He really was tall. His white shirt was open at the neck beneath a black dinner jacket and his bow tie hung loose around his collar. He looked incredibly sexy.

He gestured towards his companions. "Please, come and join us."

He stepped closer, gazing into my eyes. "You're really not intruding," he added.

"Welcome," said another, softer voice, yet just as rich as the man's. His dance partner had joined us at the edge of the lawn.

She reached out towards me and I couldn't resist. She took my hand and led me across the grass to the table where their friends were waiting.

I looked at their finery, suddenly embarrassed by my own casual clothes. My loose walking trousers and muddy walking boots. My thick hooded jacket seemed almost too warm now and under it I just wore a loose, long-sleeved t-shirt. "I'm really not dressed for a party," I said.

"Nonsense," said the man. "You're fine as you are." He pointed to a seat. "Please…"

I sat and one of the other men offered me a glass. He was also tall, but not quite as tall as the dancing man, and he looked older but was still handsome and very dashing in his black-tie evening wear. "Have some wine," he said, picking up a bottle from the table.

"Oh. No, thank you," I said. "I'm driving."

"Oh, go on," said the dancer. "One little drink won't hurt."

"No, really," I insisted, "but thank you." I smiled up at the older man.

"Very sensible," he murmured, smiling back.

The third man leapt up from his chair and grabbed my hand. "Well, if you won't drink," he said in a light, merry voice as he pulled me to my feet, "then you can dance!"

He was the youngest and the shortest of the three, but still taller than me. His hair was ruffled but thick and gold in the lights from the house, and his bow tie was slightly askew, giving him a handsome, boyish look. His eyes sparkled as he pulled me into an embrace like a vice. I tried to pull back from him but his arms held me trapped.

"Please! Let me go. I don't want to dance!" I tried to push him away but it was useless.

The first man took my hand. "Now, Rupert. Let the lady go. She's just arrived, after all. Give her time to get settled before you subject the poor creature to your two left feet."

He gently pulled my wrist and my captor grudgingly released me.

My saviour led me back to my seat. "Now," he said, "I think introductions are in order." He sat down and poured drinks for everyone.

"Rupert, you've just met. This other reprobate is Arthur." The older man nodded politely.

"This," continued my host, indicating the woman he'd been dancing with, "is Arthur's wife, Suzanne. And over there," he said as he pointed to the other woman, who had not yet spoken but had been staring at me since I'd arrived, "is Petronella, my little sister."

He looked at me and leaned forward, taking my hand once again. "And I," he said as he kissed my fingers, "am Tobias."

Petronella put down her glass and glared at me. "Now, who, exactly, are you?" she asked, settling back in her chair. Her dark eyes glittered a little too brightly and her mouth was a thin curve as she smiled. She was also beautiful, but in an artificial, made-up way. Her golden hair hung in neat, loose waves that framed her narrow face as it swept down over one shoulder. It looked stunning against the deep lilac silk dress she wore.

"Oh, I'm sorry. I'm Anna," I said.

"Anna!" Tobias smiled. The way he said my name gave me butterflies. "How splendidly perfect."

"Thank you." I laughed. "I was named after my grandmother."

"I'm sure she was perfect too," Tobias said, resting his arm across the back of my chair as he leaned in.

I looked up at him. He was staring with an almost wolf-like intensity. I could almost see him salivating. I shivered but I wasn't sure why. This man excited me in a way I'd never felt before, but something made me wary of him.

Rupert stood up again and reached a hand towards Petronella. "Come on, Nelly, dance with me. This is supposed to be a party. Let's not waste this totally brilliant band your brother has hired."

Just then the music, which I hadn't noticed had stopped, started again from inside the house, a lively rendition of 'In the Mood', the Glenn Miller classic that my grandmother had loved issued out through the open French windows. I loved it too and I couldn't help my foot tapping in time.

"You see?" Tobias said, leaning even closer. "You do want to dance." He stood up and held out his hand.

I shook my head. "No, please I'd rather just sit and watch for a while, if you don't mind."

He bowed his head. "Of course, you still need time to relax a bit. We're complete strangers after all." He smiled disarmingly and the butterflies swirled again. "However, I'd like to change that state of affairs." His dark blue eyes searched mine and my pulse quickened. There was no doubt I was attracted to this gorgeous man, but still, something about him made me wary.

I took a deep breath and turned, facing the table to include the older couple sitting opposite. "I really am sorry to have barged in on your party," I said.

"Don't worry about it," Tobias said. His voice was as lovely as he was. Deep and rich, like velvety chocolate. It seemed to flow over me and I felt a little more at ease each time he spoke.

"It was the same with Suzanne and Arthur here," he continued. "They just wandered in by chance one evening, and it's like they never left. Isn't that right?" He looked across at Arthur, who I thought for a moment looked a little uncomfortable.

The moment passed and he smiled charmingly. "It certainly is. Life seems just one long party here, I can tell you!"

"Indeed," Tobias said, still holding Arthur's gaze.

The music stopped, and then Petronella and Rupert returned to the table. Petronella elegantly lowered herself into her chair while Rupert threw himself into his with a loud sigh.

"Phew," he said, grabbing his wine glass and emptying it with one gulp. "Your sister is a real whirlwind when she gets going!" There were a few polite chuckles and I smiled.

"So, what do you do, out in the real world?" Tobias asked.

"I'm an English teacher," I said.

"How wonderful," he muttered, still watching me. "To open young minds to all the possibilities of the world. And…your husband?"

I smiled. "Oh, I'm not married. I live with a couple of other teachers from my school. They're single too." I had no idea why I volunteered that information, but Tobias reached for his drink with a somewhat satisfied smile.

"In fact," I added. "I should probably go. They'll worry if I'm not home soon."

"Well, let them worry!" he said. "Tomorrow is Saturday, so I'm sure you don't have work. They'll just assume you're out having fun. Sometimes it's good to let go and do something out of character. It stops people taking you for granted."

He sounded so plausible but I couldn't stop the strange niggling feeling at the back of my mind. I cleared my throat. "So, how about you? Do you work?"

Tobias gave me an amused smile and Rupert laughed loudly. He seemed to do everything loudly.

I felt myself blush. They were clearly very rich and probably didn't have to work. Some families were 'old money'. Maybe this was one.

Arthur picked up his wine and sipped it. "I was a doctor, in our old life." Suzanne flicked her gaze at her husband before looking down at her hands. Tobias and Petronella both stared at Arthur, their eyes hard. Rupert looked at each of them in turn with an amused smirk.

"But I'm retired now," Arthur added with a tight smile, staring back at Tobias.

"Retired?" I remarked. "You don't look old enough!"

The strange tension passed and the party atmosphere returned as Tobias laughed. "Oh, he's much older than he looks, I assure you."

Rupert grinned at me. "Well I, darling, don't do anything so vulgar as working." He leaned back and folded his hands across his stomach. "I," he announced, "am a writer."

"Really?" I said. "What do you write? Maybe I've used some of your work in my class."

"Oh, he's not published," Petronella said. "He only says that because he thinks it makes him sound like a hopeless romantic!" She laughed and leaned over to kiss his cheek. "Which, of course, he is."

Tobias cleared his throat. "Well, now that we all know each other better, you have no excuse not to dance with me!"

I looked down at my feet. My walking boots were lightweight, but big and clumpy. "I'm really not dressed for dancing," I said as I laughed.

He narrowed his eyes as he appraised my attire. "Well, then let's find you something more appropriate, shall we? Nella, darling, surely you have something our guest could borrow. Would you?"

Petronella glanced over her shoulder as she moved past us to the dance floor, dragging Rupert with her. "I'm dancing," she stated with a pout.

Tobias grabbed her arm as she twirled away and dragged her back around. "Be a good girl please," he said with a tight smile.

Petronella bowed her head. "Yes, of course. Sorry, Tobias." He released her and she took a step back, rubbing her wrist. She scowled at me and glided off with a whirl towards the wide open French doors. "Well come on then," she snapped.

I opened my mouth to protest but Tobias cupped my chin and looked deeply into my eyes.

"Please, I insist," he whispered. "For me." He smiled. "It is my birthday, after all."

"I..." I couldn't help myself. I swallowed and found myself following Petronella.

When I got back to the party, Arthur was sitting watching as the others danced. I turned around and watched the small swing quintet playing in the huge ballroom behind me. Even without an audience, they were putting on a good show. The sax and trombone players were swaying their instruments from side to side in unison and the drummer's head bobbed in time to the music. The big double bass throbbed to the beat and the trumpeter led the melody from the front. They were amazing.

I jumped as someone touched my arm. "You look stunning," Arthur said.

I turned to him as I felt heat rise in my cheeks. "Thank you," I said. "Who wouldn't look stunning in this dress?"

The soft folds of pale green silk hung in a way that made my figure look as I'd always wanted it to but never quite achieved. My red-gold hair, which had been tied back for my walk, now hung around my shoulders in soft waves.

Petronella's feet, it turned out, were the same size as mine and the silver peep-toe shoes she'd lent me fit perfectly, almost as if they'd been made for me. The heels were high enough to accentuate my ankles but not so high that I couldn't walk in them.

"Come and dance," Arthur said. "Keep an old man company."

He led me out onto the terrace, wrapped an arm around my waist, and held my other hand in his. He held me close enough to dance comfortably, but not too close. It was all very proper, and very 'Forties', I thought.

As the music soared and I whirled around, Arthur gave me a strange smile. After a few moments, he pulled me closer and spoke into my ear. "Don't get caught up in this," he said quietly.

I frowned at him.

He smiled. "Just…don't let it carry you away."

I was about to ask what he meant when the music changed and Tobias took my arm.

"Sorry Arty, I'm cutting in." He held me at arms length and looked me up and down. "Perfect," he said and pulled me towards him for the next dance.

Eventually, the band stopped playing and we all went in, since it had become quite chilly outside.

The ballroom was huge. The walls were covered with murals of dancers and musicians in baroque style dress. The high ceiling was decorated with gold panels and arched beams. Four giant chandeliers hung down, glinting and sparkling from the flame-shaped bulbs.

The musicians, apparently finished now, were dismantling their instruments and carefully packing them away.

Rupert, obviously not wanting the party to end yet, wheeled in a large, old-fashioned gramophone from somewhere and was soon sorting through a pile of 78's.

Somewhere, a clock struck a single note.

One o'clock. In the morning? Oh, god! How long had I been here? What was I going to tell my housemates? My phone was upstairs in my jacket. I would have to go and find it but I had a raging thirst. I looked around for a drink but the only thing on offer was champagne and I really didn't want that.

I walked out of the ballroom into the main part of the house in search of a kitchen. I left the main hallway and walked around the back of the wide staircase. A smaller passage led down some steps. At the bottom, I found an old-fashioned scullery. It had a sink with a tap and faded wooden worktops with utensils and pans neatly arranged.

I really needed a drink first; after that I would get my phone to let my friends know I was okay.

I searched the cupboards until I found a glass, which I gratefully filled with water. I was about to take a much needed sip when Arthur suddenly rushed in and took it from me. "Hey!"

"Don't," he said urgently, tipping the liquid away.

"What the hell…"

"Don't drink or eat anything. If you do, you'll never be able to leave."

I stared at him. "What on earth are you talking about?"

He grabbed my hand and led me back along the wide hallway then into a large lounge. On the walls were several big portraits, including those of Tobias and Petronella.

"Look at them," he said.

"Family portraits," I said flatly. "What about them? Not unusual in a house like this."

"Look closer."

I looked at him and he nodded. I took a step toward the pictures. They were beautifully painted. The colours were rich and glossy, the features detailed and incredibly accurate. They were very lifelike.

I glanced back at Arthur in confusion. "They're beautiful, but I really need that drink now."

He stood in front of Tobias's picture. "Do you know when this was painted?"

I looked again at the portrait. "Well, he doesn't look much older than about twenty, so I'd guess about twenty years or so ago?"

Arthur pointed to the corner of the picture. There was a name, presumably the artist's, and a date.

I shook my head and pulled away from him. "That's ridiculous. It says 1923. That's almost a hundred years ago!" I laughed. "That can't be right. It just can't!"

Arthur closed his eyes. "It is." He gave me a pitying look. "He was born in 1902. That was his twenty-first birthday."

My breath caught in my throat. How could that be? "That's not possible. He is not a hundred and twenty years old! I mean, this is his fortieth birthday party."

I looked at Petronella's picture. It was dated 1933, ten years after Tobias's. The portrait was as beautiful as she apparently still was. Her hair was shorter, a neat bob that curled around into sharp points against her cheeks. Her thin red lips were pouting. She looked so young, without the slightly jaded look she had now. She was stunning in a silky pale green dress. I realised with a shock it was the same dress I was wearing now.

I shuddered. "She said this was an old dress, but…"

"She's ten years younger than Tobias. It seems the family marked special occasions with portraits."

"What..?" The edges of the room seemed to darken and I staggered. Arthur caught my arm and led me to a sofa.

"I don't understand," I said. He sat me down and took a seat beside me. "Is this some kind of sick joke?"

His face darkened. "It's no joke."

I shook my head, trying to stop the spinning. "And I suppose you're going to tell me you were born in eighteen-something-or-other," I snapped. My hands were shaking and I realised my whole body was too. The room felt suddenly cold, freezing, in fact.

Arthur laughed. "Me? No, I was born in the twentieth century. 1955, actually."

I shook my head again. "But…that would make you sixty-five. Surely you're not that old."

"I'm fifty. Time is different here. Suzanne and I have been here for fifteen years now. We did the same as you, happened to hear the music and wandered in." He paused and looked down, clasping his hands between his knees. "We were welcomed, like you, and we joined in the party, but we aren't what Tobias needs."

I looked at him. "What do you mean?" I asked, but I had a good idea.

"He's looking for someone special. You see, there's Suzanne and I, and Rupert and Nella are…close. But…"

"Tobias is alone," I finished. I got up and walked towards the doorway, Arthur a step behind me.

I looked around at the plush sofas and the high, ornate ceiling. The fine furnishings and decorations were rich and expensive. I could think of worse places to be stranded for eternity.

"I know what you're thinking," Arthur said. "We thought we'd love being here forever. But it's not how you imagine.

"Tomorrow…" He glanced at the tall-case clock standing against one wall. "Sorry, today is the sixteenth of September…"

"Yes, I know that!"

"…1942."

I swallowed. I still didn't quite believe all this but Arthur was very convincing.

"At seven minutes past four," he continued, "this house will be bombed by the Germans and everyone in it will be killed. It might seem all very splendid here, and it is, just for one night each year."

"But, how can that be? Surely, if you're here, you're here. All the time."

"You'd think so. But it's not like that."

Laughter burst from down the hall and Arthur pulled me further into the room. "All we have is just this one night. Every year. For the other three hundred and sixty-four days we are…I don't know. Ghosts, I suppose, shades. We're stuck here, on the grounds, but the house is gone. We see people walking through the woods every day, but…they don't see us. Then, when the fifteenth of September comes around again, we celebrate Tobias's birthday until we're bombed back into oblivion and we stay there until the next September fifteenth."

I sat silent, my mind in a whirl.

He reached over and patted my hand. I felt the warmth of it and grabbed it.

"But you seem so real," I said.

He laughed quietly. "I think we are real, for this time. But in just a few hours, we won't be. Not for another year."

I stood up and walked to the portraits. I gazed up at Tobias. He was stunning. His bright blue eyes stared down at me with an intensity that shook me, even from the painting.

"Would it change if I stayed?" I wondered aloud. "Would we all stay here if he wasn't alone anymore?"

Arthur came and looked over my shoulder. "I don't know. Perhaps, if you're the right one. It hasn't worked yet, though."

Cold dread spread through me. "You mean there have been others?"

He glanced over his shoulder. "Look, you may be in real danger if you stay here. Please, you must go."

"What happened to the others, Arthur? Why aren't they still here?"

He closed his eyes for a moment and shook his head. "I-I don't know. All I know is that when the bombs start and we all come downstairs, the women are no longer here and Tobias...he seems to be, I don't know, stronger, more solid somehow."

My stomach lurched and the room began to spin again. "How?" I asked, dreading the answer.

Arthur paled a little. "I think he uses them to become more real. I don't know how, I never have enough time to find out. But I think he uses them to give him...life."

Bile rose in my throat and I struggled to swallow. "How long has he been doing this?"

"I don't know, longer than we've been here. But I think he's trying to finish this cycle, one way or another." His face filled with concern. "I think he thinks you may be the one who will give him that chance."

He turned away. "I don't know what will happen to this place, to us, if he manages to escape. Maybe he gets to leave and live a new life outside this nightmare, or maybe we all just stay here for eternity. Or we all disappear, I don't know. But I'm damn sure that whatever the outcome, he will not let you go."

"And if I'm not 'the one'?"

"Then I think he will kill you. Use your life force like he has the others." He gripped my shoulders. "And you won't come back next year. They never do."

"Arthur! Anna?" The shout came from the direction of the ballroom.

We stepped back into the hallway.

"There you are!" Tobias strode towards us and put his arm around my shoulders, pulling me to his side. "I should ask what you two have been up to, sneaking away from the rest of us, but Arthur here is a happily married man who adores his wife, isn't that right, Arty? So I'm assuming it's all been very innocent." He stared at Arthur before turning his gaze on me. I felt his eyes bore into my soul.

I smiled up at him. "I went to get a drink of water," I explained. "All that dancing made me thirsty!"

Tobias smiled, satisfaction and relief all over his face. "Very good," he purred. He looked into the sitting room. "You've been looking at the portraits?"

"I just needed to sit quietly for a few minutes." I indicated the pictures on the sitting room walls. "They're magnificent."

Tobias smiled but it didn't quite reach his eyes this time.

"Well," he said. "It's time for cake! We'll dance again later. And there's plenty more champagne for everyone."

I glanced at Arthur as panic began to creep through me. Cake? What possible excuse could I have not to eat it?

Tobias led us into the ballroom, and sure enough, there, on a small table was an enormous tiered birthday cake with candles all over and thick, brightly-coloured icing in various shades. It was the gaudiest thing I'd ever seen.

"Isn't it splendid?" Tobias exclaimed. "Nella made it for me, with her own bare hands! Such a wonderful sister!"

"There are exactly forty candles," Petronella announced with an almost childlike pride.

Tobias stepped up to the cake, took a deep breath, and blew. All the candles went out in one go. I smiled and clapped along with the others, but my heart was racing.

Tobias laughed and stumbled a little. "Oops! Too much champers!" He laughed again, longer and louder than before.

Suzanne started to cut the cake, handing small slices to the others. She walked towards Arthur and me with two plates. She handed one plate to her husband and the other to me. She gave me a slight, worried smile, picked up my piece of cake, and took a large bite. I smiled gratefully. She was with us.

Tobias and Petronella were laughing as the young woman grabbed a handful of cake and shoved it into Rupert's open mouth.

The icing smeared across his face and Nella shrieked in delight while Rupert chewed noisily.

Casting a quick glance at them, Suzanne reached out and touched my face. I frowned and then realised what she'd done when I felt a tiny blob of icing just under my lip. She quickly finished the cake, then handed me the empty plate just as Tobias looked over at us.

He turned away from the younger couple and came over. My heart missed a beat, I was sure he'd seen.

He stopped in front of me. With slow deliberation, he reached out and wiped the icing from my face. Staring into my eyes, he put his finger into his own mouth and licked it clean.

He pulled me into his arms and started to sway to a soft rendition of 'Moonlight Serenade'. "I do hope you'll stay here," he said. "I'm so glad I found you. I've been waiting for someone like you for a long time." His words were slightly slurred and his eyes just a little too bright.

My heart still pounded, but right now, in the arms of this beautiful man, with his words in my ear, I couldn't be sure it was entirely from fear. Looking deep into his eyes, I could imagine staying here, with him, forever.

He leaned down and his lips found mine. His kiss was deep and urgent, and I felt my own mouth responding.

When we broke apart he gazed down at me. "Be mine, Anna," he whispered. "Don't ever leave me."

He turned away for a moment and the spell broke. I was filled with a sudden coldness that bit to the core. This was all wrong. This man, so beautiful, was dead.

I knew in that moment I had to get away. I had a life outside, with people I loved. A job I adored. I was not ready to leave it behind. Not for a long time.

Tobias suddenly grasped my wrist and pulled me with him. "Dance with me," he demanded. His grip was like iron, I had no choice.

He pulled me close and wrapped me in his arms. "Don't resist," he whispered. "It won't help you."

He stared into my eyes again and I felt my defences crumble. My body seemed to take over and leaned into him. His strength held me up and my feet moved with a will of their own.

He looked away and I caught sight of Arthur, standing by the table. He gave a slight nod and I came back to myself.

I dug my nails hard into the palm of my hand behind Tobias's back. I had to stay alert.

"Let's have a drink," I said. I knew it was a risk but it was the only thing I could think of to get away from him.

"Splendid idea," Tobias said.

He let me go and grabbed two glasses and a bottle of champagne.

"Let's celebrate!" he cried.

Rupert staggered to his feet. "Not me. I'm done in, old man. I need my bed!"

"Good idea!" Petronella said with a giggle. She followed him but turned at the door and looked at me with a sly smile. "Maybe we'll see you in the morning."

I took the glass of champagne that Tobias offered me. He held my gaze as I lifted it to my lips.

As I was about to take that fatal sip, Suzanne suddenly stumbled into me and knocked the glass from my hand.

The drink went all over me, soaking my dress.

"Oh, my god! I'm so sorry, Anna! How clumsy of me."

Arthur rushed over. He picked up my now empty glass and put it on the table.

Tobias looked furious for a moment, but it passed and he smiled disarmingly.

"Never mind," he said. "There's plenty more."

Suzanne took my hand and led me towards the door. "Let's get you cleaned up," she said.

Once out of the ballroom, she ushered me into the kitchen. I glanced up at the big round clock on the wall above the vast oven. It was almost five minutes to three.

Suzanne handed me a towel and I dried the stain as much as I could.

"Listen to me carefully. Tobias assumes you've eaten and had a drink while you've been here, and that you can't leave. In a while, we will all go to bed. Arthur says Tobias goes to the girls' rooms once he's sure we're all asleep." She gave me a reassuring smile. "Don't worry. I've put something in his drink. He should pass out before he gets a chance to come to you. As soon as it's safe, Arthur will take you back to the edge of the garden where you came in.

You must hurry to get away from here. You don't want to be near when it happens."

I stared at her. She spoke so calmly about her impending death, as if it were an everyday occurrence. But for her, I supposed that's exactly what it was.

I nodded dumbly. I couldn't think of anything to say.

We went back into the ballroom and Tobias immediately came to me. "One last dance, I think, before bedtime. You will stay, won't you?" It wasn't a request.

Once again, he locked me in his arms and we danced. The music had a quick beat and we whirled around the floor. Arthur and Suzanne danced too, both of them flicking glances at me each time they passed.

When the music finally stopped, Tobias, now quite drunk, pulled me close and kissed me again.

This time all I felt was cold. Perhaps the drink or the drug Suzanne had put into it dulled whatever spell he'd had over me, but I felt no attraction now, only revulsion.

"I really think I should go home," I said. "My friends will be worried. I never stay out all night."

The wolfish smile was back. "It's far too late now. You can't go home."

Suzanne began to gather glasses so I moved to help her.

"No, leave them," Tobias said, waving his hand widely around the room. "The servants can do it in the morning. That's what I pay them for, for god's sake!"

"You have servants?" I asked, alarmed. I hadn't seen any but the thought of more people who would lose their lives this night was horrifying.

"Of course I have servants. I couldn't run a house like this without them! The Parkers and their girl live in the lodge near the gates."

A strange feeling of relief flooded through me. I had often passed the lodge house on my walks. It was still intact and sat by the main road now. The gates were still there, too.

Tobias came over and wrapped his arm around my waist. "Come along, my angel. I'll show you to your room."

His eyes were intense as he stared at me. I swallowed my panic as I glanced away.

He guided me to the stairs, with Arthur and Suzanne just behind us.

"I hope you'll be comfortable in the guest room," Tobias said quietly. He leaned in closer. "Of course, if you feel lonely, I am very happy to keep you company."

I moved my head back and tried to look shocked. A few hours ago, I would've been flattered that a man such as this would have any interest in me. A few hours ago, I might well have accepted his advances.

"I am not that sort of girl," I said as firmly as I could. My voice was steady even if my heart was racing and my hands shook.

His smile widened. "How absolutely perfect you are!"

He stumbled a little on the top step and laughed. His eyelids looked heavy when he blinked.

He showed me to the room, kissed my hand, and backed away with a small bow. Then he turned and led Arthur and Suzanne along the hall.

I closed the door behind me and looked around the opulent bedroom. The ceiling was high and decorative, with a large rose surrounding a genuine crystal chandelier. Long, heavy satin curtains hung to the floor, held back by navy cords contrasting the duck egg blue material.

I closed them across the French window, which I noticed led out onto a small balcony. The bedroom walls were covered with heavily patterned paper in white and blue, which took on a slightly yellow/green tinge in the dull light from the bedside lamps.

The bed itself was huge and high. A thick navy eiderdown covered expensive-looking white cotton sheets and the many matching pillows looked plump and comfy.

I went to the large dark wooden wardrobe and opened it. My heart sank. It was empty. So were the drawers of the matching tallboy beside it. My clothes, and more importantly my phone, were still in Petronella's room.

A sudden knock at the door sent my heart racing and the breath rushed from my lungs. I stood where I was, I couldn't move.

The door opened a crack and relief flooded through me as Arthur's face peered around it.

"Come, now," he said urgently. He looked at his watch. "We've only got about fifteen minutes to get you out of here. We must hurry."

"My clothes, my phone. I can't find them," I said.

"No time. Sorry."

We hurried from the room and crept along the hallway.

"Tobias is asleep," he whispered. "I heard him snoring. Come along, we should be safe." We carried on, heading for the staircase.

"Just where do you think you're going?" The voice came out of the darkness behind us but I recognised Petronella's snide tones.

Arthur and I turned as she sauntered towards us out of the gloom, the gun in her hand catching the light from the stairwell. "My brother will not be happy about this. He thought you were his friend, Arthur."

She stopped directly in front of him and stared. Then she turned to me and stepped in close, her face just inches from mine. "Not so perfect now, are you?"

She turned away and stood at the top of the stairway, blocking our path, the gun now pointing at my chest.

"Did you really think you would be able to escape?" she asked. "Congratulations on avoiding the food and drink, by the way, I did notice that." She looked slightly impressed. "I would've thought after a whole night of dancing you would be parched, my dear."

At the mention of drink my throat constricted and my tongue stuck to the roof of my dry mouth. The sight of the gun had my heart hammering and I struggled to catch a breath.

Petronella noticed my discomfort and smiled her cruel, thin smile.

I swallowed as well as I could. "Please, Petronella. Let me go," I croaked. "I have a life out there."

"A life?" she said, shrilly. She waved the gun in the air as her temper flared so suddenly I took a step back.

"What about my life?" she spat. "The life I should have had?"

She shook her head, screwing her eyes shut. "I should've been married, had children. But I can't have that life now, so why should I let you have yours?"

Arthur glanced at his watch and shifted his weight anxiously.

Petronella rushed up to him and grabbed the lapels of his jacket. "Don't you see? We can end this. Or rather, Tobias can. You heard what he said, she's perfect! With her it will all be over, once and for all. No more bombs."

Arthur stared at the woman's face. Conflict battled in his eyes but he finally shook his head.

"No. No more. This has to stop. We have to let her go. Nella, you can never have the life you want. Don't you understand that? No matter what happens tonight, we will all still be dead."

Petronella stood staring at us, the hand holding the gun now down at her side. "Do you know how I die?" she asked in a low voice. She looked up, there were tears on her cheeks. "Of course you don't. The rest of you die instantly. The moment the bomb hits, you're all dead. But not me. No!" She turned away, shaking her head.

"No," she whispered. "Four hours." She turned back to face us. "Four hours of agony, with a shard of glass the size of a dinner plate in my side. That's how I die. Every time. In pain, in darkness, and fear."

She spoke quietly, but the anguish in her voice radiated out.

"Nella," Arthur said as he reached out to her, "I'm so sorry, but it doesn't make this right. We can't let your brother just go on killing these women."

Petronella's face crumpled. "I can't go through it again. I just can't."

It seemed like slow motion as she raised the gun and pointed it at her own temple. "I don't want to be afraid anymore."

Arthur leapt towards her. "Nella! No!"

The crack of the shot echoed through the night as Petronella fell slowly back and tumbled, almost gracefully, down the top few steps.

I opened my mouth to scream, but I couldn't find the sound.

Suddenly, Arthur grabbed my arm as doors opened along the landing.

"Come on," he growled and pulled me down the stairs past Nella's bloody body.

He continued to drag me until at last we made it out into the early morning air.

Once outside, my body responded and I ran with Arthur.

Above the sound of our breath, another sound crept in. The unmistakable drone of aircraft engines began to fill the air.

Arthur stopped and looked up. "They're coming," he stated. He looked at me and smiled. "I can't come any further. I have to be back there, with my wife. I can't leave her alone."

I swallowed the tears that threatened. "Of course." I nodded. "Go. I'll be fine from here."

"Good luck," he called as he ran back towards the house.

"You too," I said to the empty air.

The planes were closer now, almost overhead.

I turned and ran for the trees.

Just as I reached the edge of the woods, a low whistle filled the air followed by the brightest flash I'd ever seen.

There was an almighty boom, terrific heat and a massive push that sent me flying, and...

....The lights were too bright. My head hurt.

"Welcome back to the land of the living," a deep voice beside me said.

My eyes opened to see a man bending over me, a small light in his hand. He looked a lot like Tobias and my chest tightened. "What did you say?"

The man stepped back. "I just meant it's nice to see you awake at last. You've been asleep for quite some time. It seems you hit your head pretty hard out there."

I noticed then that he was younger than Tobias had been, and his eyes were brown and not so intense. His name tag read: Dr. Toby Crawford. Toby, Tobias?

"I'm sorry," I said shakily. "I think I had a bad dream."

The doctor shone his light into my eyes and 'hmm'd'.

"Right," he muttered.

Up close he smelled really good. No wonder he was in my head! I must have noticed him before I passed out.

He stood up straight again. "Now, let's see. Do you remember your name?"

I blinked. "Yes," I answered.

"Okay, good. Could you tell me, then? Because we don't have a clue who you are!"

I stared at him.

"You didn't have any ID or anything much really, when you were brought in. Not even a phone."

"I must've lost it," I said, frowning. "My name is Anna Jarvis. What happened to me?"

"Well, Anna Jarvis, you were found wandering around the woods in the early hours of this morning. You passed out when the ambulance arrived. You've been in and out of consciousness since you got here, muttering on about a house and a bomb and someone called Tobias. It must've been some dream!

"Now, apart from the bump to your head, you don't appear to have any other injuries. I don't think there's any lasting damage but I'd like to keep you for a while longer, just to make sure."

"I can't leave?" An unreasonable wave of panic swept through me at the thought.

The doctor frowned. "Of course you can, I'd just rather you stayed a while longer, that's all."

The panic drove deeper into my core. I felt a ridiculous sense of claustrophobia that I had no control over.

"I'm sorry," I said, getting out of the bed. "I have to get out of here."

I stumbled. The doctor caught my elbow and held me up.

"Calm down," he said. "No one is going to keep you here against your will. If you really want to go then of course you can." He sat me on the bed and looked at me closely. "I'd rather you didn't leave until tomorrow, but if you must, at least wait until your head clears a bit and you can stand up properly. Give it another hour or so, please."

I lay back down on the pillows and closed my eyes. He was right. I wasn't going anywhere yet.

He pulled the blanket over my legs and smiled. "Thank you," he said. "I'll come and check on you in a little while. For now, get some rest."

I knew I was being ridiculous. It must have been a dream. I had obviously seen the doctor when I came in and had turned him into Tobias. I didn't like to think what it said about my psyche to have made him into such a monster. And as for the house? I knew the woods well but as far as I was aware there had never been such a place. And yet...

I vowed to research it as soon as I could, just to make sure.

A couple of hours later I was feeling much better. I'd called one of my housemates and she was on her way to the hospital.

Dr. Crawford returned and gave me some forms to fill in, which he seemed exceedingly pleased that I could manage.

He smiled as I handed him the paperwork. "Thanks," he said. "You certainly look much better now. I think you can go, but I want you to make an appointment at Outpatients for tomorrow. And if you have any blackouts, disturbed vision, nausea, or vomiting in the meantime, I want you to promise to come straight back here."

"I promise," I said.

He nodded. "Very well." He smiled and scribbled something on my notes. "Your clothes, such as they are, are in the locker beside you."

He looked down at me, putting his hands in his pockets. "Well, goodbye, Anna Jarvis. Please be more careful in future and I would suggest you dress more appropriately for the woods next time." He winked and left my cubicle, pulling the curtain shut behind him.

I frowned, I always dressed appropriately.

I opened the small cupboard next to the bed and leaned in to get my clothes.

I stopped. The world tilted as I slowly pulled out a long, pale green silk dress and a pair of silver, peep-toe shoes.

What if a broken piece of you was left behind, far out of reach? With telepresence technology not so far away, allowing senses and actions to be felt anywhere, decisions of the past can be revisited again. This story explores Amla Ghosh's journey to recover the telepresence machine she piloted years ago, crashed on an icy moon and keeper of her most powerful memories. Explorer first, mother second, the metal memorial relives key moments of Amla's life, just as regret colours its awakening sensors.

# *Roy Sarkar*

Roy Sarkar was born in Brampton and grew up in Saskatoon, finding his window into worlds through his first job at the local public library. He worked in software for too long before realizing words were more inspiring than code. Still with keyboard and mouse in hand, he works as a copywriter and content marketer, and is the winner of the 2020 Muskoka Novel Marathon's Best Adult Manuscript.

# From Above

by Roy Sarkar

There was nothing above me except the weight of worlds. Tears frozen beneath my eye, body broken, indistinguishable from the wreckage where I lay. Jupiter's heavy presence threaded through the maelstrom raging in the sky above but the planet itself was unseen. Beyond the atmosphere lay Saturn and Mars and Earth, along with the billions who called them home.

A mirrored helmet came into view, the protective gear of a rescue marine. I saw my own face, a sleek metal oval stencilled with serial numbers and pockmarked with debris, a lone eye sitting dead centre. Flanked by cracked sensors that used to tell me everything and now nothing. I had no voice to complain because the speakers from the bottom half of my skull sat ten metres away.

Unseen and unheard, the sky was crowded with electromagnetic oceans, gravitational waves, and subatomic grains yet to be catalogued by humans. Earth had been studying Jupiter's moons for over a century, yet I was the first to make contact with the largest one, Ganymede. On a mission to explore its surface, the unusually dense magnetic storms between the massive planet and tiny moon were hard to predict. The brutal forces drowned out my thruster exhausts like breaths in a tornado and tore off parts of my body like so much flotsam. Out of control and spiralling towards the frozen landscape, the last thing I remembered was the great plumes of ice and rock thrown into space as my titanium exoskeleton careened into the icy surface.

I do not know how long I was offline. While one marine rebooted my power systems, the other surveyed the crash site. They reconnected my neural core and spoke to each other of a larger rescue vessel on its way to tow me home. Climbing atop the broad surface of my chest, they communicated their surprise to one another, wondering if the faint activity in my brain was something new or simply old commands stuck in a dying loop.

No such luck, I knew. My speakers were damaged, but if I could talk I would tell the marines that she was on her way.

The Huveane decelerated within sight of the red giant, the pressure building within Amla's chest and forcing her tired eyes open. The only constant about in-person space travel was that all of it was terrible, and she would be glad to leave these cramped quarters and recycled air for the open skies of home. There was nothing worse than being locked inside a fragile can of metal bolted to pods of explosive fuel with little control over any of it.

Her berth was a tiny cube of seamless white panels with no sense of ceiling or floor until she put a finger to the wall. Wide ribbons of inky blackness spread out, lighting up with status displays and the outline of a hatch. The deceleration pressure meant they were only hours away from Ganymede, which also meant she had no more excuses to hide from the rest of the crew.

The Huveane was Earth's finest, a sleek Diefenbaker class cruiser that was the fastest way to spin around the solar system if you weren't a rich merchant or a richer government official. It had been launched after a UN naval ship had sent two marines down to Ganymede to investigate a faint homing signal. They had found an old, nearly destroyed Strider unit, its body half submerged in the moon's icy surface. They had restored enough of its higher functions to deem it movable, but they needed an operator to connect and command it again.

Amla's chest tightened at the thought of her past life. She had operated that Strider unit for ten years in the service of the

Corporation. Built to travel space and dive into oceans, Striders could only be operated by a small percentage of the population and, even then, most burned out due to the intense stress of constant mind to machine contact. But Amla was unique; her brain could handle more and her body could stay connected longer.

Unlike most pairs, Amla was given the longer missions; the ones with nebulous goals. Exploration, conservation, and preservation had been her operational parameters. From the comfort of her telepresence unit in Tokyo, she had been Earth's best operator while also juggling a marriage and family back in Canada.

Until Ganymede.

Amla may have been the best, but she took risks. It was the nature of pushing the boundaries of science and exploration. Until Ganymede, no other Strider operator had been involuntarily discharged from the Corporation's service. After the accident, people forgot that she had been the best; she was simply absorbed into the rest of humanity's ocean.

It took months for Amla to recover. The physical damage to her brain healed quickly but the strain of being ripped from the virtual universe of the Strider and into the reality of an earthbound life was almost too much to bear. Her brain had racked up years of operating time tethered to the powerful processors and strong limbs of her Strider. She had gone wherever she wanted and been the first to witness stunning, terrifying things.

Her Strider had travelled to the tallest mountain ranges in the solar system and dived deep into the trenches of Earth's oceans. Humans had originally built the machines to explore but found themselves pushing for commercial and military goals instead. Only Amla's mental and physical fortitude allowed her to serve the original intentions of the program. In their time together, Amla and her Strider had discovered new sources of food for an overburdened planet and tested new sciences in the perfect physics of space.

The crash forced her to leave behind her titanium body and multimodal sensors that saw everything with perfect clarity. Post-Ganymede was a prison of fragile flesh and a lost humanity that had forgotten how to cope with life on Earth.

Once grounded, Amla had to re-learn that her human brain wasn't as fast as a fusion-powered neural core and her body was no longer impenetrable. She had to navigate the frontiers of people that had moved past her long absences and single-minded devotion to work. Her husband, Subho, had grown distant and their son, Somu, had aged past the need to sit on her lap.

Everyone in her life had figured out how to move on from the crash while she was stuck in a dying loop tied to a machine she had destroyed millions of kilometres away.

I remembered the good times.

The marine standing atop my chest kicked down hard, presumably thinking she could dislodge the ice from my limbs or jiggle some internal connection back to life. Instead, she reared back as her foot rang with the impact against my armour. My rescuers were desperate to reactivate me quickly, likely because the moon's environment was degrading their protective gear and affecting the electronics inside their lander. From their communications with each other, I could tell they wanted nothing more than to go back to their ship and blast off home.

Casting my failing sensors above was a revelation. If my damaged memory was correct, I was still on the side of Ganymede that faced away from Jupiter. Sensing the emptiness of space through the moon's thin atmosphere, I knew I had been lucky. My operator and I had flown through space and swam through oceans while other Strider units were building lunar hotels and mining asteroids. Some pulled cargo tubs or fought each other in space, all at the fleeting whims of humans they had never interfaced with. A few units disappeared, never returning to Earth, as their operators lost control of their minds.

Unlike them, I had flown first over potential colony sites and last over old battlegrounds. I had walked beneath mountains on Mars and dipped my sensor-tipped hands into the thick soup of Venus. I had rescued families from their stranded space yachts and recovered Strider units overcome by systems failures. Through it all, my operator had never let mundane, unremarkable things take over our life together.

Once, a merchant powerful enough to contract the Corporation hired us to map out a new yacht route between Mars and Saturn. We had spent weeks soaring through vast stretches of space, taking our time to chart the perfect path. The merchant desired safety and fuel efficiency; my operator took advantage of Jupiter's gravity to set a new speed record to Saturn.

We were never warriors, builders, or workers. My radiation-discoloured skin and the impact dents across my body came from exploration, not labour. My data uploads back to Tokyo were always sent to researchers, scientists, and engineers, never the military.

Processing what was left of my internal records, I remembered those times and knew I was lucky that our missions were always about exploration and service and never about power or control.

Strange, though, given that I was never programmed to recognize luck.

Amla felt the vibrations inside the Huveane increase as she pulled herself along the corridor rails, feet floating behind her. The rescue ship had started to toss and turn on the approach to Jupiter and the uniform white walls of her room hadn't done her stomach any favours. She was meant to be free outside, not confined to the cramped volumes of a tiny tin can.

Outside the bridge doorway, she heard the ship's crew's speaking in precise tones with each other. Navigating space was tricky business; barreling down towards Jupiter required pinpoint coordination and communication. Amla looked out an observation window and into the infinite depths of space. Her Strider could take her anywhere out there, slipping easily through without disturbance. This hot and overworked ship assaulted her senses.

She pushed herself off the ceiling and down into the Huveane's small bridge, spotting the greying fringe of the captain's hair immediately. He was standing over the shoulder of Susanna Jessup, the ship's navigator, both studying the multicoloured panel in front of them. Lina Otero was strapped into one of the pilot's seats up front, fingers dancing across her flight joystick and thruster controls.

"If we burn here and here, we can compensate for those pinch points." Captain Menon traced a path around an image of Jupiter on the navigator's display. Orange-red lines representing magnetic and gravitational fields created a hellish landscape surrounding the planet. Looking out the pilot's windows, Amla saw the clean bright arc of Jupiter against the deep blackness of space with no hint of the tremendous forces at play. Ganymede was there somewhere, waiting to reveal its damaged bounty.

"Miss Ghosh, nice of you to join us," the captain said, indicating the vacant seat beside the pilot. "We're just plotting our entry into Ganymede orbit. You wouldn't happen to have any tips, would you?"

Otero coughed, looking away from her flight controls to shoot the captain a dark look. Menon shrugged and gave Amla a sheepish grin. The last time she was here, she had lost the Strider due to the same energies that now threatened the Huveane.

"Sorry, of course." He gestured at the maelstrom of hazard zones on the navigator's display. "I meant that you know the area better than any of us. Any help would be appreciated."

"Thank you, Captain, but I don't remember much about the crash." Amla pushed herself toward the empty seat beside Otero, her body bouncing off the wall as the ship rocked around them. "I tried to find a safe corridor to Ganymede but the environment changed faster than I could keep up. The Strider's automatic protection system kicked me out as soon as it detected a collision, well before we hit the surface. Besides, I'm sure the conditions now aren't the same as they were back then."

The details she remembered weren't worth mentioning to the crew. The thrill of maximum thrust as she pushed the Strider through the gravimetric violence of the space between Ganymede and Jupiter. She could feel the electricity running along her limbs as the machine's sensors fed back an accurate, if greatly muted, impression of the turbulence along the Strider's exoskeleton. Her optics had picked up the landing site just as a massive shift in the electromagnetics overloaded her navigation systems, causing the safeties to cut off her thrusters. The sudden loss of momentum had left the Strider even more vulnerable to the chaos.

The last thing she remembered was a shockingly vibrant blue-orange atmosphere, as the last of the Strider's telemetry was sent back to Earth before its neural core kicked her out.

"Yes, you're correct, of course." Captain Menon's voice brought her back to the Huveane. Amla's head bumped the ceiling above the co-pilot's chair as the ship bucked again. "Careful, this baby isn't nearly as smooth as your old Strider unit." Smiling, he turned back to Susanna to continue plotting their flight path.

Amla pushed herself down and strapped into the co-pilot's chair, tilting her head to get a better view out the front windows. Jupiter was gorgeous. Milky-white bands hundreds of kilometres wide rippled beside streams of red and spots of orange. The whole scene looked like flowers in continuous bloom. She looked over at Otero, who was focused on her instruments and oblivious to the masterpiece outside.

Amla saw the readings on the pilot's console and frowned. "Captain, I'm having doubts about my value here." She turned back to look at him. "The Strider's telepresence chamber didn't work on Earth — what makes you think it'll work under these conditions?"

Captain Menon looked up from the navigator's display. "It's not me who thinks it'll work here, it's the team back at the Corporation. Since they're paying the bills for this trip, I'm doing what they say." Studying the swirling colours and text on the readouts before him, he added, "I didn't ask why they wanted to recover this old unit, but I have to say it's exciting to be one of the first humans out this far. After you, of course."

Amla nodded but didn't say anything. She had asked the Corporation why they wanted her on this recovery mission, so long after the crash. Their response was some nonsense about asset protection and parts recovery but that didn't seem genuine. The cynical part of her thought they wanted the Strider's flight data recorder to pin liability on her. A small part of her wished it were so, as then there would be concrete evidence for her loss. Not just some random accident caused by amorphous reasons that still ran through her head over and over again.

Subho had always said she spent too much time thinking of outcomes, not enough time focused on the here and now. It was why she spent half her life training for and operating the Strider. Travelling space in its metal body offered nothing but options. Home was like wearing too-tight leggings that could tear at any moment. The possibility of never finding joy in flight again was overwhelmingly painful.

The captain pressed a control that beeped in satisfaction. "I think we got it, Susanna. Either this route works, or we find out very soon that we should've turned left back there instead of right."

Otero made a disapproving sound, her fingers gripping the flight controls tightly. "By 'we' you mean, 'I hope Otero compensates for any errors in calculations with her superior piloting skills and cat-like reflexes', right?"

"I'll take my sensor data over your animal brain anytime, Otero." Jessup cracked her knuckles and let her fingers fly over the navigation controls, dumping corridor entry plans to the pilot's computer every few seconds.

"This is where the fun begins, Miss Ghosh." Otero reached out to shut down the ion thrusters, causing everyone's bodies to lurch forward in their harnesses. Amla grunted as pressure built up around her chest. Flying inside a tin can was a harsher experience than existing as the tin can yourself.

"Dammit, Lina, warn us before you do that next time, all right?" The captain punched the back of the pilot's chair before giving Amla a sympathetic grin. "I'll never get used to that myself, Miss Ghosh. It's a wonder any of us survive these trips." Otero coughed again, shaking her head.

"It's okay, Captain Menon, I've gotten used to regular space travel over the past weeks." Amla pushed against the inner walls of the Huveane, settling deeper into her chair. "I'm sure we'll be just fine."

Otero looked sideways with a grin.

Years ago, my sensors had found a lost balloon in the sky above Saskatoon, dim orange against the bright clouds. Shifting my eye downwards, my operator pinpointed the perfect landing spot in her backyard. We had missed too many birthdays, so it was lucky that my maintenance cycle on Earth coincided with her son's first day as a seven-year-old.

River Heights spread out like a checkerboard, each home looking no different from the next. But only one had balloons tied to the fences surrounding the property. Red, green, yellow, pink, the decorations popped through the desert of prefabricated residences and browning parks. Far to the south, a once-great river lay drying and cracked, its path consumed by office towers and industrial complexes.

I zoomed in my targeting sensors to see Somu giggling and running around behind the house, blowing bubbles through a bamboo loop in his tiny hands. Subho was sitting at the table sipping ClearBeer and eating śaibāla cutlets with our neighbour, Mila

Bando. She and her son, Dimpy, were dressed in festive clothes, matching the colourful kurta worn by Somu. Subho wore a plain sweater and pants, his perpetually cold body at odds with the high prairie temperatures.

Dimpy chased Somu around the yard, trying to catch the trail of bubbles while soap spilled out of his own bottle. They both looked up as my engines roared and the ground rumbled. It was rare for civilians to get this close to a Strider and people around the neighbourhood emerged from their homes and fences in wonder. My titanium body went vertical and descended into our yard like a giant action figure, thrusters kicking up grass and blowing food off the table. My metal feet spanned half the lawn, sinking into the ground and forcing the kids to leap onto the stone patio. I stood taller than the house and cast everything into shadow, balloons and all.

Subho's eyes tracked me the whole way, narrowing as I took over the yard. Somu was beside himself, the bubbles and his friend Dimpy forgotten. He knew what Mommy's job was but seeing her Strider up close was surely blowing his young mind.

I'VE COME TO CELEBRATE A BIRTHDAY TODAY.

I bent my torso forward, the exoskeleton's head nearly touching our roof. Subho stood up in alarm while Mila stepped around my feet to retrieve the fallen plates and bowls. Focusing my eye in and out, pretending to search, I activated my spotlight to point at Dimpy.

ARE YOU THE BIRTHDAY BOY?

The poor kid trembled and shook his head no, pointing slowly at Somu. My son, apparently unfazed by the giant robot in his backyard, looked like he had been handed a box of sweets from his favourite store. I moved my spotlight over to him.

ARE YOU THE BIRTHDAY BOY?

I zoomed in on his face, snapping high-resolution images to download and savour later. Somu jumped and shouted as he realized the towering Strider had come just for him. He ran around the perimeter of my feet, reaching out to touch the cool titanium skin. The folds of his kurta flapped under the residual heat of my thruster exhausts. "Ma, come out of there! Come see me!" He came around front and craned his neck upwards. "Ma, come down here!"

I CAN'T. I'M AT MY OFFICE.

He looked me up and down in confusion. "But you're here. I can hear you." My operator had decided to send her real voice directly through the speakers instead of the synthesized vocalizer system that translated her thoughts into my words.

Subho cleared his throat and set down his beer, walking over to kneel beside our son. Somu was knocking against the hardened metal of my toes, trying to find a doorway into the interior of my frame. There was no such thing. My sensors picked up a crowd forming around the house with people holding up devices and tapping their temples to turn on their camera implants. It would only be a matter of time before the news drones showed up. Even less time for the Corporation to review and approve the footage.

"Ma's very far from here," Subho said, pulling our son closer to him. "She's in Japan, remember? This is just the…the vehicle she controls to do her job. Like a pilot at the airport controlled our flight to India last year." His voice trailed off as he looked up into my eye in frustration.

"But a pilot sometimes goes with the plane," Somu countered, his voice soft. "Why can't ma just open the door and come out?"

IT'S LIKE OUR VIDEO CALLS. I'M SPEAKING TO YOU FROM FAR AWAY BUT I CAN SEE AND HEAR EVERYTHING YOU DO.

Somu's face fell.

Mila Bando, ever the people pleaser, assessed the situation and stepped forward. Telling the kids it was time for birthday cake and kulfi, she waved up at me before ushering them into the house, closing the door with a long look at Subho. More people from the neighbourhood were entering the yards beside ours and filling the street. Some of them were meeting in person for the first time. Subho glared at them and his damaged lawn with equal disdain.

"You should've told me about this. How could you think bringing this machine here was a good idea?" He kept his voice low so the neighbours wouldn't hear but every word echoed loudly inside my audio processors. "It's hard enough having birthdays without you but now I have to clean up this mess and deal with this." He waved his hand at the people peering over our fence and the rapidly approaching news drones in the sky.

Dialling down my speaker volume, I knelt my massive frame as far as I could without damaging more of the lawn, bringing my speakers closer to my husband. "I thought he would like the surprise."

"You were wrong."

Amla swore and threw off her telepresence harness, the headset clattering to the floor of the Huveane. The ship bucked and groaned around her, making it difficult to jab a finger at the comms panel.

"Captain, I'm getting no response at all." Releasing the safeties, she stepped out of the Strider's operating chamber, tied down to the floor of the cargo bay several decks below the bridge. It felt like the ship was pitching and changing orientation every second, caught in the gravitational grasp of Jupiter. It was only Lina Otero's skills at the pilot's controls that had kept the ship going this far.

"The Corporation's theory isn't working," Amla said into the comms panel. "Either the atmospheric mess is preventing signals from getting through or the Strider's completely dead. Even on minimal power, we should be getting a handshake or locator beacon."

Menon's voice crackled through the speaker. "Relax, Miss Ghosh, we're in clear communications with the marine rescue party on the surface. They said the unit's in bad shape but giving off a signal. Weak, but it's there." He paused to confer with the bridge crew. "We'll send the tug down to retrieve the unit and try connecting again up close here."

Amla didn't like the sound of that. "Captain, the only way to get the Strider off the surface is to use its own thrusters to break free of the crash site. Your tug isn't nearly big enough to lift five thousand kilos off the moon and break through all the turbulence between us."

The Huveane dropped suddenly, reinforcing her point and forcing Amla to kick her feet under the operating chamber to keep from flying into the ceiling. She bit her lip waiting for Menon's response, running her fingers over the warm fabric of her telepresence harness. She didn't actually know the tug's lift capacity but was hoping the crew was too busy to figure out the numbers.

"All right." Menon sounded dubious. "What do you propose?"

"Help me move the operating chamber into the tug." Amla hoped she sounded more confident than she was. She placed the harness back onto her head. "I'll go down and get her myself."

One marine leapt towards her ship, evidently hoping to escape the electromagnetic storm building around us. The other sat kneeling on my chest, hands stuffed into one of my maintenance ports. Jupiter and Ganymede were killing us slowly and even I knew that my life was not worth two humans.

I felt a snap inside me, my rescuer swearing to her friend over the communications channel as my diminished sensors fluttered and went dark.

Fragments from the past floated inside my dying neural core.

I remembered my operator guiding me through the briny gloom of the Pacific Ocean, navigating the Kermadec Trench, searching for creatures older than humans and promising cures for the viruses of our age.

Another time, she brought me into high orbit above Venus, avoiding its corrosive clouds to survey the landscape beneath for a future crewed mission. Ignoring my sensor alarms, she dropped me into low orbit and dipped my fingers into the atmosphere, savouring the sensations and harmonies of a wholly different planet.

We floated in the nothingness of our solar system, waiting for the right moment to kick in thrusters and chase comets.

I saw Somu's eyes go wide with joy as I told him the Corporation had fired me.

Halt memory. Begin diagnostics.

I never had that conversation.

Amla was terrified. Hurtling through space in control of a Strider was one thing, quite another to drop onto Ganymede inside a shaking tin can. Locked in the belly of the Huveane's tug, with no windows or displays, she had little sense of direction or speed, no sensor feedback to tell her what was coming up.

She swallowed and hit the comms to the cockpit of the tiny tug. "Otero, I'm spinning up now." The pilot's only response over the speakers was a gleeful shout. At least someone was enjoying the ride down.

Amla snapped the safety frame of the Strider's operating chamber closed and pulled on the telepresence headset. There was a flash of light and she saw her son's eyes go wide with joy as she told him the Corporation had fired her.

"What the hell?" Amla blinked and checked the status readouts. All normal. The tug lurched and Amla's head cracked into the wall. Forcing herself to breathe slowly and focus, she took off the headset and felt around for any damage.

Her fingers dipped into the thick soup of Venus' atmosphere, the toxic acids and extreme heat cutting into her flesh.

Amla squeezed her eyes shut, blocking out the memory and the violent lurching of the tug's cargo bay. Gently lowering the headset back onto herself, the Strider's operating interface kicked in immediately. A vast, empty darkness and the distant beat of her own heart took over. Amla reached out as she had done a thousand times before, seeking the thread of connection that would pull her into the body of the damaged Strider.

As her consciousness broke through the barrier between real and virtual, Amla's whole body convulsed in pain. Her arms were broken and her face shattered. Cold unlike anything she had ever felt penetrated deep into her bones, spreading out from the icy shards of Ganymede embedded in her back. Her mind filled with the memories of a life encased in metal. More time spent in the bleak loneliness of space instead of the gardens of her own backyard. Time spent studying comets and asteroids rather than seeing Somu go to school, ride his bike, and read his first book.

Operating her Strider had never felt like this before.

Within the inky depths, she saw a form take shape. Pushing forward with her feet — or was it activating her thrusters? — Amla moved closer. She saw an orange balloon floating in the sky above Saskatoon.

Or was it the glowing eye of her Strider unit staring back at her?

Joy! I flew through space again, watching the surface rush closer, shaking and twisting between mighty Jupiter and tiny Ganymede. My body was more fragile than it should be, encased in a thin metal envelope and filled with humans, slow to respond. But still, I flew.

I was also trapped in moon ice, my solid metal body broken and cold.

A tiny connection snapped into place. Then another. My vision bloomed and cleared as thousands of telepresence links came online between me and my operator. I could see the marine jump off my chest as a small spacecraft fell towards us. It was a rescue tug but it was also me up there.

Then came incandescence as my thrusters ignited.

Elation flooded Amla's body as she felt the Strider break free of Ganymede's icy grasp. The unit wasn't entirely functional, and bits and pieces broke off to spin away, but she wasn't entombed anymore.

The rescue marines waved as the Strider rose onto its feet, then jumped away as the massive exoskeleton shuddered and swayed unsteadily on the moon's surface.

The Huveane's tug hovered as thick cables sprung from its belly, Otero guiding them to clamp onto the Strider's broad shoulders. Amla ran through what diagnostics she could. The damage was extensive enough that she knew the unit would likely never fly again but she couldn't rule out other possibilities.

She coordinated the Strider's thrusters with the tug's engines, minimizing the shearing forces as the two spacecraft pushed away from the moon's surface. Space and stars filled Amla's vision and the Strider's image processors, as did Somu's face as he looked up at them with joy.The machine's recent memories flooded into her brain. They may never let her fly through space again but there were infinite journeys waiting back home with her son.

There was nothing above any of them anymore.

Years ago I had a close friend that was deeply into Japanese street fashion, particularly lolita. It seemed no matter where she traveled, there was a lolita community eager to welcome her. Digital streaming has made Japanese media widely accessible, but clothes have to make the physical trek here, so cultivating a wardrobe is time consuming and expensive, an adventure all on its own. If you were lucky, you'd get the chance to make the pilgrimage to Tokyo, particularly Harajuku, and shop in person, returning with packed suitcases and enthralling tales.

In a world where most commercial products qualify for next-day delivery, there's something romantic about travelling halfway across the planet to buy stockings in a tiny boutique. I've always wanted to write something that captured that journey, but could never make getting there as exciting as being there.

When I heard about this anthology, I again started to think again of Harajuku. How could I make getting there thrilling, and suitably fantastic? I couldn't, I decided, but why did *getting* there have to be part of the story at all? Why couldn't the character just step through a portal and *be* there?

I ran with that. It couldn't be a single portal, it would have to be a string of them, a journey through places as much as to one place in particular. What would make this trip an adventure and not just a travelogue? Maybe they're travelling illegally. Maybe these portals make illegally travelling across the world as easy as hopping a subway fare, but with far more serious consequences if you were caught.

As the journey came together in my mind, I began to think more about the world, about how a failed alien invasion lasting only a few hours could change the world in both miraculous and disastrous ways. And it became clear that this journey wasn't just about where the character was going, but what they were trying to leave behind.

Why is travelling so exciting? Someone living in a scenic small town might find a trip to a large city to be a magical experience, just as someone from that city might find a trip to that village magical. If both places are worth travelling to, then why ever leave? I think it's because we learn things about ourselves as we travel. Some of who we are is shaped by what's around us, so when we travel we're not just going somewhere new, we're becoming someone new, at least for a time. I hope that when you get lost in this story, you experience a little bit of that yourself.

# *Taylor Calder*

Taylor Calder is a physician in Toronto, Ontario. He primarily writes near-future science fiction, where ordinary people take on extraordinary challenges to find their place in the world. When he's not writing or working you can find him building Gunpla, playing classical guitar, or delving through used book stores in search of new inspiration.

# The Harajuku Crevasse

by Taylor Calder
*For my Doki*

It was easy to portal hop to the Harajuku Crevasse, Natalia had told her. The real one, not the shit-ass digital diorama where she and Noa killed time. You hopped until you got to Atlanta. Then you hopped Atlanta to Nairobi, Nairobi to Neo Toronto, Neo Toronto back to Atlanta. "Why back?" Noa had asked. Natalia had smiled. Natalia liked when Noa said something she thought was stupid. The second hop was to the secure Atlanta sub-terminal, which you could only get to from Neo Toronto. From there you could hop a portal to Hokkaido. Hokkaido was the only place where the portal networks of the Greater Pacific Republic and the poisoned rest of the world touched. From there you took a transit portal to Harajuku Station and slid down to the Crevasse. Easy.

Noa's avatar swiped a pair of neon leggings. They broke into a splash of symbols, rolling cats and hearts – the leggings had been successfully added to her basket. "Sounds intense," she said. "Sounds hard, I mean." At fifteen she didn't have a lot to compare to, but it seemed harder than laying around a mouldy farm house, finding ways to make her life go by faster, which was all that she knew. She was a few years too young to remember the invasion.

Natalia frowned. You could barely see her actual person past her sunglasses, her platinum odango, and her swirling green and pink dress like cotton candy being spun, but she was there and she was frowning. "You don't want to come visit me here?"

"I do, it just doesn't seem feasible, is all." The digital crowd was thick. She had heard that the real Crevasse was a lot shallower, and not nearly as long – the Others' beam had hit it at an oblique angle. "Sides, this one's better."

"This one's fake as shit. Didn't expect you to be fake too."

Noa's aunt Kayleigh had flown in the final mission against the Others. A blade of white light had just sliced through Japan and so it was go go go now now now. There was only one ship, and they needed to destroy it before it could call any alien reinforcements. So they nuked the shit out of it, five or six times over, right there in orbit. The bits of it that fell to Earth ended up doing more damage than the beam, a lot more, but Aunt Kayleigh was adamant that it had to be done or else they'd have gotten nuked first.

Aunt Kayleigh would always laugh as she told the second part of the story, about how when they opened up the wreckage none of it made sense at all, like it had been designed by a committee of idiots. The thing was the size of Hawaii and was filled with these weird twisted platinum things, which eggheads called statues, but she called bullshit. That was why they hit Harajuku first – the Others were dipshit artists, and had assumed that the place on Earth with the highest concentration of its own dipshit artists had to be its centre of power.

Harajuku rebuilt itself in that excavated crevasse within a year. A few years after that they finally figured out how the Others had arrived so abruptly. The Portal Drive.

It was raining the night Noa snuck out. Dad was out with some woman and Aunt Kayleigh was drunk, their own ways of making their lives go by faster. She had packed clothes in a tiny bag she had ordered in the fake Harajuku, from a boutique in the real one. She was excited to see where it had come from, like she was bringing it home. The damp grass cushioned her fall from her window. Outside the farmhouse she unlocked her bike and started pedalling down the mud road. Only seventeen kilometres to Youngstown.

Visiting a portal port was like driving on a freeway next to a cliff – stay within the proper lines and you'd be fine, go two feet the wrong way and you're dead. There were the local portals that were used everyday by suits going to work and kids on field trips, so accessible they quickly stopped being miraculous. And adjacent to them were portals you were never, ever allowed to take, portals to places so far away that just getting there used to be considered an adventure.

It was for their own good, they were told. The world was divided into containment zones, and if you went outside your zone you risked exposure to a variant contaminant that you could bring back. So you could leave if you promised never to come back, right? No, unsanctioned travellers leaving their containment zone risked death or imprisonment, so travel was restricted for their safety. And the punishment for unsanctioned travel was the termination of your only source of escapism – the severing of your neural tether to the net. As a deterrent, they said. For your own safety, they said.

Noa almost threw up outside the portal port. She tossed her bike in a ditch, the act that had finally made her appreciate the magnitude of what she was about to do. The only person she knew who had been allowed to take a portal legally was her Aunt. If they caught her both the real and the fake Harajuku would be lost to her forever, but if she didn't do this the real one would be lost anyway. The tiebreaker in her decision making was the memory of Natalia calling her fake – if she gave up now, she'd have to spend the rest of her life knowing Natalia was right, and that pissed her off.

The double glass doors of the portal port opened as she approached. It was a specific kind of decrepit that felt nostalgic – rows of empty storefronts with shadows remembering the signage that had once been there, linoleum floors that had been cleaned but not maintained, all their scuffs and cracks pristine. There was a wall to wall barrier field, a faint sheen you'd only notice if you knew to look for it. Beyond it were the portals, just two of them, one to Toledo and one to Atlanta. She had expected them to be humming doorways of arcane energy, but they were more like dirty windows.

A white sphere rolled in circles between the portal stages. A security ball. It was just her and the ball in the port, as far as she could tell.

The port spoke directly to her mind through her tether. How can we help you? it asked. One passage to Toledo, please. She had practiced thinking it all day yesterday, practiced clearing her mind of any thought other than her desire to buy a ticket, knowing that the terminal AI was engineered to detect deceit when it parsed your ThoughtCast. Three bubbly notes chimed in her mind – the transaction had been processed. The barrier parted to allow her to pass. The shimmer rejoined behind her.

She felt sick, stomach sick, like the one and only time she smoked a cigarette. The filthy window to Toledo was up five particle board steps painted black, like her school's drama room. The filthy window to Atlanta was atop identical steps, a few yards to its right. The Sphere made lazy circles around both windows, even lazier ones when she came close. Did it know what she was going to do? She was trapped in a paradox where trying not to think about her intent to hop meant that she was thinking about her intent to hop. Maybe she should just go to Toledo. It wasn't Harajuku, but it had to be better than here. But what the hell kind of way was that to live your life? Just a string of slightly less shitty 'here's'?

She thought of Natalia calling her fake. Of herself twenty years from now, drunk on the same couch Aunt Kayleigh was sleeping on now.

Screw it, she decided.

The Sphere commenced its manoeuvre as soon as she broke for the Atlanta portal, bowling straight at her. Shit, it was fast. It was too late to stop, too late to turn, so she jumped. Legs out and hands beneath her, she leapfrogged over the Sphere as it rolled under her. By the time it had reversed its momentum and begun to roll back, she was already up the stairs and pushing through the portal to Atlanta.

There was no sense of travelling, or even having travelled. She was just there, in Atlanta, pushing through assholes in business suits. Was she the asshole? Probably, actually yeah she was for sure, but if she stopped to think about it she was dead. The Sphere was still after her. So she channelled Aunt Kayleigh in her jet, thinking only about what needed to be done and how fast she could do it. She could leave the question of right or wrong to the dipshit eggheads.

Noa shouldered through the crowd. The Ball was more delicate, rolling through the spaces Noa created and over the chunks of mud falling from her boots. Atlanta was one huge perfectly white open space, the way she had pictured Heaven in Sunday school. Focus, she told herself. The gate to Nairobi was three portals down but across the aisle. The people she pushed through seemed more offended by the mud than her pushing, like they had never seen it before.

Metal on tile. More balls bounced toward her, one bearing down the sloped terminal walls like a half-pipe. She ducked as it soared over her. She kept running. Nairobi doesn't have a portal extradition treaty, Natalia had said. Once you get there you can take a breather, but don't stop before then.

Thank God, there was no crowd in front of the gate to Nairobi. This set of stairs was carved from one large chunk of stone. She jumped to the portal platform in a single bound, bypassing them completely. Holy shit. Holy shit she was doing it. She couldn't believe her fortune, that no one else was going to Nairobi. It seemed too good to be true.

It was.

Noa had heard a lot about Nairobi's portal port. How the whole thing was on water, and you could take a boat from gate to gate. How if you weren't careful you could be swept over a waterfall that fed the city below.

What she had not heard was that it was an endless black void, that as soon as you pushed through the portal you'd be falling, falling, falling through a space darker and colder than any winter she had known. She hadn't been told that she'd fall for so long that she'd stop praying to land safely and start praying to just land at all.

Was this real? Maybe she had been caught and the Sphere was projecting this torture through her tether, the way the fake Harajuku had been, a lifetime ago. But it was cold either way. She was falling too fast for the tears to stay on her face. I'm sorry, she thought, I'm so sorry, I'm so so sorry. Hoping that somewhere, something would accept her apology. But instead she continued to fall. Long enough that she couldn't even shiver anymore. It took so much concentration to breathe that she didn't see the point of it.

Her speed was changing. She had enough left in reserve to open one frosted eyelid. Two slender arms were wrapped around her. She couldn't feel them. Be still. The voice came directly through her tether. She didn't recognize it, or its accent. Whoever it was, they were wasting their words – Noa couldn't do anything but keep still, even if she wanted to.

The arms moved in circles to produce heat. A second pair of arms joined them, making the same motions. It felt nice. Like standing twenty feet away from a bonfire.

She blacked out wishing she could get just a little closer to it.

Her Dad was singing. The song he liked to sing to her when she was little, a shanty about an ill-fated group of privateers, which he explained were like pirates, which he explained were people that rode around the sea in boats and took things from other people on other boats. She had asked him once if people still sailed those seas. Not anymore, he had said. Not since that thing fell to the ocean and contaminated it. What did contaminated mean? The best he could explain was that it made the ocean sick. That was why Mom got sick, and that was why they couldn't go for long car rides anymore. He had kissed her on the forehead, told her not to worry, that he would fix up that attic to look like anyplace she could want to go.

He never did. And each year that attic buckled more, the wood increasingly disillusioned with the burden it had been given, of being a substitute for a world she wasn't allowed to see.

Noa awoke in a sweat, fearing that the roof was finally coming down on her.

But there was no roof above her, not even what she could call a ceiling. Just a flat plane of water. Water that wasn't held up by anything, but rippled casually, like an empty swimming pool. Was she strapped into a bed upside down? It was so hard to lift her hand she half-forgot why she was doing it, but when she let go it fell back down toward the bed. Away from the water.

This was a headache for another time. She fell back asleep.

The next time she woke up she was much less tired and much more thirsty. Nothing had kept her in her bed aside from her own exhaustion, and there was no clear source of water in the crystalline room other than the ceiling. She stood on the tips of her toes on the bed to reach it. Her index finger broke the surface tension and a few drops slid down her hand.

The water rippled, annoyed. A shadow flickered behind it. When the surface became still the shadow pushed forward. Tendrils flowed around it. Hair. The figure drew closer. It opened its eyes.

Noa screamed. The figure screamed too, but not out loud – it screamed directly through Noa's ThoughtCast. It swam back the way it had come. Was it afraid? No, it was embarrassed.

Either way, her ass was out of there. She found her bag, her shoes, and her strength, and all she needed now was a door. Too bad that was the hardest part. The room was uneven, like a cave made of prismatic resin. The only way out was through the pool above her.

She stood on the bed and jumped. She got barely up to her shoulders, paddled upward like her life depended on it, because for all she knew it did, but fell back down, nostrils full of water, jean jacket soaked. Her eyes stung. She told herself it was just the water, but it wasn't. It was knowing that she was stuck here. It was knowing that she would never see Harajuku, smell the cotton candy, see the throngs of limbs decked out in black and neon. It was knowing that Natalia was right about her. But it didn't have anything to do with missing her dad, or her aunt, or home. She was glad even, glad that at least she wouldn't die never having left Ohio.

Please do not cry. I will open a path for you.

The way the resin reflected light made it hard to judge distance. She had no idea how vast or small this room was, but a point in the wall began to split, parting like a curtain, exposing a hallway made of the same stuff.

"Can you please do something about the walls?"

The light dimmed and the walls settled into a deep blue, what she had been told was once the colour of the oceans. In the hallway was the person she had seen in the water.

Was it a person?

They looked close enough to human for Noa to see her as a set of exceptions. They looked like a girl close to Noa's age, except they had four arms, except their hands had six fingers, and except their eyes were nearly solid black with just the barest promise of sclera. Their nose and mouth were small. They looked like a doll. They were wearing a pink printed dress adorned with a carousel motif, propped up with a petticoat, stockings, leather shoes. "Are you – are you wearing sweet lolita?" Sweet lolita was an old school Harajuku fashion that had come back. Noa hated the name, but loved the look.

The figure nodded.

"Are you, like, an – alien?"

The thin lips formed what might have been a frown. I am. It came through her ThoughtCast. I am sorry, I –

"Huh? Why would you be sorry about that?" The figure did not have an answer, but Noa could feel notes of embarrassment, of shame, of fear. "Hey, I like that print," she said, pointing at the carousel. "Where did you get it?"

The figure mimed sewing with all four of her hands.

"No shit? I mean, really you made that?" Another nod. "Can you like, talk?" The figure shook their head. "Then can you at least talk to me with your mind or whatever? I don't like guessing games."

Of course, I apologize deeply, I just do not wish to make you uncomfortable. I –

"It's cool, really. Do you have a name?"

The alien started to shake their head before catching themselves. It is Aoi. Please let me make you comfortable. I can dry your clothes. I can feed you. If you are afraid of me, then I can do these things while allowing you to remain in isolation.

"I'm not afraid," Noa said, but she could tell from the background noise in her ThoughtCast and the beating of her heart that neither of them believed that.

While Noa dried, Aoi made soup. While Noa ate, Aoi watched from halfway across the table, exactly ten feet away. If Noa moved an inch toward Aoi, Aoi would move an inch away, and if Noa moved an inch away, Aoi would move an inch closer – the distance between had to be kept exact for reasons Noa didn't understand, but was sure she would find annoying if she did.

She couldn't think of a compliment for the soup. It tasted like chalk and got stuck in her teeth. "Thanks," was all Noa managed. Those black pupils continued to stare. Noa wondered if Aoi had fallen asleep, if they even did sleep.

There was a deep creaking moan, like the waking of an ancient creature. If Aoi had been asleep they were awake then, running fast toward the sound. They ran with their back perfectly straight. Noa wiped her mouth and followed them through the cavern. She heard rushing water and felt wetness at the tip of her runners. Wherever Noa was, it was filling up.

A jagged bolt of fear through her ThoughtCast, Aoi's fear, not fear for their own life but fear of losing something important to them. The water reached the top of Noa's ankle socks when she found them in a room filled with statues. There was a breach in a curved ceiling far above them, in what she now saw as the hull of a ship. Aoi's hands desperately wanted to find their grip on one particular statue, the figure of an Other that looked much like Aoi, but their fingers would slip each time.

"Are you out of your mind? You're going to drown!"

As if to reply, Aoi stood tall and stared at the breach in the ship's hull. For a moment the flow stopped, as though plugged by something invisible, but the torrent burst through it, whatever it was, and Aoi was left to push.

"Jesus," Noa said. She had no idea why Aoi needed to move the statue, but she trusted that it wasn't just for the hell of it. Whoever or whatever Aoi was, they could have killed Noa a million times over. With the water at her lower shins, she trudged over to Aoi and pushed the statue from the opposite end.

It was lighter than she thought, and soon buoyed on the water. That made it easy to push but the water hit their waists without any sign that what they were doing would stop it. Until Noa looked back and saw that the open chamber was pinching itself off at the middle, like a cell dividing partitioning the two of them off from the breach. The two sides joined in a long-awaited kiss, creating a semi-transparent wall, and there was a shudder as the ruptured cell was jettisoned off.

The water drained quickly, sinking into the floor. Aoi climbed onto the base of the statue and sat against its legs. Noa was too exhausted to be pissed off about risking her life for a piece of art, but the intent was there, and Aoi wrapped all of their arms around themselves defensively, as though they could tell. Mother, they said, freeing an arm to stroke a chrome calf. She died a long time ago. This is the only image of her I have left. I am sorry. I am sorry.

And Noa remembered her own Mom. More clearly than she had in years. She remembered pulling at her pant leg when she got home from work, how she always took the hint to pick Noa up, no matter how tired she was.

Noa wiped her eyes and climbed up with the assistance of two of Aoi's hands. "I'm glad we saved her." They sat close to each other, keeping warm in their damp clothes, as the last of the water skulked away.

Aoi was a lot more talkative after that, like they had been holding back the whole time. Aoi confirmed that they were one of the 'Others', a fact they divulged only with great shame. Aoi's face didn't move much but their emotions came through Noa's ThoughtCast clearly, like background music. Aoi was the offspring of one of the crew members of the ship that had attacked Earth. Were they military? No, Aoi explained, they were artists. Their nation back home created works out of whole planets, but never inhabited ones. The beam they had swept through Harajuku was meant only to collect data on a particularly intriguing artistic locus, but due to a technical malfunction the beam that fired was the one they used to sculpt planetary objects instead. This malfunction also eliminated their ability to escape. When the nations of Earth counterattacked, they didn't know what else to do but defend themselves, to try and end the conflict. Aoi's mother had ejected them from the ship before it had been nuked, or rather, part of the ship split off and dove into a large body of water.

"Are we, like, under the ocean?"

Aoi nodded.

"So why was there a portal leading here?"

There wasn't. You entered a portal with no exit coordinate, and fell into shunted space. That is where I found you. This vessel also has a portal with no exit.

"The hell is shunted space?"

It's difficult to explain. Portals can't eliminate the space between two points. Instead they 'shunt' it elsewhere. Imagine a door leading to a long hallway leading to a second door. You could make the trip from Door A to Door B shorter by rearranging space so that the hallway comes after the doors. Or put the hallway elsewhere in the house entirely. That way the total space is preserved. What you fell through was the shunted, preserved space.

"Oh," Noa said, not meaning that she understood, but rather that she no longer cared to. "Thanks. For saving me. I was actually trying to portal hop to Harajuku." The emotion that came through the ThoughtCast was complicated, a boat of jealousy sailing over an ocean of guilt. "Have you – do you ever leave here?"

Aoi shook their head, sadly, Noa thought.

A thought flashed in Noa's head. "Do you want to go to Harajuku with me?" Those pupils dilated, crowding out what little white space there was in Aoi's eyes. The hands had paired into fidgeting partners again. "I mean, you probably can't stay here forever, right? Don't you want to see it?"

I don't deserve to. I don't deserve to. I don't –

"Forget about that. You're miserable here, I can tell. And we both wanna get to the same place. Oh, and don't forget that this ship is falling apart, and eventually you'll drown. So, like, do you have a better idea?"

I do not.

So don't be fa – so let's go."

What if they find me?

"What if you stay here forever and ever, making soup and stitching dresses, until you die?"

No. I can't. I can't. I –

"Jesus, fine. Then at least take me home! It's your fault I'm here!" It had barely left her lips when she knew it was wrong – she was the one who had gone hopping, breaking who knows how many laws, just because she was too stuck up for rural Ohio. All Aoi had done was rescue her, feed her, and give her a place to rest. But it was too late, she could feel Aoi's guilt like the chill of the shunted space. Her stupid mouth had affirmed fifteen years of self-loathing. She felt like shit. She felt like Natalia.

And worst of all was the feeling, clear as crystal through her ThoughtCast, that Aoi didn't blame Noa for any of this at all.

Aoi's portal was cleaner than the ones at the ports, less a dirty window and more a shimmering pool. Aoi could only take Noa back to Atlanta, to the portal that had led her to the shunted space, a limitation for which they apologized more than once. As Noa planned out her future hops she found where she had messed up – the portal to Nairobi had been moved during a port expansion.

Natalia's intel was sixteen months out of date, which Noa was sure meant something but she was too tired to figure out what. Aoi worked forty-three hours straight to calibrate the portal, during which Noa ate soup and looked at statues. Did Aoi need to sleep? Noa didn't know, but she could tell when someone was exhausted and Aoi was exhausted. Their shoulders sunk, their eyes were half closed, and at times they would pause in the middle of working, like a frame buffering, like they had forgotten what they were doing.

The portal shimmered above what they had used as a dining table. Noa looked at the portal, then at Aoi. "Are you going to be okay?" Noa had asked this half a dozen times, and usually the answer was Don't worry. But this time was different. I wish you a safe journey, Aoi thought. I wish you happiness. And I am sorry.

The word 'sorry' blossomed in Noa's mind, it had been encoded with a meaning beyond the semantic. Aoi was sorry for the damage their people had done. Aoi was sorry for scaring her when she swam through the pool at the ceiling. Aoi was sorry that they couldn't go with Noa. That last part wasn't directed at Noa, but from Aoi to herself.

"What are you gonna do after I go?"

Aoi strained to keep that a secret, but the straining itself came through the ThoughtCast, and that was enough for Noa to understand. Aoi's existence down here was a secret, her portal undiscovered. The moment Noa went through that would no longer be the case, and the same people who had nuked their ship would know that one of them had survived and exactly where to find them. Aoi would be dead within an hour, if they were lucky. Captured for experimentation if they were not. Aoi knew this, and still they had worked through two whole days just so Noa could get to Harajuku.

Please. The portal can only sustain itself for a short time.

It was there again, Noa's rage. When her Mom died people kept asking her how she was coping with feeling sad, but her sadness hadn't felt like sadness, it felt like being pissed off. Pissed at the world for taking her Mom when Moms were supposed to see you grow up and get married. Aoi was dying too, slowly being crushed under the literal weight of the world above them, and if Noa stepped through that portal alone then Aoi would die a lot faster.

"The hell with that," she said. Noa seized Aoi's lower right wrist. "Follow me." Aoi almost tripped coming up the table but Noa refused to let them fall. "We can chill in Nairobi. We'll be there in a minute tops. Okay?" She didn't give them time to answer. Noa pulled Aoi along as she leapt through the portal, and Aoi followed.

Atlanta.

The brief chill of shunted space, and Noa was once again in that vast white portal port, trying not to be impressed. "There. We jump through that one." She had to tug Aoi twice to get them to move – Noa didn't know if they were tired or scared or in awe, but whatever it was Aoi needed to cut it the hell out.

Three Spheres rolled down the curved wall opposite them – one of them was covered in mud. The Ball from Youngstown. It had been waiting for her. They jumped off the side of the stage. Aoi moved slowly at first but quickly outpaced Noa and Noa was the one being dragged. The balls rolled to form a line between them and the portal they needed. Aoi swiped her hand. The Spheres scattered like billiard balls.

"Holy. Shit." Noa could only spare two syllables per breath. "How did. You do."

Aoi squeezed Noa's wrist to tell her that it wasn't the time. They leapt up the stage and pulled Noa up with three of their arms. By the time the Spheres had regrouped, Aoi and Noa were through the portal.

Nairobi.

Aoi collapsed as soon as they made it through. Noa tried to hold them up but the momentum was too obstinate, so it was all she could do to protect Aoi's head from hitting the ground. Aoi's eyes fluttered, their breathing loud and out of sync, like each lung was working on its own, if they even had lungs. "Aoi?" She brushed their cheek, then slapped it. "Aoi! Aoi!"

A strong hand pressed on Noa's shoulder. "Are you hoppers?"

The woman standing above her looked like she was edged with gold, the way she blocked the sun. There was a moment of panic before Noa recalled what Natalia had said – Nairobi was a safe zone. Noa nodded. The woman knelt down, checked for Aoi's pulse, and then looked very serious. "I'm very sorry, but your friend is – "

Aoi coughed. Their lower left hand moved to cover it. Noa waited for the woman to scream, to call for help, but instead she covered Aoi with her cloak. "Your friend needs treatment. I am a physician. Will she be safe to go outside? I can take her to the hospital where I work." Noa didn't know, but said yes anyway.

It was then that it burst from the portal, the mud-covered Sphere. A guard in black armour caught it with a net before it hit the ground. "Nairobi is a sanctuary zone," they said. They threw the Sphere back through the portal, mud and all. An electric car arrived. A second guard helped Noa and the doctor load Aoi into the back, and then the four of them drove off. Noa held Aoi's hand and Aoi squeezed it back, weakly.

The guard drove into an artificial stream and over a waterfall. As they floated down Noa saw the city, a garden of crystals rising out of the clearest water she had ever seen.

Their guardian angel was Dr. Aluna Luna, but she told Noa just to call her Aluna. She was just on her way to Milan for lunch when she found Noa and Aoi. Aluna was very smart. She picked up on what Aoi was almost immediately.

"Did she escape from captivity?"

"No. Well yeah, but not that way. It's like this." Noa explained everything, starting from the bike ride through the rain and the mud to the Youngstown portal, all the way to now. She even explained that Aoi didn't seem to like to think of themselves as a she, which made Noa embarrassed, correcting someone who was so much smarter than her, but Aluna didn't yell or throw a bottle or do anything Noa expected. The whole time they watched Aoi float in the centre of a dim chamber. Noa had never seen a hospital like this – had never seen a hospital at all, actually. When she was done with her story she looked to Aluna in anticipation of her judgement.

Aluna ran her tongue along the inside of her lips. "Here is what we're going to do," she said. "Your friend, they're very similar to us. Blood, DNA, electrolytes. I don't know if they arrived here that way, or if it's an adaptation, but in my documentation I am going to write that they are an unregistered variant. A mutant. There will be an investigation, but not with any urgency. If she – sorry, if they recover quickly, you two will be gone before it gets underway."

"You won't turn them in?"

"Turn them into what?" She winked. "Go. Eat something. I'll keep an eye on your friend."

Nairobi made Noa embarrassed for thinking that the Atlanta portal port was Heaven. Each building was a singular crystal entity, each street was – well, there weren't streets, just rivers and gardens and small stages with portals to other parts of the city. She had to use her ThoughtCast's internal drawing app to create a map of the portal network so she wouldn't get lost. She bought an eggplant sandwich and sat in the shade of what her ThoughtCast told her was a Jacaranda tree. A group of girls her age passed by. She was learning to be better about her jealousy, about not being mad that she had been born in Ohio and not here, about being grateful that she was lucky enough to see it. She knew Aoi well enough to know that even if they died here in the hospital, they would be grateful for the few minutes she got to spend outside their sunken ship. If anything happens to you, Noa decided, I'll make it to Harajuku for both of us. I'll see as much of the world as I can. When she was done with her sandwich she traced her path back to the hospital.

Aluna was still there. She motioned for Noa to be quiet with one straight finger. "They're awake."

Something released inside of Noa, some ugly jagged thing she had been holding on to. She didn't know what to say. She sat in a chair to try and think of something, but within seconds she was asleep.

When she woke up her neck was killing her. It was Aoi who shook her awake. Noa hadn't had any more luck thinking of anything to say, so she hugged Aoi's waist as tight as she could. It seemed to get the message across.

An hour later Aluna discharged Aoi, and bought them and Noa portal passage to Milan. "Thank you," Noa said, "but I'm really sorry you wasted your money. We weren't going to Milan."

"The fare will get you through the door. After that, well, whatever portal you two walk into is your decision, isn't it?" She winked at them again.

The portal to Milan in Nairobi's portal port was across from the portal to Neo Toronto. Aluna must have deduced the path they were hopping to Harajuku. The stairs to Milan were packed. The stairs to Toronto were empty. Aluna thought of everything.

"Ready?" Noa asked. Aoi smiled and nodded.

They crossed the aisle and ran up the steps.

Neo Toronto. The alarm started right when they stepped through the portal.

The portal port was packed full of assholes in black armour with guns that carried themselves like the cops back home. Was there a war happening that she didn't know about? No, this was just how things were here. Noa raised her arms, the way she'd been taught to do when cops started yelling. Aoi clearly hadn't had the same set of formative experiences. Her fear was as clear as the stream in Nairobi.

"Hands up! Hands up now!" Their guns were up. The one closest to her had bad skin and a beard, like the guys her Aunt dated.

Shit, her Aunt! "I'm Colonel Kayleigh McClinton's niece! Please help me, I'm Colonel Kayleigh McClinton's niece!" She was gambling on her aunt's name carrying some weight – she and the other pilots who flew the mission that took down the Others were heroes, for a while, until the true extent of the damage was known, the combination of the nukes and the alien wreckage poisoning the planet. But among a certain group – namely, assholes – she was a martyr figure. She used to show up on the news sometimes, before ThoughtCasts took that over. Noa tapped her toes against the side of Aoi's foot. It'll be okay, she thought, hoping that Aoi could hear.

They were told to keep their hands up, but instead of them being shot or arrested the terminal waited for someone with the proper level of authority to arrive. A colonel, she picked out. He drove in a white motorcycle that made no noise, even when it slid to a stop. He looked like the pictures of her Dad from when he was in the service. Everything about the Colonel was sharp angles – hair, face, clothing. She really needed to play the scared-little-girl card, so she thought about the last time she saw her Mom, just a corpse that hadn't realized it was already dead. It did the trick. She started to cry. Aoi mimicked the sound as well as she could.

The Colonel knelt down in front of Noa even though he wasn't that much taller than her. "Do you girls know that you have travelled outside your allowed zone?"

Noa nodded and Aoi mimicked it.

"That's ten years confinement and a permanent severance from the net. Do you understand?"

Noa knew this routine. They hadn't earned any sympathy from the Colonel, but they had earned his pity. That was fine. She could work with pity. "It's just – my, my Mom – she – she wanted to see China, before she – she died..." The mucus was flowing now. "She got sick, and..." Her words collapsed into diaphragmatic spasms. The Colonel broke eye contact, uncomfortable. The travellers in the terminal were uncomfortable. The tears kept flowing, to keep everyone uncomfortable. Noa was never much of an actress, but it wasn't hard when everything you were saying was true.

The Colonel motioned her toward him. No, not toward him, but away from Aoi. He whispered, "Did this mutant coerce you or threaten you in any way?" Noa shook her head. "Has she caused you any harm?" She shook her head again. The Colonel called a woman officer over. "Take them to the holding area," he said. What he didn't say, but what was implicit in his voice, was that she should be gentle with them.

The guard nodded. "Come on," she said. Even offered a hand to help Noa down. Same thing for Aoi, except when Aoi reached out with all four hands the woman paused, confused. That was enough of an opening.

Noa jumped on the Colonel's bike. Throwing it into reverse, she rammed the woman cop just as Aoi jumped down. "Come on!" she yelled, but Aoi was already straddled across the bike. As soon as she felt two sets of arms wrapped around her she gunned it, silently.

The cops wanted to shoot. God, they wanted to shoot so bad. Probably a lot of them had become cops hoping the time would come when they could unload on another human life. But Noa wasn't stupid, she weaved through the travellers instead of skirting around them, taunting them, daring them to risk explaining to their boss why they shot some asshole exec on his way to a power lunch. The cops were mad. They were screaming. Someone was doing something that wasn't allowed, and it was a supreme injustice that they were being denied their right to kill that person. The portal to the second Atlanta terminal was close. She could ride the bike up the ramp. Aoi squeezed her, squealed.

The front tire hit a shimmering barrier. The bike spun over itself. The port had sealed the portals with barrier fields.

It made too much sense for Noa to be mad about it, and besides, she was in the process of completing a half rotation on the bike and when it stopped it would fall on her and Aoi. She was, in fact, experiencing the last seconds of their journey together, stretched into an eternity of perception. That was fine. She could spend the rest of her life in the moment, if it meant this never came to an end.

But the expected fall didn't come. The front tire came back down. The bike bounced on its suspension. The handlebars punched Noa in the chin, which punched her out of her fugue state. Righted, she revved the bike. Time to improvise. As Noa and Aoi sped through the terminal, air cutting their cheeks, the portals closed off one by one, like shuttering windows. The whole port was sealing itself off.

And that's when she saw it. The Sphere from Youngstown, still caked in mud. It was mad, as mad as a featureless metal ball can be. It moved in a straight line toward them, with no regard for anyone or anything that might be in its path. It almost crushed a waddling toddler and plowed right through a marble pillar with no loss of speed.

The portals were sealed, the Sphere was after them, and now the cops had mobilized. Two of them steadied a large cannon. It made a thumping sound when it fired, and shot out a blob of gray mucus. Some kind of glue gun. Noa was too close to a wall to swerve. Shit. If it stuck her down at the speed she was going she'd snap her neck. She let up the throttle, so it would hit her and not Aoi.

The mucus splattered three inches away from her face, birdshit on a windshield.

No, a field. Aoi had three hands outstretched in a triangle, and Noa saw the shimmer of a barrier field. Was Aoi doing that? Was that how she tried to contain the breach in her ship? Aoi blocked two more blobs. Noa kept her speed as best she could, but the

Sphere was getting closer and they were reaching the end of the terminal. Nowhere left to go.

Nowhere.

Maybe their thoughts were synchronized through Noa's ThoughtCast, or maybe they just knew each other well enough, but Noa felt her and Aoi have the same idea – shunted space. That was the exact 'nowhere' they could escape to. What they'd do then she had no idea, but it was better than dying in a motorcycle crash.

They have set null coordinates for these portals to prevent our escape, meaning that any portal will lead us to shunted space. I think I can negate the barrier field by projecting its inverse, nullifying it, but only for a moment. And I will not be able to protect us while I do.

Noa banked hard, knee scraping linoleum, and turned back the way she had come. Blew past the Sphere and confused cops. Bore right toward the nearest portal she saw. The electric motor was under a tremendous deal of stress. That made two of them.

A blob of glue flung at them. Noa leaned left and felt it lick her ear. Close, but not close enough. The front wheel touched the ramp. The odds that Aoi would get the timing right had to be low. Noa always hated math, but she hated giving up even more.

The field flashed white before vanishing as their bike made it through the ramp, cops so close behind them that Noa could smell the glue.

Shunted space was just as cold the second time. Probably colder for the cops on bikes, who hadn't expected it. Noa watched them tumble down, the black of their bodies swallowed by the void. They sailed the nothingness on Aoi's doing, some kind of kinetic manipulation. I do not know where to take you. I am getting tired.

But Aoi had explained it perfectly clearly when Noa first showed up. They could either go to her portal in the wrecked ship, or back the way they came. "Turn us around," Noa said. "And hold on. I'll take it from here."

Noa wondered what the cops in Neo Toronto expected to come back out of that portal. Maybe they expected their colleagues to ride out with Noa and Aoi cuffed. Maybe they expected some dormant shunted creature would emerge, a mass of writhing tentacles. But Noa was pretty sure they didn't expect her and Aoi to come tearing out on the silent bike, Noa flipping them the bird. Too bad, that was what they got.

Everything the cops would do after that was too late. They were too late to re-raise the fields, too late to null the portal coordinates again, too late to ready their glue guns. All they could do was watch as the rear lights of their bike vanished into the Atlanta subterminal, the muddy Sphere close behind.

They had just made it through the portal when the Sphere bit their real wheel. Its teeth were angled inward, like a shark's. The bike dragged the sphere along before it gave up and tipped on its side, exhausted. Noa landed on her feet and pulled Aoi's to theirs as the Sphere chewed through the entire bike lengthwise. Noa picked up a length of metal from the bones of the bike and held it in two hands like a sword, putting herself between Aoi and the Sphere. When it was done with the bike it would come for them.

It was fast but Noa connected with the pipe, her best two-handed swing, barely enough to knock it away but barely enough still counted. The Sphere bounced off the wall and came back, only to be pushed away by Aoi's conjured field. It was hard to hold the metal rod – Noa was sure she had broken at least two of her fingers. How many swings, how many uses of Aoi's powers did they have left? If any?

The Sphere was dented, making it roll funny, but it was still fast and Noa knew right away she was too slow to swing, the rod too heavy. It's alright, Aoi said. And for the first time, Noa felt they were telling the truth. I saw more of your world than I ever thought I would. I did things I never dreamed I could have. And for the first time since I was a child, I'm not lonely. So it's okay with me if this is how it ends.

Noa dropped the rod without meaning to, not that it mattered. The Sphere was coming for her.

Boom. Boom boom. Three shots pierced through the Sphere, the last one splitting it in two. Noa's ears rung. Someone placed their hand on her shoulder and she screamed, although she couldn't hear it. Someone with a platinum odango and a swirling green and pink dress, standing next to her own security sphere, its autocannon smoking.

"Natalia?"

The sphere rolled away. The figure of Natalia smiled, as though Noa had said something slightly embarrassing.

"I am a virtual construct, presenting through your tether." Of course, the voice gave it away – the avatar looked and felt like a real physical body, but when it spoke it spoke directly to Noa's mind, like Aoi. "I took the form of an avatar you are familiar with. Pardon my awkwardness, I am not accustomed to unplanned arrivals. What is the purpose of your visit?"

"We, uh, we just wanted to go shopping."

Aoi approached the avatar. Noa wondered how it appeared to them, if it looked like Natalia or a one of her own species. If Aoi and the avatar were speaking, Noa couldn't hear them.

"I see," spoke the avatar, to something Aoi must have said. "And her too? How lonely."

"Listen," Noa said, "I don't care if I'm a walking chemical weapon to you, I don't care if it's illegal, I don't care if it means I am going to spend the rest of my life in prison. Okay? But I am going through that portal and you can't stop me and I don't – "

Aoi touched Noa's shoulder, and only then did she realize how hard she was shaking.

The avatar smiled again. "I believe there is some degree of misinformation. Your travel here has always been permitted by us, and you do not carry any toxic contamination. Any restrictions placed on your movement have been placed upon you by your own governing body."

"What – but – that doesn't – why?"

"If they didn't, who would stay?"

"So we can come in?"

"If you wish."

Noa looked at Aoi. Aoi looked at Noa. It is frightening, Aoi said, but less frightening than everything that has come before.

"I just want to get my fingers fixed."

That was enough of an agreement. Noa and Aoi followed the image of Natalia over the corpse of the Sphere and through the portal to Hokkaido.

The Tokyo apartment that Noa and Aoi could afford was small, with just enough room to sleep and sew. The irony of the situation wasn't lost to Noa – her journey had started with the need to escape her tiny farmhouse bedroom, and she had crisscrossed the continents and travelled to the ocean depths just to end up in another tiny bedroom halfway across the world, a mirror inversion. But it was her mirror inversion, and that made it okay. Even when she got stressed juggling everything, it was okay because it was her stress and not the stress that the universe had pushed her into.

Aoi sat at a small table, pumping an antique sewing machine. Noa paused at the door before she left, adjusting the petticoat under her lolita dress, a print that Aoi had made themselves. "I'm heading out to the meetup." Aoi continued to sew. "Do you wanna come with me?"

Noa could feel through her ThoughtCast that they did. The needle stopped. I am nervous.

"Shit, I'm nervous. Bet the people at the meet will be nervous too, meeting the mysterious anonymous designer."

I am worried they will think I am strange.

"I mean, you kind of are? But who cares? You're kind, too, and brilliant. Anyone who cares about how many arms you have is fake as shit."

Am I fake?

"You're the least fake person I've ever met."

That was enough for Aoi. Dressed in the outfits they had made themselves, Noa and Aoi strode toward the pulsing fuchsia aura of the Harajuku Crevasse.

## *Why Mirror World?*

*We publish escapism fiction for all ages. Our novels are imaginative and character-driven and our goal is to give our readers a glimpse into other worlds, times, and versions of reality that parallel our own, giving them an experience they can't get anywhere else!*

*We offer free delivery within Windsor-Essex in Canada, an all-you-can-read membership program, blind-dates with books, and you can order our novels from our online store, or from your favorite major book retailer.*

*We appreciate every like, tweet, facebook post, and review and we love to hear from you. Please consider leaving us your comments online or sending your thoughts or questions to info@mirrorworldpublishing.com*

*Thank you.*